# Taken, But
# I Want You

# Taken, But I Want You

*Krystal Armstead*

www.urbanbooks.net

Urban Books, LLC
300 Farmingdale Road, N.Y.-Route 109
Farmingdale, NY 11735

Taken, But I Want You

ISBN 13: 978-1-64556-726-4
EBOOK ISBN: 978-1-64556-738-7

First Trade Paperback Printing December 2025
Printed in the United States of America

10 9 8 7 6 5 4 3 2 1

Distributed by Kensington Publishing Corp.
Submit Orders to:
Customer Service
400 Hahn Road
Westminster, MD 21157-4627
Phone: 1-800-733-3000
Fax: 1-800-659-2436

The authorized representative in the EU for product
safety and compliance
Is eucomply OU, Parnu mnt 139b-14, Apt 123
Tallinn, Berlin 11317, hello@eucompliancepartner.com

# Taken, But
# I Want You

by

*Krystal Armstead*

# Prologue

## David "Blue" Jacobs

*2007*

"Blue, you're really leavin' Greenville?" my nigga, Lamar, asked, puffing on loud early one hot and humid August morning. Me, Lamar, Ray, and a nigga we called Turtle (because he was slow but always seemed to finish first) stood outside Lucy's, my uncle's corner store. It was our last time together. I had known these niggas my entire life. They were like brothers to me. They *were* my brothers. Man, you wouldn't believe the shit we got into together.

"Yeah." Lamar passed the blunt to me. "You already know Chrys is taking the shit hard as hell. She was just over to Miss Tiffany's house."

"And they just put her mama away too. It's gotta be hard watching your mama being put into a mental institution." Ray shook his head. He looked at me and knew I was hurting like a muthafucka.

It took everything in me not to cry in front of them. Chrystal was my heart. I loved that girl. Would do anything for her but hurt her. She needed me, but Miss Tiffany (my adoptive mother) had gotten a better job in Washington, D.C. We were finally moving out of the hood.

She wanted to be excited, but she knew that I wasn't. I didn't want to leave my boys, but mostly, I didn't want to leave Chrystal.

Chrystal was the whole reason why I survived. We had the same birthday. Christmas, 1990. We were born in the same hospital, at the same time. Our fathers were both Black. Our mothers were both white. Our mothers were best friends. Christina, Chrystal's mom, came from a middle-class family, whereas Moms was raised in the hood. Chrystal's mom wanted her; my mom couldn't care less about me. The moment my mother was released from what was then called Pitt Memorial Hospital, she decided to get rid of me. Chrystal's mother told me it was by the grace of God that she found me. Her husband, William, had just gotten back from the police academy. The transport technician wheeled Christina out of the hospital to William's car. He put Chrystal into the backseat and helped his wife into the front seat, when Christina realized she'd left her overnight bag in her room. William got out of the car and started to race back inside the building when he heard something that sounded like the faint cries of a baby. He said the noise was coming from a trash can. He went over to the trash can and removed the lid. The trash can was overflowing with garbage. The noise stopped. He thought he must have been hearing things. But as soon as he started to put the lid back on the trash can, he saw the garbage moving. He quickly removed the trash, and that's when he found me.

"That girl is gonna go crazy without you, bruh." Turtle exhaled deeply as I passed him the blunt.

"David!" I heard my uncle's voice. "Y'all better get that shit away from in front of my store. I told y'all about that shit. And get'cha ass in here. Your aunt is about to take you over to Chrystal's house to help her move."

Saying goodbye to my homies was a hurting-ass feeling. Saying goodbye to Chrystal was going to be even harder. When I got to her crib that morning, she was already sitting on her porch steps, smoking one of her mother's cigarettes.

I went over and sat down beside her, looking at her. Man, she was a truly beautiful sight to see. She had a toasted almond complexion, big brown eyes, and long dark hair. She was dressed in a tight tank top and extra-short sweat shorts. I stared at her thighs for a few seconds before looking back into her face.

"Hey, li'l cutie. My uncle, Larry, said that your aunt and them will be over in a little while to help you finish packing. Lisa said she'll be over after she drops my niece and nephew off at their grandma's house."

Chrystal nodded, not able to look me in the face. "Okay."

"Where's your nigga, Tony? He should be over here helping you pack. Man, you pick the sorriest niggas to fuck with, Chrystal." I took the cigarette from her lips and put it to mine.

"Not today, okay, Blue? I can deal with you hatin' on my dude any other day, but not today, okay?" Chrystal continued to look straight ahead.

I exhaled deeply, watching her lips quiver and her eyebrows lower. She was so angry that I had to leave. We were just about to start our senior year in high school. We were always together. You didn't see one of us without seeing the other. She kept a nigga, and you could say I kept a girl or two, but we both knew who we were really rockin' with. She was like a sister to me, which was why I never approached her on the level I *really* wanted to. My main goal in life was to keep a smile on that girl's face. I loved her with every inch of me, but I never told her until the day that I had to leave her.

"This isn't fair, David." The only time she ever called me by my government name was when she was upset. "What am I supposed to do without you?"

I put my arm around her, pulling her closer to me. "You gotcha nigga."

Chrystal scoffed. "He ain't shit. You *know* he ain't shit."

I tried not to laugh and tried even harder not to say anything.

"I can't breathe, eat, or sleep without my Blue." She laid her head on my shoulder.

I squeezed her tight, my heart going a hundred miles per hour in my chest. "Let's finish packing, Chrys."

Chrystal stacked her shoe boxes of Jordans in one box and her shoe boxes of Nikes in another box. I had spent the last few days helping her family move her mother's furniture into storage. We knew the day was coming. It had been six months since William was killed. Christina and her husband had just come from a movie and made a trip to the 7-Eleven to get gas and a cup of coffee. Both of them walked into the gas station . . . only to walk right into a robbery. Without hesitation, the shooter shot right at Christina. It went straight through her arm and hit William in his stomach. Christina's mind hadn't been right since that day. William was everything to her. He was everything to everyone. He treated me like his son, since my father never claimed me. He made sure my mother was found and arrested. Even after I was adopted, he kept in contact with me and made sure that the person who adopted me was from our city. Miss Tiffany was a family friend from church. She was strict as hell, but that woman loved the fuck out of me.

"Oh, before I forget, I have to show you something." Chrystal came over and sat beside me on her night table, the only piece of furniture left in her room.

I looked up from her photo album at her as she sat beside me, her back facing me, sweeping her long, dark hair to the side. She was showing me the tattoo she'd gotten on her left shoulder blade. It was my nickname, "Blue," inked in royal blue cursive, with a crown hanging off the B.

"Oh shit." I couldn't help but laugh, standing up, running my fingers across the newly inked tattoo. "Shit is tight."

"This way, we'll always be together." She smiled at me over her shoulder.

I grinned to myself, still rubbing the tattoo.

"I wanted to get a set of wings on the side of it, but I didn't have enough money. You know I had to sneak and get this shit done." Chrystal turned around, facing me, looking into my face.

I looked at her. Man, there was so much that I wanted to say to her. She was more than my best friend. We had each other's backs. We had each other's fronts. We had each other's everything. You know her nigga hated our relationship. You know the chicks I fucked with hated the shit out of her sexy ass. I could give a fuck. If they didn't fuck with her, they couldn't fuck with me, and it was just as simple as that. But I never approached her with my feelings. I didn't want to risk what we had. What we had was perfect. Everything in my life was complicated . . . except for our relationship. And I had to keep it that way.

"I know that nigga hates that shit." I shook my head. She didn't give a fuck about shit.

And she constantly wore that expression on her face. "Ask me, *do I give a fuck?*" Chrystal stood up from the nightstand and started packing again. "My mama just got sent to Cherry Hospital, and where the fuck is he? My best friend, whom I have known since birth, is leaving me, and where is he? All Nathan's ass thinks about is

himself. You're the only one who gives a fuck about me."
Chrystal's eyes searched my face. "You love me, don't
you?" she joked. "Just admit it, Blue."

I looked at her, not really sure what to say. I couldn't
deny it. I couldn't lie to her. "When something good
happens, you're the first person I have to run and tell,"
was all I could think to say.

Chrystal grinned. "Blue, we have *so* many memories
together. Do you remember when we stole my daddy's
car and drove to Richmond?"

"Yeah, that was last year, shorty." I watched her laughing and crying at the same time. "He whupped the shit
out of us when he caught us too. Do you remember that?
And what about the time he caught you fuckin' that nigga
Terrance in the backseat of his police car?"

Chrystal's laughter subsided. "Muthafucka, that *wasn't*
funny. He chased that boy—butt naked—down the street
with his police car sirens going off, shooting at his ass.
My daddy was crazy."

I laughed out loud. "Yeah, but he was crazy about
you. He loved you more than anything. Your father was
amazing. If it weren't for him, I would have never found
my sister when I was 4. Would have never known Uncle
Larry and Aunt Lucy were raising her if it wasn't for
your father. Your father gave me everything. Your father
gave me you. He let us grow up together. He was hard
on you, but that was because you were his only baby."
I held Chrystal's hand as she started crying. Seeing a
woman cry because of something I had done or said was
my weakness. I pulled her closer. "C'mon, Chrystal, stop
crying. I hate to see you cry."

She wrapped her arms around me, crying on my shoulder. "I miss him so much, David. We loved him so much.
My mom went crazy because her heart was broken. She
woke up every day, asking where my dad's jacket was so

he could go to work. She saw him sitting in his recliner. David, she still cooked dinner for him every night."

Man, I hated to leave her when she was broken. She was my baby. I had to say something, had to *do* something to take away the pain. "Chrystal, it's gonna be okay," I whispered to her.

She shook her head, lifting her head from my shoulder. "How am I going to be okay? My father left me, my mother left me, *you're* leaving me. I don't have anybody."

"I love you, Chrystal," I blurted out over her crying.

"What?" Chrystal looked up at me, letting go of me as I let go of her.

"I love you—you heard me," I finally admitted. "You just asked me if I loved you, Chrystal, so why are you acting shocked when I say it out loud?"

Chrystal laughed a little, tears still streaming down her face. She shook her head, going back over to her boxes to finish packing.

"Why are you laughing?" I asked her, watching her mumbling to herself, closing up one of her boxes of tennis shoes.

"Because the Black boy with the blue eyes is in love with Chrystal Alison, the girl that the niggas love and the bitches love to hate. What a combination." Making jokes was her way of covering up her pain. "You play too gotdamn much, Blue, I swear. Talkin' about you love somebody. Boy, bye. Go 'head on with that bullshit."

I walked over to her, watching her taping up the box. "Man, I swear your bitchy ass is moody as fuck. So fuckin' sometimey."

Chrystal looked at me, grimacing. "Nigga, what?"

I laughed a little to myself. "But I love it, though."

Chrystal couldn't help but grin a little.

"Always trying some crazy shit. Always fuckin' with the wrong dude. Always eating all my shit when you come over to my crib—always falling asleep on my bed. You beat me in every video game. I mean, yo, anything that I do, your ass does it better. You make better grades than me. You always cock blockin', always fighting the chicks who I date," I huffed.

"Nah, I didn't fight that bitch, Mya." Chrystal rolled her eyes, drying her face. "I spared her because she was my lab partner in science. I needed her ass to win at the Science Fair. Yeah, I whupped them other hoes because they were always talkin' shit. Not to mention, they were always keeping you out past curfew."

I burst out laughing. "Curfew?"

"Yes, curfew, gotdamn it." Chrystal watched me laughing my ass off.

"Who gave them a curfew?" I had to know.

"Me, nigga. If you couldn't fuck the hoes before 10:00 on the weekends and 8:00 on school days, then them bitches just needed to wait until the next day. You had these hoes all up in the bathroom at school and shit, all up in the janitor's closet. You have these bitches sprung. Got the hoes blowing up your cell. Then when the hoes call, you won't even call them back. *Then* the bitches would be all up on *my* phone, crying and shit, asking me to talk to you for them. Ugh." She watched me laughing at her. She tried not to laugh along with me. "Can't believe some of the hoes you fuck with. Desperate, sprung, needy bitches."

I took the box that she had just finished taping up and stacked it on top of the other box. "Yeah, I wasted a lot of time."

"Time you could have been with me?" she asked.

I looked at her. "Yeah."

Chrystal just looked at me, shaking her head.

"I didn't even mention how you look because all of that is just an added bonus. You're my road dawg. We do every fuckin' thing together. A nigga is gonna miss you like fuckin' crazy." I looked her over, trying to remember everything about her so that I wouldn't forget a damn thing, not even a freckle.

Chrystal sighed. "I don't get it, Blue. Why didn't you just tell me how you felt about me? These niggas out here ain't got shit on you, Blue. Can't shit touch the relationship that I have with you."

I took a deep breath, agreeing with her. "That's why I didn't tell you. Shawty, what we have is perfect. Not to mention, you're like a sister to me. Your parents looked out for me. Your parents practically helped Miss Tiffany raise me. You're my heart. I have to be yours too; otherwise, you wouldn't have gotten my name tatted on your back, right behind your heart."

"Did you notice the crown on the B?" Chrystal grinned. "You're my king. Always have been. Always will be. You could have just told me, Blue. You're my nigga, dude."

I couldn't help but laugh at my little shawty. "And you're my ride-or-die chick. Always have been."

"Always will be," she whispered back, shaking her head at me. "If you had told me how you felt, I swear, none of them other bustas would have had a chance, Blue. Mom would have loved to hear that we were a couple. She loves you like you were her own son. She's gonna kick your ass when she finds out about this. Damn, I'm gonna miss your ass."

I reached into my pocket and pulled out a letter that I wrote to her. I wasn't good at expressing myself verbally, but I could write my muthafuckin' ass off.

Chrystal grinned. "What is this?"

I smiled at her, nervous as hell, as she opened it and cleared her throat to read it out loud.

"*One Woman's Trash.*" Chrystal read the title and then looked back up at me. "Hmmm . . ."

"Keep reading. There's more." I smiled at her.
She looked back down at the letter.

*I never knew her, I never met her, I never touched
her, but I need her. I wanna show her that I
need her, that I miss her, wanna see her. I heard
her heart beating from the inside. How could she
leave me in the cold outside? All alone until he
found me, gave me life again, and all his sympathy. He gave me Tiffany, gave me a heart, gave
me a family. Then he gave me you, all that sassi-
ness, all that energy, all that attitude. I grew up
with you, and I would do anything for you. I would
die for you, do anything you ask me to. You're my
heart and soul. I'll never let you go. Is this love I
feel, God? I need to know. I think about her day and
night; I should have told her sooner how I felt inside. Do you feel what I feel for you? I wanna hold
you close. Let me comfort you. You gave me hope
when all I felt was pain. You revealed the sun even
through the rain. Our time is up, baby. I have to go;
I had to tell you this because you need to know. I
love you . . . point-blank.*

Chrystal laughed, then cried out loud.
I bit my lip to keep from crying in front of her.
"What'cha think?"
"I love it." She cried, folding the letter and putting it
into her back pocket. She turned to me. "And would you
believe me if I told you that I love you too, David?"
I nodded. I didn't know what my next move was. I had
been with several girls. I had no problem approaching
them. No problem running game. No problem touching or kissing or fucking or sucking. But Chrystal? She
wasn't just some girl to me; she was special. When I was

fighting, she was the only girl who could stop me. When I was mad, she was the only girl who could calm me down. When I was sad, she was the only girl who could make me smile. And when I was happy, she was the only girl I wanted to be around.

"I don't know what to do next, Chrystal," I admitted. "What do I do now?"

"Kiss me." She held my hands, pulling me closer to her.

I laughed nervously. "What? You got a nigga, Chrystal."

"Is he here?" She kissed my lips anyway, nibbling on them just a little. She had my dick on swole. "You told me that you love me. So love me, Blue, before you leave me," she whispered, licking my bottom lip and then sucking it into her mouth.

"Man, these lips." I kissed her back. Her lips were so fuckin' soft and wet. "Why did I wait so long?" I pulled her in closer by her belt loops.

"How long have you been waiting?" Chrystal giggled as I backed her up against her wall.

"Shit. I've been waiting sixteen years to get this pussy." I pulled the drawstring on her cute little sweat shorts. "So, you already *know* I'm about to dig in."

Chrystal panted in my mouth, unbuckling my pants. "What time did my people say they were coming over?"

# Chapter One

## *The Woman In My Life*

## *Blue*

*Present Day*

"Mr. Jacobs, man, I hope this is gonna be a multiple choice test because your finals be killa, son." One of my students, Francis, whined to me on the last day of class before we broke for the holidays.

Teaching was something a nigga really didn't wanna do, but it was it was the only way that I was going to be able to go to college. I got caught up with the wrong crowd, not giving a fuck about anything after Miss Tiffany picked up and moved me to D.C. with her ten years ago. I missed the fuck out of Chrystal. We kept in contact for about six months until she ended up with a nigga who cut her ties with everyone. I called everyone looking for that girl; I even took the bus back home, without Miss Tiffany knowing, a few times, trying to find her. The nigga, whoever he was, made sure no one would be able to keep in touch with her. And I went crazy. I skipped school, sold every type of drug that there was, and broke Miss Tiffany's heart. She just knew that I'd make her proud. But I was doing anything *but* that. I ran the streets all day and night. I stopped going to school. I wasn't in a gang, but most of the niggas I ran with were gang-affiliated. We got into it one night with these niggas who were posted on our block. We started shooting, they started shooting, and the rest was history. The niggas swung by my house on Christmas Day, shooting at the crib. And Miss Tiffany was sitting outside on our porch, with our Rottweiler, Man-Man.

That morning, as soon as I opened my gifts with Miss Tiffany, I was out with my boys, so I wasn't even home when she died. My neighbor called me on my cell phone to tell me what had happened. I got home to a yard full of paramedics and about fifteen people in the neighborhood who were crying and screaming over Miss Tiffany. She was just 38, bruh. It took Miss Tiffany's death for me to straighten up my life. She died on my eighteenth birthday. And she didn't have any life insurance. Miss Tiffany was a smoker with heart problems, and no life insurance company wanted to insure her. Every dime that I made hustlin' went into paying to have her buried.

I obtained my GED and enrolled in college at the University of Maryland, Baltimore County. When I couldn't afford to pay for school for four years, my counselor told me about the TEACH Grant, a grant that helps you pay for college if you teach in a high-need field in a low-income area. I wasn't about teaching no badass kids from the hood, yo. My nigga, Kameron's parents were stacked with paper and major contributors to the University of Maryland. His father spoke with the dean of the math department, and I ended up teaching precalculus at UMBC after graduating from college in 2013.

"Yeah, Mr. Jacobs, I hope you take it easy on us because that midterm was no joke." Another student of mine named Letta sighed as I handed her about ten tests. She looked up into my face, taking one test and then passing the rest on. That girl was fly as a muthafucka. She was 20, dark skinned, with thick, long hair, and had these juicy lips that looked like she could suck the fuckin' life out of a dick. It was the dead of winter, and this chick had on a tight-ass low-cut T-shirt, tight-ass ripped jeans, and open-toe stilettos.

As a matter of fact, every chick in Letta's row was dressed in next to nothing, looking like they were about to hit the club the minute school was out that afternoon. Teaching was no easy job, yo. Those chicks came to school each and every day, on time, bustin' out of their outfits, wearing outfits that I swear were made just for me. I could admit, a nigga was a handsome muthafucka. And being a handsome muthafucka in a town with women as horny and as the fine as women in Baltimore City wasn't easy. I was trying to do right by Kylie, but, man, it was challenging. I knew some of my students outside of the classroom. Before Kylie put a stop to my hanging out with the fellas, I rolled with them almost every night. And the fact that most of the females that I taught were dating some of the students that I hung around didn't stop these females from trying to throw their pussy my way. I had plenty of opportunities to smash whoever, whenever, wherever, and however I wanted to, but I never gave in. I can't even tell you how many females showed up at my office at night, offering to sleep with me so they could pass. I think I prayed to God every night for the strength to be faithful to Kylie. So far, it worked.

"Ummm," I cleared my throat, looking down at Letta licking her DSLs. "Maybe you should spend more time studying and less time trying to figure out what to wear to school." I looked her over a little. "Or should I say, what *not* to wear?"

"What you mean, Mr. Jacobs?" Letta looked around the room at everyone who was snickering, and then she looked at me. "What, you want me to take off something?"

"No, trick, he wants you to put *on* something," I heard Kylie's voice over my shoulder.

I sighed, shaking my head, watching all the expressions on my female students' faces change from flirty to "not this bitch again." I turned around to see my beautiful wife, Kylie, dressed in a red, plaid Burberry coat and matching knee-high boots. Her curly, dirty-blond hair hung over her gray eyes. She was so pretty, but that expression on her face, though. She hated me teaching. Said my class had too many hoes. Said that *I* had too many hoes after me. She'd pop up just about every day, around 1:30 p.m., to take me to lunch.

Every time my students saw me with Kylie, they rolled their eyes. Kylie was a cute, petite, but shapely, light-skinned, blond bombshell. She was beautiful beyond words, a mix with Black, white, and Japanese. She could sing. She could act (which was probably why she was such a fuckin' drama queen and could cry at the drop of a dime). She could dance. She could even work the fuckin' pole (which I found out one night after thinking I was surprising her with a pole that I had installed in the center of our bedroom). She was brilliant. She spoke Spanish, French, Japanese, and German. She was a fashion major when she should have been an engineer or an astrophysicist. Her family was richer than God; she could have attended any school in any country, but she chose to go to Morgan State University.

Yo, let me tell you how I met this girl (since you're wondering). My heart was in so much pain after I lost Miss Tiffany. It was my fault that she was killed. All I could really focus on was getting my life back on track. I still kept in touch with my niggas on the block in D.C., but I kept my head in those college books and on working a legit job. My boy Kameron—or Kam for short—was steady trying to get me to run the streets with him. His parents owned half of Baltimore. They invested in just about every major business in the city. Why Kam felt the need to run the streets and make that kind of name for himself, I had no idea. When it was time to play, I kicked it with the fellas. But when it was time to work, I hung around my boy, Darius. His cousin was the assistant manager at Olive Garden. I didn't care what type of job I got; I just knew that I needed something. I was 18 and alone. I had to move in with Darius, into a two-bedroom apartment in Baltimore City. He was going to school at Morgan State. The nigga was smart as fuck, going to school to be a civil engineer. With damn near perfect SAT and ACT scores, not to mention the above-average grades he made in high school, he could have gotten into any Ivy League school of his choice. But he chose to stay in Maryland. He had a sister who was mentally disabled named Life. She was the prettiest little girl, born without limbs. She lived in a group home, founded by Darius's grandparents, called Tree of Life, in her honor.

"A'ight, kid, my cousin, Kylie, is tough. Her parents own this franchise, so whatever she says goes, a'ight?" Darius nudged me. I had yet to meet his cousin. On the day that I went for my interview, she wasn't there. I interviewed with the general manager, Reba, who hired me on the spot. She must have asked me only four or five questions before inquiring about when I could start. They needed bussers. Shit, I didn't care what job she gave me as long as I got at least thirty hours. I would attend school four days a week, from nine to three, and then work at night. I was going to be a tired muthafucka, but shit, I needed the money.

I stood alongside the back entrance to the kitchen, watching the sexy servers walk past me, putting a little swish in their hips because me and my nigga were watching. I looked back at Darius. "Nigga, what you doing here? You don't even work here. Who you trying to holla at?"

Darius laughed out loud. "Oh, my boys that I'm mentoring from the group home are coming here. These kids have nobody, yo. Parents don't even come out to see them. Could you imagine that shit?" Darius stopped laughing, shaking his head.

I nodded. "Yeah. Shit is fucked up." I knew firsthand what it was like to be abandoned by the ones who were supposed to love you the most.

"The driver is going to bring my three soldiers here. Not to mention, my little sister is coming too. We're gonna sit down and eat. You wanna meet the kids?" Darius asked.

I shook my head. I saw some of the dudes that he worked with at the group home. I had just lost my mother, man. My heart was already weak. Seeing those disabled kids always put a strain on my heart and my mind. One of the kids that he was mentoring at the home didn't have any eyes. Why? Because the little homie pulled them out himself.

"Nah, homie, I'm good. But tell the little homies I said what's up. And kiss your sister for me. I'll meet them one day, but not today, man. A nigga is already depressed enough as it is." I shook my head.

"Darius, boy, your momma has been calling me all day, looking for your ass." I heard the sweetest voice over my shoulder, coming through the kitchen door.

I looked over my shoulder, seeing what looked like an angel coming toward me. I turned around, fully facing her, as she walked up to Darius and me. This girl was wearing a tight, button-down, baby blue long-sleeved shirt, tight gray dress pants, and black high heels. Silver-framed reading glasses sat on her nose, covering her bright gray eyes. Her curly, dirty-blond hair was pulled back into a high ponytail.

Darius sucked his teeth at her. "Kylie, yo, tell your *aunt* she needs to get your *cousin* to go run her errands for her. She knows I gotta eat with my clients tonight." Darius nudged me. "Yo." He knocked me out of my trance. "This is my cousin, Kylie. Kylie, this is David. But we call the nigga Blue because—"

"Because of these pretty blue eyes." Kylie looked in my face. She looked me over a little bit before rolling her eyes. "David, don't let my cousin get you fired. You need to get to work. Tables 211, 242, and 312 need to be bussed. If you can lean, your ass can clean." And then she walked away from us.

I watched that big booty of hers bouncing as she strolled away from us, mingling with the guests as she walked through the restaurant.

"Man, don't even think about it, son," Darius laughed.

I sucked my teeth. "What? Nigga, I ain't thinking about her. I got other shit on my mind. Not to mention, shawty looks like she has an attitude. How old is she anyway, dude?"

"Shit, 18. She's a freshman at Morgan. My aunt's husband is a fuckin' millionaire. He invented computer software that helps track storms more quickly. My cousin doesn't have to work a day in her life if she doesn't want to, yo. Her place is somewhere in Hollywood, California, bruh, not here, managing a restaurant in Hanover, Maryland. She's always trying to fit in where she doesn't. Anyway, get to work before your ass gets fired. And try not to break anything. She hates that shit," Darius tried to warn me.

Why did the first thing I did right in front of Kylie have to be breaking four fuckin' wineglasses? All the other bussers, who stood beside me, emptying their dirty dishes, were rolling, laughing at a nigga. I cleaned up the glass, throwing it in the "broken glass" bin.

"Do you have the money to pay for those glasses that you just broke, David?" Kylie watched as I threw the glass away. "You've only been here a week, and I heard you've broken at least thirty glasses already."

I looked at her, trying my best not to say anything smart back. I took a deep breath before emptying the other dishes on my tray.

"While you're in here breaking dishes, there are at least ten tables in Chianti that need to be cleaned. And pull your gotdamn pants up. Don't nobody wanna see your gray Joe Boxers, dude. Ugh." Kylie walked past me.

"Yo, why you always sweatin' a nigga?" I blurted out without even thinking. I was tired of her mouth. Though I'd only been there a week, I heard that she was dogging me out to all the other managers, telling them that she didn't like the way I walked around, mean muggin' everyone. She never said shit to my face until the day I broke those glasses in front of her. She thought I was beneath her. She knew I was from the hood. But she still should have given a nigga some credit. At least I was going to college. If I hadn't of fucked around so much while I was in school, I would have gotten an academic scholarship. A nigga wasn't stupid. I made damn near straight-A's while I lived in North Carolina. It wasn't until I moved to D.C. with Miss Tiffany that a nigga started slackin'.

Kylie folded her arms, shifting her weight to her right leg, standing there in gotdamn heels on a slippery-ass kitchen floor. "*Excuse* me?"

"Yo, you in here treating everybody like shit, telling us how we fuckin' up, and your ass standing here on a gotdamn slippery-ass floor, knowing good and gotdamn well your ass should be wearing skid-resistant shoes. You wanna dog me 'cuz my pants hang a little low, and your ass ain't even dressing up to code? You gotta lead by example, shawty. You gotta give respect to get respect." I tossed my dishes on the cleaning rack, damn near cracking another bowl. "Stop treating everyone like they're beneath you. You're our supervisor, not our muthafuckin' master, yo." I walked past her.

Everyone was looking at a nigga like I had lost my mind.

Kylie just kind of stood there speechless, watching me walk out of the kitchen and back into the dining area to finish cleaning my section.

One of the bussers, Sean, came running behind me, laughing his ass off. "Yo, dude, you can't be going off on Kylie like that. You must not need this job."

I sucked my teeth. "Man, fuck that bitch. Somebody needs to tell her ass that she ain't shit. She needs to get somewhere, talkin' all that bullshit for real. She's always talkin' down to everyone. I ain't never been good at kissing ass, and I'm damn sure not about to start doing the shit now."

I was the last busser to leave that Saturday night. Kylie was closing. And I think there might have only been about two people in the kitchen cleaning their stations so they could go home. I was in the break room, getting my jacket. When I turned around, I almost bumped right into Kylie. She just looked up into my face as I moved past her, not saying a word, mean muggin' shawty a little.

"You know, that was fuckin' rude what you said to me earlier," Kylie spoke to my back as I attempted to walk away from her.

I laughed to myself a little. "Yo," I turned back around, facing her. "*I'm* rude?"

She nodded, her gray eyes looking up at me. "Yes. Your little Baby Boy, Boys from the Hood, New Jack City, Fuck the Police attitude ain't scaring nobody but you." She looked me over. "You come around here, with your chest all poked out, with that huge chip on your shoulder. All the servers tell me that you have a nasty-ass attitude, and *that's* the reason why I stay on you."

"Them hoes just mad because I don't fuck with none of 'em." I watched her rollin' her eyes at me.

"See, that's *exactly* what I'm talking about; why do they have to be hoes?" Kylie folded her arms.

"Man, I asked one of them *hoes* in the back of the house for a towel so I could clean the table, and do you know what she handed me? A pair of panties. What type of shit do you call that? And why am I explaining anything to you? You're taking up for the bitches because you're probably just like them," I growled.

Kylie shook her head at me. "Oh my goodness, why do you act like this? You look too damn good to be so mean. What's wrong? Why are you so angry?"

"You don't know shit about me, Kylie." I looked her body over a little. Shawty was fly as fuck, but she got on my gotdamn nerves.

"And I don't want to, either." Kylie sucked her teeth, rolling her big, pretty eyes. "All I'm saying is, if you wanna keep your little job, leave that gangsta shit at home, *Blue.*"

"Man, fuck you," I snarled down at her.

Kylie's eyes widened. She went to slap me, but I grabbed her hand, slinging her little ass away from me. And shawty started crying. Like real tears, yo. Like, I broke her heart. I didn't know how to respond to that. The only thing I could think of to do was grab shawty and hold her. As mad as I was at life, I still had a heart. Kylie was a bitch and needed someone to put her in her place, but still, I should have seen straight through her anger to her pain.

Kylie buried her face in my shirt. "Oh my goodness, why do I always fall for assholes?" she muttered in my shirt.

I looked down at her, letting her go. "What?"

She looked up at me. "I just broke up with my boyfriend. I don't mean to be a bitch, but the shit hurts, you know? I'm just tired of being played by guys like you."

I shook my head at her. "Guys like me?"

"There's got to be more to you than all this attitude." Kylie's eyes searched my face. "Show me more."

I just looked at her. "What do you need me to show you?"

"Let's go," she whispered to me.

I was still lost. "What?"

"Micha can close the store for me. Do you have plans tonight?" Kylie walked past me.

I watched her hips swaying as she grabbed her coat from the coatrack. "Nah. Just studying."

"You just said, 'fuck me,' right?" Kylie grinned, reminding me so much of the girl that I was missing.

I just looked at Kylie, watching her lick her plump, pink lips. "Yeah, I did say that. I meant that shit too."

"Well, take me home and fuck me, David," she whispered, walking up to me, grabbing a nigga by the collar and kissing me like she needed my air to breath.

And fuck we did.


"I'm going to be working late," Kylie told me over lunch that New Year's Eve afternoon. We sat across from each other at Chipotle, sharing a bowl of white rice, black beans, chicken, and steak, along with a bit of lettuce, cheese, guacamole, and sour cream. Oh, and I can't forget the tortilla chips. The best part about Chipotle was that the shit filled you up all muthafuckin' day, which was good because, according to what shawty had just told me, I was going to be home alone—again—with no dinner on the table.

"Yo," I shook my head at her, stopping midbite. I put my fork down in the bowl. "Again?"

Kylie sighed. "You know we're getting ready for this big fashion showcase for New Year's. I gotta host auditions for models tonight, boo." She watched the aggravated expression on my face. "C'mon, boo. We can't keep living off a teacher's salary forever."

I just looked at her. "Yo, if you stop buying a new pair of shoes every other gotdamn day, we'll be a'ight."

"Not gonna happen, David." Kylie refused to believe she had a problem. "And I refuse to ask my parents for any more money. They've done enough. Making a name for myself in the fashion industry is really gonna help us. Soon, everyone will be wearing Styles by Kylie Luckett." Kylie dug into the rice bowl.

"You mean Kylie Jacobs." I watched her roll her eyes.

"No, I mean Kylie *Luckett*. Luckett is my daddy's name. Using my daddy's name will get us far. No, I don't want to live in his shadow, but I do want the recognition. I hyphenated my name, boo. It's not like I didn't take your name. You're still trippin' over 'Kylie Luckett-Jacobs'?" Kylie shook her head at me, watching me lean back in my chair, irritated like a muthafucka.

New Year's Day marked our third wedding anniversary. Well, we never actually had a wedding. We got married in front of the magistrate. Her parents never liked me, which made Kylie want a nigga even more. They thought I was beneath her, and I knew she felt the same thing. At one point, I worked three jobs to support her.

The only thing Miss Tiffany left me when she died was a two-story house in D.C. Kylie refused to live in it, even suggesting that I sell the house. I wouldn't, so we just rented it out. Kylie wanted to live the way she did before we were married, when her parents were taking care of her. She rocked nothing but the most expensive clothing. She had her hair done every other week. She went to the spa and had her nails done every week. She had a nigga paying for her to push a Lexus *and* a BMW, while I rode around in a Toyota Camry. She had me paying a $2,800 mortgage on a house that was too big for just the two of us.

She was going to graduate school at the University of Maryland, so she wasn't working. She spent most of her time with her friends from college, who were also fashion majors. She directed major fashion shows; I'll give her that. And she kept getting modeling gigs. I knew her ambition would pay off soon, but it wasn't helping me put food on the table at the time.

Living beyond our means was starting to get to me. I was a college professor, earning around $55,000 a year, which was hardly enough to support that girl. My pockets stayed on E just to make sure that girl had everything she wanted. And she always wanted more.

"Yo," I changed the subject, "I've been thinking of hookin' up with Kam."

Kylie looked at me with this, "*Nigga, what?*" look on her face. "If you're thinking about what I *think* you're thinking about, then you better switch those thoughts up *real* quick. Kam is nothing but trouble. I can't believe you still associate with that dude. You'd think by now you'd have a new set of friends. You're a respected college professor. As much as I hate the hoes who are always all up in your grill every time I swing by your class, I am glad that you're staying out of trouble."

"Kylie, how many times have you told me to find another job where I can make more money? The lifestyle I used to live makes it hard for me to get a job around here without that nigga's help. I told you I wanna leave Maryland, but you're so determined to stay here. As long as I'm here, I might as well do something worthwhile. Kam's got the hookup, and I want it. I'm not your typical college professor, and you know it." I looked at her, watching her run her fingers anxiously through her hair.

"David, the kind of weight Kam pushes would put you *under* the jail if you were ever caught. I thought you said that you promised yourself after your mother died that you'd never go back to that life. We need the money, but we don't need it *that* badly. Big things are going to happen real soon, I promise, boo." Kylie put the strap of her Michael Kors purse over her shoulder.

"Where you going?" I asked her as she stood from the table, looking down at the display on her cell phone.

"I gotta meet my girls. They're coming around the corner now to get me." Kylie came around the table to give me a peck on the lips. "Lata, David."

I sighed, watching her walk away. I looked up to see Letta seated in a booth with some friends. She looked up at me when she saw that I was looking at her. And she winked her eye at me. I looked away, taking a deep breath. Yo, Kylie was lucky as fuck because every time I saw Letta, my dick stood at attention. It took everything in me not to get with Letta. Kylie was never home. We hadn't had sex in at least six weeks. The best part of waking up wasn't Folgers in my cup; it was fuckin.' And I got little to none of that those days. You would've thought by the way we fucked when we first started seeing each other that we'd continue on that winning streak. But nah. As soon as we got married, the sex went from three times a day to maybe three times a *month*, shit, if that. I was only 24 years old, but she had a nigga feeling like I was 64. All I did was work, go home, eat alone, and watch muthafuckin' TV.

Kylie hated all of my friends, except for Darius. All of my niggas were single. I was the only one dumb enough to get married at 22. I was just sick of missing Chrystal; that was what really drove me to put my all into Kylie. I didn't even have a picture of Chrystal. I got rid of everything in my life that reminded me of her. I couldn't find her, and I was frustrated as a muthafucka. It was as if Chrystal fell off the radar. She wasn't on Twitter. Wasn't on Facebook. Wasn't on Instagram. My niggas back in Greenville said shawty never came back Greenville to visit, but they heard she would go to Goldsboro every now and then to see her mother at Cherry Hospital. I missed that girl. I felt like a part of me was missing without her. It had been eight years since I'd seen her, but I couldn't get her smile, that voice, that touch out of my mind. I loved Kylie, but there was no love like the love I had for Chrystal.

"Aye, homie!" I was snapped out of my trance by the sound of Darius's voice.

I looked up to see Darius standing there, looking like he was about to go to an interview. But he wasn't. The nigga always wore a suit and shit, looking like he was auditioning for *The Men In Black*. "What up, dawg?" I gave my nigga some dap.

He glanced back at Letta and then looked at me, shaking his head. "Man, your students be throwing it at'cha, don't they?"

I shook my head. "Man, this is the hardest job I've ever worked; no pun intended."

Darius laughed out loud, sitting across from me. "Word. I heard that shit. Have you decided what'cha gonna do for your birthday on Friday, homie?"

My birthday is in two days. I hated my birthday. It was a cruel reminder that life hated my guts. My mother dumped me in the trash on my birthday. Miss Tiffany died on my birthday. I had to celebrate my birthday without Chrystal every year. I hated that shit. Once Miss Tiffany died, that was a wrap. I didn't even celebrate the shit. I never wanted anything for my birthday. I could give a fuck about Christmas. All I wanted to do was smoke weed and listen to the *Chronic* album.

"Man, y'all can have that shit," I mumbled under my breath, digging into my rice bowl. "I don't know what part of 'I don't wanna celebrate *shit*' y'all niggas don't understand."

Darius sighed. "Man, you trippin.' My nigga Roosevelt is throwing a masquerade party for me tomorrow night. The proceeds will help fund a new building for Tree of Life. The building they live in has all kinds of leaks, mold, and shit. My little sister lives there. I can't have her living like that. And I'll be damned if Kylie's father pays for anything else for our family. He loves to rub that shit in. My aunt isn't any better; she swears she's the backbone of our family. Ever since my grandparents died and left her all of this money, she thinks she runs my mother's life. And Mama just lets her. Not this time. I'ma do this shit for my family. I just wanna help raise money for the kids and have a little fun at the same time. You rollin' or what, son?"

I sighed. "I don't know, yo. I don't be feeling like doing much of anything on Christmas Eve. Besides, Kylie might have plans for us tomorrow night. She has this thing where she likes staying up until midnight to eat cookies and milk. It kind of reminds me of when I was a kid and used to wait by the fireplace with my girl, Chrystal. We'd make cookies and sit by the fireplace, waiting on Santa's fat ass to come down the chimney. And Mr. William made sure that shit happened on time every Christmas. Man, those were the days, yo. I'd give anything to get those days back."

Darius gave me a sympathetic look. "Well, I don't know what Kylie has planned for y'all at midnight, but I do know that she's got a talent showcase tomorrow at Morgan State at like 9:00, yo."

I sucked my teeth. "Man, why am I always the last to hear about shit? All she mentioned was that she had a show to do on New Year's. She ain't say shit about tomorrow."

Darius shrugged. "Well, don't shoot the messenger. I'm just telling you what my momma told me. She's helping Cuz sew up most of her clothes, so I think she'd know, son." He watched the pissed-off expression on my face. "But fuck all that, yo. This masquerade is gonna be off the fuckin' chain. It's a black-and-white party, yo. And I heard that Kam was gonna bring some of his girls from Club Pop It. Nigga, is your ass rollin' or what?"

I looked at Darius. Pop It was a strip club owned by Kam and his cousin, Kavante. He had nothing but the baddest bitches working up in that club. And whatever you needed serviced on your body, those girls got the job done and did it right.

"Man, Kylie's ass ain't letting a nigga go to that shit. She finds out and the bitch is gonna cut off my dick." I leaned back in my chair.

Darius grinned, looking back at Letta and her friends. And then he looked back at me. "Your girl, Letta, works there, son."

I glanced at her and then back at Darius. "Say word, yo."

Darius nodded. "Dude, I wouldn't lie to you. I saw her ass on stage last weekend. C'mon, dawg. You won't let us celebrate your birthday. Well, let's celebrate the day *before* then. Fuck that shit my cousin's talkin' about. She always be with that shit. She's out all night, every night, and where the fuck are you? Home. Alone. Smokin' that good-good, thinking about the past and shit. Tomorrow night, we gonna do it differently. Big, *real* big."


I sat on my bed in my wife-beater and sweats, watching Kylie get all dolled up for her fashion showcase that evening of Christmas Eve. She was dressed in a skintight nude dress by Robert Cavalli. Shawty looked more like she was going on a fuckin' date than to host a fashion show, but I tried keeping my mouth shut. Watching her was just more incentive to do my own thing that night.

"Do you plan on being home by midnight, shawty?" I looked at the time on the cable box. "It's 6:00, and your show doesn't even start until 9:00. What, you got a date or something?"

Kylie looked at my reflection in her full-length mirror before looking back at me. She rolled her big gray eyes. "For you and my nosy cousin Darius's information, the show starts at 8:00. I have to be there to set up in about thirty minutes, and I'm already running late." She looked back in the mirror, tossing her blond hair over her shoulders. She'd spent about three hours straightening her curls. Her hair hung halfway down her back. I was pissed off at her, but shawty was gorgeous.

The more I looked at Kylie, the more I questioned why we were even together. We both seemed to be searching for something we couldn't find in each other. The spark we had when we first met was extinguished. Maybe it wasn't even a spark. I can't speak for her, but I knew when we met that I was trying to get over Chrystal. I needed something to stop me from going crazy at night, dreaming about that girl. I needed something to numb my heart to the pain, and Kylie did just that for a few years. Though we used to fuck like rabbits, there was absolutely no love there. I think I could actually count the number of times that we kissed on two hands. I'd known the girl for *seven* years, and I could count the number of times that we kissed. What was the fuckin' point?

"You gonna be back in time to go with us to do our Christmas Eve thang?" I asked her, watching as she swept her hair to the side.

Kylie giggled, holding the gold locket I'd given her for her twentieth birthday in her hands. "You actually like that corny shit I do every year?" She signaled me to get up and go over to her to help her latch the necklace around her neck.

"Yeah, shawty." I got up and went over to her, taking the necklace from her hands. I put it around her neck, latching the hooks together. "It reminds me of when I was a kid. It's the only really good memory I still have left about the holidays, Kylie."

Kylie sighed, pulling her hair over to the other shoulder, then turned to the side, checking herself out in the mirror. Why the fuck do y'all women look back at your ass? To see if it's still there? Or to see how good it looks, to make sure the niggas stayed watching it? Whatever reason y'all have for doing the shit, I hate it. Why you worried about what other muthafuckas think about your ass when you've got a man at home that would do whatever you wanted him to do to it?

I looked down at her round behind in that dress and then looked back at her neck. I did a double take of the shit that I saw on her pale neck. There was a big red mark on her neck—something like a tooth mark or some shit. I hadn't noticed the shit until she pulled her hair back. I grabbed her arm, startling her. "What the fuck is that?"

Kylie pulled from me, looking at a nigga like I was crazy. "What is wrong with you?"

"What's that on your muthafuckin' neck?" I asked as Kylie gasped, covering her neck with her hand.

"Oh my goodness. That pimple that I popped is *still* there?" She turned to the mirror, eying her neck. "I've been picking at this shit all day. I was hoping it would dry up before the show, but now, it's all red." Kylie rubbed it a little before covering it with her hair. "There. Now, it's covered."

I just looked at her, watching her go about her business, acting like I was just going to let the shit go. "So, you're just gonna walk out of here and pretend that shit is a breakout or some shit, right?" I asked her.

Kylie rolled her eyes, grabbing her gold clutch purse from the nightstand. "David, please. You know I have eczema."

"Eczema my ass, Kylie! That's a muthafuckin' tooth mark. Who's the nigga that's been suckin' on my wife's neck?" I watched Kylie laughing like I was playing or some shit. I slowed my life down a lot since I met this girl. She was lucky because the old me probably would've snatched her up by her neck.

"Boy, bye. I'll see you later." Kylie laughed, heading out the door of our bedroom.

"So you just gonna walk the fuck off while I'm talkin' to you?" I asked.

"Aren't you *watching* me walk away, David?" Her heels clanked against the stairs as she descended the staircase.

I just let shawty go. There was no use in arguing with her. I'd stopped fighting with her months ago. Shawty thought I was weak. Nah, I just didn't care. She wanted me to fight her, wanted me to chase her, wanted me to jack up her ass. But I always kept my cool. I just let shawty do her because I'd eventually get tired of her.

All the late nights and her not returning my phone calls started to add up—quickly.

The sex had tapered off. Three years into our marriage and shawty was tired of a nigga. She could have just told me it was over. She didn't have to hold on if she was ready to let go. And the truth of the matter was, I wasn't even mad. Why wasn't I angry when I should have been? I went and jumped in the shower, got fresh as a muthafucka, dressed in black from head to toe in my Dolce & Gabbana, and rolled the fuck out.

"Here, Blue, put this on." Darius handed me a black mask to put on my face just as we pulled up in front of the Marriott Hotel in downtown Washington, D.C.

I scoffed, taking the mask from his hands. "Dude, I'ma feel like Zorro in this bullshit."

Darius's older sister, Amanda, was in the backseat of his white Mustang. "Boy," she laughed, scooting to the edge of her seat. She leaned over me, her perky breasts in my face, as she grabbed the mask from my hands. "It's a masquerade. Have you ever been to one of these?" She placed the mask over my face, covering my eyes, and tied it around my head.

"Nah," I laughed a little.

"Well, anything is liable to happen at a black-and-white masquerade party. You'll recognize the strippers *or* the ones who plan on having sex because they'll be dressed in red."

I looked back at Amanda, who was wearing red, and shook my head.

"Then men are dressed in black. And the ladies who only came to have a good time will be dressed in white. Most of the people here are planning on getting laid by someone." Amanda sighed in my ear. "So I guarantee most of these girls will be in red."

I looked over at Darius, who was dying laughing. "Nigga, what? Y'all brought me to a fuckin' swinger party? This is some fuckin' orgy shit?"

"Fool, hush." Amanda bopped me on the head and then sat back in her seat. "I'm trying to find my boo, Rashaad. He said he'd be wearing a blue mask tonight. And no, it's not a swinger party. It's just a place to free all your inhibitions if you choose to. These strippers are bad. You know Kam sells sex. These girls do it all. There are going to be all types of people here who don't want anyone to know they're here. Ya know—lawyers, doctors, police officers, judges, senators, shit, probably even some pastors. The masks help spice things up a bit. Sleeping with someone when you have no idea what they look like is an orgasm in itself."

Darius looked at me, seeing that I wasn't really feeling the situation. "Dude, didn't you just tell a nigga that Kylie had a big-ass hicky on her neck but tried to play the shit off?"

"Just 'cuz she's fuckin' off doesn't mean I'm about to do the same shit, nigga. I have time invested into this shit. Seven years with this girl." I tried to talk myself into believing that I gave a fuck about our nonexistent relationship.

Amanda scoffed. "Seven long, *miserable* years at that, bruh. That girl has been bleeding you dry for years. She's my cousin and all, but you know I can't stand that bitch. Your sexy ass can do a lot better, boo."

I shook my head, not trying to hear that. The girl I wanted was nowhere to be found, so I was good where I was at the moment. "I don't have time for games. I just came here to support the cause. You said the proceeds go to your group home, nigga. So that's why I'm here." I looked back at Amanda. "So don't try to hook me up with any of your slut-bucket friends either, a'ight?"

"Not even Letta?" Amanda grinned.

I sighed, thinking about it for a second before responding. "Nah, not even Letta."

Amanda looked into my face. She shook her head. "You and them gotdamn blue eyes, boy. That gives you away every time. Everyone up in there is gonna know it's you. Here." She handed me what looked like a Mardi Gras mask, with only tiny holes poked where the eyes were. "Take that Zorro mask off and put this one on, boo."

"I'm good, yo. Did y'all not hear what I said? I said I'm not fuckin' *shit* tonight," I exclaimed, tossing the mask back to her.

Damn, that thought changed up real quick from the moment we walked up into the party. Amanda wasn't lying; of all the women in the room, I think only about seven of them dressed in white. The rest had on some of the skimpiest red dresses I'd ever seen. I mainly stayed by the bar. Darius went off to mingle. My nigga bought me and a few more of our boys Burberry silver watches for Christmas and made sure that the niggas wore them that night so he'd recognize us. About eight of our homies showed up to support Darius. It didn't take long for all eight of them to join me at the bar. And it didn't take long for all eight of us to get drunker than a muthafucka. I drank until my gotdamn vision was blurry.

"Awe, shit," my nigga Columbus whooped and hollered, looking over in the direction of the double doors to the banquet hall.

We all looked in the direction that everyone else's gaze was glued to. It was Kam and Kavante, walking through the spot dressed in black and red, with about twelve of their girls wearing black masks and dressed in red lace lingerie. Lingerie that was damn near nonexistent. Some of these girls wore *edible* lingerie. Others wore sheer lingerie. One of the females had an ass so damn big that it looked like it *ate* her gotdamn panties. I never heard niggas scream so gotdamn loud in my life. I brushed off the shit, turning back around to finish my bottle of Hennessey. Half of them females who worked for the nigga were in my precalculus class. Damn shame.

"Man, y'all can have that shit." I drank straight from the bottle. "Can y'all believe I teach half of the females who work for this nigga? I can call almost each and every one of those girls by first, middle, and last name."

"Nigga, shut up. They're about to draw." The youngest nigga in the crew, my student, Francis, elbowed me.

I looked at him, my vision hazy as hell. "What drawing?"

"You know they took our tickets and put them in a box as soon as we walked through the door, yo." Francis shook his head, watching me drink from my bottle to the last drop. He was 21 and able to drink, but he was the designated driver, so he didn't drink that night. "Man, y'all need to ease up on all this fuckin' liquor, man. Y'all throw up in my Durango, I swear, y'all just bought that bitch."

"Man, whateva, nigga. Yo, Blue, they're about to draw a name from the box. And whoever's name gets picked gets to get a butt-naked lap dance from Rain, yo." Columbus whistled, watching the strippers strutting past us.

"Who the fuck is that?" I asked, finally eying the strippers my gotdamn self. One of them looked at me, blowing a kiss. I could barely see, but drunk or not drunk, mask on her face or not, I'd recognize those dick-suckin' lips anywhere. That was Letta.

Columbus looked at a nigga like I was crazy for not knowing shawty. "Rain is Kam's biggest moneymaker. That girl can perform all types of magic tricks with that pussy. Last week, she pulled this string of pearls out of her pussy and stuck that shit in my mouth, son."

While my niggas were praising him, I think I threw up in my mouth a little bit.

"Nigga, you gonna catch something fuckin' around with them hoes at the club." I shook my head at that freaky muthafucka.

"Well, if I do, nigga, it will be worth it. You don't know what this chick can do. Shit, you've never seen, yo. I'm telling you, everything about this girl is sexy from the tattoos on her back to the tattoo she has stamped across her pelvic bone." Columbus was excited out of his mind thinking about this chick. "Her ass gets butt naked every night, but you couldn't tell until she turns around. She's got tattoos covering her titties and a damn rosebush tattoo covering that pussy. She's bad as fuck. You'll see, nigga."

And a nigga did see. I had never won a gotdamn thing in my life. You know those fuckin' enter-to-win-this-fuckin'-brand-new-Lexus contests they used to have at the mall? I would always put my name on about a hundred slips of paper and would never win shit. But that night, at the Marriott, at a fuckin' get-laid-by-a-stranger party, my name was drawn from the box. My niggas were happy as a muthafucka, damn near pushing me down in that chair in the center of the banquet hall.

I leaned back in the chair, a glass of Blue Motherfucker in my hands. My boys were happy as hell for me. They were tired of seeing me moping around about Kylie. Though I thought I wasn't mad at her at first, the more I thought about how much time I wasted, the more pissed that I grew. I drank to drown out my anger, but it really wasn't working. I wasn't in the mood for shit . . . until Rain took the center of the floor.

My niggas weren't lying about shawty. She was sexy as fuck. Long, flowing, dark hair. Bronze-colored skin. Tattoos covered where her lingerie didn't. A sparkling red mask covered half of her face. All you could see were her lips. Those juicy lips. Her juicy lips were painted pink, making them look like a gotdamn bubble-gum-flavored banquet lollipop. She didn't look me in the face, but she looked my body over as she danced her way over to me, taking off her bra and then her panties along the way. Yeah, that pussy was covered with a tattoo that was a rosebush in the shape of her pelvic bone. It almost looked like she was wearing panties, so she didn't look naked at all . . . until she turned the fuck around and bent over, touching her toes.

"Nigga, I told you," I heard Columbus shout from across the room.

"Gotdamn!" I scooted to the edge of my chair, watching that booty jiggle and that pink pussy open wide. I thought I was gonna bust in my pants. She had a butterfly tattoo on her right ass-cheek that looked like it was flying, its wings fluttering when she clapped her ass. She made that pussy pop, made it open and close, made it fuckin' *talk* to a nigga.

It didn't take long for the people who circled the dance floor to zoom in on us, surrounding her to get a closer look. At that point, I had tunnel vision. All I could see was shawty's pussy talking until it started to drip. That shit turned me on so fuckin' bad. And just when I began to reach out for it, she slid back into my lap, her back facing me. She started grinding her hips, working the shit out of my dick. The sweet smell of this girl's pussy filled the air around me. I was in a trance for a second or two before realizing the scent was kind of familiar.

And then, she pulled her long hair over to one shoulder, showing the tattoos sprinkled all over her back. And there it was. I was drunk and my vision was fuckin' with me, but as soon as I saw the tattoo, I *knew* it was her. I grabbed shawty by the hips, looking at the "Blue" tattoo on her back with that crown dangling on the B.

"Chrystal?" I whispered to her when I really felt like screaming her name.

The girl gasped, instantly getting up from my lap, looking down at me, her pink lips quivering. "Blue?" she whispered . . . I think.

# Chapter Two

## *Eyes Like Mine*

## *Blue*

I awoke to the sound of a dog panting in my ear and to what felt like a drill pounding in my head. "What the fuck?" I yelled out as my face was covered in dog slobber. I opened my eyes to Darius's Saint Bernard, Goliath, licking the fuck out of my face. "Nigga, come get this bitch!"

Darius ran into the living room, dying laughing, getting his big-ass dog away from me. "Sorry, nigga, she's in heat, yo. She usually fucks the shit out of the sofa, but you're lying on it, so . . ."

"Yo," I sat up on the couch, rubbing my head, trying to remember everything that had happened the night before. "What happened?"

Darius sat on the sofa across from me. "Well, we got thrown out of my own benefit."

"Why?" I asked, wiping my face with my shirt. I was dressed in a white T-shirt and gray sweats. I didn't even remember changing. "The fuck y'all niggas do?"

"What the fuck did *we* do?" Darius frowned. "Man, you swore up and down that you knew Rain. You went to

confront Kavante, and all hell broke loose. You don't remember punching the fuck out of the nigga? You don't
remember me and our crew having to fight just about every one of their homeboys? Someone called the police,
but we had already rolled out before they arrived. You
know good and gotdamn well you don't need shit else on
your record. Kam pulled a lot of strings to get you that
job at the university. What the fuck does a professor—a
young, respected, *Black* professor at that—look like fighting muthafuckas? The police stay ready to roll down on
us, and you gave them a reason last night. I had to send
my sister to get the money for me and take it to the Tree
of Life this morning."

I looked at him. "Chrystal?" I tried my best to remember, and she was all I could think of. "I was fighting the
niggas over Chrystal?"

Darius nodded. "Yeah, you kept calling Rain 'Chrystal,'
telling her to take her mask off and shit. She kept trying
to tell you that she didn't know what you were talking
about. That's when you grabbed her, and that's when
Kavante jumped in. Boy, you were going off. Who is this
girl, Chrystal? Every year, around this same time, you
bring her up."

"You know that one person you always think about, no
matter who you're with?" I rubbed my head, not remembering a damn thing from the night before after I saw the
tattoo on shawty's back. I was drunk as a muthafucka.
Maybe I was just seeing shit. Darius looked at me. "Yeah?"

"That's her," I admitted out loud for the first time.

"Well, you must've really loved this girl because your
ass tried to lay that nigga's head into the ground when he
told you to take your hands off of her." Darius laughed a
little, watching the confused expression on my face. "And

Kylie has been blowing your gotdamn phone up since last night, yo."

I cringed at the thought of Kylie calling my phone. "Awe, shit," I yelled out. "It's Christmas."

Darius laughed, watching me get up, damn near stumbling over the table. "Yup. Happy birthday, nigga."

"Shawty is gonna be pissed, yo. I don't even celebrate this shit, but it's a big deal to her. Her parents are supposed to be coming over this afternoon for lunch and shit. Not to mention, my sister, Lisa, is coming in town." I started to panic.

Darius nodded. "Yeah, I think I saw her number on your phone too."

"Fuck," I shouted. "She flew in from California last night. My sista is gonna kick my ass. I was supposed to pick her up from the hotel this morning. Fuck my life, yo."

"Nigga, calm down." Darius laughed a little. "I already talked to Kylie. I told her that we went to a benefit for the Tree of Life last night. I told her that we had a few drinks, and one of your students drove us home. She was pissed, but she'll be all right. I talked to her about an hour ago. She went to get your sister. And she said that a few of her friends from college were going to be at the crib tonight too, just to give you a heads-up."

I sat back down on the couch, leaning back, covering my face with my hands. I was tripping. I kept Chrystal on my mind 24/7, but at Christmas, it was always worse. I was drunk out of my mind the night before. Did I *really* see shawty? Was she really there? Was Kam's cousin really selling the fuck out of my homie? I wanted to let the shit go, but I couldn't. I'd never been up in the club, but I'd heard enough just listening to the females that I taught talk about the shit they'd do to trick the niggas at the club out of their dollars. Not to mention, my own homeboys who'd get paid Friday and be broke by Monday fuckin' around with that club. Chrystal, a got-damn stripper. I was gonna put a stop to that shit. I'd try my damnedest to give it a few days to go check out the scene, though. Let things between me and Kam's cousin cool off. When I'm mad, all I can see is red. I had no recollection of what I did the night before, but just thinking about shawty working at that club made my blood boil.

"Man, I've got to be trippin', homie." I uncovered my face, anxiously running my hands through my hair.

Darius looked at me, his thick eyebrows knitting together. "It's Christmas, Blue. Not to mention, it's your birthday. Enjoy the day. Don't go bringing up the past. Talk to Kylie about whatever y'all are going through. I've known you since high school. I fucks with you because you've always had my back. I was the nerdy nigga whose paper everyone copied off of. You were the only person back then who didn't use a nigga. You got to know me, taught me how to get girls, gave me a little bit of your swag . . ." He watched me, laughing a little. "You were knocking niggas over, toting all types of choppers . . . .38s, 9 mms, 4-fives and shit. You've changed. I don't know anything about Chrystal or the life you had before you left North Carolina and moved here, but what I do know about you is that you don't play about who you love."

I looked at him, Chrystal's body flashing through my mind. That was my shawty. I didn't know why she was rollin' with Kam or his fuckin' cousin, Kavante, but I was gonna take her from that nigga—by any means necessary.

"Leave the shit alone. She said she wasn't Chrystal. She told you to back the fuck up, so you need to do that. Take care of your situation with Kylie, nigga, and leave the past where it is." Darius got up from the couch, watching me leaned back on the sofa, my face balled the fuck up. "Come on; take a ride with me."

"Nigga, Kylie keeps blowin' up my phone. She said that her parents are on their way. 'Where the fuck are you—'" I watched as Darius drove past the Tree of Life wooden sign, which led down the driveway to the group home that I told him over and over again that I didn't want to go to. I looked at his grinning ass. "Darius, I told you I wasn't ready to come to this depressing-ass place, didn't I?"

"Man," Darius drove down the driveway, through the woods to the group home. "You've been saying that shit for the past four years, yo. I ain't trying to force these kids on you. I'm about to pick up my little nigga, Payton. He was adopted at birth by this older couple, the Watsons. His adoptive father died when he was just 2 years old, and his adoptive mother had a stroke about four years ago, leaving her in a wheelchair. So, here he is with us, yo. He's the smartest kid I've ever met, but he's got a temper on him, boy. Little homie is deaf and blind, which I know has to be frustrating. I've never seen the nigga open his eyes. We call him 'Pretty Boy.' He's got that curly shit like you, homie." Darius laughed at his own corny-ass jokes. He saw that I wasn't laughing but just anxiously looking around at the duplexes of the group home. "Dude, it's Christmas, I'm just dropping him off with his adoptive mother. She misses him. She hasn't seen him for a few weeks because she was in the hospital."

I exhaled deeply as Darius pulled up in front of one of the duplexes. A health technician was outside the house, struggling with this little boy. The little boy was kicking and punching ol' girl, his eyes shut tightly. Darius's windows were rolled up, but you could hear that little nigga's screeches clear as day. I looked at Darius.

Darius exhaled, shaking his head, watching little man fighting with all of his life to get away from the worker. "Well, that's Payton. You gonna help me get him in the car, or what?"

I looked at Darius like he had lost his mind. "Nigga, no. That's *your* job. Shit, I'm just along for the ride, yo."

"Man, c'mon," Darius huffed, getting out of the car, walking up the sidewalk to get Payton's fighting ass. "Hey, Corina Dorsey."

"Don't 'Hey, Corina Dorsey' me, Darius." Corina rolled her eyes, trying to block Payton's kicks and punches. "Come get this boy before I lose my job!"

I sat in the passenger seat, laughing to myself, watching both of them trying to tame the little nigga. He ran from their asses. A boy, who was blind and deaf, ran around the yard, dodging every tree and even dodging the two of them from grabbing him. When Darius finally caught up with little homie, the boy pounded on his chest and kicked him in both his shins. And then, the little boy began to cry out. He was angry. He was hurting. That's why he was fighting. I could feel little homie's pain. He probably missed his mother. I know I missed mine, even though I'd never met her.

I exhaled deeply before getting out of the car.

Corina watched me walking up through the grass, making my way over to them. She raised her hands. "Watch out, sweetie, okay? This little boy is strong as hell."

I wasn't paying her any mind. I wasn't scared of no scared little kid. He had to be about 8 or 9 years old.

Darius was right; he did resemble me a little. We were about the same complexion with that jet-black curly hair. The boy cried out as Darius tried to grab him close. He pushed Darius away with all of his might.

"Chill, Payton Alison!" Darius yelled, grabbing Payton's hand, placing it over his hand that was signing to blind, deaf Payton.

Alison—that was Chrystal's last name. Everywhere I went seemed to remind me of shawty. I tried to shake her, but how could I? When we were kids, Chrystal used to always make a nigga play house with her. She was the mom, I was the dad, and her ugly-ass Cabbage Patch doll was our baby. Every time we played house, she'd give our baby the same name, Payton. Man, I was drunk as fuck the night before, but I could've sworn I saw a tattoo on her arm that said "Payton" too.

I walked up to Darius, watching him block the little boy's punches. And just when the little boy went in to punch Darius again, I grabbed his fist. The little boy let out a shriek before grabbing my hand with his other hand. Tears raced from his eyes that were clenched shut.

Darius looked at me and how I examined the boy, inspecting his face, his hair, and everything about him. "You all right, bruh?"

"Yeah." I looked at Payton for a few seconds. He looked so familiar, like we'd met before. "Who is his birth mother?" I had to ask.

Darius shrugged, looking at how calm Payton had suddenly gotten. "I don't know, but I heard she still keeps in contact with Payton. I can find out."

"Yeah, you do that." I sighed, about to let go of Payton's fist. But little homie had a death grip on me.

Darius and Corina laughed a little, watching Payton holding on to me.

Payton signed something in my hand.

Darius looked at whatever it was that he was signing, and then he looked at me.

"W-What was he signing?" I looked at Darius, who had a confused look on his face. Then I looked at Corina, who looked just as confused as he did. "What?"

"He said, 'Hi, Daddy.'" Corina spoke up before Darius did.

I looked into little homie's face as he struggled to open his eyes. After a few blinks, his eyes were wide open. And they were as blue as the afternoon sky. I tried to let go of Payton's hand, but he wouldn't release mine. His eyes danced across my face, as if he were looking at me.

Darius looked at Payton and then back at me. "Whoa . . ." Darius was in shock. "I told you little homie looks like you. I've worked with little homie for four years, and this is the first time I've seen him open his eyes. They are blue as a muthafucka." Darius watched Payton continue to look into my face as though he could see me, signing "daddy" in my hand again.

Man, I didn't have any kids, but damn it if that little boy didn't look like a nigga. From the black hair to the blue eyes that the woman gave me, who threw me into the trash can.

"I thought you said he couldn't see." I was still in awe, looking at him.

"He has nystagmus. It's a condition of involuntary eye movement." Corina looked back and forth between the two of us, who were looking at each other. "He *does* look like you."

"Payton Alison . . ." I whispered to myself, examining his face again.

"C'mon, son," Darius tried to laugh off the situation. "We gotta get little homie over to his mother's house. I'm glad you were able to calm him down. You're gonna have to come around more often to see little dude, huh?" He watched the expression on my face change from awe to "Nigga, stop fuckin" with me.' He just grinned.

I looked back at Payton, rising to my feet, still holding his hand that relaxed from the fist it was balled up in. Payton held my hand tightly in both his hands, closing his eyes again.

It was a long ride back home to the city. Darius didn't say much after he dropped Payton off at his adoptive mother's house. It was hard as hell trying to pry that little boy's hand away from mine. He didn't want to let go, and a part of me didn't want to let him go either. I watched as Darius had to carry the little boy into his mother's house, kicking and screaming again. After about fifteen minutes, Darius came back outside and hopped in his ride. I wanted to ask him if he'd gotten the chance to ask about Payton's birth mother, but truthfully, I was scared to know. It was bad enough that the boy was blind and deaf, but to have his mother abandon him like that . . . Where was she? Why wasn't she raising him?

We made it back to my place just in time to run smack into Kylie and her mother in the kitchen, cooking. When Kylie's mother saw me, she rolled her slanted eyes at me and then went back to placing cookies in the oven.

I took a deep breath before saying, "Hi, Mrs. Luckett."

"Umm-hmmm," she muttered under her breath, even rolling her neck to herself.

Darius smirked. "Good afternoon, Aunt Sheryl. What's up, Kylie?"

"Hey," she muttered, glaring at me. "Daddy is in the living room with his nephew, Tommy."

"Well, well, well—if it isn't my handsome little brotha. The fool who stood me up at the airport." I heard my sister Lisa's voice behind me.

I grinned, turning around to face her as she ran into my arms. "What's up, White Girl?" I squeezed her tight in my arms before letting her go. My sister was a beautiful, tall, light-skinned woman with auburn hair and blue eyes. She looked damn near white. Family members always said she looked like my birth mother. I missed her. I hadn't seen her since last Christmas. She was in the marines. I was glad to see her safe and home.

Lisa pushed me in the chest, grinning at me. "Boy, the next time I call your ass, you better call me back." She looked at Darius. "Hey, Darius." She went up to him, giving him some love as well. "You had my brother out late, drinking, huh? Are you to blame for my brother showing up late on his birthday?"

"Uhh," Darius laughed nervously. "Nah, sweetie, but you can blame it on the alcohol, though."

"Still corny, huh?" Lisa laughed.

Kylie walked up to me, tapping me on the shoulder. "David, can we talk?"

I glanced over at Mrs. Luckett, who was staring back at me, her arms folded, shaking her head.

Kylie and I stood across from each other in our bedroom, looking at each other, eye to eye. She stood there with her arms folded. "David, it's Christmas."

"I know what day it is. And?" I shrugged, not really giving a fuck what she had to say.

"And?" Kylie pushed me on the shoulder. "*And* you knew my parents were coming. *And* you stayed out all night without calling me. *And* Darius said y'all went out drinking. *And* it's fuckin' Christmas. *Your* muthafuckin' birthday. The first Christmas and birthday we haven't spent together since the day we met."

"Oh," I found the situation hilarious. "*Now* you wanna get fuckin' sentimental? Were you sentimental when *you* were the one hanging out all night, coming in drunk as fuck? Did my birthday or any of that shit matter to you when you let that nigga put that fuckin' bite mark on your neck?"

Kylie pushed me in the shoulder again. "David, this is a *rash*. I have them all over my body." Kylie pulled up her tight navy blue sweater, showed me similar rashes on her abdomen and her breasts, and then she turned around, showing me the rashes on her back. "See."

I looked her over a little as she let down her shirt. And then I looked back into her face. I cleared my throat. "Have you been to the doctor?"

Kylie nodded, her gray eyes coated in tears. "She said that it's a common skin change that happens during pregnancy."

My chest damn near caved in. "Pre—" I couldn't even get the word out of my mouth. I watched Kylie start to cry. She knew I wasn't happy. I didn't even try to pretend that I was. I didn't talk about it, but Kylie was pregnant when we got married. She'd lost the baby shortly after we were married. Then she was pregnant again, not too long after that, and we lost that baby too. Losing those babies was painful for both of us, and I didn't want to try again anytime soon, if ever. Not to mention, we were struggling enough as it was. We must have only had about $2,000 saved in the bank. I was the only one bringing in any income. We'd barely had time to have sex. We didn't make love; we fucked. We had quickies. And when we did happen to have sex, I wasn't even sure either of us liked it. We didn't spend any quality time together, except for the lunch we ate together every afternoon. When we first met, we were all about sex. All about being happy. All over each other like magnets. But for the past year or so, we were about everything *but* each other. And Kylie was pregnant again. Fuck.

"We don't even talk anymore. I barely see you" was all I could think to say to her.

Kylie scoffed, drying her face. "That's all you have to say to me, David? I'm about six weeks pregnant, and all you can say is 'We don't talk'? 'You barely see me'? Are you *serious* right now?"

"What do you want me to say, Kylie?" I had to ask her.

"That . . ." Her lips quivered. "That you're happy."

I exhaled deeply, shaking my head at her. "Kylie, shawty, we've lost two babies in three years. Happy? I'm hurt, Kylie, not happy."

Kylie's lips quivered. I didn't want to hurt her, but I wasn't feeling another heartbreak. I couldn't go one year without some crazy shit *not* happening on a nigga's birthday. And it was just about to get crazier.

"Kylie," Mrs. Luckett broke the tension between the two of us. "Your friends are here."

Kylie sighed, drying her face with her hands. Then she walked past me.

I grabbed her hand, pulling her back to me. "Wait, babe, I'm sorry. I'm just shocked. I'm just worried, that's all."

She slipped her hand from mine. "Don't be sorry, David. My friends are here. Maybe they'll be a little more caring than you and my mother."

I looked at Kylie as she rolled her eyes at me before leaving. That was the reason why Mrs. Luckett rolled her eyes at me when I came into the kitchen—as if she needed any more reasons to hate me.

I took a quick shower before heading down the stairs to meet Kylie's loud-ass friends from college. I had come into the house looking like the day before. I threw on a white T-shirt and covered it with a plaid gray, white, and black button-down, short-sleeved shirt. I slid into a pair of black jeans and slipped on my black-and-white Nikes. Every time I wore my jewelry, I had to hear Kylie's parents saying a nigga looked like a rapper or a pimp or some shit, so I left it on my nightstand. I sprayed on the Ralph Lauren cologne that Kylie gave me for my Christmas and birthday present last year.

Finally, I walked down the stairs, hearing laughter. Lisa stood at the foot of the steps, turning around to face me as I met her at the bottom of the steps. Her green eyes grew bigger, and she slightly shook her head at me, nodding in the direction of Kylie and her friends, laughing in our living room.

"What's up?" I whispered to my sister, looking at the shocked expression on her face.

"Boy, oh boy," she whispered, shaking her head at me. "You're gonna trip; I *know* you're gonna trip. *Please,* don't trip."

I scoffed, walking past her into the living room. There, Kylie sat on the couch, across from her friends from college. All four of her friends stood from the couch when they saw me.

"Baby, these are my girls from college. This is Tori, Jordyn, Brook, and Tela. And my girlfriend is in the bathroom." Kylie introduced her cute friends from college.

"What's up?" I watched them all giggling like little schoolgirls.

"Oh, my goodness, Kylie—you didn't tell us how handsome your husband was. That face, those eyes, the way he dresses—good Lawd!" Tori gawked at me.

"We wouldn't have even known you were married had it not been for that ring on your finger. You have no pictures of this dude anywhere in your phone, your wallet, *or* on your Facebook page," Tela called her out.

I looked at Kylie. I'd sure never met any of her friends from school. It seemed as though she'd purposely held her events on nights when I had other plans or during school hours when she knew that I had to teach. I didn't fuck with Facebook, so, of course, I didn't know about the shit she posted on her page. All I knew was that the only life Kylie and I shared was the life we had together at home and on my lunch break.

Kylie rolled her eyes. "That's because I don't want y'all bitches gawking at my husband like y'all are now. Jeez. Put your eyes back in your head, Tori, damn . . ." Kylie looked at me looking at them, still wondering what was wrong with Lisa.

"Happy birthday, by the way." Brook was the second person outside of Darius to tell a nigga happy birthday.

I nodded. "Thanks." I looked over at Mr. Luckett, who sat in Kylie's favorite recliner, looking like a Black version of the dude who played on "Masterpiece Theater."

"Oh, didn't you say it was your friend's birthday today too?" Kylie's cousin, Jeff, asked.

Kylie looked at me as I looked at her. "Yeah, but just like Darius here, she doesn't like to celebrate it. I swear, you two have a lot in common but never even met." Kylie looked over my shoulder as the door to the bathroom in the hallway opened. "It's about time, Rain. I thought you fell in."

"Girl, stop." My heart skipped about ten beats at the sound of that voice. "Y'all got me out of bed so early this morning that I didn't get to do my makeup."

I was scared to turn around and look at her. I knew it was her. I think I even felt her presence before she opened her mouth. I turned around to see Chrystal walking toward us. *There goes my baby,* my heart said to my mind. Chrystal was dressed from her coral silk blouse to her sequined heels in Oscar de la Renta. Her long hair was pulled back into a ponytail. She was gorgeous. She was my homie. She was my everything. And she was right there in my living room.

Chrystal gasped a little, stopping in her tracks when she saw me. There she was, in that same bubble gum-colored lipstick she wore the night before at the masquerade. Her lips quivered a little, but she continued walking toward me, stopping in front of me, glancing at Lisa, before looking back at me.

"Rain, this is my husband, David." Kylie proudly introduced her to me. "David, this is my girl, Rain."

Chrystal laughed a little. "Husband, huh?" She glanced at Kylie, shaking her head at her a little, like they were slick checking each other on some inside joke or something. Chrystal looked back at me and then stuck out her trembling hand to shake mine. "Nice to meet you, David." She tried to grin, but her eyes watered instead.

It took everything in me not to grab shawty closely, kiss her, and tell her how much I missed her in my life. But I was there in front of my wife and her family. A part of me didn't give a fuck about any of that. Chrystal was standing there. I hadn't seen shawty in eight years. My heart was as happy as a muthafucka that she was okay.

But at the same time, all I could think about was Chrystal popping that pussy out there on the dance floor.

I glanced back at Darius, whose eyes were as big as saucers. Not because he knew that she was my long-lost friend, but because he knew her from Pop It and couldn't believe she was best friends with my wife. I looked back at Chrystal, taking her hand in mind, more like grabbing it. "What's good wit'cha, *Rain*?" I shook my head at her, looking her over a little, before she slipped her hand from mine.

Sitting across from Chrystal at that dining room table that evening was killa. I tried my best not to look at her, but every time that I looked up, she was staring at me with that ever-so-intense stare of hers. Shawty always saw straight through me.

"So," I watched her take a sip of her iced tea with lemon, "It's your birthday too, huh?"

"Ummm-hmmm." She glanced at me.

"She doesn't celebrate it, though. It was years before we even found out that her birthday was on Christmas," Jordyn called her out.

I looked at her. "A lot of bad things have happened in my life on this day too, shawty. So I feel you. Not really much to celebrate in my opinion."

Chrystal nodded in agreement, her bright brown eyes sparkling.

"Me and this girl have known each other for about as long as I've known you, David." Kylie nudged me. "I was 18 and had just started managing Olive Garden. We went to Morgan together; we were roommates staying in the Honors dorm, Harper-Tubman. Oh, those were the days, boy. And we're going to graduate school together. And me and Rain are sorority sisters too, boo." Kylie laughed, digging into her lobster ravioli. "The rest of these bitches decided not to pledge."

"Girl, bye." Brook rolled her eyes. "The only reason either of y'all pledged was because of that Q-Dog that y'all were fighting over. What was his name again? Ka—"

Kylie cut her friend off. "We weren't fighting over anyone. Do we really have to go there, Brook?"

"Did you really have to start it?" Brook rolled her eyes, putting a big chunk of pumpkin pie into her mouth. "Always talkin' shit. Got me cursing in front of your parents."

"So," Chrystal butted in, "how did you two meet?" She looked at Kylie and then back at me. I knew it wouldn't take long before shawty started to question my relationship with Kylie.

Kylie looked at me before grabbing my hand, intertwining her fingers in mine. "We met while I was assistant manager at the Olive Garden that my family owns. He was a busser. Had the worst attitude ever. He wasn't afraid to put me in my place. I hated his arrogance but loved it just the same. Even though I didn't want to give him my heart, he took it. And three years ago, we were married. Well, it'll be three years come New Year's."

Kylie's mother scoffed. "Married? I don't recall going to a wedding."

Kylie rolled her eyes, sighing. "Mother, do we have to do this today? I told you, David and I are going to save up to have a ceremony. We're going to do it on our own, without your help."

"New Year's is you guys' anniversary?" Tela questioned. "But isn't that your fashion showcase? So, when will you guys have time to celebrate? Is he going to go to your showcase with you? I'm pretty sure this showcase is ruining whatever plans this handsome man planned for his bae."

I grinned. I couldn't help but find it funny that Kylie's friends were on a nigga's side. I did find it funny that she'd be cool with planning a fashion showcase the night of our anniversary. Obviously, I wasn't important to her anymore. She had dreams of making a name for herself without involving her parents. Shit, even me. I wasn't even a part of her dream.

Kylie rolled her eyes. "Mind your business, Tela. We'll figure it out."

I glanced over at Chrystal, who was picking over her food.

"Rain? What kind of name is Rain?" I shook my head to myself, changing the subject. "Sounds like a stripper's name to me, shawty."

Everyone looked at me.

I looked up at Chrystal, who looked at me like she wanted to smack the shit out of me.

Kylie nudged me. "David . . ."

"'Rain' can't be your real name. What's your name, shawty?" I had to ask Chrystal. I ignored Kylie's push. I had to change the fuckin' subject. There was no point in arguing with Kylie. She was always right. Knew every gotdamn thing. I wanted to know about Chrystal. *Needed* to know what she'd been up to besides poppin' pussy.

Chrystal grinned a little, looking up at me. "Chrystal Jayda Alison. I go by 'Rain,' and yes, it *is* a stripper's name. I go by 'Rain' because, whenever I step into a room, it's raining money." She glanced at Darius, winking her eye at him.

Darius looked at me and then back at her. He realized that shawty's name *was* Chrystal. He also recognized the last name. He had to look at shawty a minute to register the fact that she had the same last name as Payton. Darius muttered to himself. "Oh shit . . ."

Chrystal raised her eyebrow at me. "You judging me, David?"

Darius shook his head at me. "He hates the strip clubs. Won't step foot in one, but I have a feeling that's about to change."

"I ain't mad at'cha; I ain't judging you." I tried ignoring Darius. "Twerkin' on the pole to make tuition, huh? I can't knock your hustle. Before I was teaching, I was slangin' drugs, totin' choppers, and everything else. Me and my boys used to chop through them streets, fuckin' up shit. The lifestyle isn't much different. But there comes a time when you have to give it up and walk away before you hurt yourself or your loved ones, you feel me?"

Chrystal's eyes watered.

"So," I changed the topic, "tell me where you from, shawty."

Chrystal grinned at me.

Everyone looked at me, looking at her.

You should have seen the irritated expression on Kylie's parents' faces. They hated to hear about my past. They hated that Kylie even married someone with a past like mine. And they seemed like they didn't care too much for Chrystal either, but tolerated her because she was Kylie's friend.

"You have a cute little country twang to your voice. It sounds familiar. Like home. I know you're not from around here." I had to put her on the spot.

"I'm from North Carolina." Chrystal shook her head at me before digging back into her food. "Greenville." She glanced at her girls, who were looking at her, watching me singling her out. "You sound like you're a ways from home too. Where are you from, David?"

"Greenville, shawty." I grinned. "Moved here in 2007."

Kylie laughed a little. "Boo," she squeezed my hand tightly in hers, "y'all are from the same town. Did you know each other?"

I avoided Kylie's question. "So, how long have you been up here? *What* brings you here?" I had to know.

Kylie nudged me. "David, stop interrogating the girl. Haven't you asked her enough questions? What's wrong with you?"

I looked at Kylie. "I don't know anything about any of your friends. And your friends obviously don't know anything about me. They didn't even know that you were married, Kylie. I've known you since 2009. We got married in 2013, and your friends had no idea that we were married. You wanna talk about *that* instead?"

Kylie just looked at me, unsure of what to say. She sank back in her chair, gritting her teeth, looking at Chrystal.

"Shawty said she's from my hometown, so I just wanna know what brings her here." And I looked back at Chrystal for answers.

Chrystal shook her head at Kylie. "Nah, Kylie; it's okay, boo." She looked back at me. "I was going through a lot during my senior year in high school. My mom was put away in an insane asylum. My best friend left me. My family members spent all of the money that my father left to my mother when he died. After getting into it with my aunt and uncle, I moved out on my own. The guy I was seeing during my senior year went off to college and never looked back. I started hanging out with an older guy that my family disapproved of. After seeing this guy for two months—no sex, no nothing—I came to find out that I was pregnant."

I placed my fork down on the table, looking at her, not saying a word, though I wanted to.

"He really couldn't care less that I was pregnant at that moment. He said he had plans for me. Said he wanted to wait until I was 17 to sleep with me because he wasn't trying to go to jail; he was 28. And on my seventeenth birthday, he took me over to his place and got me drunk.

I didn't want to sleep with him, but he made me. Told me afterward that I was his, and I wasn't going anywhere. This guy had me into all sorts of drugs. I fucked that baby up and myself too. I did so many drugs and partied so hard that I sent myself into early labor. I had him when I was just six months pregnant, on January 15th, 2008. I watched that baby suffer. I thought he wasn't going to make it. He was the size of a water bottle when I had him." Chrystal struggled not to cry.

Her friend Tela rubbed her back, but Chrystal signaled her that she was okay.

"I was strung out when I went to the hospital. The doctors talked me into adoption, which really didn't seem like a bad idea. I wasn't living right. I was into all sorts of shit. I stopped going to school. All I did was smoke, fuck, and drink. Not to mention, shoot up, pop pills, and snort shit up my nose. I let this nigga control me with drugs. The doctors introduced me to a social worker, who told me she would find the best parents for my son. I had no other choice but to give him up. This guy promised me that he would get me into dancing, modeling, and everything. He took me from my family, moved me to New York with him in this raggedy-ass apartment. It didn't take long for him to start beating me. Didn't take long for him to start telling me that I had to help pay the rent. And when I say help pay the rent, I mean he had me selling my body. I tried to run away from him. But everywhere that I went, he found me. It wasn't until I was 18 that I got the strength to run away from him. I don't know how, but I got a Christmas card the day before my eighteenth birthday. It came from my son's foster parents, whose address was in Severn, Maryland. Inside was a Christmas card with his picture on it. He was 10 months old in the picture. Beautiful as ever. And alive, after what I'd taken him through." Tears slid down Chrystal's face.

Severn, Maryland? That was where the Watsons lived. Payton was her son. He had to be.

"So, how'd you get here? How the fuck did you get away from this crazy muthafucka?" I still continued to ask through her pain.

Kylie nudged me, glancing at her parents, who always acted like they'd never heard a muthafucka curse before.

Chrystal laughed a little, drying her tears. "Life is funny. You see, something terrible happened the day that the picture arrived. When Lawrence—that's the pimp's name—would leave during the day, he would lock me my room, waiting on the next trick. I would have sex with about five men or more a day. Sometimes ten." Chrystal watched my temples twitch. "If I refused to have sex with them, Lawrence would beat and then rape me in front of the men.

"That Christmas Eve, I sat alone in the room, sober, not drunk, not high, just drowning in my own thoughts. There weren't any drugs strong enough that day to fight the pain that I was feeling. I needed a way out. The door to my room flew open around 11:00 that morning. In came this guy who had to be about 30 or so. He was high as hell. And I already knew when I saw him that he was about to torture me."

"Oh God . . ." Mrs. Luckett cringed, getting up from the table and going into the kitchen.

Chrystal watched her leave, and then she looked back at me. "I already knew that day that I was gonna stab a muthafucka. The one thing that Lawrence let me do was shave so that I would be nice and clean for the tricks. So, that day, I slipped a razor under my tongue. As soon as that muthafucka lay on top of me, I was going to slit his neck. And that's *just* what I did. I slit the muthafucka's neck, and as soon as the blood squirted out of him, I pushed the muthafucka off of me and raced out of my room, grabbing my sweats and shoes that were on the floor. The man screamed out, calling for help as I scrambled through the kitchen for the money that Lawrence always kept in an empty baking soda box. I found $950 in the box and darted out the door, wearing nothing but a tank top and underwear.

"I ran smack into the mailman. He saw all of the blood splattered on me, but he handed me the mail anyway. I knew he heard the man screaming in my apartment, but he went on about his business. And I ran out of the building, putting on my clothes along the way. I tossed the mail, all except for the card addressed to me. I hopped into a cab and told the driver to take me to the bus station. When I saw my baby's picture, I knew exactly where I was headed."

I exhaled deeply, leaning back in my chair, feeling like shit for even asking her what she'd been through.

"I arrived in Baltimore, Maryland, that evening. I had about $900 left, but no ID on me. Not to mention, I'd lost the envelope with my son's address on it and his picture. I must've left it on one of the bus seats. On the back of the card that my son's foster parents sent me was their phone number. I just sat and cried on a bench outside the bus station. It was Christmas Eve, and I was all alone. Nowhere to go. I walked right into the middle of traffic and was hit by a car." Chrystal looked at Kylie.

I looked at Kylie.

Tears slid down Kylie's face. She looked at me, nodding. "My mother hit her. She was banged up pretty badly. Ended up staying in the hospital for about three weeks. I visited her every day. She told me that she had nowhere to go. My mother was already feeling some type of way about hitting her, so she let her stay with us. And we've been friends ever since. But," Kylie looked at Chrystal. "Boo, I had no idea what you went through. You never talk about your past. And I had no idea that you had a son. You never told us about him. I've known you for almost seven years. Where is he?"

I looked back at Chrystal, who was getting up from the table. "Where you going, shawty?" I asked her.

Chrystal shook her head, drying her face. "This-This is too much. I had a great time, but I can't do this. I really didn't mean to ruin dinner. Sorry, Mr. Luckett. Tell Mrs. Luckett that I didn't mean to ruin Christmas by talking about things I know she disapproves of." She looked at me. "It was really nice meeting you, David."

Mr. Luckett looked at me, frowning at me like it was *my* fault that dinner was ruined.

I looked at Darius, who was sitting back in his chair like he didn't know what the fuck kind of shit he was walking into. I had told him that I knew the girl. He could tell by the way that I was prying into her life that I knew her. Lisa was sitting there at the table, trying to hide the fact that she knew Chrystal too. She looked at me, her eyes telling me not to let her leave.

I just wanted to know how shawty ended up in Baltimore. I watched shawty go into the hallway to get her coat from the coatrack. I looked back at Lisa, who mouthed, "You're really going to just let her go?"

"We haven't even exchanged gifts," Tela exclaimed. "Y'all are just gonna let her go?"

"It's David's fault. Why did you have to go digging up dirt?" Kylie nudged me.

I just looked at her and then up at Chrystal, who was walking out the front door.

"Man, forget Rain. She's always running off when we ask her about her past. What she reveals explains a lot about her, though. Explains why she can deal with working at that dumb-ass club," Tori said, watching me get up from the table.

Everyone looked at me. Kylie was still holding my hand and refused to let go.

I looked down at her. "Shawty, let go of my hand."

Kylie scoffed. "What are you doing?"

"It's my fault that she's leaving, so I'm gonna go apologize." I slipped my hand from hers.

"David, really, she'll be fine. I'll call her later." Kylie watched as I pushed my chair up under the table.

I shook my head at her. She never gave a fuck about anyone's feelings but her own. "You just gonna let'cha friend leave? When she's upset?" I asked, walking away from the table.

"Chrystal," I walked down my porch steps, calling after Chrystal as she walked to her car that night.

She turned around, watching me walk toward her. She grinned a little, looking over my shoulder as if she were making sure that no one saw us talking to each other.

"It's been a long time, Blue." She looked me over a little. "*Too* long." She looked back into my face, her brown eyes sparkling.

"Yeah. Eight years, shawty." It was hard to look at her without thinking about all that we had gone through together . . . without seeing her bent over on the dance floor . . . without asking her who Payton's father was when my heart already knew.

"Eight years, four months, and two days, but who's counting? Right?" Her bright brown eyes shone under the streetlights.

The last time we talked, Chrystal's mother was being put in a mental institution. Her mother hadn't been the same since her husband was murdered. Chrystal watched her mother deteriorate rapidly in such a short amount of time. I couldn't tell you how many times I had to stop Chrystal from trying to end her pain in whatever way she could. Whether it was fuckin' with niggas who meant her no good, drinking to drown in her memories, doing whatever drug she could get a hold of to get high above her memories, or using whatever sharp object she could to end it all.

I still remember the day I left shawty, like it had just happened yesterday. I remember her lips all over mine. I remember those three seven-minute rounds I spent in heaven with her, banging her ass up against the wall of her empty bedroom. I wanted to grab Chrystal and kiss her so badly, but it hurt too much, as it was to see her face again. There I was, about to have a baby with Kylie, when the girl of my dreams was standing in front of me.

After all we'd been through—shit, after all *she'd* been through without me—Chrystal still looked untouched. Like she'd finally gotten the wind beneath her wings. She was driving a clean, black Mercedes-Benz. Everything from the earrings in her earlobes to the boots on her feet cost a grip. Working at Pop It was probably how she'd made her way through school. As good as she looked, I'm sure she had a nigga. Why he let her work at that club, I had no fuckin' idea. But I hoped the nigga she was with kept a smile on her face because she deserved it.

"I didn't mean to go digging up your past. I know it was hard to talk about," I said, watching her hair blowing in the wind. Man, I wanted to grab and hold her, but I knew I was being watched.

Chrystal shook her head at me. "Blue, it's okay. I don't tell too many people my business. Especially those bitches in there, your wife included. They all talk too fuckin' much. I had to tell you what I've been through so you know what I have been dealing with without you. It was important for you to know my journey so that you'll know where I have to go. It may not be the job of my dreams, but I see it led me back to you, the *man* of my dreams."

I just looked at her, my heart pounding in my chest.

"Blue, you look *really* good," she whispered, her eyes sparkling.

I disagreed. "Not as good as you do."

"Life has taken a toll on me . . . I'm not the same person anymore," Chrystal whispered, her voice quivering in the wind.

"But you look the same to me," I whispered back. "*Better* even."

"Looks can be deceiving . . ." Chrystal let me know.

But my heart wouldn't listen. Or maybe it just didn't care. I was just so glad to see her and hear her voice after so long. That smile. Those eyes. That hair. Damn, I missed that girl.

"It feels *so* good to see you." Chrystal's lips quivered. "It's been hell without you. A lot has changed."

"I see that," I agreed, glancing over at her car and then back at her.

"I think we should exchange numbers." Chrystal took her phone out of her back pocket.

As much as I wanted her, I shook my head. "Nah, Kylie ain't having that. You should know how she is. She just said that y'all went to college together at Morgan State. That y'all were roommates. That y'all graduated together. That her mother helped you get on your feet. And now, y'all are in graduate school together? This shit is wild, yo. Man, I can't believe we've been this close all these years."

"So, if you don't wanna lose touch, Blue, gimme your number." Chrystal grinned. She still wore that same conniving smile she had always worn. The girl was sneaky as a muthafucka. Always had something up her sleeve.

I looked back at my house. My sister, Lisa—the only one in the house besides us who knew of our history—stood in the window, watching. I looked back at Chrystal. "Nah. I don't think that's such a good idea. You know it's not."

Chrystal's eyes searched my face. "Do you still love me?"

"Do you even have to ask?" I didn't hesitate to answer. "You're *seriously* asking me that bullshit?"

She grinned, her face flushing a little. "Well then, it *is* a good idea."

I hesitated, taking a deep breath. It took everything in me not to ask about Payton or the club.

Chrystal rolled her eyes and smacked her plump lips. "You always were a scary little somebody." She took a pen out of her pocket, grabbed my hand, and started writing on my wrist.

That touch of hers, boy, still had a nigga. Yup, I was in trouble.

"I'm only scared when it comes to you, shawty." I watched her writing on my wrist.

Chrystal grinned, looking up at me as she put her pen back into her pocket. "You're gonna call me, right? Don't have me sitting by the phone, waiting for you to call. I know how you do, Blue."

There she was, making jokes, when she knew the situation we were both in hurt like a muthafucka.

My heart wouldn't let me let her go without asking her. "What are you doing working at that muthafuckin' club, shawty?" I finally asked her.

Chrystal looked up at me. "What are *you* doing married to stuck-up-ass Kylie?"

I took a deep breath, not wanting to explain that I ended up with Kylie because I was trying to get over missing her.

Chrystal grinned, shaking her head at me. "Looks like we both got ourselves into a situation that we didn't want to be in, but it was convenient for the time being." She turned around, walking away from me.

I grabbed her wrist, pulling her back to me. "Where you going? There's so much more that I need to know about you. I still have questions."

Chrystal looked up at me, her lips quivering. "Haven't you asked enough questions?" She already knew what I was about to ask her.

"What's our son's name?" I asked her. I didn't even have to ask her if the baby she had was mine because I already knew in my heart that he was.

"Pa-Payton," she whispered, yanking her wrist from my hands.

My heart beat out of control as I watched shawty hurry as fast as she could to get into her car and ball the fuck off.

# Chapter Three

## *VIP*

### *Chrystal "Rain" Alison*

I flew down 295 on the way to Severn. My tears blurred my vision. I started bawling so hard that I had to pull off to the side of the road. I hadn't seen my baby, Blue, since I was 16. I missed that boy so much that it hurt. Literally. What hurt the most was that I kept our son from him. I didn't want him to know what my lifestyle did to our baby. I didn't want him to know that I let some pimp manipulate me into leaving my family behind, into dropping out of school, into selling my ass, pussy, lips, and hands on an hourly basis. I couldn't let Blue see what I'd become without him.

I got my GED a few months after being released from the hospital, after Kylie's mother ran over me with her Jaguar. By the summer of 2009, I was enrolled at Morgan State University. By fall, I had moved into the college dorm with Kylie. I worked my ass off, and I think I even partied harder. Going clubbin' was how I met Kameron Price, or Kam for short. Kameron was this rich, thick, muscular gangsta muthafucka whose family ran the city of Baltimore. His family was into some of everything, and so was he. He was into the drug game pretty heavy, but he was also in college. He was book *and* street smart. He was also a Q-Dog, who also attended Morgan State, and he swore up and down he was running the Qs. I needed money, and I needed it fast. He got me a job working as a bartender at Pop It, a club he owned with his cousin, Kavante.

I worked there for nearly two years before the thought of dancing in that club even crossed my mind. One night, I was just having fun with the girls, dancing on stage. From that day on, Kavante thought I should dance for him. It didn't take Kavante a good month before he realized I was his top moneymaker, and he started sending me out to parties. After a while, men were asking to pay top dollars to sleep with me. That was where I drew the line.

That was . . . until I met Mrs. Watson, my son's adoptive mother. It took me awhile to find her. Kameron helped me find her. He paid an investigator to trace Mrs. Watson's name all the way back to the hospital where Payton was born. She was still using her name from her previous marriage, which was why I couldn't find her. It took me until my son was 2 years old to find them. And when I did, I didn't like what I saw. Mrs. Watson's house was falling apart. Her husband had just died, and she fell into a deep depression. My beautiful baby boy was the only thing that kept her holding on. The insurance policy gave her just enough money to bury her husband and take care of a few household expenses. You already know that I wanted my son back, but how could I even approach her, asking about him when he was all that she had?

Payton was so smart. He was blind and deaf, but his touch, smell, and taste senses were heightened. He could tell who you were by your scent and touch. He was 2 years old and could stack blocks by the letters. He was putting puzzles together. He could walk to me from the other end of the room without bumping into anything. He learned to read braille at the age of 4. Mrs. Watson claimed that he kept his big blue eyes clenched closed until I came around him. I wanted the best for my son and the woman who raised him. I couldn't let them live in that old raggedy-ass house.

I agreed to work for the Prices (what the conceited muthafuckas liked to call themselves). I decided to entertain specific clients, but I'd always ask him to have a few other girls come with me. He would send my girl, Letta, who went by Candy (because she swore up and down that her pussy tastes sweet), Robyn, who went by Justice (because she studied law), and Francesca, who went by Fancy (because she rocked heels with everything, even sweats) with me. He gave me the nickname Rain because whenever I stepped inside the club, he knew niggas were about to spend that gwap. Twenties, fifties, and hundreds were flying everywhere.

Doing some of everything at that club paid my way through college. I had three foreign cars sitting in my driveway. Shit, it didn't take me a month to make the down payment that I needed to move my son and Mrs. Watson into a bigger and better house. I paid for Mrs. Watson to have a housekeeper. I paid for Mrs. Watson to have home health aides stay with her twenty-four hours a day. I paid for Mrs. Watson to have someone drive her wherever she needed to go. And I paid to put my talented and gifted baby into a school for deaf and blind students. Everything I earned had a price—a Kam and Kavante Price.

By the time I started my second semester in college, I was living in a two-bedroom condo with my classmate-turned-best-friend-for-life, Robyn. Robyn was my ridah. I could always count on her. She didn't have any family.

She was pretty much on her own, and I was pretty much all that she had. She said her mother threw her out of the house as soon as she started having sex at 15. I knew where she was coming from. Once I started dealing with Lawrence—a man twice my age—my aunts, uncles, and everyone else pretty much cut me off.

Robyn and I met during my freshman year in college and have been tight ever since. We just connected. I even took her back to North Carolina with me every three months or so to visit Mama. Mama was off the deep end. Ya know, a lights-on, nobody's-home type of situation. The health technicians at Cherry Hospital told me that I was the only person from the family that she recognized and acknowledged. I'd play Spades with Mama, she'd braid my hair, we'd watch movies, and she'd introduce me to her friends who were just as loony as her. She loved me. She knew I wasn't living right. Every time I visited her, I would bring her diamond earrings, bracelets, watches, or necklaces. And she would never take them. She'd always tell me, "*You're* my diamond. Don't you ever forget that."

Robyn was the only person I'd ever told about Payton. I was so ashamed of what I had done to my baby. Robyn could relate to me. She had two kids who were taken from her when she was 17. She was homeless, living on the streets with twin baby girls. She stayed in a shelter for six months until they helped her find a place to stay. Her children were asleep one afternoon, so she left them at home to run up the street to the corner store to grab some bread and snacks for her babies. When she got back home, the maintenance man was in her apartment with her two kids. He reported her to the police, telling them she'd left her kids alone in the apartment for hours, though she was only gone for about ten minutes or so. She was charged with neglect, and her children were taken from her and placed into foster care.

The kids' foster parents were in the military. They were 15 months old when she lost custody, and she hadn't seen them face-to-face since then. The foster parents moved to Germany, where they'd been stationed for eight years. Robyn was hurt, but she kept her head in the club and immersed herself in those college textbooks to keep her mind off missing her kids. Meanwhile, no matter what I did, I couldn't keep my mind off of my little boy, who was less than half an hour away from me.

Four years earlier, Mrs. Watson had a stroke, leaving her in the hospital for weeks. Her home health aides couldn't handle Payton. He fought them every chance that he got. He loved Mrs. Watson, and he loved me. Without the two of us, my son went crazy. Mrs. Watson completely lost feeling in her left side, leaving her wheelchair bound. Taking care of Payton on her own became a challenge, and she contemplated putting my son in a group home. She hated the way that I lived and refused to give my son back to me. I couldn't blame her.

My lifestyle was pretty crazy. I couldn't tell you how many stalkers I had. One followed me damn near a whole month. He knew when Robyn wasn't there. He waited until she was gone for the night to break into my apartment while I was asleep. The only reason I heard him come in was that he knocked over the crystal vase on the bookshelf alongside the window, which he had broken through. I went for my 9 mm under my pillow, and as soon as the nigga made it to my room, I shot him in his face. Turns out, the man had committed three rapes that weekend. If I hadn't gotten to him, the police would have. That was just the first attempt at rape. But there were many others.

Robyn and I had to move. That still didn't help. It got to the point where I had to hire a few security guards to work for me. My nigga, Quincy, owned a twenty-four-hour security guard service. I paid him to ensure his security guards stayed parked outside my condo 24/7.

With all that Robyn and I had going on, there was no way that Mrs. Watson was letting Payton go anywhere with me. She told me that she wanted him to stay at the Tree of Life, a group home not too far from her house. She gave me a brochure and the contact information to call to sign Payton up for their services. Of course, Payton didn't want to go. He argued with me about staying with me. Some of it I understood, some of it I didn't. I had taken a few classes to learn sign language and read Braille, but I still couldn't keep up with my son. The month my son moved into the group home, he was 5 years old, signing, using language that adults used, and reading at a sixth-grade level. He had a temper just like his father, always ready to fuck up something. And he loved just as hard, just like his father.

"Girl, why the fuck did you leave me with them bitches?" Tela's voice yelled through the phone after I'd finally stopped crying enough to drive.

"It was getting to be too heated in there," I admitted, driving down the highway.

"Yeah. It was obvious that David had you in your feelings, girl. But you could have at least stayed to open the gifts we brought you for your birthday. I didn't wanna have to come by your job tonight to drop them off. The muthafuckas could have at least given you Christmas off. Money-hungry muthafuckas," Tela scoffed.

I sighed, shaking my head. Could you believe them muthafuckin' tricks at the club were so thirsty for us girls that they'd leave their wives and kids home just to see us dance? Or in some cases, get us to do thangs to them that their wife stopped doing years ago? If they spent more time with their wives than with us, then their marriages wouldn't be fuckin' dysfunctional. I couldn't begin to tell you how many bitches came to Pop It looking for me, ready to fuckin' cut my ass over their husbands. It wasn't my job to look at their man's hands for wedding rings. All I looked for was the money in their hands. But I would admit that the situation was growing old. If I didn't make about $15,000 a month, I swear, I would have quit years ago. But I needed the money to help pay Mrs. Watson's bills, as well as my own, to cover my son's schooling, and to keep my son in the group home. I had to take care of them.

I was in college, and I really don't know why. I graduated with a bachelor's degree in Business Administration and Management Information Systems. I couldn't find a fuckin' job because the field was so competitive. Not to mention that, upon graduation, if you don't have all those gotdamn computer programming certificates, you damn sure ain't getting a job. The muthafuckas never mentioned that shit. They just made making an average of $70,000 after graduation sound really good. But after working at Pop It, that sounded like chump change. I made that much in six months, shit. Nevertheless, I continued on to graduate school with my college girls. They knew what I did and didn't judge me, though I'm sure they wanted to.

"Yeah, I'm going in tonight around 10:00. Gotta pay these bills." I turned off at the exit to Fort Meade.

"Girl, I told you to go down and apply at Northrop Grumman. My cousin works in human resources there. She can hook you up with a job," Tela mentioned for the fuckin' tenth time that month.

"You know I gotta pay the Prices back all the money they loaned me." I rolled my eyes. If she wasn't talking those kinds of dollars, then I wasn't going to make that kind of change. "Can I make $15,000 a month working there?"

"No, but you don't have to sell that gorgeous body of yours every night, *Rain,*" Tela scoffed. "I don't knock your hustle, but I'm worried about you and Robyn. Y'all don't need to work there. You both are smart, *beyond* beautiful girls who don't need to do this shit. Is Robyn gonna continue to strip when she becomes Robyn Michelle, Esquire? She gonna fuck her defendants too? And you, what will *your* son think? Chrystal, you have a *son.* You never told any of us about him."

So much for not being judgmental. I dried my tears. I couldn't even deny what she was saying. "Tela, boo, I gotta go. I'll talk to you later, okay?"

"Think about what I said, babe, okay? You're priceless." And Tela hung up.


I sat, misty-eyed, watching Mrs. Watson's home health aide, Qiana, french-braid Mrs. Watson's waist-long silver hair that morning in her toasty living room. Mrs. Watson looked so small and frail, but she was so happy to see me and even happier to see me enjoying my time with my beautiful son.

I sat next to my baby, Payton. He sat with his head on my shoulder, his curly black hair grazing against my chin, unwrapping the Christmas presents that I bought him. I brought him books, his favorite. My little nerd! His hands ran across the braille titles of each book.

"*The Great Gatsby, Great Expectations,* and *A Raisin in the Sun,*" I whispered to my baby. To the world, my baby was deaf. But between him and me, we shared a language that only our hearts understood.

Payton smiled up at me, his blue eyes searching my face, that cute little gap between his pearly white teeth. He signed, "Thanks, Mama." I could tell he was excited by how fast he signed before giving me the tightest squeeze.

"Oh, you're welcome, baby." I kissed him on his fore-head. Then I looked at Mrs. Watson, who was smiling at us, tears racing down her pale cheeks. "So, Mrs. Watson, how has my baby been doing in school and at the group home?"

"Oh, he's doing wonderful in school." She dried her face. "He is making straight-As. They are moving him to the gifted and talented classes once school starts after the holiday. This boy is going to be something great, just like his mama still has the chance to be."

I sighed, not really in the mood for her lectures. "And in the group home, how is he doing there?"

Mrs. Watson shook her head at me, knowing I was trying to stay on the subject that I was on instead of switching to my line of work that she particularly didn't like. "Well, outside of fighting the staff members, I guess he's doing fine. He hasn't opened his eyes for anyone but you until today."

I looked at Mrs. Watson, my heart jumping in my chest. "Up until today?"

"Oh, and he's become particularly close to his mentor, Darius." Mrs. Watson avoided the question. "They get along so well together." Mrs. Watson smiled as Qiana finished braiding her hair.

"Darius?" The name sounded familiar.

"Yes. He's a nice-looking young man. Smart, handsome, going to college. His family owns the group home where Payton attends. Surely you've heard of him . . ." Mrs. Watson watched me trying to figure out where I'd heard his name mentally.

And then I remembered. Darius Newhouse, Kylie's cousin on her mother's side. He was one of Robyn's reg-ular customers. Not to mention, he seemed to be Blue's close friend. I pretended not to know this dude, who showed up to see Robyn at least six days a week. Robyn claimed she didn't give a fuck about the nigga, but he was the only client she had sex with in the past year.

My mind was going in circles. It was already mind-blowing to know that Blue had been right under my nose for the past seven years. And married to Kylie, of all people. All I could think about was him being married to the woman, having no idea who she really was or the shit that she was into. We should have been together. We had a son together. Wait—Payton. *Has he seen Payton?*

My eyes widened, watching Mrs. Watson laughing to herself. "Wait . . . Did Darius come here with a f-friend?" I stuttered, watching Qiana hold a mirror up so that Mrs. Watson could see her perfectly laid hair.

"Oh yes, honey, this is lovely." Mrs. Watson admired herself in the mirror. "Now I can invite my friends over for tea."

"Mrs. Watson." I needed Mrs. Watson to stop feeling herself for two seconds and answer me. "Did Darius have someone with him when he dropped off Payton?"

"Well, the friend didn't come inside, but he had to help bring Payton to the house. From the moment Payton got out of the car, he was fighting to get back in." Mrs. Watson looked up at Qiana, who nodded in agreement.

"Yes, me and the other awake-overnight staff, who left this morning, had to help bring him in," Qiana sighed. "Payton hugged the man so tight around his waist, we had to pry him off."

"S-So," I stuttered, "you met the friend, Mrs. Watson?"

Mrs. Watson shook her head. "No, like I said, he didn't come inside. He just brought him to the yard, and the staff helped Darius bring him in. But Qiana met him."

"He looks just like Payton," Quiana hesitated to say.

"Did you tell my son?" I whispered, the tears already trickling down my face.

"No, sweetie, but he already knew." Mrs. Watson looked at her adopted son.

I looked down at Payton, who was looking back up at me, his hands grabbing my face.

"He was screaming and kicking and yelling, signing, 'Daddy, please don't leave me.'" Mrs. Watson tried her best not to cry, but she couldn't help it. "When I finally got Payton to calm down by telling him that you were on your way, I asked him how he knew the man with Darius was his father. He kept signing, 'I could smell him. He smelled just like me. His skin felt like mine. I could feel his heartbeat. It's the same rhythm as mine.'"

Payton let out a happy cry, signing, "I saw my daddy today."

I couldn't take it. I didn't want my son to believe that we abandoned him. It was hard enough explaining to him why I could never take him with me. Why I had to leave him. Why he couldn't see my face or hear my voice. I didn't want him to think Blue left him when neither of us even knew at the time that I was pregnant. Blue saw me that Christmas Day, asking me all those questions to try to figure out whether the little boy he met that day was mine. He wanted to hear the words come out of my mouth. Blue didn't seem angry at me, but it seemed like he felt sorry for me. I was so angry at myself and what I'd become. I didn't want either my son or Blue to see me that way.

I grabbed my son's hand, signing in his palm. "No, Payton, that was not your father."

Mrs. Watson and Qiana both looked at me.

Payton looked up at my face, shaking his head in disagreement. "Yes, it was, Mama," he signed back.

I cried out, signing back to him. "Listen to me," I spoke aloud as I signed. "He is *not* your father."

Payton shook his head at me, digging into his pocket, taking out a picture, and he shoved it into my chest.

I took the picture from my son's hand and held it to my face. It was a picture of a young white girl holding a newborn baby in her arms. The woman looked a lot like Mrs. Watson. She had long brunette hair, blue eyes, and deep dimples. She held the baby tightly in her arms. Although she was smiling, you could see the pain in her eyes.

"Is this your daughter?" I asked Mrs. Watson.

"Yes. Rosy Jacobs." Mrs. Watson hesitated.

I looked up at her. "Jacobs?"

"Jacobs is my maiden name." Mrs. Watson watched me laughing to myself, handing the picture back to Payton as I started to catch on to what was going on.

My mother mentioned Rosy Jacob's name several times, even while being a patient at Cherry. Rosy was her best friend since childhood, who she thought had abandoned her. Rosy was Blue's mother.

"So, wait a minute—do you mean to tell me that the woman in this picture is *my* David's mother? Payton's grandmother? *Your* daughter?" I tried to get up from the chair, but Payton grabbed my arm, pulling me back down.

"I couldn't tell you, Chrystal; please don't be upset." Mrs. Watson watched the tears streaming down my face. "You probably don't even remember her, but—"

"I remember the bitch threw my best friend in the trash after she gave birth to him!" I exclaimed. "I remember my father said he personally found and arrested the bitch, even though they let her ass go."

"She also delivered your baby at Pitt Memorial Hospital. Her name is Rosy Watkins. Or should I say, *Dr.* Rosy Watkins? She's married." Mrs. Watson cried, watching me cry out loud. "She called me on the phone as soon as she saw you in the delivery room. She said you look just like her best friend, Christina. And she knew as soon as she delivered Payton that he was her grandson. Said he had David's eyes and the same frown he had on his face when he came into this world. When she found out that you were giving him up for adoption, she called me."

I couldn't believe it. This bitch threw my best friend in the trash. If it wasn't for my father, he would have died in that trash can—right in front of the hospital. A beautiful baby boy, thrown away with the trash, like he *was* trash. But who was *I* to talk, when I pumped my son's veins full of drugs, forcing myself into premature labor, causing my son all types of health problems, outside of not developing correctly. He had an artificial lung. Not to mention, artificial valves in his heart. My son wasn't supposed to have lived. I was trying to kill myself and ended up hurting my son in the process. The only difference between Rosy and me was that I went back for my son, and she didn't. He'd never even seen her face, not so much as a picture of her.

"She never came back for him." I cried, looking down at my son, who pressed his face against my chest. He knew I was hurting. He started crying with me.

"She felt like she'd already caused enough damage. She was living a crazy life in those days, honey. Men, drugs, sex, prostitution—not that much different than you're living right now." Mrs. Watson watched me holding my son in my arms. "You're afraid to confront David because you're afraid to let him see what you are. You're afraid he won't love the person you've become. And that's the exact way that his mother felt about him. I'm not saying that she was right to throw him away, but she felt like he was better off dead than knowing her. Her boyfriend was chasing her, threatening to kill her *and* the baby."

"Has-has she met Payton? Has she stopped by to see him?" I asked, watching Qiana pat Mrs. Watson on the shoulder before leaving us to fix Mrs. Watson some hot tea.

Mrs. Watson nodded. "Yes, she stopped by on Thanksgiving."

"What about Blue, I mean, David? Has she seen her son? Does she know he's here?" I had to know.

Mrs. Watson hesitated. "She's seen him. She came up here in 2008 for Miss Tiffany Lyon's funeral."

My eyes widened. When I didn't see Miss Tiffany at Blue's place, I just assumed that she didn't like Kylie or something. I had no idea that she was dead. But then again, I hadn't been home to Greenville in a minute, nor did I keep in contact with any of my family members or friends back home to know.

"When did she die?" was all I could ask.

"Christmas, 2008." Mrs. Watson watched me cry aloud. "Rosy wanted to meet the woman who raised her son, but she was afraid to face her. She wanted to see David face-to-face without him knowing who she was, so she showed up at the funeral. Said she saw him, even gave him her condolences, but he never looked her in the face. He was too distraught and too hurt to pay her any attention. She probably blended in with the other couple of hundred people who attended the funeral." Mrs. Watson watched me kiss my son on the forehead before I got up from the couch where I had been sitting.

Payton yelled out, grabbing my hand, signing. "Mama, it's only 5:30!"

I looked at the time; it sure was 5:30 on the damn dot.

"Where are you going?" he signed.

I held his hand, placing it over mine, and signed and talked out loud. "I have to work tonight. I will stop by the group home sometime this week to see you, okay?"

The tears that ran down my son's face broke my heart. "Give my dad Grandma's picture, okay?"

I cried, grabbing my son, holding him close. "See you later, Little Blue," I whispered before letting him go.

"Ma!" Payton yelled out my name as I made it halfway toward the front door.

I turned around, looking back at him signing, "Happy birthday, Mommy."

There I was, drunk as a damn skunk, sitting in front of my vanity mirror at Club Pop It that night. I didn't know what kind of pills Fancy had me on that night, but I was as high as a damn kite. I had to get fucked-up. The club was packed that night. Everyone knew it was my birthday. There I was in nothing but nude underwear and a nude tanzanite-sequined bra, with a diamond-studded crown sitting on top of my bone-straight hair. A party of twenty men was coming to see me that night in VIP. The same twenty men who came every year on my fuckin' birthday. They wanted a slice of my "birthday cake," if you know what I mean. And that night, I wasn't feeling it.

"Girl, you've been sitting there, staring at your phone for two hours." Letta walked over and sat down beside me on my vanity bench.

I looked up at her. She was just as tore up as I was. "Don't you get tired of working at this dumb-ass fuckin' club?" I asked her.

She shrugged. "Yeah, but it pays my way through college. So I can sit at the very front of Mr. David Jacob's classroom every day and stare into those pretty blue eyes of his. That muthafucka is gorgeous. I don't even like 'em pretty and pink, but that red muthafucka can get it. I mean, *all* of it."

I looked at her. "David Jacobs?"

"Yes, my professor. The finest nigga on campus, girl." She nudged me. "You know, bitch-ass Kylie's husband." Letta rolled her eyes. "If he only knew what type of bitch he was fuckin' with. I'd snitch if it weren't for your nigga, Kam."

I laughed out loud. "*My* nigga Kam? Girl, bye. Kam is *old* news, *Kylie's* news."

I can't say that Kameron and I were ever a couple, but we did have sex a few times. It took me until the end of sophomore year in college to realize that Kylie was fuckin' around with Kameron too. As a matter of fact, I caught the two fuckin' in the dressing room at Pop It on Christmas Eve, 2011. Turns out, *I* was the home wrecker. That Kameron was supposed to be *her* man. No one ever mentioned shit to me about the two dating. As far as I knew, Kameron was dating everyone. His dick had been in every pussy up at Morgan State, so it shouldn't have surprised me.

The last time I checked, the two were still fuckin' around. They were the break-up-to-make-up couple. That was why I looked at Kylie the way I did that day at dinner; the bitch was playing Blue. I had never seen a picture of Blue in her wallet, on her Facebook page—no-where. She kept that nigga under wraps. Or at least she'd never told me about him, and we were supposed to be friends. She'd been seeing Blue for years, married to the nigga for almost three years, and fuckin' Kameron's big, long dick-having ass. I caught the two fuckin' in the utility closet about three years earlier. I wasn't sure if Kylie was still messing around with Kam, but what I did know was she was fuckin' around with him when she shouldn't have been, which was around the time that she said "I do" to Blue.

"Well, Tela told me that y'all went over to the profes-sor's house for Christmas dinner." Letta watched my eyes water as I picked up my lip gloss, applying Candy Apple Red lip gloss to my plump lips. "She said you bailed on her as soon as the professor started asking you twen-ty-one questions about your past. She said they found out some shit they never knew about you. Shit that explains a lot about why you are the way you are now. Said you were saying a lot to a nigga you've never met before. Tori said y'all couldn't take your eyes off of each other."

I sighed, blotting my lips, glancing at her before looking back in the mirror. The drugs I was on had me so jittery that I couldn't even put on my mascara. I should have known Letta's prying ass would catch on. I wanted Robyn to be the first person I talked to about Blue, but there was Letta, dragging it out of me.

Letta took a deep sigh before taking the mascara applicator from my hands. After I turned to her, she held my chin in her hands. I closed my eyes as she applied a coat of mascara for me. "Girl, y'all are from the same hometown." She applied a thick coat to my left eyelash and paused to look at me for a reaction. "Do you know the professor, sweetie?"

I didn't say anything, but trying to hold back the tears caused my nose to flare and my lips to tremble.

"Chrystal? You know him?" Letta tried to whisper, but the excitement in her voice made her whisper sound more like a damn shriek.

I opened my eyes, looking into her face, her big brown eyes peering into mine. "We grew up together." I watched her shaking her head.

"Girl, close your eyes so that I can do your other eye." She exhaled deeply. "You and this bitch are always fighting over some nigga, I swear." She applied a thick coat of mascara to my eyelashes.

"What?" I exclaimed as she blew on my lashes to dry them. "I had no idea that she was married at all, let alone that she was married to a man that I grew up with. My parents practically helped raise that boy." I felt Letta brushing eye shadow over my lids.

"That's wild, yo." Now she was blending makeup over the crease of my eyelid. "What are the odds of this shit happening?"

"Tell me about it. And why did the first time running into him again have to be him seeing me at that fuckin' masquerade party?" I shook my head a little, my heart stampeding in my chest. "Could you imagine poppin' your pussy in front of a nigga you swore up and down that he would never catch you doing that shit? He must think I'm the biggest ho ever."

"Nah. I bet he thinks that his homegirl is just working hard to make them coins." Letta continued to blend my eye shadow. "What was it like growing up with this nigga? He got a big dick, don't he? I *know* he does."

I tried not to laugh out loud, but I had to. She always had to lighten up the mood. "You're so stupid."

"Girl, I know you're feeling like you're in the Twilight Zone. Were y'all friends or were y'all *friends?*" She nudged me.

I sighed. "Boo, I don't even know what we were. But I know what we could have been if he hadn't left. I know I wouldn't be *this* bullshit."

"Stop downing yourself, Chrystal. But now that y'all have seen each other, are y'all gonna hide the fact that y'all know each other from Kylie? I know I would. She kept shit from us. The only reason why I knew that bitch was even married to my professor was because I saw her picture on his desk in his office." Letta sighed to herself. "I've been trying to holla at that muthafucka since school started in August."

I opened my eyes, lifting my eyebrow at that horny trick. "Bitch, *what?*"

She laughed out loud. "Girl, bye. That nigga is bae. You can't blame a sista, for real. Everybody wants that muthafucka. You should see the way them bitches at school stay on that nigga's dick. I had no idea that he was yours."

I shook my head, shrinking back against the back of the vanity seat. "Nah, he's Kylie's."

Letta looked at me and smirked. "Whatever. All I can say is that working for Kam and his cousin, Kavante, helps me pay my way through college. I'm 22. It took me four years to get into college. You know my record is fucked-up. I have all kinds of charges that keep me from getting a job, let alone getting into college. If it weren't for Kam and his connections, I would've never gotten the chance to go to college. I'd do anything for that nigga. I'm telling you, he's the only reason why I haven't told the professor about Kylie. Kam loves that ho."

I pursed my lips.

Letta rolled her eyes. "Well, she's the main chick. Brings in all types of clientele for Kam and his family. Her family knows everyone. Two rich muthafuckas on the same team makes a dream team. She looks down at the professor. He works hard to make his money, girl. The bitch doesn't realize that the nigga she's married to used to get that bread. I heard he started out as the 'lookout' boy when he was 11."

I shook my head. "He was 10."

Letta nodded. "See there? The dude was *the* corner boy. I heard the nigga used to be beatin' that block, knockin' niggas over. That's how he met Kam. I heard he even killed a few muthafuckas for Kam. It wasn't until his mother died that he gave it all up. I heard fuckin' with Kam and them hood niggas is what got his mother killed."

My heart was on full stampede then. "*What?*"

Letta's big eyes searched mine. She nodded. "Yeah, girl. This gang shot up his mother's place in broad daylight. She was outside on the front porch. That shit broke that nigga all the way down. I heard he was a wild nigga; couldn't tell his ass shit. I mean, he went from street nigga to schoolteacher. Teach me, nigga, teach me." She fanned herself just thinking about my boo—ol' thirsty ass.

I rolled my eyes. "You thirsty? Need some water? You have got to be tired from all the stalkin' that you've obviously been doing." I had to joke to hide the pain I felt from hearing that my boo lost the only mother that he knew outside of my mother. Damn. I can't believe I missed that. He needed me, and I wasn't even there for him.

Letta rolled her eyes at me, admiring the work she'd done on my face. "Girl, that nigga stays the fuck in the house 24/7. And the one day that he decides to come out and play, he runs into you."

I just watched the grin form on Letta's face.

"Chrystal, you need to get to work on taking that nigga from that bitch. Though something tells me, he's gonna come and take *you*." Letta nodded, agreeing with herself the way she always did.

I shook my head, the tears already starting to slide down my face. I never let any of my friends see me cry, but seeing Blue that day had me deep in my emotions. "He hasn't called me, Letta. I gave him my number this afternoon, and he hasn't called me."

Letta quickly dried my tears. All eyes were already on the two of us. The bitches were already hating hard because we were about to get paid out of the yin-yang that night. Just me, Robyn, and Letta were going to work the VIP room that night. It was my birthday, and the niggas were supposed to help me celebrate.

"Don't let these bitches see you crying. You're strong, Chrystal. Always have been." Letta patted my face dry, making the tears come even harder.

That was Blue's and my thing when we were younger. When either one of us would say, "Always have been," the other would finish by saying, "Always will be."

"Rain, it's showtime," I heard Robyn's voice over my shoulder.

Letta and I turned around to see Robyn standing there in this crop top and thongs made of gold herringbone chains. Her gold Jimmy Choo stilettos rose five inches from the ground. Her dark hair was in a curly updo. She was too sexy. And the strippers rolled their eyes, smacking their lips at her as she strolled over to me.

She rolled her eyes and sucked her teeth. "Bow down, bitches. Take a picture or something. Damn. If you spent more time out there on stage and less time hatin' and tryin'a to figure out what *we're* up to, maybe *you'd* make more money. All them niggas out there, surrounding the stage, and about six of y'all bitches are back here pouting because Kam gave us the VIP room tonight. Get out there and get that paper. Clap that ass, pop that pussy for them coins, and, Tina, you need to tuck that gut in before you head out there."

A few girls laughed, getting up from their vanity seats, and went upstairs.

Tina, the chubby one of the crew, stuck her middle finger up at Robyn (though she *did* suck that gut in). "Fuck you, bitch."

"Nah, I don't fuck girls. I'm strictly dickly, ho. Now, take ya ass on upstairs." Robyn hugged me around my neck, watching me and Letta laugh at her crazy ass.

The pills were starting to really kick in. I could barely stand up from the chair.

Letta caught me, wrapping my arm around her neck and her arm around my waist. "You good, Chrys?"

I nodded, though I wasn't. Last year, I made about $10,000 on my birthday. Don't ask me what type of things I had to do to get that money because I honestly can't remember. I just knew that I woke up the next morning in a tub of ice, and every hole in my body was swollen. I wasn't up for it. I wanted to go home. All I could think of was the look on my son's face when he asked about Blue and the look on Blue's face when he asked about our son.

"No, wait, I can't do this." I shook my head, trying to go back to the vanity mirror and sit down.

Letta grabbed me. "Come on, boo. Nothing is gonna happen this time that you can't handle. I promise. We're just dancing tonight. I might suck a dick or two, but that's about it. And Quincy's ass is gonna be there."

Robyn shook her head. "No, Kam told Quincy that he couldn't come to the VIP room tonight."

Letta and I looked at Robyn.

"I don't think we're gonna need security anyway. Darius just called and said he's coming tonight with his crew. Said something about bringing some nigga named David." She watched my eyes widen. "Every time I see Darius outside of the club, he's always around Kylie's husband. Isn't his name David?"

I looked back at Letta, who was smiling from ear to ear. "I told you, bitch" was written all over her face.

You should have seen those niggas drooling, howling, whooping, and hollering as the three of us strolled into VIP that night. VIP was set up just like a bachelor's studio apartment, more like a penthouse suite. There was a bar (worked by one of the bartenders who only stripped on the weekend), a kitchen, a hot tub, a pool table, a sixty-inch flat-screen TV, a DJ (also a gotdamn stripper), and a king-sized bed. There had to be about thirty muthafuckas in that room that night. I was gonna kill Kam. When I could see straight, that is.

Though Quincy wasn't allowed to come inside the club, I peeped him in all black, standing alongside the bar. A few of his security guards were scattered throughout the club. Quincy Greg was crazy about me. I didn't know if you'd call it love that he had for me, but he really cared about me. Did everything he could to get my attention. He hated the fact that I worked at the club, but he knew, as stubborn and independent as I was, there was no talking me out of it. So he didn't even try. He saw some shit he should have never had to see me do. He stood outside of the Champagne Room plenty of nights that I gave head, hand jobs, pussy, and ass a few times to muthafuckas. There were a few rooms that had peepholes so that people who paid a seventy-five dollar fee could catch about a three-minute live glimpse of us girls doing whatever to niggas. Do you know how much money Kam and Kavante made off that shit? Too much, that's how fuckin' much. The shit we did in those rooms, boy . . . Can't tell you how long I stayed in the showers most nights to wash the cum residue from my face and hair. Quincy should have been disgusted by me, but he wasn't. I wanted to like Quincy, but my heart was always with Blue, making it hard for anyone else.

"Look at all this ass!" Jimmy, this fuckin' cop that visited the club on the regular, smacked me as hard as he could on the ass, gripping my ass in his hands, pulling my body up against his as Johnny, Jimmy's partner in crime, slammed the door behind us.

I was high as hell, stumbling over my own two feet. I tried to smack his hand away, and before I knew it, Jimmy had both hands behind my back, slapping cold handcuffs on my wrists.

"Nigga, what the fuck?" Robyn squealed as two niggas snatched her up. "Y'all really gotta do my girl like that? It's her birthday. She's supposed to be getting star treatment. Take that shit off her."

"Oh, I'm just making sure she doesn't get away this time." Jimmy grabbed my body up against his, breathing down my neck. He smelled just like a twenty-four pack of fuckin' Bud Light. The last time Jimmy was at the club, he was put out. He paid for five minutes in the Champagne Room. I teased the nigga for a good four minutes and fifty-five seconds. And just when I put the head of his pink dick in my mouth, his time was up. And he wasn't trying to hear it. He was living proof that not only were Black men hung. He had the biggest dick on any dude I'd ever seen, white or Black. And a muthafucka as cocky as he was shouldn't have been blessed with a dick that humongous. He shoved his dick so far down my throat that I threw up all over him. There was no way that he should have been allowed back in the club. But throw a couple stacks at Kavante, and it was "fuck our safety."

"She's gonna give me a piece of this birthday cake, if I have to *take* that shit." The muthafucka grabbed me by my hair with one hand and then bent me over the pool table, damn near snapping me in half. He pressed down on my back with all of his might, pressing my body down hard on the pool table.

I squealed out as the perverts whooped and hollered.

"Oh, hell nah, nigga!" Robyn tried to approach me, but she was blocked by the assholes who wanted to see Jimmy take my shit. I may have given oral to about three of the twenty in that room. Most of them wanted a piece, but I never gave them more than a dance or a peep show. They couldn't wait for some big shots with money to invite them to a party so they could finally get a piece of the action. What had my life turned into?

"It ain't this kind of party, y'all! You ain't about to force her to do shit she doesn't wanna do." Letta started to press the alarm switch that was on the wall beside her, but Johnny snatched her up by her wrist, pulling her body up against his. She looked up into his face, shaking her head. "Who the fuck is policing the police? Why the fuck did Kameron even let you niggas in here?"

"Because Kameron *owes* me. I let him slide on paying me the $10,000 that he owes the department. The ten grand should be enough to cover me having my way with her. Shit, with all three of you if I want." Jimmy let go of my hair, sliding my panties down over my ass a little.

I tried to rise up from the pool table. Tried to kick the nigga in his shins with my stilettos. But the more I fought, the firmer he pressed me against the pool table. He pressed down on my back so hard, I thought he was going to crack it. "You're hurting me!" I screamed out, the room already starting to spin around me.

"I'm gonna get me a piece of this birthday cake. When I'm done, the rest of the fellas want a piece of your red velvet cake too. Ain't that right, fellas?" Jimmy smacked me on the ass as hard as he could again, damn near making my knees buckle.

"Damn right!" I heard muthafuckas cosigning with that pig.

"Every nigga loves birthday cake." A few of them even sang the lyrics of "Church" by B.J., the Chicago Kid.

My heart was doing a full stampede in my chest. And just when I felt Jimmy start to slide my panties all the way down, a loud commotion sounded from behind the door to VIP before it burst wide open. I turned my head toward the door, seeing about ten men dressed in all blue from head to toe burst through the doors, flooding in like ants. And in came Darius, dressed to impress, in his suit and tie, as usual.

"And *this* is VIP." Darius glanced at me, bent over the pool table, before he looked back over his shoulder.

When I saw Blue walk into the room, mean muggin' the shit out of everyone, including me, I just knew my heart was going to fly out of my chest.

Blue looked around at everyone in the room before looking back at Johnny, who stood alongside the door. "What's good, Johnny?" Blue nodded toward him.

Why did it not surprise me that Blue knew the cops? As kids, Blue stayed in trouble with the law. He knew just about every cop in Pitt and Wayne Counties. As a matter of fact, Blue and his crew had the muthafuckas on payroll. I'm sure his life in Maryland and D.C. was no different from it was back home.

Johnny hesitated, looking over at Jimmy, who still had my body pressed against the pool table. Then he looked back at Blue. "Nothing. Just enjoying my day off. You must be here to join in the festivities. Grab a seat." He grinned. "You gotta wait your turn, though."

Blue looked over at me, eyeing my panties that had dropped to the floor. Then he looked over at Letta, who pushed the guy who had her hemmed up against the wall off of her. Then he looked at Robyn, who was surrounded by a group of niggas who were ready to strip her completely naked.

Then Blue looked up at Jimmy, who had no intention of letting me go, and then around the room at the rest of the thirsty niggas. Blue grinned a little, shaking his head to himself. "What's up, Brandon, Anthony, Trenton, Greg, Martin, Tommy? Shit, half of the muthafuckas from my 9:00 and 11:30 precalculus class are in this bitch." Blue walked through the room, all eyes on him. "What's good, Lamar, Jerome, Tyrone, Tyson? Look at Mike's fat ass . . ." He looked Letta over in her barely-there outfit and shook his head at her. "Letta . . ."

"Yo, professor?" One of the men who sat at the bar called out to Blue. "You never come to this club. The fuck you doing up in here for, bruh? And with these niggas you rollin' with at that?"

Every time I saw them boys in blue, I knew there was going to be some shit. And everyone in that room knew it too. Blue was a natural-born leader. He'd never join a gang; following the leader shit wasn't in his blood. But he had no problems making friends with gang members. He always had a way of getting muthafuckas to work with him or for him. He hadn't changed a bit.

"I was about to ask you little niggas the same thing. Y'all were gonna rape these three girls. Is that what y'all came here to do, Lamar?" Blue wanted to know.

The dude at the bar, Lamar, shook his head. "Nah, bruh."

Blue looked at Jimmy, who still had me bent over, ass in the air for everyone to see. "That's not what it looks like to me. If you weren't gonna violate these females, it sure seems like y'all were gonna stand by and watch the shit happen. So, since you wanna witness some shit, I'ma show you some shit. Take notes, muthafuckas." Blue kept his eyes on everyone, backing up, making his way over to Johnny, who still stood alongside the door. "How much did you pay for shawty and her girls? Because whatever you paid for them, I can get you ten times that amount. I know you need your money. You know cops don't make shit. I know because me and my niggas used to have you niggas on payroll."

Jimmy chuckled. He stopped pressing against my back, but instead, he yanked me up from the pool table by my hair. "I don't need your money, Professor. *This* is what I need. If you came to see Rain dance, she's busy right now. You're gonna have to wait your turn, just like everyone else," Jimmy snarled, gripping my hair so hard that I could feel some of it tear out at the roots.

Blue's nostrils flared. "Yo, Johnny?" Blue called out to Johnny, who stood behind him, right by the door, scared like he knew something was about to go down after the shit Jimmy just pulled. "I hope y'all muthafuckas are off duty for the rest of the night."

Johnny laughed nervously behind him. "Why is that?"

Blue looked at me being manhandled by Jimmy, the veins in his temples twitching and pulsating the way they always did when he was fired up. And once that nigga's flame was lit, blowing it out wasn't easy. "Because I don't think y'all muthafuckas are gonna wanna get back on the clock after this shit . . ."

Everything that happened from that point on happened rapidly. The next thing I knew, Blue turned around, slamming Johnny's head into the wall, face-first, blood splattering everywhere. Before Jimmy or anyone who came with him, for that matter, could make a move, all you heard was one gun cock—the boys in blue had their 9 mm Berettas drawn.

Jimmy laughed out loud, looking over at Johnny laid the fuck out on the floor. He looked back at Blue. "The last thing you need on your criminal record is another assault on a police officer charge."

"The last thing *you* need on your *vital* records is a death certificate, muthafucka." Blue walked toward Jimmy, his gun aimed in his face . . . Gun aimed in a very well connected, get-away-with-murder police officer's face.

"David!" Darius called out to his friend, watching Blue walking up to Jimmy, pointing his gun at his temple. "Yo, we didn't come here to kill anybody. We came to get your girl, and then roll the fuck back out. David, come on, man, chill."

Blue's gun was already cocked, locked, and loaded. All he had to do was squeeze the trigger, and Jimmy's ass would have been nonexistent.

"You better get that gun out of my gotdamn face, David," Jimmy growled.

"You better get your gotdamn hands off of *her*," Blue growled back, digging his gun into Jimmy's temple.

"Take the cuffs off of her and put shawty's panties back on, muthafucka. You were just gonna take her shit? And these muthafuckas was gonna watch a nigga do this shit to her?"

I was looking at Blue, watching his light skin turn red. As kids, Blue would go days without talking. He would go into these trances around our birthday. All he thought about was his mother and why she left him to die in that trash can. I believe Blue prayed every night, thanking God for allowing my father to find him and bring him to me. There were days when David was so calm . . . quiet. Like, the scary kind of quiet. The quiet where you'd forget his ass was in the room. All of a sudden, he'd say something, scaring the shit out of you. He was a ticking time bomb just waiting to explode, and when he did, I swear you didn't want to be anywhere in sight. Once that nigga was turned up, there was no turning him back down.

I remember watching that nigga fight back in school. He wouldn't stop until he saw blood, until he damn near put the other muthafucka in a coma. The only way to stop that fool from killing the other person was to jump my ass straight in the middle.

"Blue!" I squealed, watching Blue's finger over the trigger, trembling with anticipation. I looked up at Blue's face. "Blue, please . . . don't," I whispered.

Blue looked into my face, his expression softening a little . . . until he looked me over a little, eyeing my panties on the floor. He glared at me before looking back at Jimmy. "You have five seconds to uncuff her or else this bullet is gonna drill a hole through your muthafuckin' skull."

As mad as he was with Jimmy and the men around who could watch a girl get raped, I knew he was more mad at who I let myself become.

Jimmy's ass looked more embarrassed than scared. Embarrassed that some young, Black college professor was putting him in his place in a room full of people who were afraid of him. Jimmy came to the club almost every night, starting shit. Because he was a white police officer, he thought he could do what the fuck he wanted to do to whomever he wanted to do it to.

Jimmy reluctantly took his key out of his pocket. He snatched me by my wrists, unlocking the handcuffs before snatching them from my wrists. Then he looked at Blue before backing off a little.

Blue still hadn't lowered his weapon. "I'm letting every muthafucka in this room know to keep their gotdamn hands, dicks, lips—*any* muthafuckin' thing off her. As of today, her job here is done."

My eyes widened. "Blue, you can't—"

"Can't what, *Rain*?" Blue lowered his weapon, signaling his boys to do the same. Then he looked at Jimmy, who was mean mugging the fuck out of him. "I'ma get you, nigga" was written all over Jimmy's face. "What? Nigga, you got something to say?" Blue started to make his way over to Jimmy, but I grabbed his arm. Blue snatched away from me, pushing me off him. "Don't fuckin' touch me. Pull your gotdamn panties up. I really can't even get mad at the niggas for violating you when you put yourself in this fucked-up position. I swear, if I see you back in this club, I'ma shut this muthafucka down. Get your girls and let's roll the fuck up outta here."

I never felt more like a ho in my life, though it shouldn't have taken Blue to do it. Shamefully, I put on my panties. Blue's eyes were glued on me until I pulled them to my hips. I looked up at Letta as she pushed her way through the men surrounding her. She grabbed Robyn's hand, pulling her along with her.

"Party's over. Y'all might as well head back upstairs where the basic bitches are, fellas." Robyn had to throw her comment in before heading out the door with Letta.

"By the way, I'm posting your final grades on Monday. All y'all muthafuckas failed precalculus. Take that shit over next semester." Blue grabbed my hand, pulling me out of the VIP that Christmas night.

# Chapter Four

## *My Lane*

## *Chrystal*

"Blue, calm down," I sighed, sitting in the passenger seat of my own BMW that night. Blue had Darius trail behind him to my apartment in his car, while he drove me home in mine. I passed out the moment we left VIP that night. I wasn't sure if it was the amount of drugs in my system, the excitement of the events that happened that day, or a combination of both. Regardless, my mind, body, and soul had reached their limit that night.

"Calm down? The fuck you mean 'calm down'? I haven't seen your ass in eight fuckin' years, and when I do, I see your ass poppin' that pussy for muthafuckas!" Blue sped down 295 on his way to my condo in Hanover. "If I didn't come get y'all hoes, them niggas would've raped the fuck outta y'all."

"*Hoes?*" Letta resented that from the backseat.

"Yes, Letta—muthafuckin' hoes." Blue wasn't taking back what he said.

Letta shook her head at him. "No respect-having-ass nigga."

Blue looked back at her like she was crazy. "Respect? Give a nigga something *to* respect. I just call the shit how I see it. Fuckin' and suckin' niggas every night for a couple of stacks. All on YouTube and shit, giving niggas head. My niggas showed me a picture of both of y'all bitches going down on Johnny, the same nigga whose face I busted a little while ago."

"A'ight, now, Professor, you're fine but *not* fine enough to be calling us bitches and hoes and shit." Letta smacked her lips.

Blue scuffed, shaking his head, glancing back at her. I knew that "I can do and say what the fuck I want," glance.

He was always cocky, and my boo had every right to be. Did I like being called a ho or a bitch? No, but was I acting like a ho? Yes.

Letta sighed, sinking back in her seat. "Okay, maybe you *are* that fine, shit, but that's still fucked-up. You have no right to judge us, Professor."

"No right to judge you?" Blue merged onto the Route 175 exit toward Arundel Mills Mall. "Y'all out here fuckin' and suckin' niggas like it ain't nothing. I heard about y'all. Shit, my niggas showed me the shit on the internet. They showed me a video of y'all homegirl, Fancy's, face all in Rain's pussy, ass, and shit. The whole world can see this shit. As soon as I saw it, I called my niggas back home in Greenville, and do you know what they told me?" I felt Blue looking at me.

I just looked out the window, my pulse quickening.

"They told me that they already seen the shit. That they didn't wanna tell me that my girl was a gotdamn stripper-ho, gettin' faded on the regular, just so she can numb herself to the shit that these niggas do to her every night." Blue was hot as hell. He was gonna get in my ass, and he wasn't going to let up.

"Professor, ease up, okay?" Letta took up for me. "We work hard to afford these cars, these clothes, these shoes, this Brazilian weave in my gotdamn hair, these diamond-studded gel nails, these new titties, this ass, these thighs, these condos, these trips around the world, these long vacations. Celebrities from all over the world ask for us. Shit, groupies ain't got a gotdamn thang on us. Most of us get paid in a month what you get paid in a year, Professor. And if that means that sometimes we gotta go home with busted lips, busted asses, nuts all over our faces, then well, it is what the fuck it is, nigga."

"Well, Letta, you can do what the fuck you wanna do, but Chrystal's days in that muthafucka are over." Blue looked at me as my car came to a halt at a stoplight.

I looked at Blue, lifting an eyebrow at him. I was too high and too drunk to argue with his ass. I just waved him off. "Whateva, muthafucka."

"You trippin', Chrystal." Blue laughed to himself as the light turned green, and he took off rolling in my car again. "You show your ass in that club, shawty, and I'ma show mine. Believe that shit," he scoffed. "Does your son know you do this bullshit?"

Letta gasped. "Hold up, hold up, hold *up!* You have a son?"

I sighed, not responding to her, but responding to Blue instead. "Mind your own business, Blue."

"Mind my own business? *You're* my business. My *son* is my muthafuckin' business, Chrystal," he shouted at me.

Letta was having an information overload in the backseat. She had to unbuckle her seat belt for that one. "Wha-wha . . ." She couldn't even get her words out at first. "Hold up, wait a minute, rewind, pause, play that shit in slow motion, please. What did you just say? Your *son?* You have a son with the professor? Y'all had a baby together?"

I looked at Blue, pissed that he'd aired my dirty laundry. The only reason why Tela, Tori, Jordyn, or Brook knew about my son was because I was vulnerable at Kylie's

Christmas dinner. I had to tell Blue what was going on in my life since he'd been gone. Robyn knew everything about me. I didn't want any of the girls at the club other than Robyn to know my business. They talked too much. As much as Letta couldn't stand Kylie, she'd eventually get pissed enough at the bitch to rub in the fact that Blue and I had a child together.

"I saw little man today at that group home. He looks just like a nigga. He can't see, he can't hear, but he *felt* me. When Darius dropped him off at his *mother's* house—" Blue was trying to call me out for my lifestyle, and I had to stop him.

"I *am* his fuckin' mother, Blue." I wanted to smack the shit off that gorgeous face of his.

"Then *act* like it. Why the fuck is he going to Mrs. Watson's crib on Christmas instead of yours then? Why the fuck is he staying in a group home? Why the fuck is my son blind and deaf if he's supposed to be someone that you care about? Your *lifestyle* fucked up our son, Chrystal. He's with her because fuckin' niggas for money means more to you than having custody of your son. You abandoned that boy the same way that my mother abandoned me. You're just like her," Blue screamed at me.

Blue had barely stopped the car at the next stoplight when I opened the car door and hopped the fuck out. I refused to let him continue to make me feel guiltier about myself than I'd already felt.

"Fuck this shit," I muttered to myself, putting my hood over my head as I strutted down the sidewalk, walking as fast as I could.

Blue's crazy ass pulled up to the curb, flicked on the emergency blinkers, and got out of the car. "Chrystal," he called out, slamming my car door shut.

"Leave me the fuck alone, David," I yelled, not even looking back when I heard his footsteps trampling behind me.

"The fuck you going, Chrystal?" Blue caught up with me, grabbing my arm, yanking me back to him, quickly turning my body around to face his.

I looked up into his face as I tried to push him away from me. "This is *my* life, Blue. You *can't* tell me what the fuck to do with it."

"See, that's where you're wrong. You're *my* life, Chrystal. And I'll be damned if I watch you throw yourself to the wolves like this." His grip on my arm damn near cut off my circulation.

I looked into his face, trying my best not to cry. Then I shook my head. "No, your life is Kylie."

Blue shook his head at me. "Shawty, I'm not even supposed to be with her, and you know that shit. Just like you're not even supposed to be living like this."

I cried out, "Things have changed. We're *not* the same. You have a wife. You're a college professor. I have a son who is smart, talented, and gifted. I work my ass off to provide for him and Mrs. Watson. I work hard to put him through private school. I work hard to pay for Mrs. Watson's nursing staff. And I work hard to pay for my son's stay in the group home. I'm not proud of what I do, but it provides for my baby boy. I fucked him up with the drugs that I was on back then. When you left Greenville, shit changed. Shit that you would've never let happen to me happened to me, David. I had nowhere to turn but to drugs, but to my boyfriend, who only turned out to be my pimp. When I had my baby, I gave him to someone who could provide for him better than I could have. Lawrence controlled everything that I did. The reason why I never went back to Greenville is that the same boys you call your friends were among the first to pay to have sex with me. And do you know who they paid to have sex with me? Your *uncle,* who owned the corner store."

Blue's eyes searched my face as he slowly released his grip from my arm. "What?"

"He said I needed to stop fuckin' niggas for free. That niggas would pay to sleep with me. And to prove it, he asked a few of your friends how much they would pay to sleep with me. Four of your friends paid $150 each for five minutes of my time. And this was *after* I found out that I was pregnant, Blue," I hated to admit. "Lawrence is your cousin, a child your uncle had outside of his marriage with this woman who lived in Delaware. Your uncle is the one who introduced me to Lawrence." I watched Blue's facial expression turn from anger to pure rage.

"Next week, we're taking a trip home, shawty." Blue tried to calm his tone down a little.

I shook my head. "It's the past, Blue; just leave it alone."

"How is it in the fuckin' past when your ass is still doing something that my uncle started? My own flesh and blood would let his own son sell *my* girl? I'ma put one in that muthafucka—blood or not. Just tell me one thing—did that muthafucka make you sleep with him too?" Blue asked, gripping my arm again.

I sighed. "Blue, just let it go. I could have called the police, but I didn't. I have to take some blame for this. I was the neighborhood ho, and that's what I was treated like once you left, David. This is just who I am."

Blue shook his head. "Nah, not anymore. Not if I have anything to do with it. I'll do whatever I gotta do to help take care of you and my son, but I swear, you're not going back in that club, shawty. Where is your nigga? You can't tell me you don't have one. I heard about you and some nigga named Quincy. The weak nigga lets you do this shit? I'ma have to have a talk with that nigga too."

"Why don't you just go home to your wife and let me live my life? I don't belong to you, David," I cried out.

"So, who do you think you belong to? That club? Kam? Kavante? That money you make every night? Those niggas who do what the fuck they wanna do to you and your friends every night? Is the money worth all of this? I know what it's like to feel all of this financial freedom. There is no other feeling like it; trust me, shawty, I know. To have everything you want, not to have to ask anyone for shit, to control muthafuckas, to live it up every day and gotdamn night . . . I had tunnel vision like a muthafucka. If it wasn't about that paper, I didn't wanna hear shit. But it was that same tunnel vision, gotta-stay-getting-this-paper attitude that got Miss Tiffany killed," Blue tried to tell me, but I didn't want to listen.

"Blue, I don't wanna hear this," I cried, trying to pull away from him, but he pulled me in closer.

"She moved us to D.C., not only because she got a better job there, but also because she was trying to get me away from the life that I was living in Greenville. You remember the shit we used to get into. Robbing niggas, breaking into stores, selling drugs. Yeah, and I saw my uncles pimping women." Blue watched the tears sliding down my face. "We've both seen a lot that we shouldn't have at a young age. Miss Tiffany tried to get me away from my street lifestyle, but I wasn't trying to hear her. She tried to give me everything, so I wouldn't have to feel the need to go out in the streets and get it. I was so angry at life. I wanted my mother, and she wasn't there, and I took it out on Miss Tiffany, a woman who was already depressed because she couldn't have kids of her own. She loved me like I was her own, and I never showed her that I appreciated it. She's gone, and it's all because I was stuck on getting money and doing what the fuck I wanted to do. You're not only hurting yourself by living like this, but you're also hurting your son. *Our* beautiful son. Look at you—high as a gotdamn kite." Blue looked me over, seeing that my mind was far from anything that he was trying to tell me. "Get'cha ass back in the gotdamn car. I'm takin' you home."

I stumbled into my condo that night, Blue following behind me. He was supposed to be heading back out with Darius to take Letta back home, but instead, he sent Letta, Robyn, and Darius about their business. Darius left Blue's car, and they all hopped in Robyn's ride, on their way to get into their usual trouble. Blue was determined to make sure I sat my ass down somewhere that night. It was 11:50, and Blue knew Kylie was blowing up his phone every five minutes, looking for him. But he couldn't care less. After he got tired of feeling his phone vibrate in his pocket, he turned it off, tossing it on my coffee table. I sat there on my Ralph Lauren Desert Modern Sectional sofa, kicking off my heels, watching Blue dig through my cabinets and refrigerator. I watched him preparing coffee in my coffeemaker. It reminded me of when we were kids, studying for finals. Blue would make the best coffee, shit that would keep you hype enough to pull an all-nighter. And I knew once I saw Blue make that coffee that he didn't intend on leaving me that night.

"Kylie is gonna kill you, Blue." I kicked my feet up in my chair, taking off my jacket. You have no idea how badly I wanted to tell him about Kylie. I was mad that he'd even fuck with a bitch like her, let alone marry her. I wanted him to see her for who she was, but I also wanted him to discover her on his own. The truth would eventually come out. Now that Blue and I had found each other again, truths would be revealed regardless, on both ends.

"It's your birthday; you're supposed to be spending it with her, not me." I felt light-headed as I leaned back on the couch, sitting there in my spaghetti strap tank top and skinny jeans. Once we left VIP that night, Blue made all three of us change, right in front of Kam, before we left the club. Surprisingly, Kam kept his cool. Didn't say shit. But I knew that if I didn't show up the next day for work, he was coming for Blue.

I looked up to see Blue walking toward me with a cup of coffee and a Hostess cupcake that had a candle burning on top of it. It took everything in me not to cry. When we were kids, he'd always show up to my house early the morning of our birthday with a box of matches, two candles, and two Hostess cupcakes. It was the sweetest thing ever, and he still remembered what it meant to me. He was mad at me, but he still loved me.

Blue came over and sat beside me on the sofa, setting the cup of coffee on the coffee table and holding the cupcake between his fingers. "Sorry, it's a little squished on the sides; it was in my coat pocket." He grinned a little, examining the cake before looking at me looking at the cupcake.

I couldn't even say anything. I was choked up. Too much hurt for one day, I guess.

"Make a wish," he whispered to me, holding the cupcake to my lips.

"You . . ." I whispered before blowing out the candle.

Blue grinned, taking the candle out of the cupcake, putting it to my lips so I could lick the icing from the candle the way I did when we were kids. I took the candle from his fingers and licked the icing while I watched him take the first bite out of the cupcake. Then he put it to my lips so I could take the second one. I missed him. I couldn't believe he was sitting here, in my living room, after not seeing him since I was 16. His face hadn't changed a bit. It was still handsome. Still pretty. Still had that slit in his left eyebrow where he had stitches after getting into a fight with one of the boyfriends I had in the eleventh grade who made the mistake of putting his hands on me. And those blue eyes, the kind of eyes that always drove the girls crazy at first glance.

I reached for my jacket, taking out the picture that my son had given me, and then I handed it to Blue. I watched him licking the cream from his fingers, examining the picture for a few seconds. "Who is this?" he asked.

"Your mother," I whispered to him.

Blue was silent for a few seconds, eyeing the picture. His eyes glossed over, but he didn't cry that night, at least not in front of me. "Where did you get this?"

"Payton." I ate the rest of the cupcake. "I found out today that Mrs. Watson is Payton's great-grandmother, Blue."

Blue looked up at me, his eyes searching my face.

I nodded. "Yeah, she's *your* grandmother."

Blue slowly shook his head. "Yo, this is too much. First, I see you bent over for a nigga, naked in front of hundreds of people. Then, I meet the most beautiful, smartest, loving little boy, who looks a lot like me, at a group home, fighting with all of his might to get to me. Now, come to find out that the boy is mine . . . Next, I find out that my wife is friends with a girl who, still to this very day, I can't get off of my mind. She's been right here, in my face for seven years, and I had no idea. And now, you're telling me that my own grandmother has been raising the son that I never even knew that I had?"

I hesitated, watching him starting to go off.

"Did they *know* I lived here in Maryland, Chrystal?" Blue asked, his eyes searching my face.

I nodded. "Yes. She told me today that your mother was at Miss Tiffany's funeral."

Blue's eyebrows lowered, intertwining. "They knew I was here, they knew that *you* were here, and they knew we had a son together—and never contacted me to tell me? Why?"

"Because of me. Because of my lifestyle. Because of the way they knew you lived back then. Your mother's name is Rosy Watkins, and she's a doctor. She delivered Payton. I had no idea that she was your mother until today." I watched Blue get up from the sofa. I got up, grabbing his arm, watching him move about anxiously. "Blue, your grandmother has been *so* good to our son. Please don't be mad at them. I was mad at first too, but then I realized that she did right by my baby because they were trying to do right by what happened to you. Your grandmother loves our baby and refuses to let me get him because of the way I provide for them. Just go talk to her one of these days. Go see your son. Go see your grandmother."

Blue looked at me, searching my face, his expression calming . . . a little. "Does—" Blue hesitated. "Does he know that I didn't know about him? He *does* know that I'd never abandon him if I had known about him, right?"

I shrugged. "I didn't get a chance to explain anything to him. Once he gave me the picture, I just kissed my baby and left. He really loves you, Blue. You should have seen his face when Mrs. Watson was talking about you. You should stop by and see him sometime. He would love to see you, Blue."

Blue nodded. "Yeah, little homie fought with everything in him to get back in that car with me and Darius, yo. It's funny because my homie has been trying to get me to go to that group home since I was 18, but I could never bring myself to go. It's so depressing, ya know, seeing those kids like that. These kids are just victims of what their parents took them through. I couldn't subject my heart to that. Had I gone, I would have seen my son years ago."

I looked at Blue. "I didn't mean to hurt our son. I love Payton."

Blue just looked at me, his temples twitching a little. "Payton was our baby's name when we were kids."

"What?" I dried my face.

"When you made a nigga play house with you at recess, our play-baby's name was Payton David Jacobs." Blue tried to lighten the mood a little, which only deepened the wound. "You remember that shit? Old ugly-ass Cabbage Patch doll. You always had a nigga doing the most."

My baby was supposed to be a Jacobs. Not an Alison. He wasn't supposed to have my maiden name. Blue and I were supposed to be together. I wasn't supposed to be a stripper who sold her body at least four out of seven days a week. He wasn't supposed to be married to Kylie, a woman who was in love with a thug, but probably only married Blue to make her first love jealous.

"What are you doing here, Blue?" was all I could say, watching him drink from the coffee cup that he made for me.

"Just wanted to get you alone for a little while. It's been a long time since I've seen you. Just wanted to talk to you in private. There's so much I wanna say. I don't even know where to start." Blue exhaled deeply. He was about to question me again about my life without him, but he was rudely interrupted. And a part of me was glad.

My phone vibrated in my jacket pocket. I went over and got it, looking at the display. It was Quincy. I knew he was calling to see if it was cool to stop by. He stopped by just about every night. I looked up at Blue. "It's Quincy."

Blue sat back on the sofa, leaning back like he wasn't going any damn where. "So?"

"*So* I think he's about to come over." I watched Blue unzipping his jacket.

"Good, I need to talk with that nigga anyway." He took off his jacket, laying it across the arm of the sofa.

I shook my head, really not in the mood for any more shit that night. Blue always took shit to a whole other level when it came to me. I can't lie; I was the same way about him, but too much had already happened that day to go starting anymore shit. "Talk to Quincy about what, Blue?"

"About him not being man enough to step up, do his job, and take you up out of that club." Blue looked at me like I was crazy for questioning him. "The fuck you mean? No real nigga would have his girl selling her pussy period, point-blank, end of story. Oh, I'm sorry, I forgot—you like fuckin' with sorry-ass niggas. Wouldn't know what to do with a real nigga."

Oh, I wanted to go off on him. I wanted to tell him what type of bitch that he had, but I let him go on dogging me because he'd soon find out just what kind of wife he had. I grinned, shaking my head. "Quincy is a good guy. I'm not about to let you talk shit about him. You just did good. You brought me home, gave me my favorite cupcake, made me this awesome cup of coffee, and now, you wanna dog the only guy in my life who really gives a fuck about me?"

Blue looked at me like he was hurt, like he regretted coming to my place, like he couldn't believe he was trying to make things right with a girl who was content with doing wrong. He took a deep breath before getting up from the couch.

"Blue, wait, I'm sorry. You know what I mean." I watched him putting on his jacket again. "I mean, he's the only guy in my life right now who looks out for me. Me and you haven't seen each other in eight years. We haven't been friends in years."

"And whose fault is that?" Blue zipped his coat. "I looked for you for years, shawty. Yes, I moved away, but a nigga never stopped thinking about you. To this day,

I still dream about you. Every year for eight years, on Christmas, I prayed to God that you were safe, that you were happy, and that you hadn't forgotten about me. A nigga has been hurting for eight gotdamn years, and the sad part about it all is that I'm hurting worse now that I finally get to see you again than I was when we weren't around each other. As kids, you were my favorite person to say 'hello' to, and the hardest person to tell 'goodbye.' I wanted to be around you twenty-four-fuckin'-seven. You *forgot* about me, Chrystal."

I shook my head. I didn't. "No, Blue, I never forgot you."

"You didn't remember me either." Blue searched my face for a few seconds before laughing a little. "I'm trippin,' coming up in your life, risking my own to save yours. From this day on, I'm gonna have issues with the cops for the way things went down at the club. They gonna fuck with a nigga all because I'm in my feelings about a girl who doesn't value herself as much as I do. If you wanna work at that club, go ahead, I'm not gonna stop you. My bad. You're right; it's your life. You've been doing the shit this fuckin' long. All on pornos and shit, yo. Do you if you want to. I swear, I'ma back off. My wife is at home, pregnant, and I'm here, worried about you."

My heart came to a complete stop in my chest for what felt like a full minute. "She's preg—" I couldn't even say it. "When did she tell you this?"

"Today, before Christmas dinner. She told your girls today too after you left." Blue watched the hurt expression on my face. He was probably hurt more than I was. "The day after I run into you, Kylie tells me she's pregnant. It's kinda like she knew saying this would be the only thing keeping me from leaving her for you."

My heart finally went back to its normal rhythm. I watched Blue make his way toward my front door. "Blue, you deserve better than me. And you damn sure deserve better than her." I watched him unlock my door so that he could leave me. "Blue, I still have that letter you wrote me. You know, with the 'One Woman's Trash' poem you wrote? I read that poem every night."

Blue lowered and shook his head.

"Thank you for still caring about me," I whispered, walking up to him, watching him struggle with thoughts of staying with me that night or going home to his wife. The wife who didn't deserve one piece of him—funky bitch.

"Thank you for the cupcake," I said to his back, watching him attempt to turn the knob.

Blue took a deep breath before turning around to face me. He looked down into my face, examining my chin like I had something on it.

"What? What is it? Is there something on my face?" I started to rub my chin, but he grabbed my hand, pulling me to him. I gasped.

"I'll get it off. You've got some cream on your chin," he whispered to me.

I looked up at him as he bent over to kiss my chin, more like suck my chin, his teeth grazing against my skin just a little. My clit tingled. I gripped his jacket in my free hand, taking in the five-second moment. It was the sweetest moment I'd ever experienced. His lips grazed against mine as he straightened up. Oh, I wanted to hold him. We had yet to hug each other. I was waiting for him to hug me, but he didn't that night. But he put his lips on me, and that was more than enough . . . for the time being.

Blue looked down at me, his eyes searching my face. "Tell Quincy that I gotcha home safe, no thanks to him. Sorry-ass nigga." Blue let go of my hand and walked out.

***

"Bitch, you and the professor—*my* professor—have a *baby?*" Letta exclaimed the next morning in Hollister. You already know we were going to hit up every store in every mall in the area the day after Christmas.

I sighed, trying to avoid the stares from Fancy and Letta. Robyn just flipped through the panties and bras, acting like she wasn't a part of the conversation. She already knew my secrets. The only new information she received was the fact that Kylie's husband was my son's father. Robyn didn't care too much for Kylie, but she hung around her because I did. She didn't care the least bit that I had a child with Kylie's husband. In fact, I think she was excited, waiting for some shit to go down between the two of us, so that she could jump in it too.

"C'mon, can we talk about something else? Yes, we have a baby. Yes, my son is in a group home. Yes, my baby is deaf, blind, and beautiful. Yes, I had a child with Kylie's husband." I put it all out there. "Damn, talk about something else because the answer to all your fuckin' questions is gonna be 'yes, gotdamn it,'" I huffed.

Fancy shook her head. "And I heard the bitch is pregnant too."

"It's probably not even the professor's baby." Letta rolled her eyes, popping her lips. "I heard that she was back to fuckin' with Kam again. It's been a minute since I saw the two together, but that don't mean shit. How often do we see Kam at the club, and how often do we kick it with Kylie? The only time I see the ho is when she pops up at the university to eat lunch with the professor. Did you tell the professor about Kam and his wife?"

I just searched through the brightly colored underwear. "I could use a pair of these lime-green panties."

"Bitch, don't play. Did you tell your *man* that his *wife* is fuckin' off on him?" Letta snatched the panties from me, tossing them back on the display table.

I looked at her. "No, I didn't tell him. It's none of my business. Me and Blue are just friends, maybe not even that anymore. He's not my man; he's hers. No matter what they have going on, he's not mine anymore. I already know I'll be hearing from her soon. Blue is the realest nigga I know. He'll tell her about us. Quincy even knows about us."

All three of my homegirls looked at me.

The night before, Quincy came over as normal to place his security guards outside my house. He came to my condo, asking about what went down at the club. He wanted to know who Blue was and why he felt compelled to play Superman. To Quincy, I was a grown woman who could do what I wanted and would stop on my own when I had enough. Not to say Quincy didn't care, but he saw my vision and the life I wanted to live. He didn't know, until that night, why I had to work as hard as I did. I told him about my son and that Blue was his father.

Quincy was a very handsome, dark-skinned guy with a smile that could brighten the darkest night. He came from nothing. Grew up in a rough neighborhood, without a father, barely had a mother, and broke—ya know, the typical Black male story. However, what wasn't typical about him was that he put to use the one thing that had always gotten him into trouble. He was always fighting the niggas on the block. If anyone needed to whup a muthafucka's ass, they'd call on Quincy. It didn't take long for a rich person who needed a bodyguard to see Quincy fighting at a club. And the rest was history.

Quincy was crazy about me. Could have any female he wanted, but he wanted me. I never led him on. I told him from the moment he kissed me a few years ago that my heart beat, but it didn't feel anything. That I was empty. That there was only one man who knew what to do with my heart. It wasn't until Christmas night, 2015, that he found out Blue was that man. And it broke his heart. He played it off cool, but I knew he was hurt. I'd usually let Quincy stay the night with me, if only just to hold me, but that night, we talked for a few minutes, and I sent him on his way. I stayed up all night, staring at that cup of coffee that I was supposed to be drinking . . . with Blue.

"I know Quincy was feeling some type of way about that." Robyn shook her head. "I told you that you should've never slept with that boy. You put that pussy on that nigga, and now, you've got him sprung. You know we got that 'nigga-stalk-me' pussy."

I rolled my eyes at her, trying not to smile. "Girl, shut up. How you gonna try to put me on blast when you fuckin' around with Darius? You claim you don't like him like that, that he's just a client, yet he's the only nigga you've been fuckin' in *or* out of this club for over a year."

Robyn rolled her big brown eyes.

Letta agreed. "Yeah, I'm sure that pussy curves to the shape of his dick right about now, homie."

I laughed a little, glad the heat was off of me for a few seconds. "The only reason why you let the nigga pay to sleep with you is because you just want everyone to think that he's only your client. Shit, you're content with lying to yourself about your feelings for him. You know good and well that if you told that nigga you were his girl, he'd make you quit working at this club."

Robyn pushed past me, going to the other side of the table to look at the panties that were on sale, ten for five dollars. "Bitch, whateva. Don't change the subject. This ain't about me. This is about *you* and your little love child with your friend's husband. You already know she's gonna approach your ass. Just give her a few days, and she's coming for your jugular. But don't worry, Rain. I gotcha back, though." Robyn held up a pair of neon-blue panties. "Yes, these are cute. I think the fellas will like these. Gotta get that money tonight, ladies. I gotta put down on this new Mercedes that I saw at this showcase in D.C. last week. We have a party of thirty coming to VIP tonight. A bunch of high rollers too. As far as I know, there will be no fuckin' tonight. Just dancing. Kavante told me to round up a few girls. I told him he already knew my crew was down."

"Oh, I'm in." Fancy raised her hand.

"Me too, boo," Letta nodded.

Robyn looked at me. "You workin', sis, or are you really gonna do what your boo told you to do?"

Letta nodded. "The nigga *did* tell you to stay your ass out of that club or he was gonna come up in that bitch and turn the muthafucka out."

I sighed. "Nah, he got mad at me last night when I told him to leave so Quincy could come over. He basically told me to go about my business. Do what the fuck I want. That if I wanna fuck niggas on the regular, devaluing myself, then go ahead. Have a nice life, bitch."

Fancy laughed out loud.

We all looked at her.

"Girl," Fancy threw her long, jet-black hair over her shoulders. "I don't mean to laugh, but didn't y'all say the nigga busted up in VIP, smashed Officer Johnny Rowland's face into the wall, aimed a gun in racist-ass Officer Jimmy Copeland's face, and then told all *three* of you hoes to get the fuck out of the building? That doesn't sound like a nigga who was playing to me, boo-boo."

I shrugged. I wasn't so sure. He looked pretty serious when he walked out of my front door the night before. One thing that I knew about Blue was that he was afraid of loving anyone or anything. Admitting that he loved me the day he moved to D.C. must have been the hardest thing that boy had ever done. He was always afraid to admit that he loved or liked anything too much, worried that he might lose it. That was his main reason for trying his hardest not to love Miss Tiffany. We all knew that he cared for her, but I think a huge part of him felt guilty for never once telling her that he loved her. I believe the only reason he told me was that he knew it would be the last day we were going to be around each other. He wouldn't have to face me. He wouldn't have to face his feelings. Anger, hurt, pain, and rejection were feelings that he'd learned to deal with. Love was something that didn't come easily to him.

"It's Hard Out Here For a Pimp" played over my cell phone's speakers. I rolled my eyes before taking my phone out of my purse to answer it, knowing it was Kam. "Yes, Kam?" I huffed.

"What are you wearing?" Kam's sexy voice serenaded through my phone.

I rolled my eyes. "My 9 mm. Now, what do you want?"

Robyn looked over my shoulder, shaking her head. "Nigga, how you gonna call on the cell, rollin' up on us at the same time?"

I sighed, already feeling Kam breathing down my neck. I turned around, facing him. There he stood, tall, brown, handsome, thick, dressed in all-black Giuseppe from his baseball cap to his high-top sneakers. Always sexy and fresh to death, and I couldn't stand it. He had so much swag and sex appeal. I think every one of the four of us standing before him had had sex with the nigga at least once. And judging by the way the two hoes behind the cash register were gawking at him, I'm sure he already fucked their brains out too.

"What'cha want, Kameron?" I asked him, eying him as he licked those thick lips of his. The same lips that used to suck the shit out of my pussy daily a few years earlier.

"Let me holla at'cha for a minute." He grabbed my arm. "Excuse us, ladies." He winked at my girls before leading me out of the store.

We sat on a bench outside the store, facing each other. "What is it, Kam? I'm supposed to be meeting Quincy tonight to go out to eat, so don't even ask me about working tonight. He didn't get the chance to take me out for my birthday, so he's taking me out tonight." I watched Kam chuckle to himself. "What?"

"You know good and gotdamn well I'm not worried about no gotdamn Quincy. Quincy, who?" Kam stopped laughing. "He's not shit to you but a bodyguard. You've had the nigga's nose wide open for years and have yet to let him wife you. The nigga I'm concerned about is David Jacobs."

I just looked at Kam, crossing my legs, watching the tassels on my brown fur Tims dangle. "Why is he of any concern to you?"

"He was really in his feelings at the club last night, not to mention at the masquerade party. You said you didn't know the nigga, but by the way he snatched your ass up last night in VIP, it's obvious that you do." Kam watched me jiggling my car keys in my hand, not giving a fuck about the shit he was talking about.

"So what, nigga? What does my private life have to do with you?" I rolled my eyes.

Kam smiled, amused by my inability to give a fuck about the shit he was talking about. "I pay the police department a lot to stay off my ass, and you got your nigga down there, policing shit. When your private life becomes public in *my* muthafuckin' place of business, then it has *a lot* to do with me. I've known Blue for years. The only reason why he's working at that college is because of me. The only reason he has a gotdamn bachelor's degree and is about to start college in January to get his master's degree is because of me. The only reason why he's not in jail for his past is because of me. I have carried that nigga's life in my hands since we were in high school."

Kam got on my muthafuckin' nerves. It wasn't enough that his family ran the city; they also had to have the streets under control.

"So, how long have you been fuckin' around with Blue's wife?" I watched Kam's expression change from cocky to "Bitch, you better stay in your lane." I shook my head at him. "That's the shit you need to be worried about. I'm not into wrecking homes. I don't fuck people who just got married. When I caught you and Kylie fuckin', she was dating Blue. The two were *engaged*. Tell me that I'm lying, Kam."

"I put food on the nigga's table. It's because of me that he's even with Kylie. She ran to him back in college after she found out that I had been sleeping with you. She couldn't stand the little nigga and only fucked with him to make me jealous. But you know, I could give two fucks back then. I've changed, though. And she's changed too." Kam watched me roll my eyes and curse under my breath. "Kylie and I haven't slept together in a minute, not that it's any of your gotdamn business. But I still care about her. She gave a nigga hundreds of thousands of chances, even after she started dating the nigga—shit, even after they were married—to get my shit together. I missed out on a life with her, but I accompany her to all her fashion events. Shit, *I'm* the reason why she gets to run *any* of these events. It's my connections that will take her far. Blue can't do shit for her but sit his ass down and watch her shine. She loves that nigga, even though he can't do shit for her. A few years ago, I asked her to leave him, and she wouldn't. *That's* how I know she loves him. So, I backed the fuck off. And I'm gonna need you to do the same."

I just looked at him.

"She doesn't know about your past with the nigga, but I do. I knew when Blue snatched up your ass at the party the other night that he knew you. Shit, I knew when I helped you find Mrs. Watson that Blue was your child's father. I didn't tell you because I didn't want to hurt Kylie. I fuck with Blue because he used to shut niggas down back in the day. He had the streets on lock. I could trust him with my life. When he started dating Kylie, I flipped. He didn't know I was fuckin' around with her, but I was still pissed. When I found out that you had a baby with this nigga, I'm not even gonna lie. I put you to work in my club so that he could find out you were working for me. I had no idea it would take the nigga this long to find you, though. Shows how much Kylie and the nigga communicate, doesn't it?"

My eyes widened. I tried to rise, but Kam pulled me back down. "You had me working in that club just to piss off Blue? *Not* to help me take care of my family, but so Blue could find out I'm a prostitute?"

Kam grinned. "He fucked with mine, so I fucked with his. That's just the way the game goes, ma."

"I'm too old for games, Kam. I bet you won't see me at that club anymore." I tried to pull away from Kam, but he dug his nails into my arm. "Okay, Kam, do you *really* wanna cause a scene out here? Get your gotdamn hands *off* me."

"How much is your son's tuition? How much do you pay to keep your son in that group home? What about the staff at Mrs. Watson's house? How much are you paying per semester to get *your* master's degree? What about the insurance on those foreign cars in your driveway?" Kam tried to break me down to nothing but bills that needed to be paid. "If I didn't pay you the ends that I do, who the fuck would take care of the woman who's taking care of your son? She's never going to give him back to you. She's gonna give little homie to the state, and you know it."

I just looked into his face, my heart racing.

"Who pays for those expensive clothes on your back? The jewelry on your neck, ears, wrists, and fingers? Who pays for your son's schooling? Who pays the mortgage at your condo? Who paid for that house your son lives in? Who just paid to send you and all of your friends to Jamaica for two weeks?" Kam tried to act like I wasn't working my ass off (literally) to pay for my lifestyle.

"This pussy paid for it, muthafucka," I growled at him.

"No, *my* pussy paid for it," he growled back. "Don't forget that. After all I did for you, I fuckin' *own* you. *All* of you. If that muthafucka comes in my club talking shit, I'ma blast the muthafucka. He's gonna have problems with the Baltimore City Police Department because of the shit he pulled at the club if he comes back to my spot. I can call them off, but if I see you anywhere near him, it's game on. Kylie is having this nigga's baby. She doesn't need you having this nigga reminiscing about what could have been. That shit between y'all two muthafuckas is *over*. Fuck with your nigga, Quincy, and stay away from that girl's husband. Consider this your final warning." Finally, Kam released my arm and stood up from the bench.


"You look amazing." Quincy looked my body over as he pulled out my chair to sit down at Fogo de Chao Brazilian Steakhouse in Downtown Baltimore City.

I smoothed out my camel-colored, sleeveless, leather dress from The Row and sat down in my chair. I grinned back at Quincy as he pushed my chair in. I loved the outfit I was wearing. The dress, the beige Jimmy Choo heels, and the white gold Rolex, to match the white gold bracelet I bought for him for his birthday a few weeks ago, were birthday and Christmas presents from Quincy.

He always spoiled the hell out of me. To me, he was just a friend whom I occasionally had sex with to take the edge off missing Blue. He was a great guy, but I didn't allow myself to catch feelings for him. After the shit that happened with Lawrence, not to mention the confusion that Kam caused between Kylie and me in college, I just didn't have the strength to give love a shot. The only thing that stopped me from reaching out to Blue all those years was because of the shit that went down when he left me in Greenville, not to mention what I did to his son.

Don't think I didn't feel guilty for practically stringing Quincy along when I knew how he felt about me, because I did. He sat across from me that night, watching me check out the menu. He was so handsome. His hair was dark, close-cropped, with a smooth wave pattern. He had the smoothest chocolate skin. And he always smelled heavenly. His voice was really mellow and smooth. A part of me wished this dude didn't like me so much. He was too good for me . . . could get any chick he wanted. Whenever this dude stepped into the club with his security guards, you could hear the panties drop. I'm talking strippers *and* the female clients who visited Kam's club. He knew I wasn't ready for a relationship with him, or anyone, for that matter. He left the door open for me to stay in his life or walk out of it if I so chose. And my ass was standing in his doorway, blocking traffic. I should have done what my girls said and just backed off, but I didn't. He was a sexy muthafucka, but my heart belonged to Blue, the man who was married to a girl who was supposed to be my close friend.

I sighed, setting the menu on the table, just staring at it, really not hungry. I couldn't stop thinking about what Kam said earlier at the mall. I knew if I stepped foot back inside that club, Blue was going to show his ass, regardless of what he said to me when he left my condo. Before

Blue and I expressed feelings for each other, we were best friends. He tried keeping me out of trouble, even though I always seemed to keep him knee-deep in trouble. I guess our story hasn't changed much.

As soon as the server brought over a bottle of Lapostolle Merlot, I poured myself a glass.

Quincy laughed a little. "I thought you wanted a taste of southern Brazil, ma. You're over here about to drink this whole bottle, and we haven't even gone to the salad bar yet."

I sighed, setting down my glass, licking the sweet wine from my lips. "I was waiting for that drink all day, Q."

"I see." He watched me licking my lips. "Did you wanna try the seafood? It's amazing. 'Light, classic, and with a Brazilian twist.'" He read the description from the menu. "Or how about the mango Chilean sea bass or the grilled spiced shrimp skewers?" He watched me pour a second glass of wine. He sighed, leaning back in his chair. "Rain? I brought you here to spend a little time with me, but it looks like you're spending more time with your thoughts. What's good? What's going on? Talk to me."

I looked up at him. Before I could open my mouth to speak, a server walked by, bumping my chair, bumping me into our table, knocking my wineglass over. Red wine spilled all over my lap and shoes.

I swiftly stood from the table.

"Oh my goodness, ma'am, I'm *so* sorry!" The server apologized quickly, snatching a linen from her apron pocket, and handing it to me.

I shook my head, waving my hand. "It's all good. Don't worry about it, hon. Quincy, boo, I'll be right back."

I made my way to the bathroom. I was saved by the spill. I sure didn't feel like talking to him about life at the club or my life before I started working there. I stood at the bathroom sink, grabbing paper towels from the dispenser. I sighed, running water over the paper towels, and looked at myself in the mirror as I wiped down my dress.

And then, some laughter made its way into the bathroom. I looked into the mirror, seeing Kylie, Tela, and Brook entering. I rolled my eyes to myself as they caught sight of me standing in the mirror, wiping my clothes.

They stopped in their tracks a little before coming over to the mirror.

Tela was the only one happy to see me. She rushed over to me, throwing her arms around me, looking down at the wine spilled on my shoes. "Hey, boo, what happened?"

"Ummm," I looked over at Kylie and then back at Tela. "The server accidentally spilled wine on my clothes. But it's all good. It's replaceable. What are y'all doing here?"

"Oh, just stopped in to grab a bite before we go to rehearsal for Kylie's fashion expo, which is in a few days. Those outfits look amazing, girl. I'm telling you. Are you coming?" Tela nudged me.

"The fashion expo is invitation only," Brook spoke up.

I looked over at her, then back at Kylie. I knew Kylie was in her feelings about Blue's and my conversation at the dinner table on Christmas. Not to mention, there was no telling what Blue told her about us. I'm sure she wanted to know where he was the night before.

"So, I'm not invited, Kylie?" I asked her before tossing my wet paper towel into the trash can.

"Why, so you can steal the show there too?" she muttered under her breath before looking at her flawless reflection in the mirror.

"What? What was that? I didn't quite hear you." I moved in closer to see if she'd repeat her smart-ass remark.

"She said," Brook started her usual instigation, "you're not about to steal *this* show from her."

"The fuck is that supposed to mean?" I started to step to Brook, but Tela pulled me back. "No, Tela, don't pull me the fuck back." I looked at Brook. "I wanna know what the fuck you mean by that."

"So, you and Blue, y'all used to date?" Kylie asked, facing me.

I shook my head. "Date? No, we grew up together. We were more like sister and brother than anything." I rolled my eyes at Brook, who was eyeballing me like she was ready to get her ass beat. "My parents helped raise him. My father found Blue dumped in a fuckin' trash can outside of the gotdamn hospital."

Brook shook her head. "Bullshit."

I rolled my eyes over from Kylie to Brook. Brook never really liked me. Shit, she barely liked Kylie, but Kylie was popular. She was the girl every girl wanted to be like. Kylie was light-skinned, damn near white, pretty, smart, and her family was rich. She didn't have to want for anything, which is why I found it amusing how she'd ended up with Blue, a man who'd struggled all of his life to get anything he wanted.

"Brook, don't get'cha ass beat." I had to let her know I was sick and tired of her shit. I looked at Kylie. "Kylie, you better get'cha girl."

Kylie shook her head at me. "I'm still trying to wrap my mind around the concept of you two sitting at my dinner table, acting like you two muthafuckas didn't know each other."

I shook my head at her, rolling my eyes. "Boo, it's not even like that. It was an awkward situation. I hadn't seen Blue since we were 16. We were just friends then, and we're just friends now. So, you can get that look off your face."

Kylie looked at Brook, whose lips were pursed. And then she looked back at me. "David says there was more between you two."

I just looked at her. Kylie was into playing games. She was the type of person who liked to fuck with your head. She would pretend to know shit she didn't just to get people to confess shit to her. *Should I tell this bitch that we have a son?* I thought to myself. The bitch would have gone for my head if she knew that Blue and I had a son, so I knew he hadn't told her.

"That tattoo on your back. You said it was to symbolize a gang you were in while in Greenville. But the whole while, the 'Blue' tattoo on your back represented *my* Blue. On his name, you have a crown dangling from the 'B.' On David's chest, he has a queen's crown tattooed over his heart. And do you know what's right in the center of the crown? A gotdamn 'C,'" Kylie let me know before she folded her arms, shifting her weight to one leg.

I tried not to grin, but I couldn't help it. "He was my king, and I was his queen. Two peas in a pod. Bonnie and Clyde. Whenever he called, I was always down to ride. He was like my brother. We weren't a couple, so don't start tripping, Kylie."

Kylie wasn't buying it. "Stay the fuck away from my husband, Chrystal. Do you hear me? You wanna keep your job, you wanna stay in college, you wanna *breathe?* Then you stay the fuck away from *my* husband."

I couldn't help but laugh out loud. "Was he your husband when I caught you and Kam fuckin' at the club? What year was it that you stopped fuckin' with Kam again? If I'm not mistaken, it was *while* you were married to Blue. Refresh my memory on how the whole husband-wife thing works again."

Kylie tried to get in my face, but Brook pulled her away.

"If Kam is who you love, then that's where you need to be. Blue has been rockin' with you for damn near seven years, Kylie. And the whole while you're with him, you're fuckin' around with Kam's lying, cheating, cocky ass.

Blue is good to you. I know he is because he was the best friend that I ever had. Blue used to be young, wild, and free—you couldn't tell him shit. He used to have a group of bitches after his ass in high school. He's amazing, and I would kill to trade places with you right about now. He was my best friend, and I swear I had no idea that he was your husband, Kylie." I had to let her know.

"I find it funny that you said the same thing about Kam back in college when you were fuckin' around with *him*." There Brook was, throwing salt in old wounds.

"Kam lied to both of us." I ignored her and just focused on Kylie. "He didn't tell you that he was having sex with me, and he damn sure never mentioned to me that he was having sex with you. You keep everything so private, so how would anyone know anything? It took us almost three years to know that you were *married* to Blue. That your last name is *Jacobs* and not fuckin' Luckett anymore. You hid your relationship with Blue because you were hoping to get back with Kam. You, a stuck-up, rich bitch having a courthouse wedding? Please . . . You did that shit because you didn't want Kam to know you were married. When did you tell him that you were married?"

Kylie's eyes narrowed.

"You don't have to answer that question, Kylie. She's trying to turn the subject back around on you when the subject is *her* and the reason why she didn't want you to know that she and David were in a gotdamn relationship." Brook continued to instigate.

I looked at Kylie.

Kylie sighed, knowing there was really no avoiding the question. She knew that she was wrong. "After I had my first miscarriage two years ago."

I nodded, watching Tela gasping for air.

"Yeah, after you lost *Kam's* baby, *right?*" I questioned Kylie.

Now Tela and Brook looked at her.

Kylie sighed. "Yes." She looked at her friends and then back at me. "Nothing I did to get this muthafucka's attention ever worked. David was out of the country on a business trip. He was in Paris with a few of his colleagues from the university. He was gone for about three weeks, and it wasn't until a week after he'd gotten back that I found out I was pregnant. When I told Kam about the baby, he couldn't care less. Said it wasn't his when he knew that it was. I was so stressed about the entire situation that I lost the baby a few weeks later. I never even mentioned it to David. I just took that as God's way of telling me that I was doing a good man wrong and that I needed to stop chasing after Kam, a man who obviously didn't want me.

"It wasn't until about a year and a half ago when Kam came to his senses and tried to get me to leave David. I wouldn't. Kam was my first love. When I met David, Kam and I were going through some things. Not just when I found out that you two were sleeping around, but there were other bitches too. I knew that Kam and David were friends, and that was what made me go after David."

Tela shook her head at Kylie. "That brutha is fine. You're crazy, Kylie. He is *so* not rebound material."

Brook looked at me. "But to me, it seems as if Kylie was the rebound too."

Kylie scoffed. "I don't know about all that. All I know is that David and I are trying to make things work. I have stopped having sex with Kam. No, I haven't told David that Kam and I do business because I don't want David to know where my money to fund my shows comes from. I made mistakes, but I've learned from them." Kylie watched the "You're so full of shit" expression on my face.

"What year was it when Blue got that tattoo on his heart?" I had to ask.

Tela laughed a little. "Girl, you're trippin'."

Kylie looked at me like she wanted to smack the shit out of me, but she answered the question. "After we vacationed in Cancun two years ago. He said the 'C' was for Cancun, but last night, he told me what it meant. I could really care less what it means, Chrystal. David and I are having a baby. So, whatever it is that you *think* he still feels for you, you might as well get that shit out of your head. And stay the fuck away from him. You and I are supposed to be friends. After you found out that Kam and I were supposed to be dating, you backed off. So, I expect you to do the same now that you know that David and I are married. You have no reason to stay in contact with him.

"Leave the past alone. If I see you anywhere near him for any reason whatsoever, well, let's just say it won't be pretty. You know what your life would be if it weren't for Kam or my family. You're *nothing* without us. And just like we gave you a new life, we can take it away . . . Stay in your lane, Chrystal." Kylie pushed past me on her way out of the bathroom.

Tela looked at me before going after her friend.

Brook looked me up and down before looking back into my face, grinning.

"Hold up, wait." I sighed, taking a huge breath before coming clean. I didn't want to hurt the bitch, but she had it coming. Talking about staying in my gotdamn lane.

All three of them turned around to face me.

"I wanted to reach out to Blue for years, but I didn't because I didn't want him to see the person I became. Don't think for one second that Blue ever stopped looking for me. You were just a distraction from me, Kylie. While you were out there chasing Kam, Blue was praying that I'd find my way back to him. And now that I'm here, I promise you, I'm *not* going anywhere." I approached the three of them at the bathroom entrance.

Kylie glared up at me. She knew a bitch was crazy. She knew it was going to take all three of them to fight me. She saw me fighting bitches at the club. She knew I'd slice her throat and then go back to doing me like the shit didn't even happen. She was crazy, but she wasn't *that* crazy.

"You heard what I said, Chrystal. Stay away from him."

"Payton David Alison." I called out my son's name.

Kylie looked at me, her eyes widening a little. "What did you say?"

"Payton David Alison—that's my *son's* name. *Our* son's name. *Your husband's* son's name." I watched Kylie's light skin flush red.

Tela shook her head at me.

"So you see, Kylie, *Brook*, and Tela, this is *my* lane that Kylie's driving in. *I* control this muthafuckin' pace. In the words of Lil' Kim, 'You might be where he's at, but oh, best believe, I'm where he wants to be.' I'm not into wrecking happy homes, but you need to know that if I wanted 'your' David, I already have him. Don't sleep on me, Kylie, not for a second." I pushed past Kylie and left the bathroom. "Talking 'bout stay in my lane. This bitch got me fucked up."

# Chapter Five

## *I Can't Pretend Anymore*

## *Blue*

I couldn't think straight the afternoon that Chrystal left my house. I must have sat on my front porch for damn near an hour, just staring out at the spot where her car was once parked. I couldn't believe she'd been so close yet so far away for damn near seven fuckin' years. Why didn't I communicate with Kylie more? I would have known who her friends were. Why didn't I listen to Darius when he tried to get me to go with him to the group home? I would have seen my son.

"Baby bruh, you all right? It's getting kind of chilly out here. I mean, it *is* Christmas, bruh." I heard Lisa's voice over my shoulder.

I exhaled smoke through my nose. Yeah, a nigga was smoking weed out on the front porch. Fuck Kylie and her gotdamn parents. It was *my* house, but the way Kylie had everyone thinking, you would've thought *she* ran the show. Her parents thought I had a drug problem. I was prescribed medical marijuana for migraines back in high school. A nigga couldn't sleep. Had nightmares every night. Smoking was the only way I could get any sleep or any relief from the pain.

Lisa sat down beside me, her eyes tracing my profile.

"I can't believe it's her, sis." I shook my head.

"I know, right?" Lisa laughed a little. "What are the odds of your li'l boo being friends with your wife? Y'all two stuck together like glue back in the day, boy. Couldn't separate the two of y'all for nothing. I bet you even sent this girl texts while you were out on dates with other girls, huh?"

I just looked at her.

Lisa shook her head. "Dude, don't try to deny it. That girl has always loved the fuck outta you. She dissed those muthafuckas that y'all went to school with. She'd go out on dates with muthafuckas and then call *you* when the muthafuckas dropped her off back at home."

I laughed a little. I couldn't deny what my sister was saying. Shawty was stuck to a nigga like glue. And I hated seeing her with anyone. As soon as my date was over, I was calling or texting shawty. And the same went for her. She was as bold as a muthafucka; she'd be out on dates with dudes, texting me, "Man, come get me when this lame nigga drops me off." And I did too, laughing all the way to her place.

"Every time I see this girl, I fall in love all over again." I had a hard time saying that, but I had to let it out.

Lisa sighed. "I know. Shit, we *all* knew that you were in love with this girl. I was the first one you called when you proposed to Kylie, and what did I tell you, David? I told you *not* to marry her, right? I told you that one day you'd find Chrystal again, didn't I?"

I nodded. "Yeah. I just wish I had been more patient. Or more attentive to Kylie's life. Kylie kept me out of her personal life for years. I never even bothered to visit her while she was going to Morgan State. Every time she went out and showed out with her girls, she'd do the shit when I had other plans. If I had rolled up on her, I would have seen Chrystal years ago, Lisa. *Fuckin'* years ago."

"Well," Lisa sighed. "Shoulda, coulda, woulda. You got tired of waiting, you got tired of longing, and you got tired of being alone. So, you married Kylie, a girl you have absolutely nothing in common with. Y'all know absolutely nothing about each other after seven *long* years, bruh. You had no idea of the company she kept, and she had no idea that you even *knew* a girl named Chrystal Alison. If y'all two communicated better, then you would have known about Chrystal years ago, David. Not to mention, this girl didn't even tell her friends that she was married to you. What bitch doesn't tell her friends she's married to a guy who is as handsome as my little brutha? A chick who's waiting for someone else to come along, *that's* who. Something isn't right with Kylie—I told you that shit from jump, David."

I looked at Lisa as I held the smoke a little before letting it out through my nose and mouth. "You think shawty is cheating on me too?" I asked.

"The bitch is doing something." Lisa shook her head at me.

"Today, I found out that me and Chrystal have a son together, Lisa." I was reluctant to say because Lisa was already looking at a nigga like I fucked up big time.

She looked at me. "That baby she was talking about is *your* baby, David? I thought you said you'd never sleep with this girl, that you'd never do her like you did the other girls. You got this girl pregnant and then bounced, David?" Lisa mushed me in the head.

I shook my head. "Nah. The day I left Greenville, we slept together. She hadn't slept with that nigga, Nathan, for weeks before we slept together that day. She said she wanted it, so I gave it to her. We went about three rounds before her family showed up that day to help us finish packing. And that was the last time I saw shawty."

Lisa was in shock for a few seconds. "How do you know he's yours, though? Could've been anybody's." She saw the "Why the fuck you gotta go there?" look on my face. "Come on, David—you and her both were straight-up hoes back then. It's like you two were in competition with each other. I think she had you beat though, bruh."

"Man, why you always got jokes? I saw this little nigga. He lives at the group home that Darius's family owns. He looks just like me, from his curly hair to his bright blue eyes. You can even ask Darius. There's no way I could deny that little boy if I wanted to. Man, you should see him. He's beautiful. He's mine. He's *ours,* Lisa," I admitted.

Lisa just shook her head back at me. "You gotta tell Kylie."

"Shawty is gonna flip." I took another puff from my joint.

"Flip ain't even the word, David. She doesn't even know that you two know each other. Not only do you have to explain how you know Chrystal, but you also have to explain that y'all had a baby that you didn't know you had. Oh, I'd love to be a fly on the wall watching y'all have *that* conversation." Lisa laughed out loud.

I waved her off. "I'll worry about Kylie later, yo. If she was worried about my conversation with shawty, you know she'd be all in my grill right about now. I'll let it marinate for a minute. I went to this masquerade party last night with Darius. My nigga Kam had all of his dancers there too." Images of the night before flashed through my mind.

Lisa made a face. "Dancers?"

"Yeah, he owns this strip club downtown. Shit, it's more like a fuckin' brothel than a strip club. If a nigga is paying, those girls will do anything. Dance, suck, fuck. And guess who dances, sucks, and fucks for the muthafucka?" I held the joint between my fingers, taking another puff.

Lisa looked at me. "Who?" she asked. By the irritated expression on my face, she could tell who I was talking about. Her light eyes widened. "*Chrystal?*" Lisa watched a nigga's facial muscles start to twitch.

I was pissed. I tried to hold it in, but I couldn't. I was gonna turn that muthafuckin' spot out that night. I knew that was where Chrystal was running off to.

"David, I already know what you're thinking, and you can't save this girl. How do you know if she even *wants* to be saved? You always did love them hoes, boy."

I was ready to smack her ass. "Man, you're lucky you're my sister, Lisa. I'm telling you, say something else about her."

"Boy, what? Are you *serious?* Did you *not* just tell me what she was doing for money? How long has she been working there? What makes you think she *wants* to leave?" Lisa tried to reason with me.

I looked at her as if she were crazy. "Fuck you mean? She doesn't have a gotdamn choice."

Lisa shook her head at me. "Always thinking you're running somebody. You can't save this girl if she doesn't wanna be saved. Shit, did she *ask* you to save her?" Lisa exclaimed.

"Yeah, she did, when she poured her heart out to me in front of everyone at that muthafuckin' dinner table," I yelled back.

Lisa looked at me like I was getting loud with the wrong one. "Who the fuck do you think you're talkin' to?"

"I'm talkin' to *your* bright ass." I wasn't backing down to her. She always thought she could whup a muthafucka. "We ain't kids anymore, Lisa. You put your hands on me, you better be prepared to get laid the fuck out. I'm not playin'."

Lisa laughed out loud. "Boy, ain't nobody scared of your li'l pretty, blue-eyed T.I., August Alsina-lookin' ass! The fuck you gonna do to me? Be prettier than me?"

I tried not to laugh, but she always had jokes. "Play too gotdamn much. I ain't fuckin' with your foolish ass. A nigga is not in the mood to play right now."

Lisa's laughter subsided. "Li'l bruh, I know you go hard for this girl, but you need to slow your roll. Kam doesn't look like anyone to fuck with. I only met him twice, but his name is ringing from coast to coast. Leave that girl where she is. You're a teacher."

"Yeah, I'm about to teach some shit, a'ight. I'm gonna teach these niggas a lesson on fuckin' with the wrong muthafucka." I grit my teeth.

"David, please, don't—" She started to beg me not to go back to the old me, but I wasn't hearing it.

I cut her off. "Lisa, I love her."

Lisa's light eyes sparkled. "I know, boo."

"Then you already know I'm not having this shit." Every time I thought about Chrystal bent over, poppin' that pussy, my blood curdled. "She was supposed to be *my* girl, not Kam's ho, Lisa. I'd do anything for her, and you know that. A nigga is not gonna let her live like this. I've changed, but a nigga ain't changed enough to watch the girl my heart still beats for selling her ass for a nigga who is supposed to be my homeboy. Fuck this shit. I'm wasting time sitting here, talking, when I need to get my crew together." I stood on the porch.

"Crew? David, what crew?" Lisa looked up at me and then back at the door as it opened.

Darius stepped outside, already seeing the hurt yet angry expression on my face. He sighed, shaking his head. "Yo, *that* was Chrystal?"

I didn't even know what to say to him. I'd been talking about shawty since the day I met him. I told him how beautiful she was. How close we were. How her family saved me. The shit we used to get into. The way she had me feeling. How much I missed her. I made her sound like an angel—and there she was, working poles, dicks, and shit.

"Nigga, I've known of her since 2009. Kam took her to every single party he attended. She started as his bartender. One night at a bachelor party, I think it was her, my girl, Justice, and two other dimes danced for these niggas naked, and the rest is history." Darius watched my fists ball up. "That nigga has her doing some of everything. That's your girl, bruh? Little homie at the Tree of Life is your son? I've been mentoring him for about three years, homie. I've been trying to get you to come out there for years, son."

I nodded. "Yeah, nigga, I know, I know."

"You got that crazy look in your eyes, yo. What you 'bout to get into? Kylie just told everybody inside that she's pregnant, dude." He looked at me.

Lisa looked at me, taking a deep breath. "Shit."

I looked at Darius.

"You're about to have a baby, Blue. You need to leave that alone. Yo," he watched me taking out my cell phone, "who you calling?"

"My niggas, bruh—the fuck you think?" I scoffed, putting my cell phone to my ear.

"Oh, Lawd. I'm out." Lisa shook her head, walking back up the steps to my front door. "I swear, it's always some shit with you, Blue. Don't call me when you need bail money."

After three rings, my nigga, Tyrese, picked up. "What's good, Blue? What it do, homie?"

"Aye," I looked back at Darius. "I'm on my way to your crib."

"What's the word, homie? Some niggas giving you problems?" he asked. Tyrese stayed ready to pull the trigger on muthafuckas.

"Something like that. Get'cha niggas together. Strap up, nigga." And I pressed end on my phone.


You probably think a nigga was crazy, rolling up on the police the way that I did, huh? When it came to Chrystal, I really didn't give a fuck. I know how Johnny and Jimmy got down. They were the police, so they always thought they could do what they wanted. When I was 18 and had just moved to D.C., my homeboy, Reggie, used to have those niggas on lock. Had them muthafuckas on payroll. When he was killed by his hating-ass stepbrother, running the block was left up to me. Jimmy thought he was gonna have a nigga working for him, thought I was gonna pay him to stay afloat, but he had me fucked-up. Kam partnered up with the muthafuckas. Shit, I had too much dirt on the nigga for the crooked cops in the police department to try to run my shit.

Jimmy's father was the head of the Prince George's County Police Department, so Jimmy thought he was running shit. He did females all types of wrong. I once rolled up on a nigga raping a female who refused to show him her license. I saw the nigga snatch her out of the car, throw her on the hood of the vehicle, and rape her in broad daylight, behind a corner store. Everyone saw the shit, but no one reported him. They were scared of the nigga. I wasn't. That night when I saw the nigga pressing Chrystal down on the pool table, ass in the air, panties dropped to her ankles, pulling her by her hair, man, a nigga almost lost it. I used Johnny as an example; I tried to run Johnny's head through the cement wall of the VIP area.

I dragged Chrystal and her girls up out of that mutha-fucka, having them get dressed right in front of Kameron's ass. You should have seen the look on the nigga's face. I was pissed at the entire situation, but best believe, I was dying laughing on the inside. He took pride in taking nigga's girls, and there I was, taking three of his. My niggas in blue showed me all types of shit on the internet of Chrystal and her crew. They were worse than groupies. I can give it to her, she got paid, but some of the shit that I saw get done to these females wasn't even close to being worth the money. Taking it in the ass, mouth, pussy, all at once? Hell fuckin' nah. If I didn't love Chrystal, I'm telling you, I would've whooped the shit out of her. I was pissed that I even had to put myself at risk to save her from a life that she shouldn't have even been living.

Chrystal was a mother and was in no way living like one. Yeah, I called her a ho. Yeah, I called her a stupid bitch. Why? Because she was letting niggas dog her out. Making a gotdamn fool of herself on camera. She was beautiful. She was smart. She was clever. She could bring even the strongest man to her knees with just one look. She let her guilt of what she let one nigga do to her control her entire life. She told me that my uncle was the one who pimped her out to his son. And that made *me* feel guilty, like I should have seen it coming.

Uncle Larry ran a prostitution ring disguised as a corner store. Niggas would come to his store, buy these cards that looked like fuckin' scratch offs. The clients would scratch off the cards. The name of the female, the address where she could be found, and the cost of a night with her were on the card.

My uncle was a millionaire, but he lived like a middle-class citizen to conceal his fortune. Shit, I didn't wanna be anywhere near the nigga when the IRS came for his ass. Uncle Larry taught me and my boys everything there was to know about the world of hustle. He taught me how to sell drugs without getting caught. Taught me how to shoot my first 9 mm. Taught me how to disassemble and reassemble weapons in less than twenty seconds. Taught me how to dress. Taught me how to get girls. Taught me how good it felt to move that dope. He taught me everything I know. And the whole while, he couldn't wait to get rid of me so he could get to her. Yeah, I was gonna get that nigga in due time. When he least expected it . . . *bang*, right through his muthafuckin' skull.

Shawty was pissed at me for dragging her ass out of that club, and I couldn't care less. I softened her up a bit by pulling out a Hostess cupcake that I got from the Exxon gas station before we pulled up at her condo. It was her favorite as a kid. I'll never forget the first time I could afford to get it on my own for her. I was 6 years old with $1.75 in my pocket. I walked my ass to my uncle's corner store, bought her a cupcake, and then brought it to her house. She didn't bother saying thank you; she just snatched the shit from my hand and opened it, taking a huge bite out of it. Before I could even say, "Damn, greedy, what happened to thank you?" Shawty grabbed me and kissed me right on my lips, cake all over her lips.

Shawty pulled out a picture of my moms. I hadn't seen a picture of that woman in my entire life. There I was, 25 years old, seeing her for the first time. I wanted to hate her, but the moment I saw her face, I couldn't. The fact that my grandmother had my son all those years, knowing about me, knowing where I was, stung like a muthafucka, though. I had a feeling they kept me from my son so that I wouldn't run into Chrystal. Moms kept up with my life enough to know that Chrystal had my baby. She had to see the connection that I had to that girl. I'm pretty sure she even talked to Christina in the "crazy house." My mother made sure my son was taken care of because she felt bad that she didn't take care of me. I was hurt, but at the same time, I was a little grateful. I just wish I had gotten to know my son from birth. He was beautiful. He knew he was mine. He didn't want to let a nigga go, afraid that I'd never come back to him.

On top of that painful shit, I found out from Darius that Chrystal had a nigga named Quincy working for her. He wasn't sure if the two were dating, but wherever he saw Chrystal, that nigga was right there, watching. She was paying the nigga to protect her. How the fuck could he watch her sell herself? I don't give a fuck if she were getting paid a million gotdamn dollars; the damage to her body would cost her much more. She defended Quincy. Even put a nigga out so he could come over to see her.

That hurt a nigga to my gotdamn soul. I was willing to put my life on the line to save hers, and all she could do was worry whether some nigga she didn't have feelings for (she didn't have to tell me) was offended by seeing me. I started to walk the fuck out of her life, saying fuck it, when shawty called out to my heart, thanking me for still caring about her. She even said that she still had that letter I'd written to her when I was 16. When I turned around to face her, that damn piece of cupcake was on her chin. She went to wipe it off, but I wouldn't let her. I grabbed her and kissed it off. I wanted to kiss Chrystal's lips, but Kylie was at home waiting for me.

But I didn't even go straight home that night. I went to the Inner Harbor and just sat on a bench, staring out at the water. Every now and then, I looked down at Chrystal's number on my wrist. I wanted to call her. I could really give a fuck if that nigga, Quincy, were at her place. But I didn't. I couldn't stand by and watch my shawty just throw her body away, but I felt like a fuckin' idiot for just busting in on her life, trying to take control of it. She was the sheep that got lost. I wanted to help her find her way back. As soon as I left the harbor, I stopped by a bar and had a few drinks. I didn't make it home until around 3:30 the next morning.

And when I got home, Kylie's ass was waiting for me in the hallway, her arms folded, tears sliding down her face.

I took a deep breath, closing the door behind me, sliding my hat off my head, and tossing my coat on the coatrack. I walked past her like she wasn't standing there. And then shawty went off.

"David!" She tried to grab me, but I sort of pushed her off me and kept on walking until I made it into the kitchen. Kylie came to the kitchen, standing in the doorway, watching me dig through the refrigerator for a Budweiser, something I didn't even need because I had at least six or seven that night. "Where have you been? I've been calling you since this afternoon."

I grabbed a beer from the refrigerator, closed the door, and then popped the top. "I went out for a drink."

"Kam called, looking for you. He said that you were actin' a gotdamn fool at Pop It tonight." Kylie watched as I sat down at the bistro table in our kitchen. I leaned back in the chair, looking at her like I wasn't in the mood to hear her go off on me. "Since when the fuck do you go in that club?"

I just looked at her, sipping from my bottle.

"You went after Chrystal, didn't you?" Her eyes glared at me.

I couldn't lie to her. "Yeah."

"Why, Blue?" She walked over to the table where I sat, sitting across from me. "Why did you go after her?" She searched my face as she watched me drink the bottle until I got halfway finished with it. "You know her? The whole time that you were asking her all of those questions, you *knew* her, David?" Kylie tried to stay calm throughout our conversation, but I wasn't responsive. "You know what, David?" Kylie laughed to herself and rose from the table.

I stood, grabbing her arm, and pulled her back down to her chair. "Shawty."

"David, you know this girl?" Kylie demanded.

"I haven't seen her since we were 16, Kylie, I swear," I admitted. "We grew up together. Her parents helped raise a nigga. I've been looking for this girl for eight years. A nigga thought I'd never see her again. And turns out, she's been friends with my wife for seven years!"

"Again, I ask you, why were you at the club, acting a fool over her? Why does Chrystal working in the club have you feeling *any* type of way, David?" Kylie asked.

I didn't mean to look at Kylie like she'd lost her fuckin' mind, but she had. Whether I had feelings for Chrystal or not, no friend of mine was selling their ass at a club. "What, Kylie? What'cha mean? *You* don't feel some way about your friend working at the club?"

Kylie shook her head, "Why should I? She pays her bills. She has protection. What she decides to do with her mouth, hands, feet, pussy, tongue, *whatever*, ain't got shit to do with me, *or* you, for that matter."

I looked at her. "Kylie, you've got me fucked-up. No shawty of mine is working at that club."

Kylie scoffed. "'Shawty of yours'? *Really*, David?"

I didn't see anything wrong with what I said. "Yeah. That's my shawty. She was my best friend, and I'll be damned if I let her ruin her life for a couple of dollars. I'll go back to hustling in the streets if I have to, to help shawty pay bills, but I can't live with myself knowing that I didn't do anything to stop her from selling her body for far less than what she's worth. You can get that look off your face, Kylie, because she's your friend too, and you shouldn't be cool with her living like this."

"Why didn't you tell me that you knew her when you saw her? Why pretend that you didn't know her?" Kylie whispered to keep from yelling at me.

I took a sip from my Budweiser. "The situation was awkward enough, shawty. I didn't want you feeling some type of way about her."

"Kinda like I do now, David?" Kylie rolled her eyes at me, crossing her legs, which were looking good by the way, in those tiny boy shorts.

I just looked at her, drinking my beer to the last drop.

"David, you never once mentioned to me anything about *any* girl named Chrystal. You never talk about your life in Greenville, North Carolina, other than to say that you lived the street life. Other than to say Miss Tiffany brought you here to get away from that, only to turn you more into a street monster. You never once told me that Chrystal was a part of your life in Greenville. All you ever told me was that you've been with a lot of girls and that none of them compared to me. But that couldn't have been further from the truth, now, could it?" Kylie looked so hurt.

"Kylie, baby, you're taking this all out of proportion," I tried to tell her.

"David, do you love me?" Kylie's eyes pleaded.

"Yeah, I do," I forced myself to say, even though I wasn't so sure once I saw that tattoo on Chrystal's back that night at the masquerade party.

"Do you love *her?*" Kylie asked, shaking her head to herself. "Wait, let me rephrase that—do you *still* love her?"

I couldn't lie to her. I'd lied long enough. "I never stopped loving her, Kylie."

Kylie gasped, tears instantly building in her eyes. She got up from the table, but there I was, grabbing her again. She yanked away from me. "Don't fuckin' touch me, David."

"When I met you, I'd just lost her, Kylie. I never talked about her because I wanted to forget about her," I admitted out loud for the first time.

"Did not talking about her make you forget her?" Tears slid down Kylie's cheeks.

I shook my head. "Nah."

"Did marrying me make you stop loving her?" Kylie cried.

I shook my head. "Nah."

"David, we all have secrets, but this was a big secret to keep from me. This girl's whole life would have been different had she run back into you seven years ago. This girl was probably so lost because she was looking for you too. If you had known that she was here, this ring would be on *her* finger, wouldn't it? She'd be sitting here, carrying your baby, not me, wouldn't she?" Kylie's cheeks were soaked in tears.

I just looked at her, trying to hold her hand, but she slipped it away. I didn't want to hurt Kylie, but there was really no denying how I felt about Chrystal. I never stopped loving Chrystal. I still dreamed about her. I needed her. I wanted her. I still loved her. And I couldn't pretend anymore. Life without that girl was painful.

"I can't let shawty throw her life away at that club, Kylie," I repeated, watching her and letting her get up from the table. "Shawty needs a nigga. If you wanna be all in your feelings about this situation, then go ahead, Kylie. I've known you for seven years. I've never cheated on you, and you know I've had plenty of opportunities."

Kylie stood, her arms folded, and her face flushed. "Is that supposed to make me feel better, David? Right in the middle of dinner, you got up and raced outside behind this girl to make sure that she was okay. Oh, I should've known something then. And then you just left me here with my family—not coming back until 3:30 in the morning. Kam said that you came to his club with a whole squad of gang members, ready to shoot up the place if they didn't let you take Chrystal with you. He said you assaulted a police officer. This girl has you totally out of character. Damn right, I'm in my feelings about her. You fight *with* me, but you fought *for* her, David," Kylie cried out as I stood from the table.

I tried to approach her, but she pushed me away.

"No, don't touch me!" Kylie cried. "She's my *friend*, David."

"She was my friend too," I whispered.

Kylie shook her head at me. "David, I haven't been the best wife. I spend more time with my friends, at school,

and at my job than with you. I left the door open years
ago for someone to come in and get you. I didn't even tell
my friends that I was married to you. I just didn't think
you fit in with my friends. They're so rich and uppity. I
thought they would look down on you, so I never introduced you. Yes, I was ashamed of your past. I come from
a rich family, and you came from . . ."

"The trash can, huh?" I shook my head at her. "I'm
not the richest muthafucka, Kylie, but I know how to
make the kind of money your family makes; trust me, I
do. I just try to live an honest life. I have been faithful to
you for years, never once stepping out. I used to run the
streets, sleep with hundreds of females, and do whatever
the fuck I wanted to do. But I changed. I settled down
with a woman who really, in her heart, didn't think that I
was even settle-down-with material."

Kylie sighed, feeling a little remorseful for a change.
"I wouldn't have said yes if I didn't want you, David. At
the time, you were what my heart needed. I had been
hurt and taken advantage of, and I needed you. Over
the years, I grew bitter about past relationships and the
need to defend my relationship with you to my family, so
I stopped kissing you. I stopped touching you. I stopped
cooking for you. I've stopped talking to you. But I haven't
stopped loving you, David. Have you stopped loving me?"

I didn't know what to say to her, so I didn't say anything. I was feeling some type of way about her feelings
for me. She was just as unsure about me as I was about
her. She wanted to love me too, but something in her past
was also holding her back. We *did* have something in
common—regret.

Kylie laughed a little, drying her face. I'd broken her
heart. I didn't mean to, but I had to tell her the truth
about Chrystal. The only thing I didn't tell her was that

we had a son. That would have driven that girl crazy. She was pregnant, and I was already stressing her out enough.

"I'm sure seeing this girl is bringing back all types of memories, David. I'm sure you've always thought about how your life would have been if you two had never been separated. I'm sure these past seven years with me were erased once you saw that girl standing in your hallway today, huh?" Kylie asked, looking up into my face.

I took a deep breath before saying. "We all have that one person that we still think about, Kylie."

Kylie looked at me like I'd just told her that it was over between us. She turned away from me, her hands resting on the countertop, and she started crying like I'd never seen her cry before.

I walked up behind her, placing my hand on her back, kissing her on the back of her neck. "Kylie, I'm sorry I never told you."

"That—that tattoo over your heart." Kylie was referring to the queen's crown I had over my heart with a 'C' imprinted in the middle of it. "You got that tattoo when we left Cancun. But now that I think about it, Chrystal has a tattoo of the word 'Blue' on her back with a crown dangling from the 'B.' That Blue is you, isn't it?" she cried.

"Yeah, it is," I admitted.

"And that 'C' on your crown symbolizes Chrystal, doesn't it? Your queen? Your heart?" Kylie whispered.

I couldn't say anything.

"I wasn't prepared for this, David," Kylie cried out.

"Me neither," I whispered back, feeling like crying my damn self.

"I swear on my life, David, I'm not about to lose you to her!" Kylie cried out, turning around to look me in the face. She watched my drunken eyes coat themselves in tears. "Or maybe I already have."

I took another deep breath, not sure what to say.

Kylie cried out, pushing past me and walking out of the kitchen.

"Aye, nigga, don't you open up that window," Columbus snapped at Darius's attempt to let the windows down on the car as we cruised down the streets of Annapolis in my nigga Tyrese's Monte Carlo.

"*Don't you let out that antidote*," Tyrese sang in his Travis Scott voice.

I laughed a little. "Y'all niggas stupid. Y'all stay fucked-up. I don't think I've ever seen y'all niggas when y'all *weren't* high."

"Shit, when I'm fucked up, it's the real me. Yeah," Columbus laughed, singing along with "The Hills" playing on XM radio.

"So, where we headed?" Darius shook his head at the situation. He hated riding with them fools. He hated riding with us because he'd always hop out of the car smelling like loud. The only reason why he even hung around them seemed to be to make sure they kept me out of trouble.

"To my mom's house for a few, dude." Tyrese looked over at Darius in the passenger seat. "Moms is throwing a party today that lasts all the way up until tomorrow morning, yo. We 'bout to get fucked *all* the way up."

Tyrese's mom was only twelve years older than he, just 36 years old. And looked like a fuckin' model. It's not what you think. She was kidnapped and raped at the age of 11. By the time cops found shawty, she was already eight weeks pregnant. He took her all the way to California. The idiot took her to the mall, where a person pretending to take her picture for a modeling agency took her photo and then went to the police station.

When I told Tyrese about the shit that was going on with Chrystal, he was on that shit. It reminded him of what his mother had gone through. Ya know, in that situation that she needed to be rescued from. I don't think his mother ever recovered from that shit. She partied just as hard as we did and couldn't care less about a relationship. After what happened to her, she'd never trust another man again. The one thing that I respected about her was that she never treated Tyrese like a product of her rape. They were so close in age that he was more like a brother than her son.

It was New Year's Eve. I hadn't seen Chrystal since Christmas. I would have been worried about shawty, but I had a few of my niggas visit the club to keep a lookout for me. They said shawty was there but worked the bar that week, covering for another girl. Covering the bar meant she wasn't dancing, fuckin', or suckin', and a part of me was relieved. But my mind and heart still weren't at ease. Kylie hadn't said a word to me since Christmas night. I was pretty sure she'd approached Chrystal, and with the mouthpiece Chrystal used to have on her, there was no telling what she might have said to Kylie.

"Yo, while we're here, pull up in front of the district court." I cringed at the thought of the $180 ticket I almost forgot to pay. "Lemme go pay this fuckin' ticket before I forget."

"Yeah, dude, you better pay that shit. You already about to have PG County Police harassing you. The last thing you need is Anne Arundel County Police in your life." Columbus shook his head.

I can't tell you how many times Columbus had gotten pulled over and harassed by the AACO police. They'd have his 2016 black and chrome Jaguar towed every time they pulled him over. Did he have a license? Yes. Did he have insurance? Yes. Was his shit legit? Yes. Why were they fuckin' with him? Columbus's family was the head of the dope game in the county. They could never catch anyone in his family, but they wanted to. And since they couldn't, they'd find any reason to fuck with them. I'm talking a crack in the headlight, one headlight dimmer than the other, tags crooked, driving too close to the car in front of him, three miles over the speed limit—stupid shit.

I stood at the window of the clerk's office, waiting for the clerk to print my receipt. I didn't trust the court system. I can't tell you how many fines I paid that the court swore up and fuckin' down I didn't pay. I kept all my receipts. I made copies. Shit, I made *copies* of the copies.

"Thank you. Make sure that payment gets processed, Miss . . ." I looked at her name tag. "Dawson. Y'all don't want no problems." I grinned at her before turning around to leave the window.

And I bumped right into Chrystal. I looked her over before looking into her face. She stood before me, wearing a black hooded leather jacket, dark skinny jeans, and black, furry, knee-high boots. That girl loved Jimmy Choo. It's sad I knew women's brands the way I did. Kylie kept a nigga into fashion, so I'd know what to buy her. Chrystal was obviously into fashion too. The only difference was with the way her attitude was set up, I'm pretty sure Chrystal paid for the majority of her clothing. Her father always taught her to be independent. As children, he made sure to stress the value of hard work to both of us. Tell us not to get trapped in debt. To pay for everything in cash. To invest in minority businesses. And never to live beyond our means. Shit, I had failed William big time. But I'm sure Chrystal was racking up on the dough, saving more than she spent. She always dressed to impress, but always shopped on the clearance racks.

Chrystal grinned at me, her bangs hanging over her eyes. She had sort of an Asian/Geisha girl thing going on with her hair. She stayed fly. Looked finer than a muthafucka. There I was, falling in love again.

"Excuse me." She moved past me and went up to the window. "Hi." I could hear her smiling at the clerk. "I'm here to pay off a few speeding tickets."

I looked over her body. That ass sat up perfect in them jeans, looking like a juicy-ass apple. "Tickets? With an 's'?" I stood alongside her, still examining her body.

Chrystal laughed to herself a little, sliding the clerk at least six tickets. Then she looked up at me, grinning, them cute-ass dimples popping up on her face. "My girls sent me in here to pay their tickets. Not even gonna tell you why they don't wanna walk up in here; that's a whole other story." Chrystal looked back at the clerk.

I stood alongside Chrystal, eyeing her face as she paid each ticket separately with cash. Now that we knew each other were in the same state, it seemed as though we couldn't stop bumping into each other.

"You didn't call me, nigga," she mumbled as she slid money for one of the tickets to the clerk.

I looked at her. "What?"

"You heard me, Blue," she scoffed, looking at me. "I said your ass didn't call me." She looked back at the clerk.

I grinned. She was too cute when she was mad. "443-261-9741, right?"

Chrystal glanced at me and then looked back at the clerk as the clerk handed her change for one of the tickets.

"I didn't forget you. I was just trying to let things calm down a little. You already know Kylie is sweating the fuck out of me." I shook my head. "Shawty didn't even invite me to her gotdamn fashion show tomorrow."

"*You* too?" Chrystal laughed, sliding another ticket to the clerk. "I helped her plan this shit, and *I'm* not even invited. Me and my girls from the club showcased these clothes a few weeks ago at one of Kam's events. I even gave your girl a gold necklace with a 'Styles by Kylie Luckett' charm hanging from it. And none of us are invited. And it's all because of you."

I looked at shawty. "Me?"

"Yeah, nigga, you. What did you tell her about us?" Chrystal's eyebrows crinkled.

"The truth." I studied her face.

Chrystal glanced at me and then back at the clerk, who was acting like she wasn't eavesdropping. "And what is that?"

"That you were the missing piece of my heart," I whispered to her, watching her cheeks turn a little rosy.

Chrystal tried not to smile but them gotdamn dimples, though . . . She nodded. "Yeah, that's why she was mad at me." Chrystal looked at me, her eyes glistening. "She rolled up on me in the bathroom at the Brazilian Steakhouse in Baltimore. She had her ass-kisser, Brook, with her too. Your girl told me to stay in my lane, and I told the bitch this *is* my lane. I didn't wanna tell her about our baby, but she asked for it."

My heart damn near stopped in my chest. I just looked at Chrystal as she paid the rest of the tickets. When she'd gathered all her receipts, she glanced at me before walking away from the window. I couldn't breathe. A nigga was in shock. Kylie hadn't said shit to me in days, and *that* was the reason why. I let a little distance get between Chrystal and me before I went to catch up with her. She got to the exit of the courthouse when I caught up with her, holding the door for her. She looked at me as she walked through the doors.

"Now I see why shawty hasn't said shit to me since Christmas," I told her.

"If you're wondering why I told her, it's because she said I wasn't shit, Blue. She said, 'Just like she gave me life, she could take that shit back.'" Chrystal stopped outside on the handicapped ramp of the courthouse, then turned to me. "Do you think I like doing this shit, David?"

I shook my head. "Nah, I don't."

"I don't wanna dance for, fuck, suck, nothing for these niggas. I told Kam that I wanna go back to just bartending, and do you know what the muthafucka told me? That niggas don't want me to serve them drinks; they want me to serve them ass, lips, tongue, hands, and pussy." Chrystal's toasty skin was flushed with anger. "She hit me where it hurt, so I hit her ass where it hurt too. Stuck-up-ass bitch. Why'd you even fuck with her? What made you fuck with a privileged bitch, who thinks everyone and everything is beneath her?"

"She wasn't always like this." I watched Chrystal purse her lips. I grinned. "A'ight, she was *always* stuck-up, but me and shawty used to have fun. She used to be crazy about me, or maybe it was an act. I don't know. But she cared about a nigga, and I needed that. And . . . I got sick of missing the fuck out of you," I told Chrystal, watching her eyes water. "Miss Tiffany had just died. My head was all fucked-up. I tried to get around a different crowd, but turns out the niggas in college and in these upper-class neighborhoods are just as ruthless. Look at Kam's family, yo."

"Blue, Kam knew about us." Chrystal looked up into my face.

"What'cha mean he knew about us? Who? Me and you?" I looked at her.

Chrystal nodded. "He's *not* your friend, Blue. Don't trust him, don't trust Kylie—don't trust anybody. Kylie's got secrets too, while she's trying to throw shade on me. And I know Kam has helped you come up. Even got you into college and the job that you have now. But trust and believe, he had ulterior motives. Just be careful, okay?"

I just looked at shawty, not sure how the fuck Kam knew about her and me. Or why my relationship with her even mattered to him. "Where you headed?" I changed the conversation altogether.

Chrystal looked at her watch. "Well, I was going to stop by the group home to see my son. And then maybe pay Mrs. Watson a visit today. I think she's throwing a party tonight, but I have to work."

I frowned at her a little.

Chrystal grinned. "The bar, not the pole, I promise. It's gonna be poppin' tonight at the club, bruh. You already know your boys are going to come through. It ain't like you have anything planned tonight."

"Tyrese's mom is throwing a party tonight here in Annapolis. We're headed over there now to help set up." I felt my phone vibrating in my pocket. It was probably Darius's ass, wondering what was taking me so long.

Chrystal rolled her eyes. "I meant plans tonight with Kylie. I heard she's staying over at Brook's house tonight. They gotta get up at the crack of dawn in the morning to make sure all the outfits fit the models just right. I'm sure she knows you're kickin' it with your boys tonight."

"Yeah," I nodded. "I kick it with my homeboys every New Year's."

"Well, this year, kick it with me." Chrystal's brown eyes searched my face. "We have so much catching up to do. Stop by and chill with me at the bar. Don't leave me hanging, Blue, a'ight?"


Tyrese's mother had us help set up for her New Year's party that afternoon. Darius already let me know that his girl, Robyn, a.k.a. Justice, planned on picking him up around 6:00 that night to take him out to eat and then to the New Year's party at the club. He said he wasn't trying to hang out late that night because he wasn't trying to show up to Kylie's event the next afternoon tore up, hung over and shit. Ain't that a bitch? *He* got an invite, and I didn't. But then again, he wasn't the one who had a baby with her friend. He wasn't married to her and in love with someone else. I tried to call Kylie, tried to smooth things over a little, but she wouldn't answer my calls.

I sat outside on Monice's (Tyrese's mother's) porch, looking at the picture of my mother. I went back and forth in my head about whether I should pay Mrs. Watson—or should I say, "Grandma"—a visit.

"What'cha doing out here, homie?" I heard Darius over my shoulder.

I looked up at him as he made his way over to the steps to sit beside me.

Darius looked at me and then at the picture in my hand. He took the photo from me. "Who's this?"

"Moms, yo." I took the picture back from him.

"Your mom?"

"Yeah," I nodded, looking down at the picture. "Chrystal gave it to me on my birthday; said Mrs. Watson gave it to Payton to give to me. Mrs. Watson is my grandmother."

Darius was just as blown away as I was when I heard the news. "What? Yo, that's wild. Your grandmother has been taking care of your son? Where is your mom? Did they *know* they had your son? And if they did, I sure as hell hope they didn't know you were staying here in Maryland."

I took a deep breath, trying my best not to be pissed . . . but I was. "They knew, and they kept the shit from both me *and* Chrystal."

Darius exclaimed. "Nigga, you need to find out why."

"Man, it's because of the lifestyle that we were living. You know I was young, wild, free, not giving a fuck. And from what we heard on Christmas from Chrystal's mouth, her lifestyle wasn't much different. Come to find out my uncle is the one who started this whole thing. The nigga pimped her out to some of my own friends. It's all good, though. I got something for his ass." I sipped from my Bud Lite, which was my third one that afternoon.

"There's got to be more to this story. It's like they were purposely trying to keep you two apart, homie. Something isn't right." Darius took out a pack of Newports.

I looked at him. "Nigga, since when do you smoke?"

Darius looked at me. "Since Robyn sent me this text." He handed me his phone.

I looked at the picture of a positive home pregnancy test on the display. I didn't mean to laugh at the nigga, but the shit was funny. Those two only had sex with each other for the longest, yet swore up and down that they weren't a couple. And there they were, having a baby together.

"Well," I handed him back his phone, trying my best to stop laughing at a nigga, "you might as well go 'head and wife that, bruh."

Darius sighed, sliding his phone back in his pocket. "Yeah, I thought about that."

I looked at Darius. He was dead-ass serious. "Yo, are you serious?"

He nodded. "Yeah. I'm gonna ask her tonight over dinner."

I shook my head. "Nah, I was just fuckin' with you. Don't do that shit, yo. That was the worst mistake I've ever made. I wouldn't wish this shit on my worst enemy, son."

Darius looked at me. "That's because the heart wants what it wants. You knew when you married my cousin that she wasn't who you really wanted. You went hard for Chrystal at that masquerade party, nigga. Tried to beat the fuck out of *everyone* who stopped you from getting to her. Shit, I think *I* even took a few hits to the face over this girl that night—*that's* how turnt you were.

"Then there was Christmas dinner at your house. I have seen you around my cousin for seven years and have yet to see you look at her the way that you looked at Chrystal that day. Not to mention the night at the club. Yo, you put Johnny's ass in the hospital. When you fight for someone the way you fought for her, *that's* the person you need to keep in your life. Kylie is my cousin, and I love her, but Chrystal is where your heart lies, Blue. You need to go for yours. I don't condone cheating, but I don't condone a loveless marriage either."

"I care about Kylie. I *do* love her," I tried to tell myself.

"Man, stop lying to yourself. You've lied to yourself for seven years. And she has too, to be honest. Brook tried to call her out over dinner, but Kylie cut her off." Darius removed a cigarette from the package.

I looked at him. "What'cha mean?"

"You can't tell Cuz I told you this shit either," Darius pleaded.

"Man, what is it?" I asked.

He took a deep breath. "Her and Kam used to date in high school. Shit, in college too, from what I can remember."

I just looked at the nigga. "What? Fuck you mean, bruh?"

"They used to date, Blue. Well, she used to date *him*. You know Kam ain't never claimed no girl. She was in love with him until you came along." Darius watched the frown form on my face.

And I watched the "Shit, why did I even say anything?" look spread across his face. "Nigga, how long have you known about this? I've known you since high school, and you've *never* mentioned this shit."

"Man, you knew when you started dating Cuz that she had just broken up with her boyfriend. She called it a breakup when, in reality, she found out that he was sleeping with . . ." Darius didn't even want to say anymore, but the truth was already out.

I didn't even want to hear the rest. I already knew what he was about to say.

"Sleeping with Chrystal." Darius continued, despite the pissed off expression on my face. "Chrystal, of course, had no idea what was going on. She called it quits with Kam. I don't think Kylie ever forgave Chrystal for what happened, even though Chrystal had no idea he was even seeing her."

I took a deep breath. "So, what you're saying is that me and Chrystal just got caught up in Kam and Kylie's bullshit? So, I came into the picture around the same time that both Chrystal and Kylie ended things with Kam?"

Darius nodded, lighting his cigarette. "Yeah, and around the same time, Kam had Chrystal dancing for him. She may have quit sleeping with him, but you know shawty is a paper chaser."

I looked at Darius. Seemed to me like Kam was feeling some type of way when he found out Kylie and I were seeing each other. Somehow, this nigga found out that I knew Chrystal. Why else would he put shawty to work after he found out Kylie and I were seeing each other?

"I think that nigga put Chrystal to work in his club to get back at me, dawg." I watched Darius throw his head back in laughter.

"Dude, you trippin'. Why are you always speculating?" He grinned, shaking his head at me. The nigga always thought I was paranoid about everything.

I looked at him, not much in the mood for joking. "Nigga, ain't nobody speculating shit. The moment I run into Chrystal again, I find out Kylie is pregnant. The nigga threw Chrystal in my face when he brought her to that masquerade party, knowing I was going to be there. I already know that the only reason Kylie invited all her friends for Christmas was because she wanted to rub it in their faces that she was having my baby. Why now? She's never introduced me to *any* of her friends. She did this to prove a point to them, Darius. Something for them to go back and tell Kam."

"Blue, my Cuz loves you. Whatever she had going on with Kam was over years ago." Darius sighed deeply, already knowing where my mind was headed.

"How many years ago, Darius? Were they fuckin' around while we were dating?" I asked.

Darius hesitated.

"The nigga was fuckin' with her while we were *married?*" I stood on the porch.

Darius jumped up too. "Yo, son, chill."

"Tell me, nigga; your ass knows everything else. Don't tell me you don't fuckin' know." I pushed him.

Darius took a deep breath. "I heard—"

I cut him off. "Nigga, you *heard?*"

"A few of my frat brothers said they saw them together a few times at the club, but I just brushed it off as a rumor." Darius watched me rub my head in frustration. "Blue, hatin'-ass muthafuckas *always* spread rumors."

"Why didn't anyone tell me that they used to see each other? I never would have gotten involved with her. I ain't some fuckin' rebound nigga," I shouted.

"Wasn't she yours, though?" Darius questioned me, trying to turn the situation back around on me.

I looked at the nigga, ready to punch him dead in his grill.

"I'm just saying, Blue." Darius tried to laugh off the expression on my face. "You can't tell me that you didn't get with my cousin to get over Chrystal. And I'm not even the person to be talking to about this shit. You need to talk to Cuz."

"Hey, fellas."

We looked up to see Robyn walking toward us, dressed in a camel-colored leather jacket, white sweater, light denim jeans, and knee-high leather high-heeled boots. We were so busy talking that we didn't even notice shawty had pulled up to the curb.

"What's up, Robyn?" Darius glanced at me and then looked at Robyn.

She walked into his arms, kissing him on his lips. "Hey, boo." She glanced at me as Darius slid his arms around her. "Hey, David. Chrystal asked about you. Wanted to know if you were going to stop by Mrs. Watson's house. We just left there about an hour ago. Mrs. Watson said she wanted to meet you."

"I rolled here with Tyrese. My ride is at the crib. You mind dropping me off at the crib?" I asked.

# Chapter Six

## *Never Leave Me*

## *Blue*

I hesitated before knocking on Mrs. Watson's door that evening.

"The door is open." I heard a familiar voice calling from inside the house.

I opened the door, walking into Mrs. Watson's place. The house looked pretty festive. You could tell the woman was big on holidays. Streamers, lights, garland, poinsettias, and mistletoe were everywhere. The house was buzzing with home health aides and a few other houseguests. I closed the door behind me as a few little children whisked by me.

"David, is it?" I heard a familiar voice to my left.

I looked over to my left, in the doorway of the kitchen, to see Corina, one of the staff from the Tree of Life. "Corina? Hey, shawty. You work here too?"

Corina grinned. "No, it's my day off. But sometimes I come over to help Mrs. Watson out. She's so good to us over there at the Tree of Life. Do you know she gave me and the other awake-overnight staff $1,500 each for Christmas? I paid my light bill *and* my rent for the new year with that check."

I grinned a little. "*That's* what's up."

"Are you here for the party?" Corina asked, more like insisted. "You know Mrs. Watson's been asking about her *grandson* all day."

I looked at Corina, who was smiling from ear to ear.

"There's no denying it, is there? That little boy looks just like his gotdamn daddy." Corina's big country ass grabbed me by the hand, leading me into the living room.

There, in Mrs. Watson's living room, were about twenty guests. All white. All smiling at me. I could tell by the way she clapped and giggled that the woman in the wheelchair was Mrs. Watson . . . my grandmother.

She wheeled herself up to me. "David, meet the Jacobs. Jacobs, meet Rosy's son."

I looked up at everyone, whose smiles had faded before appearing again. I know they wanted to hug me, but they were probably just as shocked as I was.

"Hello," they greeted me.

"What's good wit'cha?" I looked at all of them.

My mother's family was gorgeous. Every last one of the women and children before me looked like they stepped right out of *Glamour* magazine. One of the little children rushed over to Mrs. Watson's side, handing her a fancy wooden cane. Mrs. Watson kissed the little boy before rising to her feet, striking the cane against the ground. Then she threw her arms around me.

"It's so nice to meet you finally, David." She cried and laughed simultaneously. "Oh, you're so handsome. Just like your father." She smiled into my face as she let go of me.

It took Mrs. Watson a few minutes to get me all to herself. She had to check on her pies in the oven, ensure all her guests were on their way, confirm that Payton was on his way over from the group home, and make sure I was comfortable in her home. I stood in her guest room, looking at the pictures on her wall. My mother was in every picture. My mother was voluptuous, curvy, and shapely, with a face that resembled Marilyn Monroe's. There were several pictures of her with children.

"So, she went and had other kids, huh? Forgot all about me and Lisa." I laughed to myself, hearing the wheels of Mrs. Watson's wheelchair squeaking behind me.

"She has a daughter, who's 19. She goes to Harvard. Studies law," Mrs. Watson told me as I turned around to face her.

I frowned a little before turning back around to look at the pictures on the wall. I came across a picture on the wall of William, a picture of him with Chrystal's mother. It appeared to have been taken while the two were in high school.

"That is my favorite picture." Mrs. Watson laughed. "It was at their junior prom. Your mother went alone and refused to have her picture taken without a date. William was a sight to see, I tell you. Every girl in school loved him, your mother included."

I looked over my shoulder at Mrs. Watson and then back at the picture.

"While William was alive, he was taken to court at least four times for paternity suits. Your aunt Drew, who raised Lisa, wanted her tested as well," Mrs. Watson sighed.

I turned around, facing her, my heart racing. "And?"

Mrs. Watson nodded. "She's William's daughter."

I shook my head. "Nah, Lisa and me have the same father? The nigga who they said used to beat on Moms. The one who they say she was running from when she dumped me in the trash. You know, Greg, Uncle Larry's brother."

Mrs. Watson shook her head. "Sweetie, William was your father too."

My heart was beating so fast and hard that I could hear it pounding. Did they keep me away from shawty because we were sister and brother? I wanted to ask her, but I was too afraid of the answer.

"On that picture of Christina at her junior prom, she had a tubal pregnancy and had no idea. She ended up in the hospital and had to have a hysterectomy." Mrs. Watson looked at me looking at her. "Chrystal was adopted. Born on the same day as you. Her mother was a young, 16-year-old mixed-race girl named Sofia Braxton, and her father was a 20-year-old white man named Ira Kravitz, who her parents didn't approve of. The girl's parents didn't believe in abortion. So, adoption was her only choice." Mrs. Watson watched a nigga rubbing my head anxiously. "You thought I was about to say that the two of you were related, huh?" Mrs. Watson giggled, watching me sit down in the recliner in the corner of the room to catch my breath. "You thought I was trying to tell you that you had a baby with your own sister, huh, boy?"

I looked at her, my heart on full stampede by now. I saw then where I got my twisted sense of humor. Wasn't shit funny about the situation. Chrystal was devastated when Christina was put away in the mental institution. She watched her mother slowly lose her mind every day. The final straw for Christina's family was when she tried to kill herself by turning on her gas stove and getting into the oven. Chrystal found her mother in the stove, and that was only because she walked into the house and smelled the bread crumbs at the bottom of the oven burning. And then there was William, who was Chrystal's heart and soul. She lost a part of herself when she lost him. She loved him, and I guess she loved me because she said I was just like her father. She thought it came from the fact that he helped raise me, but it turns out I was like him because I really *was* a part of him.

"Does Chrystal know?" I asked.

Mrs. Watson shook her head. "No, honey. Christina was told the truth years ago, but was in denial. She was blind to William cheating on her for years. Rosy was dating Greg, who suspected that she was cheating on him. He threatened to kill you *and* her if she brought you home from the hospital."

My mind was still blown. "So . . . Aunt Drew and Uncle Larry aren't related to me or Lisa?"

"No, and your uncle Larry wasn't too happy about that either. He felt deeply insulted by being asked to help raise William's children. A man who used to have the boys who sold drugs for him arrested on every occasion. You and Larry were pretty close, weren't you?" Mrs. Watson watched my nostrils flare and my jaws tighten.

I just looked at her.

"He got close enough for you to trust him and waited for you to leave to start harassing Chrystal. She doesn't think I know about her life in Greenville after you left, but I do. Uncle Larry had Chrystal raped on several occasions, while she was pregnant with your baby. She was drugged and raped the day she went into labor, David. She doesn't even remember it happened. Rosy said that when she came into the ER, she was beaten and had bruising in her vaginal area. Chrystal was so out of it when she came into the ER. Rosy said she found traces of sedation medication in her system that surgeons used to put patients to sleep for surgery. Not to mention Pitocin." Mrs. Watson's eyes glistened.

"Pitocin? Isn't that what doctors use to induce labor?" I exclaimed.

Mrs. Watson nodded.

"He was trying to kill my baby *and* my girl, Mrs. Watson?" I rose from the recliner.

Mrs. Watson grabbed my arm. Her old ass had a mean grip on her. She really gripped my arm with her cold, dry hand. "David, now you listen to me. Don't you go out there and do something stupid."

"He has my girl thinking *she* was the reason why our son was born this way. She thinks that *her* lifestyle is what put her in early labor. He's got my girl strippin' and sleeping with muthafuckas every night to put a roof over her son's and *your* head," I exclaimed.

"This is the exact reason why we didn't want to tell you two about each other. I knew that as soon as you found out, you'd go and try to kill Larry. It's over. Chrystal has a choice, and she makes that choice every night. She is not her past, and neither are you." Mrs. Watson let go of my arm. "You are a professor, teaching at the University of Maryland. You have a beautiful wife. *And* Chrystal tells me that you are about to have another baby." Mrs. Watson could tell by the look on my face that I couldn't care less about that last sentence.

"Not sure how things are going to turn out with Kylie. I feel like she's keeping secrets. Not even sure if her baby is mine, from what I heard a few hours ago. I don't even wanna think about her. Our anniversary is tomorrow, and she's not even answering the phone. Tonight, I'm just gonna concentrate on Chrystal. She's working the bar tonight." I looked at Mrs. Watson's pursed lips. "*Not* the pole but the bar. I think she's scared to leave that club. Kam's got shawty thinking he's going to ruin her life if she leaves that club. Everything she built is because of him, and she thinks he'll tear it down."

Mrs. Watson sighed. "Yeah, she told me how you and your friends came up in the club, causing a huge commotion. She said you damn near broke a police officer's face, pointed a gun in another officer's face, and then made Chrystal and her friends get dressed in front of the man they work for. You did all that, and you *still* let this girl go back in that club?"

I shrugged. "She said she has that nigga, Quincy, to look out for her, so I let the shit go."

"Young man, your grandmother is asking you to save this girl from herself. I'm old. I had to put my great-grandson in a group home because I was too afraid to let him go and stay with his own mother. Why? Because her lifestyle could get both of them killed. I have cancer in my spine, David," Mrs. Watson told me to get my attention.

I looked at her, watching her eyes water. "Does Chrystal know?"

Mrs. Watson shook her head. "No, I want to keep it that way. I don't have much longer to live. I want to give Chrystal back her son, but the only way I will do that is if you get that girl out of that club. And you do that shit tonight." Mrs. Watson wheeled past me in her wheelchair.

Titties, ass, pussy, *everything* was exposed that night at Club Pop It. My niggas were too turnt; the muthafuckas came to the club drunk. I drove by myself to the club alone so that I could take Chrystal home. Darius rode in with his girl, Robyn. Columbus, Tyrese, and about five of my homies in blue pulled up to the curb alongside me. I also had a few niggas on standby, just in case some shit popped off. Kam was nowhere in sight; as a matter of fact, Kavante wasn't in the spot either. I wasn't sure what was going on, but I was going to use that opportunity to talk shawty into leaving with me that night. You already know that after what happened a few nights ago, I was banned from the club.

Chrystal knew when she invited me that I would show up and possibly show out if I had to. As soon as I rolled in the spot, I peeped Quincy and his security guards scattered throughout the hallway entrance. Quincy was muggin' the shit out of me, and all I could do was grin. He already knew I was there to *take* shawty. He could stand by and let Chrystal have her way if he wanted, but Mrs. Watson knew I wasn't the type of guy to just stand by and do nothing. Yeah, I let her back in the club when I shouldn't have. That was my mistake. I let my pride get in the way. However, the news Mrs. Watson gave me made me think about life from a completely different angle.

"Aye, shawty," I called to Chrystal as I sat down at the bar.

Chrystal turned around, her long, curly hair flowing down her back. She wore a sequined bra under a white tank top, black skinny jeans, and sequined stilettos. I knew shawty had her pole-dancing outfit under her clothes, just in case she felt like hitting the stage. She approached me at the bar, eyeing the people she worked with, who were looking at her like she must've been crazy for allowing me up in the club. Chrystal rolled her eyes at them and then stood before me.

"You bustin' outta that shirt, ain't cha?" I eyed her smooth cleavage.

Chrystal grinned, bobbing her head a little to music playing over the loudspeakers. "*Woo, I know, I know, I know,*" Chrystal sang, in her Dej Loaf voice.

I grinned. I looked back at Quincy, who stood along the back wall of the club, eyeing both of us talking to each other. I looked back at Chrystal. "Your boyfriend has a problem with me talking to you, huh? Tell the nigga to bring his punk ass over here so we can talk about it then."

Chrystal rolled her eyes. "Get over yourself, Blue—the man is just doing his job."

"Why would you pay him to do something that I'm willing to do for free?" I looked up at her as she set a few shot glasses on the countertop.

Chrystal sighed. "Do you remember when you used to be that he-don't-wife-'em, he-one-nights-'em type of guy? The type of guy that other guys were scared to leave their girl around?" Chrystal watched me laugh out loud. "Do you remember *that*, David 'Blue' Jacobs? Because *that's* the muthafucka that *I* remember. This school-teacher, the stuck-up-wife-having-ass man before me is *not* the Blue that I remember. The Blue that *I* remember would have seen right through Kylie. Would have known she wasn't shit from the jump. Do you see Kam around here? Has Kylie called you? I bet'cha that those two are together, the night before your anniversary at that."

I just looked at Chrystal. I tried not thinking about Kylie. That was a conversation that I wasn't even ready to have with Kylie. She still hadn't returned any of my calls. The only thing she managed to do that night was send a text saying she was out with her girls from college and that she'd be out late. I had every right to not even go home to shawty that night.

"I stopped by Mrs. Watson's house," I told Chrystal as she took the order from the drooling, thirsty-ass nigga who sat down beside me.

Chrystal looked at me as she started fixing the dude's drink. "That's good. Did you see my son there?"

I shook my head. "He hadn't made it yet when I left." I watched her get irritated with the nigga because he couldn't decide if the drink she made was the drink he really wanted. The nigga already looked faded to me.

"Nigga, do you want a rum and Coke or not? Other people want drinks too," Chrystal huffed, watching the dude's eyes glued to her cleavage.

"Well, what I *really* want is my five minutes alone with you in the Champagne Room." The blue-black muthafucka licked his lips before grabbing shawty's hand, pulling her body up against the bar counter.

It didn't take me a second to jump up from my stool and put my .45 to the nigga's temple. "The fuck did she just ask you, nigga? Did she ask if you wanted some pussy? Hell muthafuckin' nah!"

The nigga threw up his hands, laughing nervously, careful to look my way, the gun aimed in between his eyes then. "A'ight, homie, it's cool."

"She *asked* you if your ass wanted the gotdamn rum and Coke, nigga." I continued to aim the gun at him as Chrystal slid him a rum and Coke.

"Yeah, yeah, a'ight." He tossed Chrystal a twenty onto the countertop and backed away from the counter, his mind not even on the drink then.

"How much change does the nigga get?" I snarled.

"Nah, homie, she's good. She can keep it." He shook his head at me as I lowered the gun. The nigga hurried his scary ass away, leaving the drink on the counter.

I looked back at Quincy and his crew, lined up against the wall, pointing at me. I looked back at Chrystal, who was giggling with one of the girls working the bar with her.

"Shit, I might as well drink this." I picked up the drink and took a sip.

Chrystal's friend was laughing her ass off behind the bar. "Your nigga got that nigga to buy him a drink." She laughed out loud.

I looked at shawty's name tag. "Fancy," I called out to her. "You think a nigga is crazy, huh?" I put my gun back in my pants.

Fancy looked me over a little and then back at Chrystal. "You two crazy muthafuckas are made for each other. Rain, I told you the nigga was gonna come back up in here, acting a fool. You hit that stage with me tonight if you want to, and this nigga is gonna shoot up the place." Fancy kissed Chrystal on the cheek and then took off her apron, handing it to Chrystal. "I gotta go change, honey. You can have this shit. Rent is due at my condo in a few days; gotta get this paper tonight." She left the bar.

Chrystal looked at me, sighing. "You can't come up in here acting a gotdamn fool, Blue. I see your niggas speckled all over this club; I ain't crazy. Kam might be out all night, but I guarantee you, Kavante will be here in a few minutes. Now, just chill out, have a drink or two, and don't kill anybody tonight, Professor." Chrystal pulled out an apple Cîroc bottle from the refrigerator and sat down on a stool behind the bar.

I grinned.

Chrystal twisted the top off the bottle and took a few sips before asking me, "So, what did Mrs. Watson talk to her grandbaby about?" She grinned at me, licking the Cîroc from her lips.

I smiled, trying to ignore those lips. "She, ummm, she told me a lot that I didn't even know. A lot about *you* that you probably don't even know, or should I say can't remember. Told me that the nigga I thought all my life was my uncle really isn't my uncle at all. And that she thinks he's the one who sent you into early labor. That they found large amounts of sedation, not to mention labor-inducing drugs in your system, shawty, the day that you had my son."

Chrystal's eyes widened, taking another few sips from her drink.

I watched shawty's lips tremble. "She told me that Uncle Larry and I ain't even related. That the man I thought was my father *isn't* my father. When I thought I never knew my father, turns out I grew up with him the entire time. That he helped raise me . . . That he dug me out of the trash."

Chrystal's eyes widened even more. She drank damn near half of the bottle before slamming it down on the counter.

I looked at her trembling hands and grabbed them in mine. "Chrystal, she told me that your mother couldn't have kids, that you were—"

Chrystal shook her head at me, squeezing my hand in hers. "David, it doesn't matter what she told you. That man who died in that robbery was *my* gotdamn daddy. He did more with me than my mama did. He helped me pick out a bra, took me to all my band and chorus practices, and taught me how to ride a bike. Shit, he even taught me how to beat the shit outta muthafuckas. He taught me *everything* I know. He loved me."

I nodded, squeezing her hand back. "Shawty, I'm not taking that away from you. I know he was everything to you, Chrystal."

Chrystal looked up at me, her light eyes watering. She shook her head at me. "And there I was, in love with you for years because you reminded me so much of him. Turns out, *you* are him."

"Mrs. Watson wants you out of here, Chrystal." I watched her roll her eyes as she slipped her hands from mine. "*I* want you out of here. You don't belong in here."

"And where do I belong, Blue?" Chrystal's eyes questioned me as she took a few more sips from her Cîroc.

"With me," I meant to think it, but said it aloud instead.

Chrystal just looked at me. "What you drankin', Blue?" She tried her best to avoid my statement. She took the watered-down rum and Coke from me. "I know you don't want this watered-down shit. I have to water it down so these niggas don't get too drunk up in here."

"Hennessy. On the rocks." I grinned, shaking my head at shawty. "I know you heard what I said, Chrystal; don't act like you didn't hear me."

"Have you tried Hennessy Privilege? You know, privileged like that bitch you're married to?" Chrystal had jokes as she scooped ice from the ice bin and dumped a few cubes into a glass. She poured the liquor in the glass and took a sip before sliding it over to me.

I laughed a little before taking a sip from my drink. "You got jokes."

"Who's fuckin' joking, David?" Oh, she *was* serious. Calling me by my name and not my nickname. "Don't try to sell me a dream, telling me that we should be together when you're married to that stuck-up-ass bitch who's been cheating on you for years, right in your face, and you never took the time to notice."

I just looked at her as I took a few more sips.

"Marrying someone doesn't make you forget about the person your heart knows that it belongs to."

Chrystal shook her head at me. "And now, you're about to have a baby by a bitch, who you care nothing about and who cares nothing about you. *But* now that she knows we have a baby together, yeah, she's about to make both of our lives hell. You just watch. But don't come around me, talking that 'we belong together' shit when she has your ring on *her* finger. As long as that ring is on her finger, there *is* no us. There's you. And then there's me. And keep that shit in your head, nigga."

I grinned. "You haven't changed a bit. Still moody as a muthafucka."

Chrystal looked at me, her bright browns sparkling under the bar lights.

"Yo, Rain, check this shit out," another bartender called out to Chrystal.

Chrystal turned around, looking at the flat-screen television that hung in the corner of the bar as the other bartender turned up the volume.

On the news was the grand opening of "Bottomless Pit," a bar and grill owned by the Moores. A family that was even richer than Kam's family, the Prices. The families were rivals, but they kept each other pretty close. I should have known that Kam would be at the event. There he was on camera, sitting at the bar, cameras and reporters in his face, asking how he liked the food and alcohol selection at the bar. And just when I got fed up with looking at the nigga, the camera zoomed out . . . and there beside him sat Kylie. Her hand in his. As soon as she realized that she was in the shot, she quickly slipped her hand from his. But not quick enough to hide the fact that she wasn't wearing my wedding ring.

Chrystal looked back at me over her shoulder, shaking her head. "What did I tell you?" she asked, looking back at the screen.

I glanced at Chrystal, then looked back up at the screen too, watching Kam snatch Kylie's hand, pulling her to him, then kissing her on live television.

Everyone at the bar looked at me. Damn near everyone sitting at the bar attended the college that I taught at. They knew Kylie was supposed to be my wife. They knew that Kam was supposed to be my boy.

I laughed to myself, drinking my liquor all the way to the last drop.

Chrystal turned around, facing me. "Now, Blue, she's not worth it." Chrystal thought I was gonna kill Kam over Kylie, but I could really care less. All I could think about was which one of my lawyer friends would handle my divorce.

Chrystal looked over my shoulder, her eyes growing bigger. "Blue!" she squealed.

I got up from the stool just when I felt cold steel digging into the back of my neck.

"The fuck you doing in here?"

I felt Kavante's hot breath singe the hair on the back of my neck. "Nigga, you know your ass isn't supposed to even be in here after that shit you pulled at the masquerade *and* the shit you pulled on my man and them in VIP the other night."

I eased my way around, facing Kavante. The fact that he had a pistol digging into my neck didn't faze me much. If Kavante were going to shoot me, he would have shot me already. I tried not to laugh out loud, looking at his swollen nose and two black eyes. Darius wasn't lying; your boy did major damage to that muthafucka's face. He deserved it. I don't remember much from that night, but I'm pretty sure I tried to get to Kam's ass, and Kavante jumped in to block me from getting to him.

"Whoa, nigga. You look like you got jumped, homie. Somebody hit you in your face with a bat or something? The fuck you do to get fucked up like this?" I tried not to grin, watching Kavante cock the gun back and then aim it at my face that time.

Kavante's face balled up. Oh, he was mad at a nigga for real. "I'm only gonna say this one more time—*get the fuck out*. You ain't got no reason to be up in this muthafucka."

"The reason I'm here is standing behind the counter. If I leave, she leaves." I peeped my niggas approaching over his shoulder. Kavante's boys were close by but hesitated to approach because my boys were closer. Tyrese and my niggas would put at least five holes in Kavante before they had a chance to get him.

"Nigga, you don't want the kinda problems that fuckin' with this ho will bring you." Kavante tried to grin, but I'm sure that swollen jaw of his hurt like hell. "You want a piece of that pussy, you gotta pay just like everyone else. Fuckin' with her comes with a price—*Kameron* Price."

Tyrese rolled up on Kavante, cocking his gun back. All my niggas made their way to the bar, all except for Darius who was busy holding Robyn back from approaching her friend at the bar.

"My boy said let shawty go," Tyrese growled, his finger over the trigger, having no problem giving Kavante a few shots to the back of his head in front of everyone at the club. "You betta get that gun out of his face. Fuck around and get everyone up in this bitch sprayed."

Kavante hesitated to lower his weapon, but he did. "You don't know what you're doing, son. Rain is under a contract. She still has four muthafuckin' years in this bitch. Do you know how much money we loaned her over the years? You must be out'cha gotdamn mind if you think we're just gonna let you walk up out of here with our girl."

"That nigga just slobbed my wife down on national television," I exclaimed. "Do you think I give a fuck about a gotdamn contract that he has with shawty?" I walked away from the muthafucka and behind the counter to Chrystal.

Chrystal's eyes watered as she slowly removed her apron.

"You take shawty out of this club, and all hell is gonna break loose," Kavante warned me. "Nigga, I'm trying to tell you."

"Fuck you and your gotdamn cousin *and* this gotdamn club." I snatched Chrystal up by her wrist. "You ain't comin' back in this muthafucka, do you hear me?" I yelled at shawty so she could hear me loud and clear.

Chrystal's nostrils flared a little, and her fists clenched, but she nodded.

"Now, go get'cha shit and let's roll out." I let go of her wrists, tossing her ass toward the back entrance of the bar.


"Yo, Rain." I heard someone call out to Rain as we left the club that night.

Chrystal looked over her shoulder and then stopped in her tracks, taking a deep breath. "Shit," she muttered to herself.

"What's up? What's wrong?" I asked before looking up to see Quincy walking toward us, accompanied by a few of his security guards. I laughed to myself, watching the nigga approaching me, like he was ready to shoot a nigga. He mugged the shit out of me before looking at Chrystal. "Rain, you really gonna quit? Really gonna leave this club? You know that Kam isn't going to let this shit die easily. You have a contract with him. The police *still* haven't found the bodies of the other three girls who tried to leave this club last year." Quincy glanced at me and then looked back at Chrystal. He scoffed, "Is this muthafucka Superman or some shit? He really thinks he can just take you from this club with no problems? Can he repay all the money these muthafuckas have invested in you? They pay for your son's school, for your son's stay at that group home, for the mortgage of the woman who takes care of your son. They paid your way through college—*cash!* They are paying for you to get your master's degree. The muthafuckas have cleared your entire police record so that you can get a job outside of this filthy muthafucka when your contract is done here. They pay for those cars you drive, the clothes you wear, and your gotdamn health insurance. These niggas have a life insurance policy on your ass, Rain. If they want you dead, they will do it *and* get paid for the shit. You really think this li'l nigga and his li'l crew can protect you? What the fuck can this nigga do for you but cause more problems?"

I looked at the nigga, who thought I was just going to let him get all in shawty's face, talking shit. "Aye, homie—I'm right here. Your issue is with me, *not* with her, nigga. Shawty pays *you* to protect *her,* but you slackin' on your job, so I had to step ta him."

"*I'm* slackin'? Looks like I've been doing *your* job for the past four or five years, bruh." Quincy called himself, trying to step to me.

Tyrese and my niggas were standing alongside Tyrese's ride, peepin' the situation. I signaled them to back down, indicating that the situation was cool before they started to make their way over to us.

"*My* job?" I laughed. "If you were doing *your* job, shawty wouldn't even be up in this muthafucka for four or five gotdamn years. Ain't no way that I could stand by and watch niggas damn near rape her every other night. I used to be the number one dope nigga in Maryland, D.C., and Virginia. Not to mention, me and my crew were running shit down South when a nigga was just in high school. Kam's ass used to come to *me* for connections, homie. The only thing I needed that nigga for was to help clear my record and to keep my name from ringing in the court system. I gave up that life when my mama was killed. You love Chrystal? You want Chrystal? You respect her?" I asked Quincy.

Chrystal looked at me and then at Quincy.

Quincy couldn't even look at her; he just grilled the shit out of a nigga.

"You don't feel *shit* for Chrystal. You don't even *know* Chrystal. All you know is 'Rain,' the girl who pays you a grip to make sure niggas don't follow her home. You don't love, respect, *or* want her if you can watch her do this shit. And she can't love, respect, or want you for *leaving* her in this shit. Just the *thought* of this girl with another nigga would have me ready to tear up some shit, and you stand by every gotdamn night and watch niggas jam their dicks down her throat." I pushed Quincy, and the security guards behind him tightened up.

Quincy signaled them to back up. He looked down at me, shaking his head, his eyes glistening with anger. He knew I was right. He could've talked Chrystal out of the shit if he wanted to, but he didn't because she was paying him.

Chrystal grabbed my arm. "Blue, come on; let's just go."
I pulled from Chrystal and yanked my arm from her
hands. "Nigga, you could've helped her, but you *didn't,*"
I yelled at Quincy. "If you haven't gotten shawty by now,
you ain't never gonna get her. So, what you need to do is
back the fuck up and let a nigga get his job back."

"You really didn't have to do Quincy like that, Blue."
Chrystal strutted through the front door of her condo
that New Year's Eve night. She let her girl, Fancy, roll out
in her car that night so that she could roll out with me.
"Like what?" I strolled through the front door behind
her, then closed the door, watching her ass pouncing in
those tight-ass jeans she was wearing.
"Nigga, you know what the hell I'm talking about.
Playing him in front of everyone in the parking lot,
then punking him in front of his boys, your boys, and
me. I keep telling you that just because you don't care
whether you live or die doesn't mean the next nigga
doesn't." Chrystal took off her fur jacket and hung it on
the coatrack in her hallway. She parked the Louis Vuitton
suitcase—which contained all of her club costumes from
her locker at the club—next to the coatrack. "You're about
to go to war with Kam over Kylie? Over me?"
I looked at her as I took off my coat. "Kylie never once
mentioned shit about having a relationship with this
nigga. She knew that we were boys. She never wanted
me around the nigga, and now, I know why. She's on
national TV with the nigga, letting the nigga kiss all
on her, and where the fuck was her wedding ring? The
ring that *I* busted *my* ass to buy for her?" I tossed my coat
on the arm of her sofa.
"I told you, baby—you thought I was just making shit
up." Chrystal shook her head at me before bending over

to unbuckle her heels. "You always were a sucker for a pretty face, though I thought you said that after that shit that happened with that light-skinned girl back in high school that you'd never ever *ever* date a redbone again in your life." She cut me off before I could say anything. "But I'll leave that alone. Kam *is* getting pretty bold, though. Taking her to dinner at the Moores' restaurant, knowing the shit would be televised. He did that shit so you could see it."

Chrystal stood up straight, kicking off her shoes. "She must have told him about our little boy. When Kam approached me in the mall a few days ago, he told me not to tell her about our son. That she was trying to do right by you. That their little 'situation' was over with. That I needed to back up and let you two be happy."

I looked up at her as she turned around and walked into the kitchen. And then I went to the kitchen after her. I leaned against the wall of the doorway, watching her dig through her refrigerator. Shawty was bent all the way over, digging through the crisper compartments. Maybe it was just my imagination, but it looked like Chrystal was twerking just a little. That booty jiggled as she searched for something to munch on.

"So, ummm, you really have a contract with this nigga?" I asked, watching as her tank top slid up her waist a little, revealing a bit of skin.

Chrystal sighed, standing straight again. She tossed a bag of baby carrots, a bag of apple slices, veggie dip, and fruit dip onto the counter. Then she reached into the refrigerator to take out a bag of chewy Chips Ahoy cookies and tossed those on the counter too. "Yeah, for the next four years." She took a bottle of water out of the refrigerator door before closing it.

"How much do you owe these niggas?" I asked.

Chrystal glanced at me before reaching up into the cabinet to take out a plate. "Well," she placed a few cookies on the plate and then popped it into the microwave, turning it on for thirty seconds. "Let's just say it's a lot. Kylie's parents paid my way through my first semester of college, including the stay at the dorm. Kavante gave me the money to pay them back. I worked overtime at the bar to repay him. Then once I saw how my son and Mrs. Watson were living, I had to put them in a new house. Once I saw how smart my baby was, we decided to put him in a school for blind and deaf students. Then I had to pay for Mrs. Watson's nursing staff, not to mention home health aides who could help take care of Payton when he came home from the group home that I *also* pay for. Kam covers all of that, and I pay him back. I get to keep 55 percent of what I earn, and they get to keep the rest. The only catch is that I have to do whatever they want me to do with whoever they want me to do it to." She took her plate out of the microwave and placed a few carrots and apple slices on it.

I just watched her as she put a little dip for her fruit and veggies on the plate. I could tell she didn't feel like talking about working at the club, especially with me. When we were teenagers, she swore on her life that she'd never be caught dead working in a strip club. That she'd never sell herself to make a quick buck. She was ashamed, and I was pissed.

She put the bags of food back in the refrigerator and continued explaining her life at that dumb-ass club. "I have a seven-day workweek, and I get off early on Sundays." She sighed. "I dance on Mondays, Wednesdays, Fridays, and Saturdays. I have to attend promotional events for other businesses that the Prices have. I have to host parties with a team of my choice. Of course, I always take Letta, Robyn, and Fancy. Despite what a lot of people may think, I've only had vaginal sex voluntarily a few times."

"*Voluntarily?* The fuck is *that* supposed to mean, Chrystal?" My temples twitched.

Chrystal looked at me before taking a bite from one of her apple slices. "Exactly what I said, Blue. I told you about the shit that Lawrence made me do when he had me locked in the house. Working for Kam wasn't much different either. I think that throughout my whole club career, I've only let a few guys hit it. Maybe three or four in five years. There were times when Kam would make me go into a room and . . . You saw what almost happened the other night, Blue. Robyn and Letta wouldn't have let it happen, though. They would have gone out fighting for me. Trust me, we've whopped several niggas and doms at the club. Anyway," she peeped the frustrated expression on my face, "I can't pretend that I haven't danced naked and teased niggas and bitches with sex objects because I have. That was my specialty. I can't say that I haven't sucked quite a few niggas or bitches because I have. That was my specialty too. I have repaid the Prices *and* saved at least $80,000. That's *my* money, and I refuse to give it to them. They let so much shit happen to me over the past few years, and that's why I hired Quincy in the first place. That money belongs to me, David."

"Damn, you must've sucked a lot of dick to save that much money *and* be able to pay bills." I couldn't help but comment on her savings.

"Just the small ones. A bitch wasn't trying to get lockjaw." Chrystal wasn't going to let me upset her.

I laughed a little, shaking my head at her. "There never has been any shame in your game. My baby girl has always been straight-up with a nigga. That's why I fuck with you like I do."

"Ugh, you make me sick. I ain't fuckin' with you, Blue." Chrystal grabbed her snacks from the counter and then walked up to me. I was blocking the entrance. She looked me over from head to toe. "You stay dope boy fresh, Professor."

"I remember when you were my sweet little girl." I looked down at her pretty face.

Chrystal rolled her big brown eyes, her long eyelashes fluttering. "That's a gotdamn lie. I was *never* a sweet little girl."

"You were *my* sweet little girl." I touched the tiny moles on her neck before looking back into her face.

Chrystal looked at me a few seconds before pushing past me and going down the hallway, into the living room. "Boy, go on, now. Always trying to spit game."

I turned around and followed behind her. Shawty had tattoos sprinkled all over her back. Flowers, butterflies, fairies, suns, moons, stars. Payton's name was on her arm. And "I Miss You, Daddy" was on her other arm. And my name was on her back. Don't even get me started on the roses covering each breast or the rosebush-shaped panties she had inked over her pelvic bone.

"When did you get all these tattoos?" I had to ask her.

Chrystal sat on her sofa, turning on her mini-stereo with her remote. She looked up at me as I sat down beside her. She sighed, setting her plate of food on her expensive coffee table that looked like it was made of crystal. "Well, I hated dancing naked on stage. Some strip clubs only required the girls to remove their tops, but the Prices don't play that. 'All Clothes Must Come Off' is on a sign at the damn entrance to the club. They make us take off everything, *and* they make us bend all the way over, touching our toes so the nigga can see inside of us too. That took a lot of getting used to. I stayed high and faded to get through it. I got all of these tattoos to try to cover up a little. The roses over my breasts are so the niggas can only see the shape of my breasts and nipples.

I stay waxed, so the roses over my pelvic bone look like panties. I just have to wear a garter belt to dress it up."

I watched her eat her fruit. "As much as I hated to find out that the girl who was dancing naked in front of all of those people was you, I must admit that the shit you did was sexy as a muthafucka. I'm still mesmerized off that shit. I can see you still bent over, poppin' that pink pussy for a nigga. You have most of my students and a few of my niggas in love, for real." I watched Chrystal trying not to blush.

"Talkin' about I was your sweet little girl . . . When?" Chrystal changed the subject. "When we were robbin' those liquor stores, just to get bottles of Hennessy?" She watched me laughing. "Or maybe it was when I talked you into kidnapping that bitch who tried to sleep with one of my boyfriends? Or maybe it was when I kidnapped *your* bitch because she was trying to fuck with one of your homeboys?"

I couldn't help but laugh out loud. I grabbed one of Chrystal's warm cookies. "Yo, remember when you burned your cousin's hair, trying to put a Just For Me Relaxer in it? Your cousin was white! You burned that little girl's scalp."

Chrystal burst out laughing. "Shut up! Remember freshman year, when you wore that gotdamn Trojan Man costume to school during Spirit Week? No more costume day for us! You had everyone going around singing, '*Trojan Man, hmm, hmm, hmm.*' Even the teachers." She laughed out loud, tears clouding her eyes.

"Yo," I laughed. "Remember when *you* posed naked for art class? I should've known then that you'd end up naked center stage somewhere."

Chrystal's smile faded. She pushed me, watching me laugh as I ate her cookie. "Don't get slapped, David. That shit isn't even funny. I wasn't naked. I had on a bikini top and bottom, and y'all just *drew* me naked. Don't try to play me." She watched me eat, and then she handed me her bottled water.

I grinned at her, taking the bottle from her hand.

The '90s jams flowed through the stereo's speakers.

*"Can't explain why your lovin' makes me weak . . ."* Chrystal sang along with SWV.

I looked at Chrystal, watching her eyes water. That song always made her cry. Made her think about the good times we had back in elementary school. As hard as that girl was, she was never afraid to shed a tear or two in front of me. I hated to see her cry. That shit always hurt me to my soul.

"So," she choked back the tears, "Mrs. Watson says I'm adopted, huh?"

I nodded. "Yeah."

Chrystal shook her head. "Why doesn't anyone love us, David?" she whispered.

"We love each other. That's really all we need," I whispered back.

Chrystal looked at me, her bright eyes sparkling.

"I bet you never thought your life would be like this." I looked around at all her lavish things, then back at her.

She sighed, dipping her apple in the fruit dip on her plate. "No. After Daddy died, after Mom was sent to live in the crazy house, and after you left me, I didn't *have* a life. Y'all were all I needed, and y'all were gone. I missed y'all. I did so much shit to try to forget you guys. I was in so much pain that I did anything I could to drown it out."

Chrystal looked at me, her brown eyes glistening. "You know I always wanted to be in the military. But my record was too fucked up to join, so here I am. I have a bachelor's degree in Business Administration, with a concentration in Management Information Systems, and I'm working on my master's degree. I just might take Tela up on her offer and have her cousin hook me up with a job at Northrop Grumman. Or I might leave this place. Go to Hollywood. I started taking a few acting classes too." She watched me smile. And she smiled back. "I have skills, boo."

"I don't doubt that you do. I've seen you act. You can be anything that you wanna be." I smiled, thinking about her performing on stage back in high school. She was pretty good. She always took the attention off everyone else on stage.

Chrystal watched me drink from her water bottle. "What about you? You are *so* not a teacher, Blue." She watched me laughing. "Seriously. Letta told me how those bitches be sweating you in class, drooling over your ass and shit. How could anyone concentrate on the lesson when they have to look at a face like yours? Sheesh. Teachers shouldn't be fine, Blue."

I laughed out loud. "Well, after that shit that happened this week, I'm pretty sure I won't have a job come Monday. Just watch. But I got you, so I'm cool. All I have to worry about is which one of my lawyer homies is gonna help me with this divorce. And don't look at me like that." I watched Chrystal shaking her head at me. "I tried to make it work with that girl. I gave her everything, and it was never enough. And now I know why. She was in love with that nigga, which is why she could never love me."

"You did the same to her too, boo." Chrystal turned toward me, curling up on her sofa.

I looked at her and handed the bottle of water back to her. "I gave her everything."

"Yeah, everything but your heart. Do you honestly think she didn't feel that shit, Blue? Your love is incredible. If she felt it, I guarantee, she wouldn't have continued a relationship with Kam. She only stopped dealing with him when she realized that he wouldn't change. But he *has* been funding her fashion shows," Chrystal let me know.

I looked at her. "What?"

"Yeah." Chrystal nodded, sipping her water.

Now I see why she never invited me to any of her events. I took a deep breath.

"Kylie sure played the fuck out'cha, nigga."

I tried not to get too upset about it.

"No, you just didn't care enough to pay her any attention. I can't even tell you how shocked I was to see you on Christmas Day. When Kylie introduced you as her husband, I damn near peed on myself," Chrystal exclaimed. "*My* Blue was married to Kylie Luckett? The girl who would do anything, or anyone, to make a name for herself? I bet'cha spent every penny you earned trying to make sure that girl lived and looked like Beyoncé, huh?" She watched me grin. "You always bend over backward for whoever you're with. That's just who you are. But maybe it's time you let someone take care of you, boo."

I looked at her. "Is that someone going to be you?"

Chrystal's eyes watered. "Blue, you don't want this. And I can't give you this. I don't want to be this person. The reputation that I have is going to take years to erase. You deserve so much better than me. You need a woman like—"

I cut her off. "Like you."

She shook her head, getting up from the sofa, and grabbed her plate of food. "No, David, not like me." Then she walked back into the kitchen.

I got up from the sofa, following behind her. "Chrystal, I still dream about you. I haven't been able to get your face out of my head."

She dumped the rest of her food into the trash can and then tossed the plate in the sink. Then she turned to me, tears in her eyes.

"I tried telling myself that I was a'ight without you. That I didn't need you. That maybe you didn't love a nigga anymore," I admitted to her. "You hid from me. Shawty, you ran from a nigga."

Chrystal shook her head. "Blue, I—"

"You thought I wouldn't love you anymore just because of how you decided to put food on your table?" I watched her look away from me. I grabbed her face, turning it toward me. "You thought that I would never look at you the same because you take off your clothes every night to take care of your family? To make sure my son and my grandmother live well?"

Tears slid down Chrystal's cheeks as I let go of her face.

"Why would you love me, David?" she whispered. "*I* don't even love myself."

"I love you enough for both of us," I told her as the grandfather clock in the corner of her living room chimed.

Chrystal looked up at me. "It's midnight . . . Happy New Year, Blue . . . My Blue." She cried. "Oh my goodness, I'm *so* glad you're back. I missed you so much."

I grabbed her close, holding her up against my chest, listening to her cry out loud in my ear. It was the first time I'd held that girl after eight years. I can't tell you how good it felt. There were no words to describe the feeling I felt, holding her and having her hold me back. Smelling her hair, feeling her heart beating against mine, listening to her cry—it all felt amazing beyond words. There was so much that I wanted to say to her. We'd been apart for so long, but our past felt like yesterday.

"Please, don't leave me again," Chrystal cried out, looking up into my face. "You promise me that you'll *never* leave me again. You're my best friend. I don't care who you decide to be with. I just know that life without you isn't worth a damn thing."

I had almost forgotten about the bracelet that I had bought her from the mall the day after Christmas. It wasn't much, but it was pretty, and when I saw it, I thought of her. It was a silver bracelet with tiny, rich violet-blue tanzanite stones wrapped around it. I let go of Chrystal, digging into my pocket for the velvet box. Chrystal didn't even look down at the box. She just continued to look up into my face as I opened the box and removed the bracelet from it. I grabbed her wrist and latched the bracelet around it. She still hadn't looked down at it.

"It's beautiful . . ." she whispered, still looking up at me. I grinned. She was my homie. Nothing mattered to her at that moment. All she wanted to know was if I would ever leave her again. All she wanted was my word that our paths would never split again.

"I'm here, Chrystal. I'm not going anywhere. I promise." I pulled her closer to me by the wrist that didn't contain the bracelet.

Finally, she looked down at her bracelet, a slight grin forming across her face. Then she looked back up at me.

I shook my head. "I know you're used to so much more. Go ahead and laugh."

Chrystal shook her head. "This bracelet is worth more than every piece of jewelry that I have." She looked down at the wedding band on my finger and then back up into my face. "Are you really ready to take off that ring?"

I didn't even realize that I still wore the shit.

"Fuck this ring. I can't pretend like I don't need you anymore. I don't think we were given a fair chance, shawty. But God has plans for us." I slid off the ring and tossed it into the trash can.

Chrystal looked up at me as I grabbed her by her waist, pulling her body up against mine. And I kissed her lips. I took those lips. Didn't even give baby girl a chance to say no. Shawty cried, kissing me back. Kissing her felt something like . . . like the puzzle piece that I've been searching for all of my life.

"I thought about kissing you today. And yesterday. Shit, the day before that too." I kissed her lips. "*And* the past twenty-five years of my life."

Chrystal cried out loud, pulling her lips from mine. She pushed me away from her, walking past me. "David, we can't do this. Shouldn't be kissing, hugging—none of this."

"My biggest mistake is *not* kissing you when I had the chance, Chrystal." I grabbed her arm, pulling her back to me. She still had a hard time believing that, after all she'd done, I still loved her.

Chrystal cried, shaking her head at me. "You were so ashamed of me. I saw the look on your face at the masquerade party and the club the other night. Not to mention, when you called me out over Christmas dinner."

I shook my head at her. "If you thought I was judging you, I wasn't. You were just doing what you thought that you had to do, shawty. I'll admit, it was hard knowing that the girl who was meant for me was out here, doing the unthinkable with niggas who couldn't care less about her. Yeah, a nigga is mad about the way you chose to live your life, but I'm back now. I'm here now. And I'm not going anywhere. I swear, I'll do whatever it is that I have to do to make up for the time I missed out on. We have so much catching up to do, baby."

Chrystal dried her tears, but it didn't even matter because the tears just kept coming. "We need to just concentrate on being friends again. That's all I need, David."

"Since the day I saw you at my house on Christmas, all I could think about were three things—seeing you again, hugging you, and kissing you. Chrystal, I love every part of you, even the part you gave away at that club." As I watched Chrystal crying, I grabbed her closer to me and dried her face. "Chrystal, I don't wanna be your friend anymore. We've always been so much more than that. Chrystal, I love you. You know I love you, don't you?"

She looked up at me, her lips trembling.

"I can't take away what happened to you when I wasn't around, but I can tell you that the shit will never happen again. And the muthafuckas who violated haven't gotten away with shit. A nigga is about to fuck up some shit, starting in Greenville." I let go of Chrystal, walking past her.

"Where are you going?" She followed me into the living room.

I grabbed my coat. "I have a lot to think about, shawty."

"Yeah." She nodded at me as I turned around to face her, putting on my coat. "You do. Whatever plans you have, whatever you decide to do, I hope I'm somewhere included in there. Just a thought. But you know I've always been a dreamer."

I grinned at her as she came up to me, putting her hands on my face. "Shawty, you *are* my plan."

And she kissed me. "I've always loved you, David. I'm so glad you're back."


My head was spinning that night as I drove back to my house in the city. Everything felt like it was closing in on me. In just seven days, my life had changed. I loved Chrystal. Yet, I couldn't help but think that I was endangering her life more by being in it than I was when we were apart. Kylie was going to make her life hell, on top of the pain that Kam was about to bring.

I don't know why I even expected to see Kylie when I got home that night. I returned to an empty house. The house was spotless, like she hadn't been there all day. I needed to talk to her, find out where her head was. She'd taken off her wedding ring, something she'd been wearing for three years. She said she was kickin' it with her girls, yet she was with Kam. On New Year's Day, our anniversary, Kylie was somewhere with Kam, letting the nigga bust her shit wide the fuck open. And there I was, leaning against the counter, trying to decide whether to pack my shit and head to a hotel for the night. I brought in the New Year with my shawty, Chrystal, so I guess that's how I was going to spend the rest of my year.

Trust and believe that I wanted to fuck the lining out of Chrystal's pussy that night at her place, but first, I wanted to set the record straight with Kylie about where we stood in our relationship. Yeah, she'd made it clear that it was over, but not clear enough. She was avoiding my calls, probably knowing I saw her ass on gotdamn television with her nigga.

I pressed play on our answering machine that sat on our countertop beside the refrigerator. I think we were the only people I knew who still had a house phone. Shit, the cable bundle was cheaper with the phone than it was for just cable and internet, so that's why we had the shit. When I didn't want muthafuckas having my cell number, I gave them my house phone number. My students had my house phone number and called the bitch all day. Many of Kylie's friends in the fashion industry also called that number. But that night, when I played the messages back, I heard some shit that I really didn't want to hear.

"Hello, Mrs. Luckett, this is Doctor Stem calling from Hillcrest Clinic." The voice message played over the answering machine.

My soul became immediately agitated. A few months ago, one of my students missed a week in class. When she finally showed up at my office, she informed me that she was taking some time off from school. She couldn't live with herself after what she'd done to her baby. She said that after she found out she was three weeks pregnant by a man married to her aunt, she made a trip to Hillcrest Clinic, an abortion clinic in Baltimore County.

"Your follow-up appointment has been rescheduled for January 15th. If you have any questions, please give me a call at . . ." I immediately pressed end. I didn't want to hear that bullshit.

# Chapter Seven

## *Shit Just Got Real*

## *Chrystal*

"I can't believe my bitch, Justice, is muthafuckin' engaged." Letta toasted Robyn the following afternoon at Fancy's studio apartment in Columbia. She had a delicious prepared lunch for us. That girl could cook her ass off. She made the kind of food Grandma used to make. I'm talking bread from scratch. My homegirl *never* bought processed food. This bitch could make her own gotdamn noodles.

"Don't forget pregnant. Let that sexy-ass nigga knock her the fuck up too." Our girl Pookie grabbed Robyn's hand, admiring (not hating on) her fancy pink cushion-cut and wide-split shank engagement ring, set in 18-karat white gold. Oh, it was beautiful. And I was so happy for my boo.

Robyn was so happy that she was crying happy tears. "I's gettin' married now, bitches," she cried out, laughing at the same time.

We—me, Robyn, Letta, Fancy, and Pookie—sat around Fancy's beautiful dining room table that afternoon, smacking on chicken of all sorts, homemade biscuits, mac and cheese, pasta salad, shrimp, cakes, pies, and some of everything else. Pookie had just come back in town after being away for nearly three months. She was a dancer and spent most of her time on the road. She was Kam's sister; he didn't play about her. He'd be pissed if he knew she was hanging with us. She was nothing like that fucker and disassociated herself from her family once she entered into the industry. Changed her name from Candace Price to her stage name, Pookie. And Pookie was straight hood. She would tell you about yourself in a minute. And I loved her.

"I *knew* you and Darius were serious. That boy worships the ground that you walk on, Robyn. You weren't fooling anyone." I rolled my eyes. "But I'm happy for you. No one deserves this more than you, boo."

Robyn blew me a kiss.

I blew her one back.

"What made you say yes?" Letta wanted to know. "I mean, come on. Y'all are *nothing* alike—have nothing in common but college. He dresses like a cross between Mr. Rogers and Kanye West, and you dress like Marilyn Monroe if she worked at the Player's Club."

"He—" Robyn hesitated. "He is nothing like the other men who have been in my life, and that's why I love him. He curses me out when I need it. And he loves me even when I'm a bitch. He couldn't stop me from grinding at the club, so he made sure that he was there every night, taking up all of my time so that I would have no choice but to sleep with him and only him. He made me love him. But best of all, he talked my children's adoptive parents into bringing my kids back stateside this year."

We all looked at her.

Robyn nodded. "Come April, my kids' adoptive parents will be stationed at Andrews Air Force Base. I haven't seen my babies in years, y'all, and Darius brought them back to me."

I think all of us shed a few tears that morning listening to Robyn tell us how much of a hero Darius had been in her life. He was corny as hell, but he was cute. He had a little style to him, and I should have figured it was because he hung around Blue. Blue rocked Jordans with everything and kept a Rolex on his wrist, and Darius did the same. Who would have ever thought that my best friend was marrying the best friend of the man of my dreams?

"Enough about me." Robyn dried her tears. "What about you, Rain?"

"What *about* me?" I took a bite out of Fancy's fluffy, flaky, buttery, make-you-wanna-slap-yo-mama-and-*her*-mama biscuits.

"Girl, yo' ass went home with Blue last night. Did he fuck the curls out of your hair, girl? Did Blue rock his bae into the new year?" Robyn grinned.

Letta looked at me, pursing her lips, watching me shake my head. "You let my professor put his dick up in the stomach, didn't you? I ought'a kick your ass, bitch."

I laughed out loud. "Letta, shut up, and, Robyn, no, we didn't have sex. After that shit he saw on the news, the only thing on that boy's mind is probably applying for divorce. Kylie's bitch ass deserved no part of my bae, for real. How did she even get him?"

"Well," Pookie smacked her lips, "I heard that David got her pregnant three years ago, which is what made him propose to her. The bitch claimed she had a miscarriage a few days after the wedding, but I think she did it to trap him. You already know she only said yes to the nigga to try to make Kam jealous. David is sexy as fuck. Who in their right mind would turn down a marriage proposal from him? If that nigga came in the door right now and said, 'Jump on this dick,' shiddddd, I'd do summersaults on that bitch."

My girls were dying laughing.

"Girl, whateva. Kam would kill your ass if you stepped foot near the nigga who stole his girl." Robyn laughed, taking a bite out of her slice of lemon cake.

"Shit, it would be worth it. I'm sorry, Rain, but that nigga could get it in any hole of his choice if he wanted it." Pookie high-fived Letta's nasty ass.

"Y'all are all types of wrong." I shook my head at the four of them, dying laughing.

"I think David is happy about seeing his wife on TV, kissing another nigga." Robyn shrugged.

"Why would you say that? He invested seven years into that bitch. Giving her everything her bitch ass didn't even deserve. He could've given that shit to me." Letta rolled her eyes. "Shit."

Robyn glanced at me. "This is his way out of a marriage that he knew he had no business being in. This gives him the opportunity to make things right with his girl, Chrystal."

I rolled my eyes, my heart fluttering in my chest at the thought of actually being able to be with Blue.

"The look on that nigga's face when he snatched your ass up behind that bar, though . . . I seen that shit from across the bar last night." Letta laughed. "He acts like your brother, being so overprotective. At the same time, he acts like an ex-boyfriend who came to get his girl back. I love it, I swear."

"You can't tell me that you're not happy that you finally found your boo. The boo you were too ashamed to talk about." Robyn shook her head at me. "That nigga goes hard for you, Chrystal. I've only met him a few times, but I could tell he wasn't happy. A part of him was missing. And I know he feels so much better now that he's found it."

I looked at my boo. She always had a way with words. Always kept tears in my eyes. I shook my head. "I can't give him this, y'all. I could have had sex with that boy last night if I wanted. He grabbed me, kissed me, and cried with me. And all I wanted was for him to promise me that he wouldn't leave me again. I can't be his girlfriend, his wife, his everything."

"Bitch, *what?*" Letta squealed. "I will beat what little black you have in you *off* your ass! Are you crazy? Like Pookie said, that nigga says, 'Jump,' you say, 'How muthafuckin' high?' That nigga said, 'Let's ride,' you say, 'Which .38 you need me to bring?'"

Letta's ass was crazy.

"I love him, but . . . I'm just ashamed of who I am. And y'all know Kam isn't gonna let him have me easily. I owe him so much money, and I'm not about to let Blue endanger his life trying to pay back that money. Blue has always been down to ride for me. I made that boy crazy. He used to be so shy and quiet before me and my cousins got a hold of him. And the rest is history. Now, even if he is a frontin'-ass college professor, he's a thug at heart. I want him, but we are far from ever being a couple," I sighed.

"Y'all niggas have a gotdamn child together. Shit, y'all *been* a gotdamn couple. And Kylie's ass *been* irrelevant, if you ask me. Privileged, stuck-up-ass muthafucka. I hate that bitch." Robyn rolled her eyes.

"So, I'm guessing that the professor gave you that cute little bracelet on your wrist, huh?" Letta teased.

Robyn looked at Letta like she had lost her mind. "Cute little bracelet? Bitch, you already know that to her, that 'cute little bracelet' is just as valuable as the engagement ring on my finger. Y'all gold-digging hoes have *no* class. I think it's beautiful. I'd rock the fuck out of it too."

My phone chimed next to my plate on the table. I picked it up and looked at the display. I had gotten a text. I pressed the text icon, seeing that I had a text from a number that I didn't recognize. I exhaled before pressing the icon to read the text in its entirety.

"Shawty, wanna chill with me?" it said.

I grinned, already knowing the text was from Blue. I started texting him back.

"The fuck you grinning so hard for?" Fancy asked.

I rolled my eyes, then sent my text. "Blue, is that you, boo?"

In seconds, he texted, "It ain't your nigga, Quincy."

I rolled my eyes, texting, "Whateva, fool."

In seconds, he texted, "I miss you."

My heart pounded. "I miss you too, love." I texted back.

"Then come to me. Let's chill. Meet me at the Baltimore Marriott. I left a key for you at the front desk," Blue texted.

I bit my lip, hesitating before texting back. "I'm on my way."

"Uh-oh, I know that face." Robyn grinned, watching me grip my phone in my hands. "What does ya nigga want?"

I sighed. "For me to meet him."

"Then go, shit." Robyn rolled her eyes. "We hang out every damn day. It's not every day that the man who assaults cops for you wants to meet up wit'cha."

They all grinned at me, watching me get up from the table and grab my coat from the back of my chair. I slid my arms into it and pulled my hair from my coat, throwing it over my shoulder.

"I hope you have on your cute panties today and not none of them granny panties you think are so comfortable." Letta laughed out loud as I pushed her on her shoulder.

"Shut up, bitch. Do I look okay?" I asked all of them as I zipped my coat. "I really wasn't prepared to meet this man today."

I was wearing a tight gray Hollister T-shirt, skinny Hollister jeans, gray knee-high socks, and knee-high Tims. I was dressed to kick it with my girls, not be around a nigga as fine as Blue.

"Girl, when *aren't* you cute? Not too many girls can look like a *Cover Girl* model wearing only mascara and lip gloss. Get'cha ass outta here, Mrs. Jacobs-in-the-making." Fancy blew me a kiss.

I walked into Blue's deluxe, oversized hotel room that New Year's afternoon, around 1:30. "Blue?" I called out, closing the door behind me. I walked through the hotel room to see Blue sitting in a chair near the window, looking over the Inner Harbor.

He was dressed in a wife-beater and baggy black sweats. Blue had a small frame, but he was always muscular and sexy as fuck. Talking about my tattoos, it looked like he had about just as many as me. He looked up at me, exhaling smoke from his nose.

I grinned, walking toward him as he stood from the chair. I walked into his arms, and he grabbed my face, kissing me, exhaling smoke into my mouth. I inhaled as his lips released mine. I grinned, exhaling the smoke through my nose.

Then I shook my head at him. "Still smoking that medicinal shit, huh?"

Blue nodded, exhaling smoke through his mouth and nose. "Migraines have gotten so much worse than they were when we were teenagers. A nigga can barely sleep."

"I understand, but this is a nonsmoking room, bae." I told him.

Blue shrugged. "So? What's your point?"

"I see you're still part of the 'no-fucks-given' squad." I shook my head, going over to the desk in the room.

Blue exhaled smoke through his nostrils. "Yeah, the same exact squad *your* moody ass is on."

I removed my jacket, hanging it over the back of the chair. Then I saw all the bags and suitcases in the room. I turned around and faced Blue, who then stood, leaning back against the wall, looking over my body a little before focusing back on my face.

"So, I'm guessing you talked with Kylie? I see you have all your bags and stuff here wit'cha. You gotcha laptop, and it looks like some of your students' work piled over there on the desk." I looked around the room and then at the nonchalant look on his face.

"Nah." Blue took a puff from his joint. He held it for a few seconds before exhaling. "Shawty didn't come home last night. I left as soon as I heard some bullshit left on my answering machine."

"What bullshit?" I sat down on the leather bench that stood at the foot of the bed.

Blue came over and sat beside me, the ashtray and half of his joint in his hands. He put out the joint and set the ashtray on the floor. He was quiet for a few minutes. I watched his temples twitch as he turned to me, grabbing me to him by my calves. I watched him start to untie my boots, then loosen the laces, one boot at a time, before unzipping them and then sliding them from my feet. He looked in my face as he slid both knee-high socks from my feet. I'm glad I had my toes done because I was *so* not used to a nigga wanting to see my feet.

"Bae?" I giggled, looking into that intense stare on his face. "What did the message say?"

"Shawty had an abortion," Blue said, his eyes watering a little.

My eyes widened. "Bae, she got rid of the baby?" I exclaimed. "Are you serious?"

"The message said that they were rescheduling her follow-up appointment. I went through the house, looking for her gotdamn planner, which she writes everything in. I found it in one of her Coach purses. And sure enough, on December 28th, shawty had an abortion scheduled. She did this to hurt me or any part of me, Chrystal." He shook his head.

"Blue," I sighed as he grabbed me from behind my knees, pulling my body onto his lap, surrounding me in his arms. "Baby, I'm sorry."

"She didn't have to kill the baby. Why would she do that shit? If she wanted to leave me, fine, she could've done that. But all Kylie's ever talked about was having kids. I'm not gonna lie; shawty was pregnant twice but lost both of them." Blue looked into my face, his hands gripping my waist. "After we lost the second one, we gave up. When she told me that she was pregnant with this one, I couldn't even be happy for her. Not only because I had run back into you, but also because we'd already lost two. I never talk about it. I knew shawty and I weren't meant to be together, and I guess God knew too. Why else would he allow her to lose two babies by me? This one makes three, shawty. A nigga could have had *four* kids. I would have loved them all, Chrystal. What would make her kill a baby?" Blue's eyes glistened.

He was really upset.

"Being with that girl has always felt like moving mountains. Everything was so gotdamn difficult. I put my all into that relationship. Yeah, I was in love with you, but I swear, I tried my damnedest to move on and make shit work with her. And all because she found out that I had a child with you, she wanted to kill the one I had with her? I know I didn't love that girl like she wanted to be loved, but I didn't want it to end like this. Not like this, Chrystal. Shawty won't even answer my calls. We're fuckin' grown as a muthafucka. You can't just ignore a nigga and expect the problem to go away. That's bullshit." Blue watched me take my phone out of my pocket and play some slow jams on Pandora. He watched me set the phone down on the stool next to us.

"Nice & Slow" by my boy Usher (like for real, I know the dude) played over my phone's speakers.

Blue looked into my face, a slight grin forming on his lips. On February 14, 2004, my father threw a Valentine's Day party for me. My little boyfriend at the time was Edward Cruise. The entire dance, he stood up against the wall and refused to dance with me. I'll never forget, when "Nice & Slow" came on, I was standing alongside the wall with Edward, pissed more than a muthafucka that he wouldn't dance with me. Blue made his way over to me, mugging the shit out of my boyfriend, before grabbing me by the hand, pulling me from the wall, and taking me out to the dance floor. There wasn't anything he wouldn't do to keep a smile on my face. I swear, that boy knew the lyrics to my heart.

I slid off Blue's lap and stood before him, reaching for his hands, pulling him up with me. Then I pulled his body up against mine as I looked into his face. I couldn't let him sit there and be upset with what Kylie had done. I knew he needed to talk, and I was there to listen, but at that moment, I had to say what I had to say to him, and I needed his undivided attention.

"I have done a lot of things that I'm not proud of, Blue. Some I remember, some I don't because I was faded at the time. I had a choice; I could have walked away from it all, but I didn't. Life without you or my parents has been tough. I hated you for years because of what Larry and some of your crew did to me." I looked up into his face.

"Shawty, I'm already on it. I'm already taking care of that shit, trust me," Blue assured me. "I made a few phone calls to a few of my homies that lived out in Raleigh. You remember Xavier and Dillon? You know them muthafuckas stay ready to rob a nigga. I sure hope Uncle Larry had insurance on his shit. And I hope his ass stays strapped because when he least expects it, we gonna get his ass."

I shook my head at him. "See, that's what I'm talking about. I don't want you risking your life to save mine, Blue. I am knee-deep in shit, and I don't want you involved. Let me handle Kam. And forget about Larry."

Blue shook his head. "Nah, they both did this shit to you because of me. Kam is feeling some type of way about me because he thinks I stepped in on Kylie. He knew about us. You said so yourself. You are *my* responsibility. You're my life, my heart. Without you, there has never been a me, Chrystal. We're in this shit together, no matter how crazy it gets."

"Kam's ass is fuckin' crazy," I whispered to him as he pulled me closer by my belt loops. "And so is Larry. Just leave it alone. Your ass needs to concentrate on teaching. From what I hear, you're good at it. Stay out of trouble, like you've been doing. These niggas are crazy out here, for real."

Blue made a face like I must've forgotten how crazy that *he* was. "Man, a nigga ain't never ran from a mutha-fucka, and I *damn* sure ain't about to pick today to start running. I got something for you, though."

Blue walked over to the desk where all his paperwork sat and picked up a set of about five or six DVDs. Then he walked back over to me, giving them to me.

I looked down at them and then back at him. "What are these?"

Blue's eyes searched my face. "Something we're both gonna need, real talk. I have the originals in the trunk of my car, tucked in the flooring, right behind the rear left light. Make copies of these whenever you can. Give copies to your girls. If you ever end up in court in Anne Arundel County, PG County, Howard, Baltimore City, *or* Baltimore County, tell your girls to give this shit to your lawyer. And if something happens to me, you're going to need them to give these to mine too, a'ight? Just trust me on this."

I nodded. I wasn't sure what he had on those DVDs, but I knew he wouldn't have told me that I needed them if I didn't. I went over and set them on the chair where my jacket hung. My heart nearly stopped when Toni Braxton's "Unbreak My Heart" flowed through my cellphone speakers.

*"Unbreak my heart. Say you'll love me again. Undo this hurt you caused when you walked out the door and walked out of my life . . ."* I sang before it even got to that part in the song. I turned around, facing Blue, who was already coming out of his tank top.

"I played this song over and over the night you left me in Greenville," I told him as I turned around to close the curtains to both windows. *"Un-cry these tears. I've cried so many nights . . ."* I whispered to myself, turning back around to face him.

Blue glanced at me before grabbing my phone from the stool, changing the song. I guess he was already depressed enough and didn't want to hear anything that was going to make either of us feel worse than we'd already felt at that moment. And when he changed the station, my song "Roni" by Bobby Brown flowed through the speakers.

Both of us looked at each other and then laughed out loud. My parents used to love this song. They would play it until the neighbors got tired of hearing it. Blue and I would be so happy watching my parents laugh, sing, and dance to this song.

I walked back over to Blue, watching him bobbing his head to the song. I knew he was about to sing a lyric or two to make me smile.

*"The truth about a Chrystal, she's a sweet little girl. You treat her right, real nice and hold her tight."* Blue smiled at me, watching me giggling at him replacing "Roni" with my name.

I looked up at his face, tears immediately sliding down my cheeks, remembering all the times we stayed up at night in the tree house that my dad built for me in the big tree in my backyard. Whenever Blue would get into those deep depressions where he'd think about his mother and why she left him, I'd sing Roni to him. I don't know, but it always seemed to cheer him up. Always made him smile. Always seemed to calm his soul.

Blue pulled me close. "Let's be clear here so there's no misunderstanding between us; you are sexy as a mutha-fucka. I loved seeing you dance out there on the floor of that masquerade party. What hurt a nigga is the fact that you were dancing for a room full of hundreds of people."

I looked up at him, loving the way that he was gripping my waist.

"You can dance, but when you dance, I want it to be just for me, ya hear me? *Just* for me, no other nigga. A'ight?" He unbuckled my jeans. "These lips are for me. This tongue is for me. These hands are for me. This pussy is for me. *You* are for me, Chrystal. Are we clear on that?"

I nodded, looking up into his face.

"Good. Now, take off this shit." He slid my jeans over my hips a little.

I slipped my shirt over my head, tossing it on the floor, alongside his shirt. I backed away from Blue, turning away from him toward the leather bench, pushing my jeans over my hips, sliding my pants down, bending all the way over, my knees touching my elbows. I had on the cute panties that I'd brought the day after Christmas from Hollister's, thank goodness.

"Clap that booty for me," Blue whispered, smacking me on my butt.

*"My heart belongs to tender Roni . . . She's my only love . . ."* Bobby Brown's voice serenaded my soul that afternoon. Stepping out of the clothes while still managing to dance sexy to the music became an art. I slid off my panties, clapping my ass cheeks together as I slid the panties down my legs.

"Pop that pussy for me again," Blue asked, smacking my ass again before gripping it in his hands. "That juicy pussy looks so pretty."

My heart pounded in my chest as I squeezed my pussy closed and popped it back open again and again and again. It took a lot of practice to develop those strong, tight Kegel muscles that I have. I used toys on stage and even in the Champagne Room for the perverts. I could insert only the head of a dildo into my vagina, and my vagina would suck the entire thing slowly in. And I could push it slowly out. Those perverts got a kick out of it. They would even lick the pussy juices off of it.

I looked back over my shoulder, watching Blue tilting his head to the side a little. He gripped my left booty cheek, spreading it a little, watching me pop my pussy. And with his other hand, he slid his fingers to my opening. I let out a sigh as he slipped a finger inside of me, then another, and another. My pussy walls clamped around his fingers. He didn't have to do a damn thing if he didn't want to. I pulled his fingers inside of me and pumped them out.

Blue laughed a little. "Oh shit," he whispered, watching my pussy do the work. He began to twist and turn his fingers, pressing them against my G-spot. Shit, my A-spot, B-spot, C-spot too. He kneaded and churned the walls of my pussy while my muscles constricted and contracted around his fingers. I hadn't been touched like that *ever*. Everyone I'd had sex with was all about *their* needs and not about satisfying mine at all. The few times that I did have sex with Quincy, he acted like he was scared. Or maybe he was just disgusted with me after the things that he'd seen me do on stage.

I moaned, grabbing my ankles, enjoying the stroke of my bae's fingers. I peeped him sliding down his pants with his free hand. His pants dropped to his ankles. Then he kicked them off.

When I felt his fingers begin to slide out of me, my pussy grabbed on to his fingers, locking them inside.

"Shawty, let 'em go." He laughed a little, rubbing my pussy with his other hand. "You are tight as a mutha-fucka, gotdamn!"

Just when I contracted my pussy muscles to let his fingers go, I heard what sounded like a package tearing open. I looked over my shoulder to see Blue biting open the gold wrapper to a Magnum condom. I immediately stood up, turned around, and faced him, taking the condom from his hand.

He looked down into my face as he slid his boxers over his hips, letting them drop down to the floor. Then he grinned because he knew I wanted to see what it had transformed into over the years.

I followed from his bright blue eyes to his eyes lingering until I got to that long, thick-ass polo sausage that hung between his legs. It was at least eight inches, and he wasn't even fully erect. I sighed as he kicked off his boxers. I had to calm my nerves. My pussy tended to contract on its own as soon as anything slipped inside it. It was to the point where putting in a tampon or removing the bitch was painful. I wasn't joking when I told Blue I'd only fucked with the niggas with the smallest dicks. Outside of Jimmy jamming it down my throat that time and the few times where arrogant muthafuckas would take advantage of my profession, I hadn't had a dick in me that was bigger than Blue's. I hated sex and anything to do with it, as crazy as that sounded. The people who wanted me were the ones whose wives didn't want them. Or men who could barely get it up, from the ones at the club to the ones who raped me in that tiny one-bedroom apartment in Yonkers.

I liked to be in control. I couldn't lose control, not even with Blue—*especially* not with Blue. He hadn't seen, touched, or heard from me in years. He was about to put it on me, I knew he was.

"Sit down," I told him.

Blue laughed a little before sitting down on the stool. I think he was just as nervous as I was, but he tried playing it off. I'm pretty sure he'd heard about me. I'm sure he'd heard that I could suck a dick until a nigga's legs went numb. And if he hadn't heard, he was sure as hell about to find out. And my song was playing too. Hell yeah, I was about to suck the skin off of that dick.

"*But you can't stop there . . . The music still playing in the background. And you're almost there . . . You can do it, I believe in you, baby . . .*" Kelly Rowland sang through my phone's speakers as I danced slowly, unhooking my bra, slipping it from my arms.

Blue looked up into my face as he leaned back, his elbows resting on the foot of the bed. I grabbed his knees, spreading his legs so that I could kneel between them. I gently caressed his inner thighs. He was pretty calm until I put my lips on the inside of his left thigh and slid one hand from his knees to his scrotum and wrapped my other hand around his dick. He quickly sat up straight, one hand caressing my shoulder and the other hand running up the nape of my neck and into my hair.

"Shit," Blue whispered, twirling my hair until he got it to twist into a bun.

I giggled a little, aroused at him tugging on my hair the way that he was. I kissed the head of his now fully erect penis before sliding my lips on it a little, just to get a little taste of him while giving *him* just a little taste of what my lips would feel like. I licked his dick up and down and around it, using broad strokes and as much saliva as I could muster. I gave the dick a few flicks of my tongue before gliding my tongue from the head until I got to his ball sack. By then, Blue was gripping the shit out of my hair as I pulled one of his balls into my mouth. He moaned as I caressed his testicles with my tongue and lips, gently applying pressure to his perineum with my fingers.

I worked my way back to the head of his penis, pulling it into my mouth, making sure to cover my teeth with my lips as I slid my way down his shaft, until my nose was tickled by the curly hairs surrounding his dick. And I worked my way back up, applying pressure against his dick with my tongue and lips. Over the years, I've learned to relax my gag reflex, so my head game was on point.

I popped my lips over the ridge of his dick, then gave Blue's penis a variety of kisses, strokes, licks, and flicks, performing each technique repeatedly before changing to the next, giving him constant pleasure. I moved my left hand up his shaft. I removed my lips briefly and used my palm to glide and twist over the head of his penis. Then I slid my hand back down and followed behind my wet lips. Oh, Blue was going crazy. He loosened his grip on my hair a little but gripped the shit out of my shoulders. I peeped up at him, watching him bite his lip to keep from screaming out.

"Hold up, hold up, shawty . . ." He tried to lift up and scoot back, but I pressed my elbows against his thighs, holding him down.

He started to release my hair and shoulder until my lips and tongue rapidly slipped up and down on the dick. His dick began throbbing in my mouth. He grabbed my hair and gripped my neck that time. "Shit . . ." He lifted up on his toes as I bobbed up and down on his dick until his toes curled.

Then I slowed down for a second, adding a little teeth to the action. I began to glide the surface of my teeth along his long shaft, trailing it with my tongue.

*"Let me lick you up and down, 'til you say stop . . ."* Silk's voice flowed through my phone, adding more fuel to the fire that I was trying my best to put on Blue.

I hummed the lyrics to the song as Blue began to thrust a little inside of my mouth. And I tugged lightly on his testicles.

"Awe, fuck . . ." His legs began to shake.

I sucked him deep into the back of my throat and slowed down my sucking rhythm as I felt several strong spurts shooting against my tongue, the roof of my mouth, and then down my throat.

Blue loosened his grip on my hair and neck and began to run his fingers through my hair as I flattened my tongue, sliding it over the underside of his penis. His body jerked as I pulled my lips from his dick, my tongue twirling around it on the way up.

Blue grabbed my face in his hands as I removed my lips from his dick, biting the head a little before releasing. Blue panted, looking down into my face. His temples twitched a little, and I already knew what he was thinking.

I looked up at the "This is the shit you learned from that club?" expression on his face. I sighed, watching him lift his leg up over me so that he could stand.

Then I watched him walk toward the bathroom, running his hands through his curly hair along the way. He was angry with me. It was going to take a lot of time for that man to be able to have sex with me without thinking about the shit I've done with other men.

I took a deep breath, getting up off my knees, and walking toward the bathroom. "Blue?" I called out to him, hearing a steady stream of what I knew was urine. He was using the bathroom when I pushed open the door.

He didn't look back at me, but I knew he felt my eyes tracing his profile. "What's up, shawty?"

I hesitated. "T-This is going to take some time, isn't it?"

He shook his dick a little bit before flushing the toilet, then looked at me as he went over to the sink to wash his hands. He just stared at me the way that he always did, as if he were fixing the words in his head so that they wouldn't come out wrong. "You can't put a price on what you just did to a nigga," Blue sighed, washing his hands.

I looked at him, watching him turn off the water before drying his hands.

"I mean, you sucked my whole dick into your mouth—damn near down your throat. You just sucked a nigga until he busted straight down your throat. And it only took you a few minutes, but it felt like forever. You did that shit so good that you made a nigga wanna tip you." Blue shook his head to himself, walking past me out of the bathroom.

I followed behind him.

Blue quickly turned around, pulling my body close to his. And he kissed my lips, sucking on them before he released my lips from his. He grabbed my face, his thumbs swiping across my lips as he looked into my eyes. "You're mine. And we belong together. The past is behind us, but I . . . I'm gonna need you to show a nigga everything you did in that club. Do it to me, every fuckin' night, and we'll be a'ight . . . A'ight?" He grinned, watching me trying my best not to cry.

I just wanted Blue to accept me. That's all I wanted. And he did.

He lifted me, wrapping my legs around his waist. "Let me just hold you for a few minutes before I dig in, a'ight?" He gently kissed my lips as I wrapped my arms around his shoulders, and he carried me to the bed. "Stop crying. I'm here. I'm not mad at'cha. It's in the past. Let's just concentrate on the here and now." He dried my tears. "I'm here." He carried me to the bed. Then he sat down on the edge of the bed, gripping my thighs in his warm hands.

I sighed, looking into that face of his that I missed oh so much. He grabbed the condom from the bench and removed it from the wrapper. I looked into his face as he put it on. "You're so beautiful, Blue, inside and most definitely outside. I missed your face so much." I held his face in my hands, kissing his lips. "I missed your lips. Oh, these taste and feel *so* good."

Blue kissed me back, sucking on my lips a little.

I looked down, watching him grab his dick. Dude wasn't playing any games. Foreplay, my ass, he might as well said. And I didn't even care. He slid the dick through my lips to the opening.

"Tell me how *this* feels." Blue pushed himself inside of me, through the tightness, through the resistance, and through the pain.

I squealed out as he put that dick into my stomach. "Oh my goodness! *Gotdamn it . . .*" I grabbed on tight, wrapping my arms around his shoulders. My heart slammed against my chest as he slid himself into me until his dick pressed against my cervix.

Blue laughed in my ear. I think the dude was actually happy that his girl's pussy was still tight after all the shit that I had done . . . That we still fit together, hand in glove. He was laughing, and I was crying. Not so much because it hurt, but because just being with him only reminded me of how much I missed him when he was away.

I unwrapped my arms from around him, holding his face instead. I looked down into his face as he held my thighs in his hands. He dried my tears, looking into my eyes. That dick filled my soul. I was almost scared to bounce on it, afraid that he would bounce back. I see why he said he just wanted to hold me for a little while. That dick was going to tear a hole straight through to my soul.

Why August Alsina's "Porn Star" had to come on, I don't know. That nigga's voice always did something to my soul. But then he had to sing to me while Blue was already up in my guts? OMG.

Blue grinned, grabbing my face, kissing me, already starting to grind his hips. "Don't get scared now. Grind with me. Take this dick in that pussy the way you took it in the mouth, Chrystal. Fuck me like you're trying to pay bills."

I shook my head, looking down into his face as he grabbed a hold of my waist, pumping a little harder, my pussy gripping the shit out of that monster. "You said you just wanted to hold me."

"I *am* holding you." He bit his lip. Oh, that bite. Sexy muthafucka. "I waited a long time for this moment, Chrystal. I'm tired of waiting. Work this dick like you work that pole, ma. C'mon, what'cha waiting for?"

I shook my head. I was really nervous, almost out of my mind. Sexual intimacy wasn't something that I'd had regularly. For the most part, I just gave head. I took drugs and stayed drunk to be able to function in that club. I don't remember the last time that I'd actually had sex while I was sober. I don't recall the last time I let someone kiss or touch me. Even when I had sex with Quincy, it was quick, and that was months ago. Robyn always teased me about putting it on the nigga, but I never really did. When it came to head, yeah, maybe, but when it came to my body, I was reluctant to give it. And Quincy always felt my unwillingness to give it my all, which made him behave the same way. I guess a part of me was always hoping Blue would return.

Blue shook his head. "Oh, you wanna play wit'cha boy, huh? A'ight . . . My turn." He gripped my waist, lifting me up, sliding me off his dick, and set me on the bed. Then he got up from the bed, facing me.

I looked up at him as he gripped my thighs, swiftly pulling my hips to the edge of the bed, causing me to fall backward on my back. Next, he stood between my legs. The bed was high off the ground, the perfect height for Blue to align himself with the opening to my soul. He gripped my legs, his hands wrapped around my knees, pulling my body up against his.

"Spread that pussy wide, baby; put those knees against your chest," he commanded, his blue eyes searching my body.

I put my knees to my chest . . . and gasped when he spread my knees apart. I watched as this dude eased himself into me as far as he could go. I screamed out as he dug in. I gripped the sheets in my hands as Blue pressed down on my thighs, gripping them tightly. This man began to stroke the shit out of me. Long, deep, slow strokes at first. He was looking down at his dick going in and out of the pussy, eying the diamond stud piercing the hood of my clit. There he went, biting that lip again. Just the look on his face had my pussy dripping like a leaky faucet.

There it was, the day of his anniversary, and here he was, with me. Kylie was going to call eventually. The bitch was already placing hell in motion. Blue was hurt, and he was trying not to think about it. With each stroke he gave me, I knew he regretted every stroke that he gave her. He sped up a little, his hands moving up behind my knees, and he gripped my legs in his hands, raising my booty off the edge of the bed. Then he wrapped my legs around his waist.

I squealed. "Hold up!" I tried to rise up, resting on my elbows, but Blue gripped my legs, pulling me farther off the edge of the bed, causing me to lose my balance and fall back onto the bed.

"Nah, I asked you to ride a nigga, but you wanted to play the hard way. So . . . let's play," he moaned, tapping that dick against my cervix.

I matched my breathing to his strokes, inhaling when he went in and exhaling when he came out. He pumped in and out of me at a moderate pace, but he still tapped against my cervix with every stroke. Butterflies, dragonflies, birds, *every* muthafuckin' creature with wings were flapping around in my stomach.

"Not a day goes by that I don't think about you, Chrystal," Blue told me. "Now that I got'cha back in my life, I swear you're not going anywhere."

My heart pounded in my chest as Blue began to pound into my soul. It felt like magic being with him. His stroke was hypnotizing. The steady, pulsating rhythm of his stroke was about to put me in a trance. He held my legs around his waist for a good five minutes before he let me back down and lay his body down between my legs, laying his warm body on top of mine. He held my body tight against his, pulling my body with his to the center of the bed, where he continued to rock my boat. Did he follow Aaliyah's advice and put that dick in overdrive? Yes—yes, he did. He worked my pussy so good that I think I actually blacked out for a few seconds.

The passion and energy that flowed throughout my body were overwhelming. Blue's body communicated with mine perfectly. Blue bit my ear, panting, moaning, growling even. His stroke triggered some of my deepest emotions. I could feel him throughout my breasts, my hands, my feet, my legs, my heart, my soul. The entire encounter felt like a screaming orgasm. He stroked fast, deep, and hard for a few minutes, then slowed his stroke to a slow, deep, and calm pace. It seemed as though with every stroke, involuntary muscle contractions rippled throughout my body. His touch, his stroke, his breathing, his technique, his very being stimulated the right nerves in just the right way. My soul was in love with his.

Blue held my body tight against his, one hand gripping my waist, the other wrapped around the back of my neck, cradling my head in his hand. He rolled over, lying on his back, and me lying on top of him. "Fuck me," he whispered in my ear, his hands sliding up my back.

I let out a sigh as Blue began to grind his hips, his dick thumping against the opening to my cervix again. I rose from his chest a little, resting my elbows above his head, my torso hovering over him. We locked lips for a few seconds as I began to wind my hips.

"Shit," Blue hissed in my ear as I started to pounce and bounce on the dick before locking my knees against his hips.

I straddled him, sitting up on it, leaning back. I rested my arms on his shins, still grinding with him.

Blue held my hips as he slid us both back on the bed so that he lay back against the fluffy pillows at the head of the bed. His eyes searched my body, dancing over every detail of the tattoos on my shoulders, breasts, stomach, and pelvis. He watched my hips grinding in a circle, giving his dick a little dance. I felt his dick sliding and gliding against all sides of my walls. I rocked back and forth. I felt him sliding his hands up my thighs until one of his thumbs found my clit. Then he began rubbing it in a circular motion.

"Blue!" I squealed.

The combination of Blue grinding with me and him stimulating my clit sent my hormones raging. I arched my back, his dick pressing against my G-spot. My body fed off his momentum. He pushed his pelvis up and toward me as I thrust down and back at him.

The feeling became too intense. I didn't want to come yet. I wanted to make it last. I pulled his shoulders toward me, so we were both upright. Then I wrapped my legs around him, molding his body into mine, slowing the tempo down just a little bit.

Blue shook his head before kissing me. "Nah," he moaned, gripping my waist in his moistened hands. "You tryin'a put a nigga on hold, Chrystal? I've been on hold for eight muthafuckin' years. Let this shit rip." Blue slid his arm around me, locking my body against his, switching positions.

There he was, back on top again. He didn't even give me the chance to brace myself for his impact. The signal went out on my phone, and the music stopped flowing through the speakers. The only sounds flowing through the room now were the sounds of our moans intertwining. I squealed in his ear as his dick swerved through my ridges. He dug into my body until I squirted, juices swirling down his thighs. Blue bit down on my neck as I dug my nails into his back.

"Yes, baby, work this pussy," I screamed out.

Blue growled in my ear as I grabbed his butt, clawing it with my nails. As he dug in deeper, my pussy clamped around his dick. Blue worked my body until my thighs burned and my calves went numb. He panted in my ear, and I screamed in his. He pumped until his body began to shake and shudder. I squealed and came just before he did. As soon as I came down from my climactic high, I started crying.

Blue sighed, kissing my neck, then my shoulders. "Ssshhhh," he whispered, breathing down my neck.

"Amazing. That was amazing," I cried.

"Hell yeah . . . Hold up; let me get my wallet. How much do I owe you?" Blue laughed, his face in my neck.

I grabbed his face, kissing his lips. "Shut up," I cried, laughing at the same time.


The sound of thunder and lightning woke me up from my sleep late that night. Blue and I had sex off and on for hours. We talked and laughed, ordered room service, and drank a little. We enjoyed each other's company, knowing it wouldn't be long before shit got hectic. There was a world that existed outside of ours that hated to see us together. It was his anniversary, and the only reason why he hadn't heard anything from Kylie was because of her fashion show. She had no idea that he knew about her getting the abortion, and I'm pretty sure he was bracing himself for the impact of their argument. She knew things with them were over from the moment she knew that we shared a child together. I had no idea what her plans were, but I did know that she played dirty. And from what I'd seen Kam do, he played even dirtier.

I was naked under the hotel sheets. I pushed my wild hair from my face to see Blue sitting in a chair, facing the window, watching the rain trickle down. A thick cloud of smoke floated around him. Ever since I could remember, Blue woke up from nightmares. I'm pretty sure over the years, his dreams grew even more frightening. He'd done a lot that he wasn't proud of. I think it was his guilt that kept him up at night. I'm sure Miss Tiffany murder didn't help much.

"What time is it?" I sat up, rubbing my eyes.

Blue looked back at me over his shoulder. "About 3:45, shawty."

"You okay, boo?" I asked, knowing that he wasn't.

He just sat there, exhaling smoke through his nose.

I reached for my bra and panties that were rolled up in the sheets. After sliding into them, I climbed out of bed and walked over to him. I slid my arms around his shoulders, and he kissed my arm as I kissed the back of his neck.

"I gotta jump back in the game again, shawty, after seven years. A nigga was a monster. I don't wanna go back to that, but I have to if I wanna pay this nigga back the money you owe. Not to mention, the nigga is feeling some type of way about me taking you—his money—from that club. Darius has been texting me, saying Kam's crew was parked outside of my crib, lookin' for a nigga." Blue looked up at me.

I looked at him as there was a light tapping at our room door, followed by what sounded like something sliding underneath it and into the room.

I slid my arms from around Blue as he got up and went to the door. He looked down at the floor and picked up what appeared to be an envelope. I walked over to him, watching him tear it open. His face started to twitch before I even looked at whatever it was that he was holding in his hands. I looked down to see a picture of Miss Tiffany lying in a pool of blood, bullet holes in her face and chest, and someone kneeling over her, his gun still aimed at her face. Though you couldn't see the assailant's face, you could see his hands. And tattooed on his hand were the words, "*Everything Has A Price—Kameron Price*." My eyes widened as I watched Blue crumble the pictures in his hands.

Damn, shit was about to get real, *real* fast.

# Chapter Eight

## *My Chick from the Island*

## *Blue*

*Washington, D.C., December 25, 2008*

"I don't get off until 6:00 in the morning, David. You've been gone all day, honey. I left your plate inside the stove. Did you get it?" Miss Tiffany called me from work as soon as the clock struck midnight, on my eighteenth birthday.

"Yeah, I got it, ma'am. And I tore it up too." I rubbed my stomach, holding the phone to my ear with my shoulder, standing over the bathroom sink, brushing my teeth. I hadn't made it in too long ago. I think we beat the block all muthafuckin' day that day. Shot up a few muthafuckas who posted up on our block, who forgot who was running things in Southeast.

"I'll be home in time to cook Christmas breakfast, hon." Miss Tiffany lived for Christmas Day. She always tried to make it special for both of us. She knew I missed Chrystal. She knew how much I was hurting without her. I was a hardheaded muthafucka, but Miss Tiffany never gave up on me. "And please remember to walk Man-Man. Every time we don't let him out, he chews at the front door. If

I see one more muthafuckin' teeth mark, I'ma kick that muthafucka's teeth down his throat. Yours too, David."

I laughed out loud. "*What?* What did *I* do?"

"You already know what I'm talkin' about, boy. Don't play. Don't let me come home to find any of those little hoes up in my house. Do you hear me?" Miss Tiffany snapped at me.

I smirked, damn near choking as I spit the toothpaste from my mouth. "Miss Tiff, come on."

"Don't 'come on' me, boy. I didn't bring you into this world, but I'll be damned if I don't take you the fuck out of it. I will beat ya little pink ass black and blue if I catch another li'l ho in your bed. You don't even know what to do with that thing you keep slingin' around," Miss Tiffany scoffed.

"Well, apparently I do if you keep finding hoes in my bed, Miss Tiffany. I'm just sayin'," I smirked.

Miss Tiffany would've slapped me in the mouth if she were in front of me. "Say something else, David, and I swear, I will knock the life out'cha ass."

I cleared my throat, laughter subsiding. "I'm sorry. I'm just playin'."

"That dick of yours is gonna be your downfall, David. Keep thinking everything is a gotdamn joke," Miss Tiffany tried to warn me. "And Mr. Abu said that you and your boys were posted up in front of his liquor store tonight."

I exhaled deeply, prepping myself for the lecture that I was about to get about hanging around with Tyrese and my crew from the hood. They stayed in some shit, always into it with street crews around the way. Whenever they needed my help putting niggas in the dirt, I was there. I had their back, and they sure as hell had mine. I had only been around my niggas for a little over a year, but I felt like I knew them forever. As soon as they knew I didn't hesitate to lay a muthafucka down for mine, they didn't hesitate to roll with me. We hung out all day, dropped out of school, and partied harder and longer than a muthafucka. Partying was how I met Kavante and Kameron. Before the cousins got hold of Club Pop It, Kavante's father, Tevin Price, owned it. It was called "Prices." And it was the liveliest spot in town. When he died, Kavante took over the club. And that was when all the trouble started.

"I told you about hanging around those little niggas, David. They are going to get you killed. I don't want to see my son on the news in some body bag." Miss Tiffany broke down and cried.

I sighed. "Come on, Miss Tiffany, don't cry. Nothing is gonna happen to me. I stay strapped. I stay ready to unload on these dudes." Flashbacks of the events that happened earlier yesterday in an alley behind the strip mall flashed through my mind. I couldn't even tell you how many niggas I left in blood that day. I didn't play about my family or about my money. I think a nigga averaged about $1,500 on a *bad* day. When I found out these niggas were stealing my clientele, posting up on my turf, me and my niggas rolled up on them. In those days, nobody snitched, so doing shit in broad daylight was nothing new. We protected our block, and the block protected us. Not to mention, my nigga, Reggie, had a few police officers on payroll. He was the whole reason I even knew Jimmy and Johnny, the crooked cops from around the way. I hated those muthfuckas, but I got away with so much shit at that age because I had so much dirt on those two that they wouldn't dare rat a nigga out.

"David, bullets don't have names on them. You're not invincible. If you live by the gun, trust me, David, you or someone you love is going to die by that muthafucka. You keep that in mind when you have those niggas posted up on *my* porch at all hours of the night while I'm at work. Mrs. Pearl next door told me that you had a party the other night. Had muthafuckas all outside, fuckin' on my front porch." Miss Tiffany went off.

"Miss Tiff, don't you have to get back to work? Your break is only fifteen—"

Miss Tiffany cut me the fuck off. "Boy, don't worry about how fuckin' long my break is. You heard what the fuck I said, David. Let me come home and find some niggas at my muthafuckin' house, and that's *your* muthafuckin' ass. It's bad enough you dropped out of school because of these niggas, but now I come to find out that you're hanging around the same people who were arrested for murder two weeks ago."

I sighed, setting the phone down so I could wash my face. She stayed going off on a nigga. The only reason why she hadn't put me out of the house was because she was scared to let a nigga go out in the world. Miss Tiffany loved me as if I were her own flesh and blood, and I never really understood that growing up. I did any and everything I could to test that woman's love for me. But no matter how hard I tried to push her away, she just wouldn't budge. She tried her best to keep me out of the streets, but every time the streets called my name, I was flying out that door.

After I washed my face, I picked up the phone again, and Miss Tiffany was *still* going off. She was the only person I knew who could argue with herself for hours. "I moved us here to get you out of trouble, David. But it's like you've only managed to get worse. You are a smart boy. You can be anything in life that you want to be, yet you choose to be a drug dealer, a killer, a—"

I shook my head, "Nah, I'm not a—"

"David, please, okay? You fuck up niggas. You must think that I forgot about the shit Reggie was into before he was killed. You didn't learn anything from what happened to him. You hang around Sister Josephine's son. That boy has gotten off on so many murder cases because they could never find the bodies to prove that he committed the crimes. As sneaky and as smart as you are, I'm sure *you* were the one who helped hide the bodies. You used to put those little niggas back in Greenville in comas. You can't tell me that you aren't involved in any of that shit that's been going down in South East. I found guns, knives, and shit in your room," Miss Tiffany exclaimed.

"You've been digging through my shit, Miss Tiffany?" I huffed.

"In *my* house, there is no gotdamn privacy. Damn right I looked through your shit. It's in my house, boy, so it's *my* shit. How do you think that stack of condoms got in your nightstand drawer? All those hoes that come over to the house, and you didn't have one gotdamn condom in that room. You need to be careful, David. I am so worried about you. You treat me like *I'm* the enemy when I am all you got, David. All you got," Miss Tiffany reminded me.

"I'm all you have too, Miss Tiffany," I reminded her.

Miss Tiffany was quiet for a minute or two before she said, "Then act like it, David. Chrystal wasn't the only person there for you; I have been here too. You're pissed at me for bringing you to D.C. and leaving her behind. She's not my daughter. I couldn't take her with me. I'm sorry that she ran off with some nigga and hasn't reached out to you. I'm sorry that you lost touch. Girls come and go, but you only get one mother, David. *One.*"

My temples twitched. I hadn't heard from shawty since around February, ten months earlier. We kept in touch for about six months after I moved to D.C. But then she stopped calling and stopped writing. No one knew where she disappeared to; that nigga she was with made sure of that. She sure knew how to pick 'em. "She's not just some girl to me, Miss Tiff. She was like . . . seeing my heart outside of my body."

Miss Tiffany sighed on the phone. "I know, honey. But you just need to face the fact that maybe she meant more to you than you did to her."

I shook my head, looking at my hurt reflection in the mirror. I didn't believe for one second that Chrystal didn't love me. I didn't know where that girl was back then, but every inch of my soul knew that wherever she was, she needed me like a muthafucka.

"I will be home around 6:30, David, and I expect you to be up, already starting breakfast. We have company coming over for lunch for your birthday, honey," Miss Tiffany told me, knowing good and well that I was going to be pissed.

I huffed. "Miss Tiff, nah, man."

"David, they're coming, and that's that. I don't have time to cook lunch, so some caterers are coming over. You know Mrs. Rogers and her daughters just opened that restaurant. They should arrive to get their money around 6:00 when they start making their morning bagel deliveries. I left the check that I wrote for them on the countertop, alongside the microwave." Miss Tiffany went on and on about her plans for that day with me.

I pretty much stopped listening when she mentioned Mrs. Rogers. I grew up with Mrs. Rogers's daughter, Niyah, up until they left Greenville when I was in the eighth grade. Mrs. Rogers's husband used to beat the shit out of her. She got tired of the nigga going upside her head and left the nigga in the middle of the night. She took her four girls with her and left her oldest three boys with their father. We had no idea that Mrs. Rogers had even moved to D.C. until Miss Tiffany got a call from her one day, telling her about a nursing position that was opening up at MedStar Washington Hospital. Niyah was happier than a muthafucka when Miss Tiffany pulled up outside of her front door the summer of 2007. I'll admit, I missed my baby, Chrystal, the moment that I left her, but seeing Niyah lifted my spirits a little.

Niyah was this sexy, deep chocolate girl from Trinidad. She had the prettiest smile and the thickest thighs. Her silky, jet-black hair grazed against her tapered waist. She was bad. That accent only added to her sex appeal. Everything she said sounded sexier than a muthafucka. And Chrystal couldn't stand her. And that was probably because the two were so much alike. I'm not even gonna lie. Niyah was feeling a nigga, but even though Chrystal and I were just friends in school, my heart was too emotionally invested in Chrystal to give it to anyone else. Regardless, Niyah was a ride-or-die chick for real. Anything I asked her to do, that girl did it. She sold drugs for a nigga, cooked pies for a nigga, transported for a nigga, fought bitches for a nigga, shot at muthafuckas for a nigga—all this before we even made it to high school. Her father was really ruthless and had the drug game on lock in Greenville. Greenville was literally Mr. Dean Rogers's neighborhood. Even after shawty and her mama moved to D.C., Mr. Rogers still had me and my boys working the block for him. I'm sure the nigga was hurt that his wife left him, but he never let that stop his hustle.

When we finally met up with Niyah and Mrs. Paulette Rogers, they were living it up in a cobblestone mansion in Georgetown. Turns out, Paulette got involved with another high roller, Reginald Sparks. This nigga had five boys—Bryson, Rico, Osias, Bates, and my nigga, Reggie. Reginald's wife died when she gave birth to Reggie. Reginald met Paulette one night when her car caught a flat tire. He always said that it was love at first sight with Paulette. Reginald came from a big family, so moving

Paulette and her four girls into his home only made him feel more secure. Paulette filed for divorce a year after leaving Maryland, and Dean didn't contest it. Dean lay low until he caught word that Paulette remarried and to a drug distributor who was much larger than him, who ran the police department as well as the judicial system.

Reginald was once a respected judge. He stepped down after being accused of taking bribes from drug dealers to have cases dismissed in court. He quit before he was fired or before an investigation was launched. After leaving the judicial system, he still had his connections with both the legal system and the streets. He was on top of the world—both worlds. Reginald thought he had it all. A beautiful wife, four beautiful daughters, five loyal sons, and a lucrative business. Little did he know that some five years later, Dean Rogers would send his oldest son to drive a wedge between the family. Reggie was killed that summer before I turned 18.

So, you're probably wondering why I never hooked up with Niyah. Well, the summer that we moved to D.C. in 2007, shawty was pregnant with her second child. Seventeen years old with two gotdamn kids. A 1-year-old and the baby in her belly. And guess who her baby's daddy was? Kavante Price. And Reginald Sparks hated the muthfucka and hated me just as much once he found out that I'd started hanging around him.

Kavante and Kam kept a nigga in some shit. They were two rich boys doing hood shit. Their family owned every gotdamn thing of any value in the state of Maryland. The cousins ran the hood because they could afford to. Reginald always told me to stay the fuck away from Kavante because he was trouble, but I wouldn't listen. The main reason why I even kicked it around the nigga was to keep an eye on Niyah. I was worried about her. She was a smart, beautiful girl, who let this nigga control her every move. Though shawty was into that street life, at least she was smart enough to graduate from high school on time. Her two babies sat on my lap, watching their mama walk across that stage to get her high school diploma. Me—not Kavante. The nigga wasn't shit. But she loved him, or so I thought anyway.

Niyah got tired of Reginald always being on her ass about Kavante and finally moved out of that big mansion in Georgetown that summer after graduation. She didn't want any help from her mother and definitely didn't want any help from Reginald, who was really only looking out for her best interests. She moved into a condo in Laurel with her girls and stayed away from her family until her mother contacted her around Thanksgiving time to let her know that she had opened up a restaurant in D.C. called "Reggie's" in honor of my nigga, her stepbrother.

"Oh, word? Niyah's coming by to get the check?" I asked. I hadn't seen shawty in a few months. She attended the University of Maryland. She still helped her nigga in the streets, but she was determined to keep her head in the books. One thing I could say about Kavante was that he may have had a temper on him, but he never cheated on that girl. He treated her like shit, but he wasn't cheating on her. Hoes were the least of her problems. Control was the issue she had with him.

It was funny because as soon as I mentioned homegirl's name, the doorbell rang.

"I'm not sure which one of the Rogers girls is coming over. Oh, I hear my supervisor around the corner. I gotta go, Blue. Just make sure you set your alarm, okay, baby? And Happy Birthday, baby." Miss Tiffany gave me a smooch on the phone. "I love you, Little Blue."

I grinned a little. "I love you too, Miss Tiff."

I pressed end on the phone before leaving the bathroom and walking down the hallway and down the steps toward the front door. Then the doorbell chimed again.

"Hold up, yo." I reached behind my back, placing my hand on the 4-five I had tucked in my sweats. "Who is it?" I asked, standing to the side of the door, about to peep through the blinds to see whose car was parked out front.

"Boy, open up. It's cold outchea." I heard Niyah's sweet voice through the door.

I grinned a little before opening the door to see Niyah's pretty face glowing underneath the porch light. I unlocked the screen door and let her in.

"Waz di scene, Blue?" She grinned at me, walking past me in her expensive black heels and trench coat. A trail of Juicy Couture perfume lingered behind her.

I looked her over as I locked the screen door and shut the front door behind her, locking it. "What's up, my little Island Girl? Long time, no see. How you been, shawty?" I watched her untie and then unbutton her trench coat.

She grinned. "You know I've been all school and no play. You need to get your head back in the books and stop playing in the streets too, boy."

When she took off her coat, yo, li'l mama had on this short, fitted cocktail dress that hugged her in all the right places. She didn't have to show any cleavage to be sexy. The dress had a boat neckline, and though the dress was short as fuck, it was still classy. Different patterns of beadwork and sequins made the dress fit for a Caribbean queen like her. The sleeves, back, and center of the dress were sheer. Man, this girl was bad, but I knew better than to fuck with her.

"Whoa." I looked her over as she handed her coat to me. "Where you coming from, ma?"

Niyah giggled a little, pushing her hair behind her ears. "A Christmas Eve party at my job in Baltimore. More like a going-away party. I was interning for the hospital, but since I'm moving—"

I looked at her. "Moving?"

She nodded, her eyes sparkling. "Yes, to Florida. I'm transferring to the University of Florida. I leave tomorrow. Well, today, after your mom's Christmas party. My mother asked me to stop by and get the check for the food this morning. I figured, since I was already out, I should come by and get it."

I just looked at her. I wasn't really ready to see her go. Shawty was down, and I liked that. I never told anyone, not even Chrystal, that Niyah was the first girl that I'd had sex with. We were 12 years old. Yeah, young as a muthafucka. At the time, Chrystal was messing around with this dude who was about 15 years old. That was really what made me go out and have sex with Niyah, on Valentine's Day at that. Niyah had a boyfriend at the time too. She came over to my place around midnight, knocking at my bedroom window, crying because her father damn near choked her mother to death for questioning him about where he'd been all night. We sat in the tree house that William built for me in my backyard—the one where Chrystal and I would stay up talking all night occasionally. Niyah was tired of her father beating on her mother. I hated seeing her crying. I leaned in and kissed her. She kissed a nigga back. Next thing I knew, she was pulling at the drawstring of my pajama pants, and I was pulling down her pants. I don't even think a nigga lasted a minute, but Niyah's ass had been down with me ever since.

I held the coat in my hands for a few seconds before hanging it on the coatrack beside me, alongside the front door. The fact that she took off her coat meant that she planned on staying for a while. I didn't see much of shawty since her stepbrother passed away. I guess I reminded her too much of Reggie. Reggie and I were niggas from day one. Our friendship was brief, but it was tight. You would have never known I'd only known the nigga for just a little less than a year when he died. We were like brothers. I think I even trusted him more than the niggas back home in Greenville that I grew up with. The way he looked out for Niyah, like she was his flesh and blood, was fuckin' amazing. He hated Kavante just as much as his father did, but spared him because his sister was crazy about him. As crazy about Kavante as she was, she must have been tired of the nigga because she was taking his two children and bouncing on him.

"So," I turned to her, "what does your nigga say about you leaving him?"

Niyah's eyes sparkled. "I didn't tell him I was leaving. In his head, the streets need him more than I do. I'm sure he won't miss me. I'm taking Ashelle and Niyima with me to Gainesville. We'll be staying with my aunt and uncle until we get on our feet. I can't sit here and watch you boys dig yourselves into an early grave. I'm scared, Blue. We've done a lot out there in those streets. It's gonna come back to us. I have babies who need me. If Kavante doesn't care about my kids' safety, then I have to." Niyah dried the tears that slid down her face before turning and walking away from me, toward the kitchen. "Fix me a drink, Mr. Jacobs."

I exhaled deeply, following her. I watched her toss her car keys on Miss Tiffany's granite countertop before digging through the refrigerator for fruit. Miss Tiffany hated that a nigga drank, but as long as I did it in her house where I was safe, and nowhere else (yeah, right), she was cool with it. She taught a nigga how to make margaritas, daiquiris, piña coladas and shit. And I was a beast at it. I started coming up with my own fruit-blended drinks. Even named a drink after Niyah called "Island Girl," which ended up being one of the most popular drinks at Pop It years later.

Niyah sat and watched as I blended, then poured her drink into a margarita glass. I grinned, watching her tuck the check that Miss Tiffany left on the counter into her bra before picking up the glass, placing it to her lips. Niyah sighed, sipping from the glass. She licked her lips, looking over my face as I sat down next to her at the bistro table in Miss Tiffany's kitchen.

"My sista and her friends are limin' tonight on Pennsylvania Avenue. I was going to head out with my babies to Florida today . . . But if you want to hang out, I'll stay a little while. It's ya birthday. I'm not Chrystal, but I am somebody, Blue." Niyah looked at me looking at her.

I nodded. "I know you're somebody."

"For true?" Niyah pursed her lips. "Then why won't you kick it with me tonight? I'm going to stay a little while, risk running into Kavante, just for you, and you won't come out. You're a real *bess ting*, boy, but you sit around the house, moping because Chrystal done lost her mind. You've always loved that girl. I saw it. *Everyone* saw it except for Chrystal. I wished that . . . I wish that you loved me, Blue. I always wished that. Everything I do is for you to love me, Blue," Niyah told me for the first time.

I just looked at her, not knowing what to say. I'd given my heart to Chrystal. She wasn't there physically, but mentally, that girl was everywhere. Yeah, I messed around with a whole lot of girls that year and four months that I'd been in D.C, but my heart was with Chrystal, wherever she was. I missed her like crazy. There Niyah was, in my face, giving herself to me, despite who her man was, and I was still waiting for Chrystal.

Niyah grinned, knowing I wasn't sure what to say. "You're still waiting on Chrystal to come back, huh, boy?"

I shook my head, lying my ass off. "Nah."

Niyah hated it when I insulted her intelligence. "Don't lie to me, Blue. You're waiting for that girl. They say if you love something, let it go. If it comes back to you, that's how you know it's for true. She'll come back if it's meant to be. But if she doesn't, you've got to move on, boy. No one like you needs to be alone. We deserve better, Blue. So let's just let all our stresses go, blaze one, and drink a little. I got some of that fiyah from the Arab store around the corner. I had to sit through that horrible music that no one understands just to get an ounce from his ass today. You know Mr. Abu stays listening to that 'kill de white man' music."

I laughed out loud, pouring myself some of my cocktail. "How do you know the music Abu listens to is talking about killing white muthafuckas?"

"Abu is Arabic. You think he doesn't think about blowing these muthafuckas up who's always giving his business a hard time? Tshca," Niyah laughed out loud. "Anyway, nigga, you wanna blaze one? The shit he sells is just as good as that medicinal shit you blaze."

I nodded. "A'ight, but we're gonna have to go upstairs to my room 'cause Miss Tiffany's gonna smell that shit as soon as she walks through the front door."

I tried to keep my eyes off of shawty's thighs and ass when she laid across my bed on her stomach. She laughed as she rolled up a blunt, and I unstrapped her shoes, pulling them off one at a time and setting them on the floor. I sat as far from her as I could, at the foot of my bed, my eyes tracing from her ankles to the base of her butt cheeks.

"Iyona said you, Tyrese, and the rest of your niggas shot up the alleyway behind Mr. Abu's store." Niyah looked up at me as she sparked a lighter, firing up the blunt.

"Man, I don't know what the hell ya sista is talkin' about. A nigga has been over in Greenbelt all day, over my man, Griffin's, crib. What?" I watched Niyah purse her lips, shaking her head at a nigga.

"Save that shit for someone who doesn't know you, Blue." She inhaled the smoke from the lit joint, holding it in for a few seconds before exhaling it through her nose and mouth. "You kill niggas who steal from you; that's just who you are. As soon as you find the nigga who took Chrystal from you, I'm sure you'll kill him too." She passed the blunt to me.

I shook my head. I really couldn't deny that what she was saying was true. Shawty knew me, in and out, probably just as much as Chrystal did. Why I couldn't love her, I don't know, but I cared about her. Didn't want to see her hurt by a nigga who controlled her every move, her every breath. She couldn't blink unless that nigga told her to. She was upset with me for not taking her from him. I knew she was. But I couldn't lead shawty on because I knew in my heart that whenever Chrystal walked back into my life, whoever I was with was getting dismissed. I couldn't do Niyah like that.

"So," I changed the subject, "I heard your mama's restaurant was doing well. We need a good Caribbean restaurant out this muthafucka."

Niyah examined my face a little as I puffed. "Yeah, it's doing amazing. You know my sisters have always been de best in de kitchen. Can outcook any bitch alive. Except for my mama, that is. Reginald hasn't said much since his son was killed, but once Mama opened that restaurant, it was like Reginald got his life back. I can't believe my own brother would do something like this. Reggie was like a brother to me; he *was* my brother. There wasn't nothing that I asked him for that he didn't make sure he got for me. He treated me better than he did his girl. My babies loved Uncle Reggie. I stopped taking them to Mama's place because every time I did, they'd ask where their uncle was. This is no life for a child to live, Blue. We saw some shit at a young age that we shouldn't have. We had to fight to live a normal life each day. I don't want my girls to fight the way we did. We're out of the hood now, Blue. But we still went right back to that bullshit. It's time to move on."

I should've listened.

"My aunt can get your mama a job at the hospital in Gainesville. Get your mama and leave with me. Please." Niyah watched me exhaling smoke from my nose. She sat up in the bed and then crawled her way over to me, sitting alongside me.

I looked down at her thighs, her dress hiked all the way up, showing the strap to her string bikini panties. She saw a nigga looking, and do you think she pulled her dress down? Nah. She watched me eyeing that phat pussy print in her panties. It had been six years since I had sex with that girl. When I first hit it, I didn't know what to do with it. But sitting beside her on the bed that night, I could think of a million ways to tap it. Niyah was my homie, though. Up until that night, I never even looked at her that way. Kavante would kill a nigga over that girl. Once I found out that she was his, I kept my distance. She didn't let the nigga tell her she couldn't come near me, but I knew better than to let her flirtation cause any beef between me and the Prices. But that day in my bedroom, temptation was calling me. I wanted her so badly at that moment that the thought of war didn't even cross my mind. I did and said what I wanted all the time, with no apologies and with no regrets. Miss Tiffany was right; all that power I had in the streets had gone straight to my head.

"Nah, shawty, we good where we at," I said as Niyah snatched the blunt from my fingers, putting it to her lips. "Why you gotta be snatchin' shit, Niyah? Damn." I nudged her.

She rolled her eyes at me, inhaling from the blunt, nudging me back with her elbow. She held the smoke in, closing her eyes, feeling its strong effect before exhaling smoke from her nose and opening her bright brown eyes. "You know the only reason I even settled for Kavante was because you never gave me you. You know that, right?"

I just looked at her.

"You were my first love, Blue, but I wasn't yours, and that hurt. Blue, I did *everything* you've ever asked me to do for you. And yet, Chrystal has always been your first choice. I bet you fucked me in seventh grade just to spite her, didn't you?" Niyah grabbed the ashtray from my nightstand to put out the blunt.

"I never told Chrystal about it, so how was I doing shit to spite her, Niyah?" I asked as Niyah sat back down beside me on the bed. "I didn't tell anyone that you were my first. I wasn't trying to have the whole neighborhood talkin' about that shit, so I kept it to myself. I respected you."

Niyah's eyes searched my face before a slight grin grew on her face, then quickly faded. "I was your first?"

I nodded. "Hell yeah, shawty. We were fuckin' *12 years old*. How many other chicks you think I was fuckin' with before you? I didn't know what the fuck I was doing. All I knew was that once we started kissing and touching, I couldn't stop until I released something in you. We were kids. Had no business gettin' down like that. We're lucky you didn't end up pregnant."

Niyah agreed, smiling at me, her brown eyes searching my face. "I know, right? It only lasted like a minute, but I swear, boy, it felt like forever. The dick felt *so* good. My soul connected with yours. I was in love, but . . . You never saw me. After that day, we were back to being friends. You didn't acknowledge the fact that my heart belonged to you."

"I did . . . I noticed. You did everything for a nigga." I unintentionally grabbed her thigh.

Niyah looked down at my hand on her thick thigh, and then she looked back into my face, placing her hand over mine. "Shit is about to get crazy. You have no idea of the people you shot up today, do you?"

I scoffed. "Some muthafuckas whose luck ran out, that's who, Niyah."

She grinned, shaking her head at me. "That arrogance of yours is gonna kill you. You shot someone's sons, nephews, cousins, whoever. I think you were set up to get knocked down, but hey, what do I know? I'm just Kavante's baby mama, the girl David Jacobs rejected because I wasn't light skinned with light eyes. You hate my dark skin. That's what it is."

I made a face at her. "What? You think I love Chrystal because of her complexion? You think I don't love the skin you're in? You got me fucked up, Niyah. All this chocolate, and you think a nigga wouldn't want this? Who the fuck *doesn't* love chocolate?"

"You. You like vanilla, muthafucka." Niyah rolled her neck at me, pushing my hand from her thigh. "You always fucked with red bitches. White bitches. Latin bitches. Asian bitches. What Black bitch have you fucked with?"

I laughed out loud. "You were gone from Greenville for three and a half years, shawty. Most of the chicks I fucked with *were* blacker than a muthafucka. I love chocolate of all flavors. I don't discriminate. I can name plenty of chicks a nigga fucked with who were dark back in the 'Ville. Since I moved to D.C., most of the dark women think a nigga is too pretty and shit. I fuck with who fucks with me. And I haven't taken it there with you because you're with Kavante, my nigga."

"Well, I'm leavin' ya 'nigga' today, as soon as the day is over. As soon as my babies open their presents at my sister's house in Baltimore. I don't belong to him anymore. We haven't had sex in weeks, and even when I did have sex with him, the only way I made it through it was to picture you in my head." Niyah turned to me, her dress pushed up around her hips, the sheer lace of her underwear hinting at the skin underneath. The pussy was staring a nigga in the face. And the cocktail was kicking in, not to mention I was blazed off of the few puffs I took from the loud.

I exhaled deeply, watching this girl pull her dress up over her head, tossing it to the floor. I looked away from shawty, not wanting to see her like that.

"Look at me," Niyah whispered.

Shaking my head, I turned it, my heart racing, looking at everything *but* her. "Nah, shawty. You got a nigga." I remembered saying those exact same words to Chrystal a year and a half earlier.

Niyah scoffed. "He ain't shit." I remembered hearing those words too.

"You got two kids with this nigga, shawty." I still wouldn't look at her.

"I know, but it's only been you, Blue. I've always only wanted you. Just touch it. I won't tell. It's just between me and you." Niyah kissed my shoulder.

"Put your muthafuckin' clothes back on." I took a deep breath as shawty sat as close to me as she could, on top of my hand, to be exact. I looked at her, whose gaze danced all over my face. Why the fuck did she have to look and smell and sound and feel so good? Shit. Fuck. I can't even begin to explain how hard it was not to give in to temptation when it was lookin' so good in my face. She sat there on my bed, in a lace push-up bra and those tiny panties. My leg started shaking anxiously as I rubbed my hand across my hair nervously. "Gotdamn," I muttered to myself, pulling my other hand from up under her, getting up from my bed before I fucked the shit out of that girl. "Shawty, you gotta roll the fuck out. For real."

"Blue, I love you." Niyah stood before me, that chocolate skin glistening, looking like a fuckin' Coca-Cola bottle made of hot chocolate. I watched this girl get completely undressed. She unsnapped her bra, pulling it from her body, and then she slid out of her string bikini panties. My mouth dropped open a little as she tossed her bra and panties to the floor. "You don't have to give it all to me, Blue; all I want is a little bit," she whispered to me before standing on her toes to kiss my lips.

I hesitated to kiss her back, my heart drumming in my chest. I think outside of her, Chrystal was the only girl I actually kissed. The rest of the chicks, I fucked them, then put their asses out. Kisses were intimate, something that I wasn't. Nothing at all, that's what shawty had on. If she had been another girl, I would've taken the pussy. But she was Niyah. Niyah was everything, but I couldn't hurt her. Not her. Not someone who was down for my every move.

I pulled my lips from hers, taking her hands from my face. "Shawty, I can't do this shit with you. You are too fuckin' dope to be someone's secret. Nah. Here." I picked up her bra and panties from the floor, shoving them into her chest. I didn't give her a chance to respond before I grabbed her dress from the bed and shoved that shit at her too. "Nah, yo, get out."

Niyah laughed out loud, shaking her head at me. "Are you for true, Blue? You're rejecting me? Again?"

"I'm not rejecting you, Niyah; I'm being honest with you!" I told her. "You're my girl, but you're not my girl at the same time. That nigga will kill me over you. You may not love that nigga, but he loves the fuck out of you. If I touch you, he's gonna get his niggas to light up my ass. If you cared so much about a nigga, you'd get the fuck on, Niyah."

Niyah burst out crying, tossing her clothes on my bed. Then she picked up her panties, sliding into them one leg at a time.

I exhaled, shaking my head as she slid into her bra. "Shawty, I'm not trying to hurt you. I know I can't love you the way that you deserve. You don't need a nigga who's in love with someone else. You deserve every piece of a nigga's heart. I'm not the one to give it to you. I'm not gonna lead you on. I'm sorry I did when we were kids. You're not just some girl I can fuck and forget about. You're special. So, go home."

Niyah cried out loud as she grabbed her dress and put it on. Then she grabbed the check from the floor, which had fallen from her bra when she took it off a few minutes earlier, and stuck it back in her bra. "I want you so bad, Blue, and you still want her." She cried, laughing at the same time.

"I can't even get just a little bit of you."

"Nope, because you deserve more than a gotdamn little bit, Niyah." I watched as she grabbed her heels. "I'm sorry that I can't be the type of nigga you're used to. Them other girls I fuck with ain't nothing but sex. You're . . ." I didn't want to say it out loud.

She looked at me as she stood there, holding her heels in her hands by the straps. "I'm what, Blue? What am I to you?"

I took a deep breath before saying, "You're who I'd be with if it weren't for her." I didn't know it then, but I fucked up when I told shawty that shit.

Niyah tried to smile, but tears slid from her eyes instead. She quickly dried them away. "Walk me to my car."

I stood alongside Niyah's bullet-blue Jetta, a black hood over my head, watching her hesitate to unlock the doors to her vehicle. She turned to me, those pretty brown eyes looking up into my face. At that moment, I wished my heart wasn't still mourning the loss of Chrystal. I was tired of losing. I'd lost the man who helped raise me, I'd lost Chrystal, I'd lost Reggie, and at that moment, Niyah was leaving a nigga for good.

"You can't wait for Chrystal forever, Blue," she let me know.

I shook my head. "Yes, I can."

Niyah sighed hopelessly. "Well, when you get tired of waiting, I'll be in Florida. This is so sad. I'm waiting on you, and you're waiting on her. I got bucket naked in front of you, was about to rock your muthafuckin' world, and you *still* wouldn't budge."

"I wanted to, shawty; trust me. But my will to protect you is a lot stronger than my will to fuck ya brains loose, Niyah." I watched her cry as she pressed the unlock button on her keychain. "Niyah? You know you're my nigga; you've been down for me foreva, shawty."

Niyah turned to me. "I don't wanna be your gotdamn nigga! I wanna be your woman, Blue. I have been workin' mad overtime for you, Blue." Shawty pushed me in the chest. "You know I'd leave that nigga for you if you wanted me. I've *always* had your back. I've *always* been down for you. I've *always* done whatever you asked."

"I know, baby, but—"

Niyah cut me off, shoving me again. "I've been here for you, doing whatever you asked of me. Where is she? Do you know? Shit, does *anybody* know where she is? All I know is *I'm* here. Just give me you, Blue. Nigga, I'm more than just an option. And I will be *damned* if you forget about me. I'm *not* a fuckin' second choice. I deserve you—I've been working this hard. Give me something—*anything*."

This girl cursed me the fuck out, her accent so thick as hell that I couldn't understand her, and the crying muffled her voice. I grabbed her face, sucking her plump lips into mine and backed her up into her car.

Niyah let out a long sigh, as if she'd been waiting all her life for that kiss. As good as she felt and tasted in my mouth, a nigga felt bad. She was crazy about a nigga, but I was crazy about Chrystal. Every bit of my soul belonged to Chrystal, but Niyah didn't even care. Fuck, why couldn't I love her? Any nigga in his right mind would have wanted a girl like Niyah, but I was stuck on stupid, in love with a girl who let a nigga make her forget that I even existed.

Niyah sucked my bottom lip into her mouth before she peeled her lips from mine. She looked into my face, her eyes glued to my lips as she swiped her finger across them. "I gotta go. If you need me, call me, Blue," she whispered.

I nodded, pushing her hair from her face. "A'ight."

Niyah shook her head. "No, Blue, I'm serious. I don't care if I'm asleep, at work, if I'm in the hospital, if I'm with another nigga, or if I'm mad at you. If you need me, I'm already there. I'ma always rock with Blue." Niyah pressed her hand against my chest, pushing my body away a little so she could turn around and get into her car.

I backed away from her car, watching her crank it up.

She looked at me, winking her eye, those brown eyes shimmering. "Happy birthday, Blue. I'm sorry that I unwrapped your present for you."

I laughed a little. "You wild, yo."

Niyah grinned. "Instead of unwrapping your gift for you, I should have let *you* unwrap me. I'll see you around, Blue. You've got my number. I'll text you my address, boo. Come visit me sometime."

I nodded. "You already know, shawty."

Tears slid down her face. She sighed before putting the car in drive, then darting off down the street.

I shook my head, turning back around, and headed back toward the house.

I must have lain in my bed a good thirty-five minutes that night, just staring at the picture of me and Chrystal that sat on my nightstand. I removed the photo from the frame, my eyes tracing Chrystal's sexy silhouette. It was a picture of the two of us at junior prom. She went with some sorry-ass nigga, and I didn't go with anyone. When it came time to take pictures, I snatched shawty from her nigga and went to stand in front of the camera. Chrystal laughed her ass off, posing for the photo, wrapping her arms around my neck as I grabbed her waist, gripping that silk royal-blue dress in my hands. Me and that girl shared some amazing memories, from robbing muthafuckas to whuppin' muthafuckas to spending the night in the tree house that William built for us in her backyard. How could Chrystal let some nigga keep her away from me? I cried every night over that girl, worried out of my mind about her. Where was she? Was she okay? Did she need me? Did she cry for me too?

All of a sudden, I was angry. My whole life revolved around that girl. I hadn't seen her in almost a year and a half, and I hadn't heard from her in ten months, and I was *still* waiting for her. My heart, my soul, my entire life belonged to Chrystal and no one else. The only reason I never acted on my feelings was that I didn't want to lose her as my friend. I didn't want to cross that boundary into a world I never knew. Girls didn't mean shit to me but sex. I never really gave my heart to anyone but Chrystal. I never really trusted anyone but Chrystal and Miss Tiffany. Those two were all I had. I was lost without the two of them. I *needed* the two of them, and everyone knew that. Chrystal knew she was my other half. She knew what she meant to me. Why would she let go? How could she let go so easily? It was time for me to let go too. I clenched the picture tightly in my hands before ripping it in half, then in fourths, then in eighths. And I threw the shit in the trash can beside my bed.

Suddenly, my cell phone vibrated on my nightstand. I exhaled deeply before picking it up, hoping it wasn't Tyrese's ass. He was talking about hiring some strippers for my birthday, and I wasn't trying to hear that shit. Shit, if I wanted a chick to dance for a nigga, Niyah was already on it. I couldn't get that girl's body out of my head. I checked the display, relieved to see Darius's name on it. I met him through some members of the church Miss Tiffany attended. Darius stayed dress to impress for any event, but he was far from a church nigga. When I was attending school, I hung with dude. Niggas were constantly testing him because of the way he dressed. That nigga may have dressed like Kanye West, but that lightweight nigga could whip a nigga like Mayweather.

"What up though?" I answered the phone.

"Aye, happy birthday, my nigga," Darius chimed through the phone.

I laughed a little. "Thanks, man. I don't see what's so happy about it, but I appreciate ya anyway, dude. Man, I thought you was Tyrese, yo. I was about to hit the ignore icon on your ass. Send your ass straight to voicemail, nigga."

"You dressed, nigga?" Darius asked.

I looked down at my wife-beater and sweats. "Hell nah, nigga. I'm about to roll one and go the fuck to sleep."

Darius huffed through the phone. "Nah, homie, let's go out."

I shook my head. "Nah, man, not you too. I ain't trying to kick it with y'all tonight. I gotta be home when Miss Tiffany gets here. She's gonna flip if I don't start breakfast. We always open our gifts together while we eat breakfast. She lives for my birthday, bruh. I can't eat with Miss Tiff all drunk and shit."

There was a call on the other line. I looked at the display. It was Niyah. I made a face before saying, "Yo, Darius, I'ma hit you right back."

"A'ight, you better. We goin' out tonight, nigga, so get dressed, gotdamn it," he said before hanging up.

I laughed a little at the fool before switching to the line that Niyah was on. "What's good, shawty?"

I heard what sounded like traffic in the background. "Baby, I'm stranded at the gas station. I went in to pay for gas, and when I came out to try to crank my shit, it wouldn't start. This is so not my night, Blue."

I sat up in bed. "Where ya at, shawty?"


I hopped in my ride that night to drive about thirty minutes away to the Exxon gas station on Route 1, where Niyah's car was being towed. She stood back from the tow truck, watching her car being mounted onto the vehicle. Her long hair flowed behind her; her arms were intertwined, trying to keep herself warm.

I hopped out of my clean, white 2008 Acura TLX. I was dressed in a gray and orange plaid, long-sleeved button-down shirt, crisp black jeans, and fresh all-white Js. Since I planned on dropping shawty off anyway, I thought I might as well step out with my niggas. But once the tow truck driver drove off and Niyah turned around, her dress flying up around her thighs, the wind blowing through her silky hair, and that smile of hers, yo, my plans switched up real quick.

I took a deep breath, leaning back against my ride as shawty pranced her way over to me.

Niyah looked me over, standing in front of me. "You always look and smell so damn good. Shit. I'm sorry to interrupt your plans, Blue, but my starter is acting up again. Brand-new fuckin' Jetta, and my starter is faulty. I had it towed to Reginald's brother's shop in Upper Marlboro. I didn't want to bother you, but I didn't know who else to call." She looked up at my face as I grabbed her hands, pulling her body up against mine.

"Your mother is coming by my spot this morning to pick up the check, right?" I looked down into her face, watching her lick her lips. Watching her do that had me licking mine too.

Niyah nodded, looking at my lips, a yearning look sweeping across her face for a few seconds before she looked back into my eyes. "Yeah. She said between six and seven . . . Why?"

I sighed. Man, what was I doing? Why was I trippin'? Chrystal wasn't thinking about a nigga. Shawty dissed me. We'd known each other from childbirth, and once I moved, I no longer existed to her. Niyah was right here. Shawty would move mountains for a nigga. She was moving to Florida. I made enough bread to travel back and forth to visit her. I would protect her from the nigga if she needed me to. I didn't too much fuck with Kavante. I only dealt with him because Kam kept him around. He wasn't treating shawty right, and shawty felt like I was ignoring her, so she was chuckin' up the deuces.

"Fuck it," I mumbled to myself.

Niyah giggled a little. "What now? What did you say?" she whispered as I slid my hands around her neck, cupping the back of her head in my hands.

"Forgive me for what I said earlier. I just don't wanna hurt you, Niyah. You're dope as fuck." I massaged her scalp with my fingertips. "Chrystal was my everything, shawty. I'm kinda lost without her."

Niyah grinned, her brown eyes sparkling. "Totally lost without her. It's cool. I can back off a little. But if you keep running your fingers through my hair like this, we're going to have some problems."

"I don't feel like driving to Baltimore," I told her.

She agreed, nodding. "What you for?"

I made a face, grinning a little. That fuckin' Trinidad slang, boy. "What, shawty?"

She laughed. "Why yuh screw up yuh face like that, boy?"

"Don't nobody know that Trini slang. Took me forever to realize *limin'* meant 'kickin' it.' You gotta speak English with me, shawty," I laughed out loud.

"I said, 'What are you trying to do?'" Niyah smiled before kissing my chin.

"Spend the night with me." I'd never asked a girl to spend the night.

Niyah's eyes widened a little. She just looked in my face, not really sure what to say. "You want me to spend the night? But you said—"

I cut her off. "I don't even care what goes down, shawty. I just want you there. I'm sorry I put you out earlier. I just wasn't ready for all this chocolate. But I'm good now. Stay with me and roll out wit'cha mom when she rolls through in the a.m." I could barely get the words out when shawty's lips saturated mine.

"Oh," she whispered between kisses, "you fucked up now, boy. It's going down."

And it did indeed.

Clothes were coming off as soon as we got through the front door of Miss Tiffany's house. This girl was every man's dream. She had no inhibitions. No boundaries. No limits to the things she did to keep a nigga wanting and begging for more. I undressed her while she undressed me. Shawty's hands stroked the fuck out of my dick while

I unhooked her bra. She moaned and squealed in my mouth as I ripped her panties from her body. As soon as I stepped out of my boxers, Niyah's eyes were on my dick. She grinned a little, gripping and working it with her hands. I tilted her chin, lifting her face so our lips could meet back up again. Shawty grabbed my hand, turned around, and led me to the staircase. She pushed a nigga down on the fifth step before turning around, sliding onto my lap.

"Shit," I moaned as she slid her way all the way down my lap, her booty grazing against my abs. I smacked her thighs as she held on to the rail and lifted herself up, grabbing my dick that had grown stiff as muthafuckin' wood. I grabbed her hips as she slid my dick through her moistened pussy lips. She sighed as I bit down on her back to keep from yelling out loud. And as soon as I felt the opening that led inside of her, I lifted myself a little from the step, sliding my way inside.

"Blue, oh, Blue . . ." She cried out, leaning back against my chest as I leaned back on the steps, sliding one hand around her torso to her left breast and my other hand down between her legs. My dick throbbed inside of her as I rubbed my fingers through her pussy lips and sucked on her neck. Her hair grazed against my face. She smelled so good.

"Gotdamn, you smell, and taste, and feel, and sound, and *look* so good!" I kissed her neck, caressing her breast with one hand and rubbing her clit in a circular motion with the other.

"You're in the driver's seat, ma. What'cha gonna do?" I whispered to her.

Niyah giggled, gripping my knee with one hand and the handrail of the stairs with the other. She started riding the dick back and forth by pushing off the rail and my knee, and pressing up from the last step with her feet.

She pressed her booty against my groin as I caressed her nipple with one hand and rubbed that pussy with the other. That was until shawty leaned forward, resting her hands on the bottom step, and then she started winding her hips, working the shit out of the dick. I leaned back, watching that pussy go up and down, and round and round on it. It looked as good as a muthafucka, watching her pussy lips suck and fuck the shit out of me. I felt good as a muthafucka, feeling the walls of her pussy pulsate and cave around me. As soon as I felt her legs shiver, I grabbed her hips, lifting her off the steps. She laughed as I swung her around so that her elbows rested on the fifth step, and I was kneeling behind her, gripping her waist.

Niyah moaned, lifting her booty, putting a deep arch in her back. "Pull my hair, Blue," she whispered, throwing her long hair over her back.

I exhaled deeply, grabbing a hold of her hair, wrapping it around my hand, tugging on it enough to make her throw her head back a little. "Throw that ass back," I groaned as I slid in and out of her, gripping her waist with my free hand. I used short strokes at first to stimulate her G-spot. Once I felt her body begin to warm up and her pussy relax around my dick, I started giving her longer, stronger strokes, tapping against her cervix.

"David," she cried out my government name, something she'd rarely done. And it was that moment that my baby Chrystal's face flashed across my mind. Her face became distorted in my mind once Niyah started to move side to side, up and down, and back to meet my strong thrusts.

I removed my hand from her waist and smacked her ass, watching that booty jiggle and my dick sliding in and out of her. I worked that pussy, had her booty bouncing up and down . . . I had shawty screaming and moaning, crying out my name.

"Oh, Blue, I'm about to come. Don't stop, baby; come with me. Come in me. Fill this pussy. Beat this pussy. I've been waiting on this shit," Niyah cried out, working with me.

"Shit," I moaned, feeling her pussy pulsating, dripping wet, fluid slipping down my thighs. "This pussy feels as good as a muthafucker."

Niyah moaned. "Shit, Blue, baby, do you feel me? You feel that shit?" Her pussy tightened before loosening around the dick, throbbing and whistling as I pumped in and out of her. Her legs gave out from under her, and she fell to the steps, her face pressed into the carpet. I wanted to see shawty's face. I let go of her hair and slipped out of her. I didn't have to say shit. Shawty turned over, facing me, her legs spread, and her feet resting on the stairs. She arched her back as I slid my arm behind her, pulling her body up against mine as I slid back into her wetness. She bit her bottom lip, and I leaned in, biting it too as I dug into her. My little Island Girl cried as I worked the pussy. I must have worked the pussy for a good fifteen minutes before I busted.

We had sex for hours, yo. From the time I brought her home until about an hour before my alarm clock went off. We lay in my bed that morning, laughing together until shawty fell asleep beside me, lying on her stomach. I looked at her face as she slept. I wanted to tell her to stay in Maryland with me, not to leave me, but I didn't. A small part of me hoped Chrystal would pop up, and Niyah knew it too. So, she held back a little. Niyah fucked the shit out of a nigga, don't get me wrong, but I felt her holding back. I think the tears she cried while I dug into her were because she knew I'd never love her the way she wanted me to.

I woke Niyah up at six so we could both jump in the shower before Miss Tiffany rolled up on us. Niyah was quiet and didn't say much that morning. I scrubbed her body down, even washed her pretty face. I lathered her hands, washing between each finger. A nigga even washed shawty's feet. Tears seeped from her eyes, and she finally spoke to me, begging me to go to Florida with her. Again, I refused, and again, she cursed me out. And the only way I could get her to shut up was to kiss her before I fucked her up against the cold tile of the shower that morning.

"Something sure smells good." Miss Tiffany came into the house at 6:45, a little after I let Man Man out in the backyard to take a piss. When Miss Tiffany walked into the kitchen, she stopped in her tracks to see Niyah helping a nigga cook breakfast.

I looked at Miss Tiffany, checking for her reaction. She couldn't call Niyah a ho because she liked the girl. But Christmas morning was me and Miss Tiffany's time. I knew better than to have shawty up in my crib, but her mother was on her way to pick her up. Not to mention, I needed help starting breakfast. Shawty scrambled eggs, fried bacon, fried sausage links, fried steak, baked cinnamon rolls, baked biscuits, and made French toast from scratch. As a matter of fact, shawty was just finishing scrambling the eggs when Miss Tiffany walked through the front door.

"Good morning, Miss Tiffany." Niyah blushed, sliding the eggs from Miss Tiffany's nonstick Rachael Ray frying pan onto a plate. Niyah was standing there in her dress from the night before with no panties underneath. Ya know, 'cause a nigga ripped them off earlier that morning.

"Umm-hmmm." Miss Tiffany pursed her lips. "Don't you have somewhere you have to be? Ya know, like . . . with your own family on Christmas?"

"My mama's on her way over with my sisters and the kids. We open presents as a family after breakfast." Niyah approached me, sitting at the bar, dressed in my white T-shirt and navy blue sweats.

Just then, we heard the sound of a car honking outside.

"That's my mother." Niyah leaned in and kissed me on the lips in front of Miss Tiffany. "I'll call you okay, Blue? Swing by my sista's to see me, okay? Don't stand me up. I'll be waiting." She kissed my lips again, and then she turned around to walk away, unable to look at Miss Tiffany as she slid her way past her and out of the kitchen.

Miss Tiffany looked over her shoulder, listening for the sound of the front door closing before she went in on a nigga. She rolled her eyes and her neck back and forth. "David Jacobs, I know you *didn't* fuck that girl in my house?"

I smirked, taking a sip from my orange juice.

Miss Tiffany scoffed, tossing her keys and purse onto the countertop before refolding her arms, her weight shifting over to one leg. "What is she doing in my house, David? Isn't she your homeboy's girl? So, we're playing pussy snatcher, huh?"

I set my glass of orange juice back down on the counter. "Come on, man."

"That nigga, Kavante, will kill you over her, David. Are you *serious?*" Miss Tiffany exclaimed.

I shook my head. "Man, Kavante ain't gonna do shit. Shawty called me late last night when her car broke down. I went to pick her up, and I brought her back here. Her mama was coming to scoop her up anyway, so I thought, fuck it, just spend the night with me."

Miss Tiffany shook her head, laughing to herself. She always laughed when she was pissed off. "Boy, you must think I'm stupid. You had that girl in here cooking breakfast. You fucked her when you know she doesn't mean anything to you but sex, just like the rest of the girls. You're *playing* with her, David."

I shook my head. "Miss Tiff, she's not like the rest of them girls. She's different. I'm not gonna hurt her. She knows the deal."

Miss Tiffany nodded. "Yeah, she knows she's not Chrystal and that if that girl just so happens to pop back in your life, you'd diss Niyah. I told you not to go around breaking these young girls' hearts, didn't I? But you never fuckin' listen. One day, your luck is going to run out, and I will be the first one in your face, talkin' about, 'Nigga, I told you so.'"

"She's leaving, Miss Tiff." I took a bite out of the crispy bacon that shawty cooked.

Miss Tiffany sighed before coming over and sitting down on the stool beside me. "I know. Her mother said she's going to school in Florida. It's a great opportunity for her. She needs a break from this life that she's been forced into. She's a brilliant girl. She's going to be some-body one day, just watch and see. Don't sleep on her, David."

I looked at Miss Tiffany. "She wants me to go with her. You too."

Miss Tiffany grinned. "If she wasn't Kavante's girl, I'd pack up my shit and go down there with her."

I just looked at Miss Tiffany.

"But she is his girl, whether or not she wants to be. She has two kids with him, David. He's not just going to let her go like that, and you know it. In your head, what happened between you may have been just sex, but in her eyes, you made love to her. And trust me when I say, she's going to be expecting you to protect her from that lunatic. Kam is your boy, David, but Kavante is his family. And when Kavante finds out you fucked with his girl, you better be ready to strap the fuck up. You can't keep going around causing problems and expect no one to come for you, David. Especially when you *sent* for them."

I wasn't trying to hear shit that Miss Tiffany was talking about. I thought I had everything under control. I thought I was untouchable and that niggas knew better than to fuck with mine, but boy, was I wrong . . . When I finally got Miss Tiffany to calm down, we sat down and ate.

There were only two of us living in that house, but you wouldn't have known that by the number of presents under the Christmas tree. On the first day of Christmas, I bought Miss Tiffany a white gold and diamond necklace from Tiffany's. On the second day, I bought her a Marc Jacobs purse and matching watch. On the third day, I bought her about ten paperbacks from her favorite author, Krystal Armstead, a new Canon EOS digital camera, and an Apple MacBook. And so on. It was going to take her all of January to open all the gifts that I bought for her. Miss Tiffany hated my hustle, but she knew I would do anything to make sure that she was taken care of. I had racks and racks of doe stored away in that house, in places no one would think to look. I paid Miss Tiffany's bills before she even received the bill in the mail. I bought her groceries. I paid to have her hair done every week. I cleaned the house. She refused to let me pay for her home because she told me that if anything were to happen to her, she wanted to be able to say that she paid for the house that she left me.

I didn't want anything for Christmas, but Miss Tiffany bought a nigga pretty much a whole new wardrobe. She stayed hittin' the numbers. Every day, she was at the corner store, buying them fuckin' scratch-offs. She must have won a good $1,000 in scratch-offs every month. And she'd go blow it at the mall or up in Delaware with her friends from work. Miss Tiffany was damn near

40 years old but looked like she was in her twenties. Everyone swore she was my older sister, not just because of how pretty and young she looked, but because of our connection. She was the realest woman I'd ever met. The only mother I knew. And that morning, she was taken from me.

As soon as I opened my tenth box from Miss Tiffany, my cell phone vibrated. It was Tyrese telling a nigga that it was time to strap up, that the niggas we'd run up on the other day had shot up our boy Demarcus's mama's house that morning. I didn't even hesitate to think. I just hopped up and kissed Miss Tiffany goodbye. She shouted for me to be back in time for lunch at one as I darted out the front door. We were too late to Demarcus's mama's house that morning. The niggas ended up killing his mother and his two little sisters. We'd started a war that wasn't going to end until everyone we loved was taken from us. I wasn't gone from my house three hours when my neighbor, Miss Pearl, called my phone, telling me that some niggas had swung by my house and killed Miss Tiffany and her dog. By the time I made it back to my home, Miss Tiffany was being wheeled out to the ambulance in a body bag. A nigga was screaming, crying, cursing, trying to get to my mama, but my boys held me back.

I knew I had to make a change. I had to come down off that pedestal that I thought I was on. I took lives, never stopping to think that a life that was important to me would be taken. Everyone knew a nigga wasn't afraid to die, which was why I lived so recklessly. They knew hurting Miss Tiffany would make me leave the streets alone. But I didn't just leave the streets alone. I disassociated myself from my niggas too, for a minute. After I spent everything I had to bury Miss Tiffany and to pay off all of her debts, I had nothing left. Everyone's face was a blur at the funeral. I think a nigga even blacked out a few times at the funeral. I was in so much pain. I shut out Niyah, who stayed in Maryland, trying her best to reach out to me. I ignored her. I totally dissed shawty. I didn't want anything to do with the streets, and that included her too. I moved in with Darius to a two-bedroom apartment in Baltimore. Niyah swung by the place a few times, but I refused to see her. Shawty withdrew from the University of Florida to stick around. She finally got tired of waiting on me and left Maryland around April of that year.

# Chapter Nine

## *Truth Hurts*

## *Blue*

*New Year's 2016*

"Okay, Blue, sweetie, calm down, okay?" Chrystal followed behind me as I went through the envelope, eying the rest of the pictures in it.

My blood was boiling as I sifted through the photos in that envelope that someone slipped under our hotel room door. Several pictures were taken of Miss Tiffany's dead body. And the first one I saw was a cropped picture of Miss Tiffany's body and the hand of the person who killed her—muthafuckin' Kameron Price. There were more pictures. There was a picture of Miss Tiffany having lunch with Kameron. There was a picture of Miss Tiffany having lunch with the nigga I grew up thinking was my uncle Larry. There was a picture of Chrystal getting off a bus in the same clothes that she described that she wore the same day that she left that nigga who was pimping her. There was even a picture of Quincy giving some nigga dap outside of Club Pop It. And just when I dug through my sweatpants pocket for my phone, about to call my niggas, I came across a picture of a woman lying in a hospital bed, beaten up, hooked to a ventilator. It took a few seconds for me to realize that the woman hooked to the ventilator was Niyah. I gripped the pictures in my hands, my temples twitching. Whoever sent the pictures was trying to get a nigga's attention. Oh, they got it all right. And I was about to get theirs too.

I turned around, walking over to where my clothes lay across the chair in the corner of the room, tossing the pictures on the bed along the way. Chrystal was too busy watching my expression, once I saw the first picture of Kameron's tattoo, that she hadn't noticed the rest of the pictures. Why was Miss Tiffany meeting with Larry? What happened to Niyah? Why was she hooked up to a gotdamn respirator and shit? Where the fuck was she? Who the fuck sent those pictures?

"Where are you going?" Chrystal hesitated to ask.

"The fuck you think I'm going, Chrystal?" I scoffed, pulling my white tee over my head.

Chrystal sighed. "Blue, you don't even know where those pictures came from. They could be photoshopped or some shit. It's been seven years—" Chrystal stopped when she saw the *I-don't-give-a-fuck-how-long-it's-been* expression on my face. She took a deep breath before going over to the bed where I tossed the pictures. As she sifted through them the same way that I did, she gasped, pausing at the picture that I didn't even have to ask was the picture of her getting off the bus.

I glanced at her as she stood from the bed, going to the next picture.

Chrystal covered her mouth, her light eyes widening. "David, this is Lawrence! Your cousin. The guy who was pimping me. Why is he—" She choked. "Why is he with Quincy?"

I exhaled deeply, sitting down at the desk to slip into my shoes. "That's what we're gonna find out, shawty. Get'cha clothes on."

Chrystal was in shock, moving on to the next picture, examining it, her eyes squinting to get a closer look. "This is Niyah. Niyah Rogers from the 'Ville. I haven't seen her since like 2009. Did you know she was here, Blue? Did you know she's Kavante's baby mama?"

"Nah." I glanced at Chrystal, continuing to get dressed. Niyah had seen Chrystal. *That* was probably why shawty was calling me for those months before she moved to Florida. I shook my head to myself.

Chrystal continued looking at the picture of Niyah. "Oh my goodness, what happened to her? Who did this bullshit to her?" From the corner of my eye, I could see Chrystal looking back up at me. "Blue? This girl was your ride-or-die chick back in Greenville, and you mean to tell me that you had no idea that she was here? That she was fuckin' around with Kavante?"

I couldn't look at Chrystal. "Nah, yo, I said I didn't."

Chrystal wasn't buying it, but she let it go for the moment. "What could she have done to deserve some shit like this? Oh my goodness . . ."

Chrystal had the exact same questions that I did. I knew all those pictures were connected in some way. I knew in my heart there was something strange about that Quincy nigga. Why would any nigga who cared about her let those niggas fuck her in front of his face? What I couldn't get my mind around was why Miss Tiffany was with Larry. She couldn't stand the muthafucka.

"Blue, these pictures are connected somehow, baby." Chrystal snapped me out of my daze.

I looked up at her slipping into her skinny jeans. I nodded, feeling my cell phone vibrating in my pocket. I dug into my pocket to grab it. "Yeah, I know," I responded to her before checking the caller ID on my cell phone. I had a few missed call icons at the top of the screen, but I ignored them, peeping the incoming call number on the display. I didn't recognize the number, but I answered it anyway. It had to be something serious for someone to call a nigga at that time of night. "Yo?"

"What it do, Blue?" I heard a familiar voice on the other end, but I couldn't get a mental image of who it was in my head.

I made a face. "Who the fuck is this?"

Chrystal looked at me.

"Pookie, nigga." Pookie laughed on the other end.

"Pookie?" I laughed a little, watching Chrystal squinting her eyes at me before throwing her shirt over her head. "What's good, homie? I ain't seen or heard from you in a minute, yo." I sat down in the oversized chair in the room to slip into my Js. Then I looked at my watch. "The fuck you doing calling so late? Or early? Shit, however you wanna put it."

Pookie laughed. "Oh, I'm only in town until later on today. Did you get my pictures?" she asked.

My heart leaped in my chest a little. "What you mean? *You* dropped these pictures off at my room?" I watched Chrystal gasp, dropping the boot that was in her hands.

It took Pookie a few seconds to reply. "I can't say much over the phone, Blue. Are you alone?"

I looked at Chrystal as her frustration made it hard for her to put on her shoes. I was sure she was wondering why her friend had access to those pictures or if she was the one who had taken them. "Nah, I'm with shawty. You knew I was with shawty when you slid that shit under my room door, Pookie. The fuck is going on?"

"Meet me at the Holiday Inn Express in Laurel. I'm in room 231. I won't be here long, Blue. I can't be here long, so hurry the hell up," Pookie replied before hanging up.

I flew down the highway on my way to Laurel. Millions of thoughts were running through my mind. I had no idea what to think, or why, all of a sudden, my world was turning upside down. I had at least forty missed calls on my cell. A few were from Darius. A few were from Tyrese. But most of them were from Niyah's stepbrothers, niggas I hadn't kicked it with since their brother, my nigga, Reggie, passed away.

My past was all of a sudden coming back to haunt me, and it all started when I saw Chrystal out there poppin' it for a nigga on the dance floor. Then I found out that I had a son, a son who was a victim of the life that his mother chose to live. Nah, Larry had no business putting her through the things he did, but Chrystal put herself out there that way for niggas to fuck with her. I wasn't there to protect her, and I felt guilty as a muthafucka.

We got to the hotel where Pookie was staying. I parked close to the entrance and got out of the car, going around to open the door to let Chrystal out of the passenger seat. Chrystal looked just as nervous as I did. I grabbed her hand, squeezing it in mine, and led her into the hotel.

"Glad you could make it." Pookie grinned at the two of us as she let us into her hotel room.

I glanced at Pookie before looking at all the paperwork shawty had spread out everywhere. The room looked more like an office than a hotel room. She looked like she'd been working on shit all night. I walked through the room, going over to sit in a corner chair.

Chrystal hugged her friend. "What's going on?" Chrystal asked. "Where did you get these pictures? Why do you have these pictures?" Chrystal slid her arms from around Pookie's shoulders.

"Well," Pookie's big brown eyes followed behind Chrystal as Chrystal went and sat at the edge of the bed, "I already know I can trust the two of you. I have known both of you for years, and I know if I tell you anything that it won't leave this room." She waited for our reaction.

I slouched down in the chair a little, watching Chrystal gesture with her hands for Pookie to keep talking.

"Chrystal, you already know that I have my law degree and am studying for the bar exam. But what no one knows is that I am also a criminal investigator for the Internal Affairs unit. And I do a little criminal investigation for a contractor. I am also an undercover dancer for a private company that investigates sex crimes within the entertainment industry." Pookie watched Chrystal's face cringe.

"So, you're not a dancer? You're a gotdamn spy?" Chrystal exclaimed.

Pookie shook her head, sitting down at the cluttered desk in the room. "Call it what you want, but I have helped put plenty of criminals away over these past few years. I couldn't tell anyone what I was. I changed my name because I didn't want the police department to know that Kam was my brother or that I was related to the Prices. And I didn't want Kam or our family to know that I work for the police department. Our family is into some heavy-hitter shit. I would have never gotten this job if they had known who my family is."

Chrystal's mind was still blown. She took off her jacket, throwing it across the bed, and anxiously ran her fingers through her silky hair. "The whole time everyone thought your ass was a gotdamn dancer, it turns out you're a criminal investigator. We saw your ass on *Dancing With The Stars* and shit."

Pookie giggled a little, taking out a pack of Newports from her leather purse. "One of the perks of doing undercover work for a contractor. I can be whoever I wanna be as long as no one knows the real me. It's fuckin' awesome. Next week, I get to be a madam. Y'all know it's hard out here for a pimp." Pookie always had fuckin' jokes when a nigga was trying to be serious and shit.

"So," I got up from the chair that I was sitting in and tossed the envelope of pictures that she'd slid under the door on the desk in front of her. "Where did you get this shit? Did you take these?"

Pookie shook her head. "No, I found them in my boss's desk one night when I was working late. Kavante's and Kam's businesses have stayed afloat this long because they are bribing people. I work for the Anne Arundel County Police Department. I'm sure my boss, Norman Berry, is one of them. He's as dirty as they come. Too bad I didn't know that when I signed up for this shit. I want to leave Internal Affairs, but I can't because, if I do, he'll know that I found these pictures. Then he'll go digging up *my* past. He has shit on Kavante, Kam, and Larry, and they have shit on him too. Everyone who works for the police department is crooked. Chrystal, Blue, y'all remember that shit. If you have any information on any of them, I suggest you burn that shit."

I scoffed, going over to the chair in the corner of the room. I wasn't getting rid of the DVDS I had of Jimmy's punk ass. I was gonna use that shit to my advantage. Once I killed every last muthafucka who destroyed my life and the lives of the people that I loved, I was gonna need that evidence.

"So, how are these pictures related, shawty? Fuck all that other shit." I flopped down in the chair.

Pookie sighed, taking the pictures from the envelope, flipping through them. "How much do you know about Larry?"

I shrugged. "I thought the nigga was my uncle all my life until the woman I just found out is my grandmother told me the nigga wasn't shit to me but someone who is about to receive a headstone."

"Well, you already know that Larry is a pimp. He pimped out several women, your mother included." Pookie hesitated to tell me that. "She didn't throw you in the trash because she wanted to, sweetie, trust—"

I cut her off. "The fuck was he doing talking to the only mother that *I* know?"

Pookie shook her head at me. "Let me get to that. This picture that was taken of Chrystal getting off the bus was taken by Kameron."

Chrystal and I both looked at each other before looking back at Pookie.

Pookie took a Newport 100 out of its box and sparked it with her gold-plated lighter. "Kavante found out that Larry sent Lawrence looking for you. Quincy is not only a bodyguard, but he's also a paid contract killer." She watched the awestruck look on Chrystal's face. "Girl, you know that nigga is too calm. Can handle any type of situation with ease because he knows that, if he wanted, he could kill a nigga instantly with his bare hands. Larry hired him to kill you."

Chrystal held her hand over her heart, her chest heaving in and out. "I hired that muthafucka to be my security guard, and you're telling me that the nigga could have killed me? I-I met Quincy at a frat party my freshman year in college. We were friends for nearly two years before that nigga became my security guard."

Pookie nodded, inhaling the vapors from her cigarette and releasing them through her slim nostrils. "Yeah, what year was it that you met him? Around the fall of 2009? Yeah, that had to be around the same time that Lawrence came up missing."

I looked at shawty. "That nigga, Quincy, popped the nigga?"

Pookie nodded. "You already know. The only reason Larry hasn't gone after Quincy is because of all the shit

Quincy has on him. Not to mention, Quincy has eyes all over Larry back in Greenville. I have a few friends in the police department watching him too, just waiting on the nigga to make the wrong move." Pookie watched the hurt expression on Chrystal's face. "If he wanted to kill you, Chrystal, he would have. I guess Quincy called himself falling in love with you; he couldn't kill you. And you already know he was paid a grip to get the job done. The only reason why he let you continue stripping and whatnot is because he knew that Kavante and Kam knew his secret, and he didn't want you to find out."

I glanced at Chrystal, watching her shut her eyes as tears slid down her face. Then I looked back at Pookie. "So, where does Kam fit into this picture, and why was Miss Tiffany talking to Larry?"

Pookie picked up the picture of Larry and Miss Tiffany sitting across from each other at what looked like an umbrella table outside of a restaurant. "Well, Kameron and I aren't Prices by blood. We were adopted. That nigga, Larry, is our father. Sick muthafucka's blood runs through my veins." Pookie cringed at the thought.

My heart pounded in my chest. "The *fuck* you mean? Larry is your *father*? Then who the fuck is your mother?"

Pookie hesitated. "The woman sitting across from Larry in this picture."

Chrystal gasped as my heart skipped a few beats.

Pookie sighed. "I think Miss Tiffany was meeting Larry that day, maybe around August of 2008, to tell him that we were his children. That we were *their* children."

I rose from the chair, shaking my head in disbelief, pissed like a muthafucka. "Hell nah. Miss Tiffany didn't have any kids. She *couldn't* have any kids. *I* was her only child; *I* was her gotdamn son. If she was your mother, then why would Kameron kill her? Why would he kill his own mama?"

Pookie's eyes glistened. "I think he was trying to kill you. Jealousy, revenge, envy . . . I don't know. Kameron found out that we were adopted around the same time that he found out Lawrence was chasing after Chrystal. There was more to why Kam and Kavante pimped your girl than because you started dealing with Kylie. Fuck Kylie. It was more because Miss Tiffany gave us up and took you into her home instead. And the fact that you, a boy who came from the bottom, owned the streets. I think he took Miss Tiffany out to take *you* out. He knew physically killing her would mentally kill you."

I sat back on the couch, slouched back in the chair, heated.

"It's hard to say if he did the shit purposely. The day that Tiffany was murdered, she was sitting on the porch, wearing one of your hoodies. I think Kavante thought she was you. Either way, he knew he would benefit on the streets from you being off them. Officer Jimmy Copeland took a picture of him shooting you. I have access to his computer files, little does he know." Pookie watched me glaring at her. "Oh yes, trust and believe the cops knew who killed your mother. Kam was paying the police to make sure that *you* never found out."

"You're calling Miss Tiffany my mother like she wasn't yours, shawty," I scoffed, hurt, not knowing how to show how hurt that I really was. I masked a lot of my pain with anger. That was how I showed how hurt I was. And I'm pretty sure Pookie saw right through me.

Pookie disagreed, exhaling smoke from her nostrils. "I never knew her. The only reason why Kam even hired Chrystal was to get back at you. Finding out Tiffany was our mother really broke my brother. He didn't want to tell me because he didn't want to hurt me. I knew in my blood that I wasn't a Price. I hated them. It wasn't until about four months after her funeral that I found out

Tiffany was my mother. That was when my background check for the internship I took in my freshman year of college, back in 2009, came back. I did a little research on my own. I found out that Larry started pimping Miss Tiffany at the age of 15—that her own mama sold her to him for a hit."

Both Chrystal and I shook our heads. That nigga was pimping everyone we knew, it seemed. That was how our parents all knew one another. I wouldn't be surprised if Chrystal's birth mother was pimped by that nigga too.

Pookie continued. "The nigga ended up having two kids with her. She was 17 when she had me and 18 when she had Kavante. Tiffany was living in a shelter at the time. And Larry was married to Lucy Drew Todd, the woman you thought was your aunt, who raised your sister. To keep her from finding out that Tiffany had a second child by Larry, he made Tiffany give us up for adoption to the Prices, a family who he was in business with. It was either give us up or the nigga was going to kill us. Tiffany bought her freedom from the nigga and gave us up to a family she knew could take care of us. Tiffany left that life alone, and members of this church in Greenville took her into their home. She was friends with your mother, which is why she took you in, Blue."

Chrystal's cell phone rang in her pocket. She sighed, taking it out of her back pocket, looking at the display. "It's Mrs. Watson, y'all. I'ma step out in the hallway to talk to her."

I watched Chrystal answer the phone, swiping her hair behind her ear as she left the room. Then I looked back at Pookie, who was taking her last puff from her cigarette before putting it out in an ashtray on the desk.

Pookie looked up at me. "Y'all skipped a picture." Pookie held up a picture that was stuck to the back of Niyah's photo. "Sorry it's so sticky. A bitch was eating

French toast and sausage when I put these pictures in this envelope."

I watched Pookie get up, come over to me, and hand me the photo. I looked it over a little. It was a mugshot of a chick who was light as a muthafucka, could have passed for Hispanic. She was really pretty, though she looked exhausted as hell. I looked back up Pookie. "Who's this Hispanic chick?" I asked.

"She's Black and Hispanic, Blue. I know she's light as a muthafucka, but she's Black. They call her Snow. She's one of Larry's girls. She's been working for him since she was 15 too. Got pregnant by this white guy who tried to take her from Larry. She had her baby at Vidant Hospital. Back then, it was known as Pitt Memorial Hospital. Her baby was taken from her at the hospital. She didn't want to give up her baby, but she really had no choice. Her baby's daddy didn't want to get her killed, so he backed off. He was six years older than Snow and couldn't tell the police he was fuckin' with a 15-year-old prostitute." Pookie watched me studying the picture. "I found out her real name is Sophia Braxton."

My eyes widened as I examined the picture before glaring down at it. She was Chrystal's mother. I looked up at Pookie. "The nigga has Chrystal's mama? Where?"

"Living in the house with the rest of Larry's prostitutes, I assume. Of course, I can't go undercover there because Larry knows who I am. But I am going undercover at another brothel, trying to get girls there to help me get her out of there before the Feds raid the place. Word on the street is that Larry is here this week on business. I wouldn't be surprised if he showed up to Club Pop It. I mean, a third of that club belongs to him. He owned the club with Tevin when he was alive, having no idea that Tevin left it to Kam and Kavante." Pookie sat down beside me, on the arm of the chair.

I sighed, lit like a muthafucka. This nigga was making everyone's life around me hell. He was going to pay. "Don't show Chrystal this shit, a'ight? She doesn't need to see this right now. It's too much."

Pookie nodded, taking the picture from my hand. "I know. But we're gonna get her mother out of there. That's a promise."

I didn't even want to know why Niyah's picture was mixed up in that pile, but I had to know at the same time. "So, what's Niyah's connection to all of this bullshit? Why is her picture in that pile?"

Pookie hesitated, then got up from the chair and went over to her cluttered desk. She flopped down in the chair, closing her eyes really tight as if she were mentally preparing herself to tell me that news. "When was the last time that you talked to Niyah?"

I sat up in the chair, resting my forearms on my thighs. I thought for a few minutes. "Shit, it's been a minute. Probably since Miss Tiffany's funeral." I watched Pookie, who leaned back in her chair, looking at a nigga like she knew what happened between me and Niyah.

"She never reached out to you after that? Y'all were pretty tight. At one point, I saw the two of you together more than I saw her and Kavante together." Pookie folded her arms then, pursing her lips.

"The fuck are you trying to say, Pookie? Get to the fuckin' point." I didn't have time for the side of Pookie that reminded me of her brother. The part that made me not want to trust her. Kam was her brother. Kavante was her cousin, blood or not.

"I did, nigga. I asked you if she reached out to you." Pookie crossed her legs and leaned back in her chair.

I exhaled deeply, leaning back in my chair. "She did . . . for about four months until she got tired of me ignoring her. You already know that after Miss Tiffany died, I cut everybody off for months. I didn't want shit to do with anyone in my life who I ran the streets with, especially not her. A girl was diggin' the shit outta me when she already had a nigga. Though I didn't fuck with her, I still had respect for her. She moved to Florida. I ain't seen or heard from shawty since my moms passed away."

Pookie looked at me. It wasn't too often that I called Miss Tiffany my mother, but she was. I was mad that she never told me the truth, but it explained why she'd often go into deep depressions. It explained why she was so hard on me at times. It explained why she was so overprotective.

"Well, nigga, you shouldn't have ignored the girl. What happened to her is because of *your* white ass," Pookie scoffed.

I made a face at her. "The fuck you mean?"

Pookie looked at the door of the hotel, listening for Chrystal's muffled voice behind it, making sure she was still on the phone before she kept talking. "Well, about a month ago, Kavante took Niyah to court in Baltimore City for custody of their kids. You already know the Prices pretty much always win in court. They granted temporary custody to Kavante until the next court date, which isn't until damn near July. I don't know why Niyah didn't just put her pride aside and ask Reginald to help her get her kids. He was a judge; the nigga has the inside track. He doesn't give a fuck about Kavante. He'd gladly help her get her kids away from that nigga. However, the court granted him custody because Niyah had ignored a previous court order to allow the kids to stay with him during school breaks, holidays, and for two months out of the summer. She would bring the kids to visit him maybe once or twice a year, but pretty much stopped bringing them up from Florida three years ago, around the time you and Kylie got married. Hey, wasn't yesterday y'all gotdamn anniversary? Ol' funky bitch. I told you about her, Blue."

"What does this have to do with the picture, shawty?" I just shook my head at her.

"Niyah came up on New Year's Eve to visit her sisters and to go to her sister Iyona's baby shower, but she didn't make it to the party. As of yesterday, Niyah's been at the University of Maryland Medical Center. I have no proof, but I think Kavante tried to kill her." Pookie watched me sit up in the chair, my hands clenching immediately.

"What would make that nigga do this shit to her?" I hissed.

Pookie shook her head at me, taking a deep breath before saying, "Well, the court ordered a paternity test on their children. Our cousin, Latrese, works as a secretary down at the diagnostic laboratory in Johns Hopkins, and she peeped the results. She called Kavante as soon as the results were in. Turns out, one of the kids wasn't his."

My heart was the first part of my body to react to the news. I felt it literally sink in my chest, pausing for a few seconds before it slowly started beating again. "Which one?"

Pookie laughed a little, shaking her head at me, her eyes sparkling. "The third one."

I looked at her, my heart on full stampede then. "A *third* one? When the fuck did she have—"

Pookie cut me off. "When she left Maryland, she was four months pregnant, nigga," she exclaimed, keeping her voice down as much as her emotions allowed her to. "The baby was born September 30th, 2009." Pookie watched me standing up from the chair, turning around to face the window, staring out that bitch, ready to bust the glass and jump out that muthafucka. "Her name is Raven; she's 6 years old and as beautiful as you can imagine. About your complexion with jet-black curly hair like yours too. Big, bright brown eyes like Niyah. Looks just like the peanut butter version of Niyah."

"Fuck," I muttered to myself.

"You slept with that girl, Blue?" Pookie rose from her chair. "Is that little girl yours, Blue?"

"I don't need to be discussing this shit with you, Pookie, real talk." I had to tell her before she got in my face. With the mood I was in, I would've knocked out the bitch.

"No, you don't owe me shit. You owe it to Niyah, who's lying in that hospital bed, fighting for her life." Pookie stood before me, even though my whole demeanor screamed whup-a-bitch. Pookie never gave a fuck. She stayed ready to fight muthafuckas, male or female.

"She tried reaching out to you for months, Blue. She wanted to be with you, and you know it. The girl told me she would straight up leave my cousin if you wanted her. When you ignored her calls, she went right back to that nigga. When she couldn't take his shit any longer, she left and went to Florida. This entire situation is *your* fault, Blue. You're the reason why I had to hold her hand while the doctors inserted that fuckin' breathing tube down her throat. The nigga beat her so bad that her throat was damn near swollen shut." Pookie pushed me in my chest. "That is *my* muthafuckin' friend in that bed, hanging on for her life. If you didn't want her, then you should've left her the fuck alone."

I just looked at her, my temples twitching. It was at that moment that I realized Pookie was nothing like her family. That she was hurt because Niyah was hurt. Niyah and Pookie were really close. They were almost like sisters. Both went hard and would ride to the death for anyone they cared about.

I exhaled deeply, watching the tears slide down Pookie's cheeks before she dried her face. "The fuck did he do to her, yo?" I asked quietly.

Pookie shook her head. "He fucked her up; *that's* what he did. Took forever to sedate that girl. They had to put her in a medically induced coma because her brain is so swollen. She's lucky she escaped with just a few broken bones, a fractured skull, and internal bleeding. Shit, the things our family does to women is crazy. Uncle Leroy Price shot his wife up the pussy when he found out she was cheating on him. Blew that bitch up from the inside out."

My blood was at 450 degrees by now. All I could do was plot in my head which group of niggas were gonna head over to Kavante's spot with me that morning.

Pookie saw the look in my eyes. "Dude, don't be so quick to move. He knows you're coming. You know it's a trap. You know she wouldn't tell him who she had sex with. You already know she'd die before she gave you up, Blue. But Kavante knows how close you were to her."

"Who took her to the hospital?" I questioned.

Pookie sighed. "Housekeeping was doing their early-morning rounds, and when they went into the bathroom, they found her in an empty tub, blood everywhere. They called 911. I was the only person the doctors could contact. Her sisters were at work when she was admitted to the hospital. They hadn't heard from her since the day before. Her mother went to Trinidad to visit her sick mother. Her stepfather, Reginald, is away on business in New York. It took me all day to get in touch with Iyona. She had no idea why her sister didn't show up to her baby shower. Her sisters are with her at the hospital now. I think they finally got in touch with Paulette last night. Her flight is expected to arrive this morning. I'm not sure if they got in touch with Reginald, but you already know that, as soon as he catches wind of this, it's war in these streets. Her stepbrothers are already on the lookout for the nigga who did this shit to her. I'm pretty sure they've been blowin' up your cell all night."

I looked at Pookie. She couldn't care less about Kavante's ass. She didn't give a fuck that I was about to tear up the block, looking for that nigga. She never really fucked with the nigga unless she had to. But Kam was her brother. And she already knew that I was about to fuck that nigga's entire world up over Miss Tiffany.

"You know that Kameron got you fired from your job this past Friday, right? You no longer have that job as a professor at the college. Chrystal's college career is pretty much over too." Pookie looked me over a little, knowing I really didn't give a fuck about none of that.

"Why are you doing this? These are your people. I don't give a fuck about them. You already know I'ma go after these niggas. You already know Kavante and Kam are about to be nonexistent in a few hours." I looked down into her face.

Pookie laughed a little. "Nigga, this is a warning. I already told you that they are ready for you. That kiss Kam gave Kylie was just the tip of the iceberg. He kissed that girl to show you that he can do whatever the fuck he wants to do. To show you that he controls your life. That whatever is yours has *always* been his. He's just waiting for you. You need to fall back a little and let the dust settle before you join Bryson, Rico, Osias, and Bates. You know them niggas are crazy. They will die trying to find out who did their sister like this. I'm risking my own life meeting you here, Blue. You need to get my girl, Chrystal, and your son out of here."

"What about Raven? He's gonna kill that little girl," I exclaimed.

Pookie shook her head. "Kavante has the kids staying over at one of the strippers' houses. I haven't found out who. But when I do, I'll get someone I can trust to get the girls out of her house." Pookie watched me shaking my head, saying *fuck all of that.* "Blue, *fall back,* I'm *telling* you."

I wasn't trying to hear her. "I gotta do something. Larry, Kavante, Kam—all of them niggas have ruined my fuckin' life. And they're taking out whatever beef they have with me on the people that I love. Nah, I'm *not* gonna let this shit continue."

"No, Blue, *you* ruined your fuckin' life. You should've left the streets and that girl alone. Miss Tiffany's gone; you can't bring her back. And killing my brother and my cousin isn't going to change that. The best thing you can do is let the police handle this. Blue, stay out of it. I swear to God that I have your back on this, Blue. You can trust me. I'm not like my brother and them. You know I'm not. If I say that I got you, then I fuckin' got you." Pookie pushed me.

"You knew when you slid me those pictures that I wasn't gonna stay out of this bullshit, Pookie. You've known a nigga a long time, shawty; don't play." I shook my head at her.

Pookie's big brown eyes glistened under the hotel room lights. "And you know me too, Blue. I'm gonna help you. You just need to hold up. Don't be so quick to move. You're gonna get everyone killed. I only told you because I couldn't hold it in anymore. When I held Niyah's hand, before they inserted that tube down her throat, she cried, whispering your name. Do you think I wanted to tell you about this shit? No, but I couldn't keep it from you any longer. This information is yours to use as you see fit. Just keep my name out of your mouth. They'll kill me for talking to you. I'm sure someone peeped me going into the hospital to see Niyah. I'm probably already dead, Blue. You need to get your girl, your son, and lie low for a few days."

Chrystal came back into the room, eyeing Pookie and me standing face-to-face. "Sorry, y'all. Sometimes, Mrs. Watson calls me late at night when Payton can't sleep. He says he has nightmares about something bad happening to me. He won't sleep unless he knows she's talking to me . . ." Chrystal closed the door behind her, standing in front of it, eying the expression on my face. "What happened? What did I miss?"

I looked at Pookie.

Pookie looked at me. "Just get'cha family and leave tonight."


Chrystal had no idea what was going on, but she knew by the look on my face that I was ready to wreck the streets until I found those two muthafuckas. I wanted to go to the hospital to check on Niyah, but Pookie was right. Regardless of whether Kavante knew there was a possibility that Raven was mine, he still knew that when her family found out she was in the hospital, I would be the first nigga they called. I wasn't quite ready to face the Sparks boys. I wasn't sure how I was going to be able to look them in the eyes and tell them that the reason why Niyah was fucked up was because of me.

"Blue, talk to me, boo," Chrystal begged me as we pulled up into the driveway outside of Tyrese's crib in Annapolis. "You're about to jump straight into this shit again? Seriously? Blue, no, please, don't do this." Chrystal grabbed my arm before I jumped out of my ride. "This life ain't for you anymore, Blue."

"Kam killed my mother," I exclaimed, pulling my arm from her hands.

Chrystal nodded, her light eyes sad. "Yes, Blue, baby, I know."

"That nigga Quincy was hired to kill you, shawty. That shit doesn't bother you?" I just shook my head at her.

Chrystal nodded. "It does. I have a few words for him. Trust me, I do. But I'm more bothered by this look in your eyes. Pookie told us to back off, and you're over here in the hood where them boys who rock blue live. These niggas are crazy, Blue."

I nodded. "Yeah, I know. They're my crew. I fuck with Tyrese and them because they fuck with me. I left the street life alone, but it won't leave *me* alone. I teach some of these kids, shawty. They're not all bad. They're just trying to make a way for their families. When Miss Tiffany was killed, they were all I had left. I need them, Chrystal. I can't get these niggas without them. They have Niyah's children."

Chrystal's eyes searched my face. Shawty could always read my mind. It was hard keeping shit from that girl. She always knew what I was thinking. "When I asked you earlier if you knew she was Kavante's baby mama, and you said nah, that was a black-ass lie, wasn't it?"

I slouched back in my seat, looking straight ahead, not really in the mood for Chrystal's interrogation, but I knew better than to keep shit from her. "My nigga, Reggie, who died a few years ago was her stepbrother. Yeah, I knew shawty was here. But," I cut her off before she cursed me the fuck out, "I haven't seen shawty since Miss Tiffany's funeral. I pretty much cut everyone off when she was killed."

"Wait, she knew you were here and didn't tell me?" Chrystal shook her head at me.

I exhaled deeply. "She tried reaching out to me, but like I said, after the funeral, I cut shawty off."

"And you think what happened to her was your fault?" Chrystal calmed down a little, only because she didn't know the truth.

I looked at her. "Nah, I *know* this is my fault."

Chrystal shook her head. "I don't see how any of this is your fault, Blue . . . unless there's something else you're not telling me."

I reached for the door, but Chrystal pulled my arm again, pulling me back to her.

"Blue, don't fuckin' walk away from me. *What* is going on?" Chrystal yelled. "You have always kept it one hundred with me, Blue. Don't switch up now."

I pulled away from her. "Shawty, this is just too much too fuckin' fast. I'm not ready to deal with all of this shit, yo. You grew up with shawty too. You already know how she felt about a nigga. And I wouldn't give her the time of day because of *your* ass. I gave you my heart, Chrystal, and did everything you ever asked of me. But as soon as I left Greenville, I was just a memory to you. I looked for you, I wanted you, I prayed for you, and you disappeared on a nigga. This girl loved the fuck out of me, and I dissed her because she wasn't you."

Chrystal laughed a little to hide her pain. "Wow. That's *really* how you feel, David?"

"Damn right, this is how the fuck I feel. Everything I have ever done has been to get over the fact that I'd lost you. Niyah came to me for help, and I turned her away. She is lying in that gotdamn hospital bed because I wouldn't save her from that nigga when she needed me to. I was too much in my feelings, wanting to ex everything and everyone out of my life. My heart was always with you when maybe it should have been with . . ." I stopped, taking a deep breath. I needed to shut the hell up before I took out my anger on Chrystal, who had already been through enough.

Chrystal unbuckled her seat belt, turning to me, searching my face. "Blue, baby, I love you. I have *always* loved you."

I looked at her, my heart slamming against my chest.

"It's not gonna be easy getting over the past, and I don't expect it to be. But I will be damned if I let you keep throwing it in my face. We have a son together, so whatever we decide to do with each other will also affect him. I should have told you about him when I was pregnant with him, but I was afraid to. I should have made some better decisions, Blue, and you should have too. I don't know what happened with Niyah, but I do know that if you had a girl who was willing to ride with you, wherever and whenever you needed her to, you should have said, 'Fuck Chrystal.'" Chrystal's eyes sparkled with anger.

I shook my head at her. "Nah, it wasn't that easy, shawty."

"You married Kylie, so evidently it was, Blue." Chrystal disagreed with me.

"I only married that bitch to move on with my life and forget about my past. I wanted to forget about everything that I did before my mama was killed. I became a family man, something I said I'd never be. I stopped hangin' in the streets. I finished school. I got my bachelor's degree. I became a college professor. I became a one-woman man. I ignored Niyah's feelings for me because I knew I'd never be able to treat her the way she deserved to be treated. I settled for Kylie because I thought you were never coming back. I had no idea that you were right here since 2008. My past destroyed my future. My past has taken everything I love from me. It's like when I left my heart in Greenville, nothing else in life mattered. I mistreated that girl, and it's coming back to haunt me." I rubbed my hands across my close-cut wavy hair. "Shawty, I dissed this girl when she needed me. After all she'd done for a nigga, I just said, 'Fuck her.'"

Chrystal had an expression on her face that was a mix of sympathy and jealousy. She felt some type of way hearing me talk about another female who obviously meant something to a nigga. Kylie, she wasn't worried about, but I believe it was at that moment that she saw Niyah as a threat.

I ignored her expression and pulled the latch to the driver's door to open it. "You rollin' with a nigga or what, Chrystal?" I asked, hopping out of my car without waiting for her response.

Chrystal took her time getting out of the car, but nevertheless, she did get out.

I stepped into my nigga Tyrese's crib, and the place was lit like a muthafucka. Those niggas stayed partying till the muthafuckin' sun came up. They were in that bitch, thirty deep, which was about half of the size of the crew we rolled with . . . what was left of us anyway. My niggas were still twisting fingers up, still repping their street colors, still doing what they did best—regulating the streets. They called themselves "the Regulators," and that was precisely what they did, 24/7. Every type of gun you wanted, them niggas had it. Street sweepin' was their specialty. They all fucked with Niyah the long way, so when I told them what was up, they were down. They never understood why I wasn't with Niyah, after all she had done for me. They never understood why Kylie was wearing my wedding ring, and she wasn't. Niyah was a part of my life that I wanted to forget, along with my thoughts of Chrystal. Trying to ex those two out of my thoughts is how I ended up with Kylie.

"Yo, you need a drink, bruh?" Columbus handed me a Styrofoam cup of whatever it was that he was drinking.

I looked at him, taking the cup from his hand. Man, I knew better than to drink anything that nigga fixed. That nigga mixed promethazine and codeine with just about everything he drank. I sniffed the drink a little, my stomach already bubbling.

"Nigga, how many Jolly Ranchers y'all put in this shit, man? Shit smells sweet as a muthafucka. There are about to be some sleepy diabetics out this muthafucka, for real."

My niggas laughed, looking over my shoulder at Chrystal as she walked up behind me. All eyes were on her for a few seconds before the niggas' minds snapped back to reality and realized she rolled in the spot with me.

I shoved Columbus. "Eyes front, nigga," I growled at him.

Columbus glanced at her again, watching her run her fingers through her hair, bringing it all to one side. "Gotdamn. Shawty looks good with or without clothes, nigga. A nigga knows the things that she can do. I can't help but stare at shawty."

"She's not here for a muthafuckin' lap dance, nigga, so get your gotdamn eyes the *fuck* up off her." I shoved the nigga harder that time in his chest.

Tyrese got up from the couch where he was sitting and rushed his way over to me before I had to hurt Columbus. "Yo, yo, *chill,* my nigga." Tyrese laughed as he and my nigga, Cruz, pulled me away from Columbus.

"Nah, homie. Let someone else up in this muthafucka say the wrong thing out of their mouth to shawty while I'm in this bitch," I shouted as Tyrese and Cruz struggled to get me out of the living room and into the kitchen.

I pushed my niggas off of me, grabbing Chrystal by her hand before turning around and walking toward the kitchen. Tyrese keeps a bad chick or two or *five* in his kitchen, preparing his product. A chocolate assortment of fine women stood around naked in Tyrese's kitchen, preparing every drug you could think of from meth to crack. I was sure he had about ten more females down in his lab in the basement. You hadn't seen a trap house until you saw Tyrese's house. Every home that surrounded his apartment for a mile radius protected my nigga. If no one recognized a car coming through the hood, they weren't coming through that bitch. Plenty of vehicles got shot the fuck up, trying to roll through the hood. And the cops knew better than to go through.

Chrystal felt right at home, not at all fazed by her surroundings. She stood alongside me, her back against the wall, watching Tyrese and Cruz sit down at the bistro table in the kitchen.

Tyrese held up his phone, showing me all the calls he'd received from the Sparks boys. "Yo, your boys have been blowin' up my phone, nigga. They lookin' for your ass."

I nodded. "Yeah, I know."

"Said somebody fucked Niyah's ass up bad." Tyrese shook his head, placing his phone down on the table. "They about to wreck these streets to find this nigga. It doesn't take a genius to know Kavante did this shit to her. He has their kids and shit. He's been trying to find shawty for years to take those kids from her. Bryson even went so far as to hook up with Quincy's crew to go get that nigga." Tyrese glanced at Chrystal before looking at me. "Kavante knows y'all are coming for him. Y'all need to play it cool. Don't let them Sparks boys get your head blown the fuck off. Stay away from that hospital. That nigga has snipers all around that bitch, bruh."

"My nigga Doug said the nigga found out Pookie was working for the Internal Affairs unit. Said she was helping the police get all the dirt on the Prices before having the police raid all their businesses. She had way more dirt on her family than her family had on the police department. Doug also said that Kavante had niggas trail her to a hotel she was staying at in Laurel. Said she met up with you at a hotel this morning," Cruz interjected.

"Fuck! No, not Pookie!" Chrystal yelled out, turning toward me, and laying her head on my chest.

I exhaled deeply, my hand gripping shawty's hip. Pookie was just as good as dead. Kavante would kill her before we could make it back to the hotel. "Shawty was meeting a nigga to put me on to some information about Kam, Kavante, Larry, Miss Tiffany, Niyah, even—" I looked down at Chrystal. "Chrystal's mama."

Cruz and Tyrese looked at me.

Chrystal lifted her head from my chest, looking up into my face. "What?"

I nodded, hating to tell her that. "Larry has Sophia. Pookie said Larry would be here on business this week." Chrystal turned from me, about to walk away, not wanting to hear anymore. I grabbed her. "Chrystal, we're gonna save her. We don't know the real story of our parents. We have both been lied to our entire lives. Pookie risked her life to tell us this shit, knowing her family would find out."

"So, what's the plan, bruh?" Tyrese interjected. "You know we gotcha back, whatever you decide. Whichever way you go, some niggas are gonna end up dead, and some are gonna end up in a jail cell. Pookie knows how to handle herself. I'm sure she got out of that muthafucka alive somehow. Just be careful who you trust. Don't mention Pookie's name in shit. Stay away from the hospital. And Rain needs to stay away from the club. You can't trust anybody up in that bitch anymore. If you go near that club, they gonna kill your friends. Don't call them, don't talk to them, don't even go the fuck back home where they know you live. You gotta son, right, Rain?"

Chrystal glared at Tyrese a little, like he knew too much about her life.

"Yeah, nigga, *we* have a son," I interjected.

Tyrese laughed a little, not even wanting to ask questions. Then he looked back at Chrystal, who stood there with her arms folded. Tyrese couldn't care less about her attitude. He was trying to help her. "Kam and his niggas are always bragging about paying for the li'l nigga's schooling and shit. They know each and everything about your ass, Rain, and will make your life hell before they let you escape them. You owe them niggas. Blue here is gonna have to work overtime to either kill them muthafuckas or pay them muthafuckas back. You need to get'cha son out of that group home today. And get Mrs.

Watson to safety. I can have one of my girls go pick them up. Don't go back over to that house, I'm telling you."

"As for Niyah's girls, I say you pick them up from school," Cruz said. "They go to that private school called Gillam. My girl's aunt is a teacher there. She's Raven's teacher." Cruz looked up at me.

I looked at him, knowing they were about to bust me out in front of Chrystal.

"Raven is the whole reason why Niyah is laid up in the hospital, with one functioning lung. Turns out little shawty isn't Kavante's child. The results were leaked to the nigga this weekend." Cruz looked up at Chrystal. "Kavante didn't like the fact that another nigga's dick invaded his girl. Another nigga was killing the pussy while he worked overtime to put shawty through school, pay all of her bills, put her children through day care and a private school. He neglected his girl, too busy in them streets. And another nigga was taking care of home. Ain't that right, Blue?" Cruz looked up at me.

Chrystal looked at me muggin' the shit out of Cruz. "Blue? What is he talking about?"

"You didn't tell her that you used to fuck with shawty?" Cruz grinned as Tyrese stood from the table, watching my fists clench, ready to reach inside my pants and pull my Glock out on his muthafuckin' ass.

"Blue, homie, *chill*." Tyrese saw the way I was looking at Cruz as he stood from the table too.

"Nigga, you ain't ready to square up with me. So, you need to sit the fuck back down," I snarled at him.

Cruz shook his head at me. "Nigga, what the fuck you mad at *me* for? You want shawty at your side, but you're not gonna tell her what's up? You're not gonna tell her that the girl is laid up in the hospital, fighting for her life, because of you? Shawty came to you for help years ago, but you weren't trying to hear that shit. You left shawty to deal with that muthafucka on her own. It ain't me you should be mad at, nigga—take that shit up with yourself, homeboy."

Chrystal grabbed my arm as I stood up straight from leaning back against the wall, ready to light straight into Cruz's ass.

"Blue, is he serious? Kavante tried to kill her because that little girl is yours?" Chrystal gripped the fuck out of my arm.

I looked at Chrystal, watching her light brown eyes blaze under the kitchen lights. The other females in the kitchen whispered amongst themselves as they whipped up that work. I didn't want to hurt Chrystal, but as dirty as Cruz was for busting me out, he was right. She deserved to know the truth.

"I don't know," I confessed.

Chrystal scoffed. "You don't *know?* The fuck you mean you don't know, David?"

"Shawty looked for him for months before she moved to Florida," Tyrese spoke up then. "She came over to my crib, looking for you just about every day, hoping to run into you, Blue. Homegirl was probably trying to tell you that she was pregnant. She didn't wanna fuck with Kavante again, but you really didn't give her a choice. That nigga was beating the shit out of her. She never told you because she didn't want you to kill the nigga and end up *under* the fuckin' jail. She was hoping you'd take her off the nigga's hands, but you never did."

I wasn't trying to hear the nigga. I was too focused on the hurt expression on Chrystal's face. God knows the last thing that I wanted to do was hurt her. It was fucked up the way my so-called boys sprang it on her, but truthfully, she needed to know. Tyrese had no fuckin' filter. I couldn't tell you how many female hearts *he* broke. The truth hurt, but my nigga, Tyrese, was the truth, 100 percent genuine. If you didn't like what he had to say, he didn't give a fuck; his conscience was clear.

"Yo, Blue." Tyrese's little brother, Marco, came into the kitchen. "One of Rain's girls just pulled up to the crib. I think her name is Robyn."

Chrystal looked me over before attempting to walk away from me.

"Shawty, didn't Tyrese just tell you not to go near them girls?" I grabbed her arm. "Stay away from them."

Chrystal tried to pull from me, but I wouldn't let go. "Blue, I'm good. I've been taking care of myself for years without you. Now, let go of my arm. You don't have to feel guilty about what happened to Niyah, and you sure as hell don't have to feel bad for what happened to me. Is that what this is? You feel bad about not saving her from Kavante, so you think you can save *me* from the muthafucka?" Chrystal smacked her lips. "Nigga, please. Let go of me now, Blue."

I wouldn't let go. "Shawty, now is not the time to be in your feelings about my past."

"Tell that shit to yourself, Blue." she hissed at me. "Go save your daughter and leave me the fuck alone."

I exhaled deeply, still gripping her arm. "I didn't know she had my daughter, Chrystal. I wouldn't have left her with that nigga had I known."

Chrystal nodded, biting her lip to fight back her tears. "Well, now you know, David. Go save your girl, both of them. And let me go get *our* son."

"C'mon, shawty, don't—"

Chrystal cut me off. "Let go of my arm, David." She finally snatched away from me, walking out of the kitchen.